GENESIS OF
ANTIMONY

GENESIS OF
ANTIMONY

S. D. M. Carpenter

Clovercroft Publishing

Genesis of Antimony

©2018 by S. D. M. Carpenter

Published by Clovercroft Publishing, Franklin, Tennessee.
www.clovercroftpublishing.com

Ship photos courtesy of The U.S. Naval History and
Heritage Command, Washington, D.C.

Edited by Lapez Digital Services

Cover and Interior Design by Suzanne Lawing

East Africa map by Erin Greb Cartography

ISBN: 978-1-945507-93-9

Printed in the United States of America

To Linda, as always.

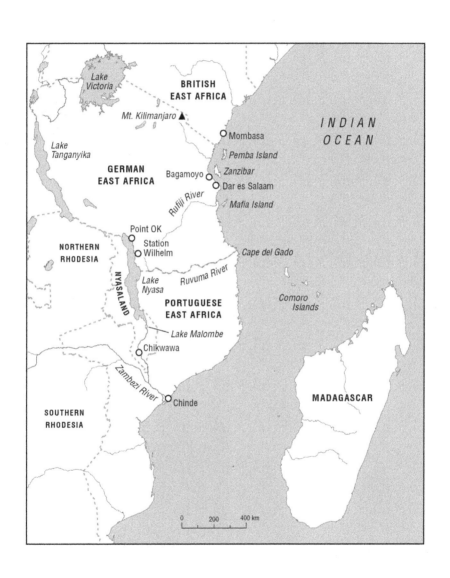

Lake
Victoria

BRITISH
EAST AFRICA

Mt. Kilimanjaro ▲

○ Mombasa

INDIAN
OCEAN

Lake
Tanganyika

Pemba Island

GERMAN
EAST AFRICA

Bagamoyo ○

Zanzibar

○ Dar es Salaam

Rufiji River

Mafia Island

Point OK ○

NORTHERN
RHODESIA

Station
○ Wilhelm

Cape del Gado

NYASALAND

Lake
Nyasa

Ruvuma River

Comoro
Islands

PORTUGUESE
EAST AFRICA

Lake Malombe

Chikwawa ○

Zambezi River

Chinde ○

MADAGASCAR

SOUTHERN
RHODESIA

0   200   400 km

PART I.
Action This Day

CHAPTER 1

A Valiant Little Warship

18 November 1914. The North Sea.

"Smoke on the horizon! Ninety degrees off the port bow, bearing...
wait...bearing 270 degrees. Contact unknown!"

"Action Stations, Mr. Braithwaite!" came the crisp order from the
captain who had just come onto the flying bridge at the top of the
ship's conning tower.

"Aye, aye, Sir." The officer of the watch (O.O.W.) turned to the seaman and nodded. Without a word and with a piercing cry of the boatswain's pipe, he called the ship to battle stations. "All hands to action
stations! All hands to action stations! All hands to action stations!"

With a clanging of hatches and heavy leather shoes scrambling
across cold metal deck plates, HMS *Halberd* prepared for battle.
Sailors just off watch rolled out of hammocks, bare feet hitting the
decks, arms flailing to pull on shoes and uniforms. As sailors reached
their battle stations, the clanking of wrenches reverberated about the
spaces as they dogged down hatches and secured scuttles. Petty officers shouted orders as gun mounts and torpedo stations came to life.
Below in the engine spaces, stokers pulled on their gloves, prepared to
fire the boilers with more coal. Speed would be needed.

"Signals, bridge."

"Yeoman, aye," came the tinny voice in reply.

"Make a signal to all ships. Investigating contact. Make best speed and proceed on assigned course." Within seconds, signal flags fluttered up the halyards in the stiffening, cold, November sea breeze.

"All stations report manned and ready," shouted the sailor from the opposite side of the flying bridge.

"Very good," responded the captain. The O.O.W. marveled at the "old man's" calm demeanor and matter-of-factness. The captain raised his binoculars, scanning for any further contacts. None. A ship's mast broke the horizon as a setting sun illuminated the waves. The O.O.W. stared, transfixed by the water's calmness despite the freshening breeze.

"Mr. Braithwaite, what do you see?"

"Nothing yet, Sir. She could be one of ours or perhaps a German," he responded.

The captain merely nodded, and, with the calm voice of authority honed by years of sea service, issued the orders to intercept. "Set course 075, 20 knots."

Braithwaite gave the order crisply, "Helm, Port 20 degrees, come to course 075. Engines ahead for 20 knots."

The helmsman responded as the ship's wheel whirled to the left. "20 degrees Port, aye."

As *Halberd* picked up speed, a white foamy bow wake formed. The destroyer heeled to port. Lieutenant John David Fairchild Braithwaite had seen some minor action before in this new war of the 20th century. The doughty, stout little destroyer had earned her battle spurs in action in earlier engagements that late summer and early autumn against German raiders of the *Kaiserliche Marine* (Imperial German Navy) attempting to either shell port cities or interdict maritime traffic along Britain's North Sea coast. But somehow, someway, this action seemed different, as if two mounted knights prepared to charge at each other at full gallop. He felt a queasiness in his gut—one that he had not even felt in his first action at sea the previous August. He squinted into the gathering dusk, fearful for what he might see.

The unknown interloper looked to be in a wide turn clearly planning to intercept the collier convoy making steam for the safety of a nearby port. Its lookouts had spotted the multiple smoke plumes to the west. As the steamers read the escort's signal, each collier poured on the coals for maximum speed—the speed of flight. *Halberd*, now coming up to battle speed, raced to intercept the intruder on what had been to this moment, a routine convoy run down from Newcastle to the Thames.

"Port 10," Braithwaite calmly ordered as the helm quickly responded. The captain's quiet demeanor infected the anxious bridge watch with an amazing calmness despite the inward racing of heartbeats and beads of nervous perspiration welling up on foreheads and cheeks. For some, this would be their first action should the unidentified contact prove to be an enemy. Braithwaite marveled at the captain's incredible calm in the face of perilous combat, certain death, and destruction.

"Bridge, lookout," shouted the anxious seaman into the voice tube from the foretop lookout station as the intruder's funnels and upper superstructure came into better view.

"Bridge, aye," responded the captain as he leaned over the brightly polished brass speaking tube. "She looks like a cruiser, Sir. Can't make the class yet."

Before the lookout had even finished his report, Braithwaite started flipping through the pages of the enemy recognition book kept permanently at the O.O.W.'s station. Braithwaite shouted into the voice tube that led up the mast to the men with the best position for observation. He knew that the entire ship would know the interloper's nature soon enough. "Very good. Stay on her."

Braithwaite stared at the stoic commanding officer who, showing no emotion whatsoever, relit his briarwood pipe. "Could be a bad night, Mr. Braithwaite. A bad night, indeed." The O.O.W. could only muster an acknowledging nod. The young naval officer knew as much. A bad night, indeed.

Collingwood, the teenaged sub-lieutenant, as the Junior Officer of the Watch, barely out of public school, but already well-seasoned, had been tracking the contact in silence, and finally had a solution to report. "Contact bears 045 degrees. Estimated course 220, speed, 14 knots."

"Very good. Well, Mr. Braithwaite, it looks as if she intends to parallel us and close slightly. Let's close with her and let our colliers put some distance between." As the orders rang about the bridge, the destroyer raced to intercept the interloper. Torpedo tubes cranked out pointing to starboard, readied for launch. At the forward gun mount, a young sailor, trembling, rammed in a round, then looked over at the chief petty officer, who in the best stoic tradition of His Majesty's senior noncommissioned officers, nodded in approval. *Halberd* reached 20 knots, closing rapidly to a firing position.

"Contact bears 020 degrees off the starboard bow, range...," the sub-lieutenant paused to re-check his calculation, "... range 10,000 yards. She looks to be a *Kolberg*-class light cruiser." In the distance, a white smoke puff from the contact signaled the fight had begun. The first rounds landed perilously close. Salt spray covered the fantail.

"This German knows his business," remarked the captain in obvious admiration. "Mr. Braithwaite, come right 20 degrees." The captain meant to close to torpedo range. Braithwaite stepped to the railing and gripped it tight, knuckles white with tension. The nervous anticipation never changed no matter how many times he had seen this before. He strode back to the chart table and opened the enemy recognition book.

"If she's a *Kolberg*, that beast has—let's see, 4.1-inchers—two forward and two aft with twelve total, plus 5-pounders. Torpedoes as well. Max speed looks to be 25 knots on all boilers." Braithwaite laid down the book and snapped the binoculars to his eyes. "More smoke. Looks like she is laying on the coal and coming up to speed."

The old man crossed his arms and grunted—a low, guttural acknowledgment as he nodded in agreement. "Come right another 30 degrees. Let's close the range."

"Right 30 degrees, aye." Halberd lurched and heeled over as the rudder bit. The sudden jerk threw Braithwaite slightly off balance. He clutched the railing and steadied himself. A moving target is hard to hit, and a zigzag pattern served them well until the destroyer reached their guns' effective range.

"Range to target?"

"I make her 9,000 yards and closing," responded the sub-lieutenant, calipers and dividers working furiously across the chart table.

"Mr. Braithwaite, I trust that your gunners know their business."

"Aye, Sir. They are the best gunners in the fleet." They are the best. In the tradition of the old navy, Braithwaite drilled the men every day, hour upon hour until each man knew his job by instinct. If a man went down, the next one stepped in and took over the functions. He served not only as the ship's navigator but also as the gunnery officer. They were the best, they were his men, his crew, his gunners. He trusted them implicitly. They were up to snuff now; the drill would tell.

"Let us hope so. Let us hope," responded the captain. He smiled and raised his eyebrows knowingly.

Amazing, simply amazing, thought Braithwaite. In the face of such great peril, the man's calm demeanor was truly astounding. It was a characteristic Braithwaite intended to emulate—that is if he survived.

"Where is the convoy, Adams?"

"Over the horizon, Sir," responded the lead yeoman of signals from next to the flag bag aft of the flying bridge, where he had been watching the colliers' retreat.

More white frothy splashes straddled *Halberd* from the cruiser's second volley. The water kicked high in the air by the blast rained down on the forecastle. "Damned close," mumbled Braithwaite as he snapped the binoculars back up to his eyes. He could now make out figures on the cruiser's open bridge.

"Both torpedo stations report trained to starboard and ready," shouted the sub-lieutenant.

"Very good," responded the captain, arms folded across his chest in an almost casual fashion. "Mr. Braithwaite, we will close to about 2,000 yards and fire two torpedoes simultaneously. Our 4-inchers should disrupt his firing solution to let us get in close to the bastard. I'll take the conn." Braithwaite concurred. His job now was to coordinate the fire control for *Halberd's* three 4-inch guns, one forward and two aft on the centerline. "Starboard 20 degrees."

"Starboard 20 degrees, aye," came the swift reply from the helmsman.

Halberd lurched hard, her boilers at full blast, turbines spinning at maximum RPM. Propellers bit into the cold North Sea throwing up great clouds of white foam and froth. *Halberd* surged into the fray.

"We'll open fire at 6,000 yards and give the Hun a lesson in British gunnery, eh Braithwaite!"

"Very good, Sir," shouted Braithwaite over the gathering whine of the hard-charging engines.

The captain grabbed the speaking megaphone, strode to the bridge rail, and leaned over, megaphone raised to his lips. "Commence firing at 6,000 yards when you have the range, chief."

The gunner's mate chief shouted up in response, "Aye, aye, Sir!"

"Mr. Collingwood, pass that word to the gun mounts, if you please." The sub-lieutenant nodded and shouted the orders into the speaking tube that ran to the two gun mounts, one forward and one aft of the forward torpedo tubes. The captain gently snapped the megaphone back into its holder and stood erect.

Horatio at the bridge, thought Braithwaite in singular admiration. *"The time has come, the walrus spoke, to speak of many things. Of shoes and ships and sealing wax, of cabbages and kings."* He wasn't quite sure why the line from Lewis Carroll's *Alice Through the Looking Glass* suddenly struck him as appropriate. But indeed, the time had now come as the destroyer charged toward the enemy. He jabbed a hand into the side pocket of his greatcoat and slowly turned his lucky guinea over and over, gently stroking the coin's smooth surface. His father had given him the coin for good luck the day he received his commission in His Majesty's Royal Navy.

"Port 10 degrees!"

"Port 10 degrees, aye!" came the helmsman's crisp reply, already spinning the ship's wheel back to the left. The shift back to port unmasked the two guns in the aft part of the ship and also dramatically changed the enemy gunners' firing solution. Another salvo from the cruiser landed far astern, safely behind the destroyer's fantail.

"Good. We have broken down his firing solution," whispered the captain to himself, breaking into a slight grin.

At mount "A" forward of the conning tower, the gunner, his right hand gripping the firing trigger, felt a small bead of sweat form on his brow. He swatted it away with his free hand. "Bugger all. No time for bloody worry," he cursed under his breath.

"6,500 yards. Off the starboard bow," came the word from an ever-increasingly anxious, but outwardly calm, Sub-Lieutenant Collingwood.

"Very good," responded the captain. "Well, John, here's to all the men who have gone before. Best of luck, lad. Make Horatio Nelson proud today," The captain admonished as he swiftly moved in behind Braithwaite. The sudden comment startled him as a nervous anticipation began to tell despite this being the next in a line of actual engagements over the preceding months. "Action, once more. God be with us!"

"6,000 yards," shouted the sub-lieutenant again from the opposite side of the bridge. The captain nodded and strode over to the forward bulkhead. Grabbing the megaphone in one quick thrust, he leaned over the railing and shouted, "Commence firing. Fire when ready!"

At almost the same time, Braithwaite popped open the voice tube to the two aft guns and gave the order to open fire on the enemy intruder. At that moment, the first round struck. It had to happen. The superior German fire control system and optics meant that *Halberd*, despite the captain's dodging and weaving, would be hit eventually. The German gunners were simply too good, too professional, too well drilled. The 4.1-inch round struck just aft the third smoke funnel near the after torpedo station. It plowed through the thin metal hull and exploded in a crew berthing compartment with a whump, causing a shutter throughout the ship. Braithwaite turned toward the captain. The imperturbable man showed no outward expression, but Braithwaite must have known that the captain inwardly seethed. No ship's commanding officer would feel otherwise. War generates rage and hatred, the necessary emotions for any warrior facing an implacable enemy. But, the captain never moved, never wavered, never flinched. In a calm voice, he simply gave his next order. "Steady as she goes. Rudder amidships."

"Rudder amidships, aye," shouted the now highly animated helmsman as his hand on the wheel felt clammy with nervous fear. It was the young quartermaster's first action. It was many of the *Halberd* crew's first action.

By straightening out the course to the exact opposite of the enemy, the captain had placed the destroyer in a position relative to the cruiser that only allowed the German to bring the two forward starboard side guns to bear on *Halberd*, thus reducing the advantage in gunnery. It also allowed for a close-in torpedo shot where any real damage would result if their aim was true. Fortunately, no one was hurt or killed as the exploding round hit an empty compartment. All the crew were at their various action stations, fully girded for battle. Braithwaite knew in his soul that this was only the first scene of a long and deadly duel. On the forecastle, a gun retorted. Acrid cordite odor blew over the open bridge. Braithwaite had smelled this odor on many, many occasions both in training and action and knew it well. His nostrils flared; his right hand trembled. It was a common reaction brought on more by nervous energy than fear.

Their initial 4-inch round landed well short of the target, but it was merely the first of many shots. *Halberd*'s gunners would soon find the target. He had drilled them day and night for any situation. Another enemy round landed close aboard. Salt spray careened over the open bridge. At "A" gun mount, the chief gunner's mate placed a soothing hand on the nervous gunner's shoulder as the loader slammed another round into the breach. "There, there, steady, lad." The chief knew that the backbone of every military organization is its senior noncommissioned leaders. He would not let the men down despite his own queasiness and dread. As the ship rolled to port, the gunner saw the enemy cruiser, dead in his sites. No arching ballistics needed now; it was a straight-on shot at close range as *Halberd* pulled parallel with the German. He squeezed the trigger and a 4-inch shell boomed as it left the muzzle. Seconds later, a cloud of ugly, orange smoke erupted from the cruiser's amidships just below the forward mast. A hit! A hit! A loud cheer erupted from the men along the destroyer's starboard side who saw the result of the well-placed shot. On the flying bridge, the captain smiled and nodded in appreciation. A hit, indeed. And so it went for several minutes as David zigged and zagged about the larger, less maneuverable Goliath. All the while, the captain angled *Halberd* closer and closer to the enemy. At 2,000 yards, he would let loose the main battery of 21-inch torpedoes and counted on speed to avoid the cruiser's own torpedoes.

"Target bears 040 degrees off the starboard bow, range 1,900 yards, course reciprocal to ours!" shouted Collingwood, who maintained a good target track.

The captain raced to the torpedo station speaking tube and shouted as loud as he could. "Torpedoes one and two. Fire when ready!"

Fired at an angle of 75 degrees off *Halberd's* starboard bow, the captain figured that, with its present course and speed, the cruiser and the deadly torpedoes would meet at precisely the desired point. A loud whoosh was heard on the bridge. Braithwaite raced to the signal platform at the aft end of the bridge just as the second torpedo left the tube, shot out with incredible pressure by the compressed air charge.

"Torpedoes away!" He trained the binoculars on the frothy white wake kicked up by the two 21-inch torpedoes. Both ran straight and true toward their intersection with the enemy cruiser. Amazingly, the German ship either ignored or just didn't see them. The cruiser made no attempt to maneuver away. Seconds passed.

For years later, Braithwaite could still hear that devilish screaming, screeching noise like a banshee as it arched down behind him. The cruiser had found its mark. A round landed square on the deck forward of the bridge just behind the "A" gun mount. Shards of hot metal and shrapnel flew in every direction, shattering men and ship as it tore away flesh and steel. Every man in "A" gun mount went down. The concussion blew the chief gunner overboard. The nervous gunner had squeezed off one more round when the blast hit, tearing his arm from his shoulder and rolling him forward along the deck only to bleed out slowly.

On the flying bridge, the wheel spun out of control as the sailor on the helm crumpled in a bloody heap. The leading signalman, who had at that moment been running forward with a report to the captain, was hit full in the face by the blast throwing him backward against a signal-searchlight. Red blood gurgled up from his punctured lungs impaled on the now jagged edge of the destroyed light. Collingwood somehow survived the blast, having been hunched over the chart table running a new round of course and speed calculations. Only his hat was blown off and some slight shrapnel bits to his scalp. Without helm control and racing ahead at nearly 25 knots, *Halberd* careened about like a sailor on leave ashore fresh from the pub. The unattended helm spun wildly, first right, then left. Amidships and below, sailors banged off bulkheads and fell prostrate to the deck, unable to maintain their balance in the wildly lurching ship.

Braithwaite, stunned and thrown to the deck, braced himself and pushed off with both arms. As muscles flexed, they became rubbery and weak. He slumped down again to the deck, unable to lift himself up. He gradually became aware of some stickiness on his right thigh. There was no pain—just a slimy, warm feeling, a stinging, warm feeling. He rolled over and raised up on his elbows. Halfway between his groin and knee, a long tear appeared in his uniform trousers covered in deep red ooze. *Thank God, not an artery. Must move. Get back on station!* Then the pain came. It came first in tiny spasms, then a general rush of horrific torment. Only later, he learned that a shard of steel had sliced through his leg and tore a gash two inches deep into the leg muscle. Pulling together all the strength he could muster, Braithwaite pushed himself onto his knees, then into a crouch, not fully erect, but enough to move forward. A moment later, he heard a wrenching, metallic screech come across the water. He glanced up in the enemy's direction. A tall geyser of water and spray spread up and over the enemy cruiser. A hit! One of *Halberd*'s torpedoes had struck home. Flames and black, oily smoke poured from the wounded enemy, billowing up from the wound. Then he noticed flame astern of the cruiser's amidship guns. The "A" mounts gunner's last shot had hit as well, exacting his vengeance for the loss of mates and his own life. Braithwaite gasped and gulped hard. He breathed in deeply and lurched forward as fast as his crippled leg could move.

"Captain, captain. We hit them. We…." The next thing Braithwaite saw haunted him for the rest of his life. On the deck just forward of the ship's wheel, Lieutenant-Commander Urquhart lay crumpled, a gash in his neck so horrible that it had almost taken off his head. Next to him lay a jagged piece of steel from the cruiser's shell, crusted in deep, dark red, clotting blood. Braithwaite fell to his knees in confusion and horror. Another round landed on the fantail. *Halberd* shuddered. Braithwaite drifted between the real and the surreal. Memories of a happy youth crowded his consciousness—memories of nanny stroking his hair, his father, imperious but gentle as well, Brighton Beach on a warm humid July afternoon, the Welsh Highlands, cool and full of budding life in spring. The *Kolberg*-class cruiser had the range. More 4.1-inch rounds crashed through the hull just forward of the main engine room tearing great gashes in the thin, unarmored steel. Seawater, cold and frothy, poured in over men and machinery. Boiler fires flickered then snuffed by the pouring water, died. Main steam to the turbine ceased as the blades wound down to zero RPMs. In the dim light, men scrambled for safety up narrow ladders. Others, hit by flying shrapnel, moved in agony or simply collapsed in death throes. Within seconds, *Halberd* began to list to port as great tons of seawater poured in. Here and there, senior petty officers shouted orders, trying to control the growing panic and at the same time, close off watertight doors to control flooding. The leading chief stoker, despite frigid seawater cascading over and around him, managed to dog down the engine room door, an act that prevented flooding of more forward compartments.

On deck, the aft 4-incher ceased firing as the gun crew furiously cranked down the elevation to counter the ship's list. But, in a desperate shot just as the gun muzzle elevated too high for any accuracy, the gunner fired another round at the demon cruiser. Amazingly, it hit the German square in an ammunition space. Ugly flame shot out and up from the gash in the cruiser's starboard side. A booming sound rolled across the water. Sailors, who moments earlier had been scrambling in panic, now froze at the sound and gazed across the few hundred yards separating the ships. All firing ceased from the cruiser.

On the bridge, Braithwaite became aware of a hand on his shoulder, shaking furiously. "Sir, Sir, please, Sir. You must come back, come back!" pleaded a panicky Collingwood.

"What… huh…," Braithwaite mumbled the only words that came to him. Slowly reality and consciousness returned. He realized where he was, and suddenly, the pain in his thigh and the acrid odor of cordite replaced thoughts of family and pleasant summers. He raised his hand to his head, then placed a palm down on the deck, pushing himself up slowly. His left leg wobbled but then stabilized. Despite the huge blood loss, he managed to raise his wounded right leg, finally standing with Collingwood's assistance.

"Lieutenant Braithwaite, the captain is gone. You're senior. You are the one, John. Please, you must take the command."

Braithwaite could only shake his head in acknowledgment. He looked over at the dead captain still lying in the dark pool of his own blood. "We can't leave him like that. Just can't." Without a word, Braithwaite limped over to the prostrate captain's body. Reaching him, he placed both arms under the man's limp shoulders and with all the strength he could muster, pulled the dead officer up by the armpits. He propped the limp body up against the forward bulkhead. Braithwaite folded the man's arms neatly in his lap, almost in a sleeping position. "You deserve better, Sir, but this is all I can do for you now."

Braithwaite only now realized that *Halberd* had lost all forward motion and was slowing to a dead stop. The list had become more pronounced. In an attempt to reach the slowly turning ship's wheel, he slipped on the deck, wet with seawater and blood. He steadied himself by grasping onto the engine order telegraph, barely managing to avoid cutting himself on the shattered glass faceplate. The arrows indicating ordered speed were bent to a 90-degree angle, another victim of the carnage. Only now Braithwaite realized that the air had become suddenly quiet. In the gathering dusk, he saw the enemy cruiser silhouetted by the flames shooting from her amidships and the black smoke that wreathed her stern. Between the last round fired by the destroyer and the torpedo hit, the *Kolberg*-class light cruiser had been mortally wounded as had his own ship. He struggled over to the speaking tube connected to main control. Flipping open the brass cover, he shouted in hopes of a response. "Engine room…bridge …engine room!" No response. He did not know of the carnage below but was now fully aware of the loss of ahead speed as a ship approached dead in the water.

At that moment, the chief stoker, who had successfully secured the watertight door earlier, arrived on the bridge, huffing and puffing with the effort and muttering under his breath, "Too many bloody steak and kidney pies!" He took three deep breaths to catch his wind. "Sir, engine room gone. Completely flooded. We took a hit, maybe even two directly at the water line. I lost many a good lad, Sir. The rest are gathering on the fantail."

"Chief, can we get any way on it all. Anything at all!"

"No, Sir, nothing. All boiler fires are out. Completely flooded. The bastard has buggered us well, I'll say that for sure. Even if we could raise steam, won't do any good. The turbines are all underwater now. And we are taking on water in the aft spaces as well. The blast took out the watertight door astern of the engine room. No hope, Sir. Just no bloody hope."

Braithwaite simply nodded in acknowledgment. "Chief, go back and see to your lads. See if there's anything to be done to stop the flooding." *Save the ship. Must save the ship.* The German cruiser had become almost irrelevant now. She had done her damage and now struggled with her own death spiral. Braithwaite placed both hands on the bridge railing. Without rudder control or forward motion, the bow had swung around to port. Slowly, *Halberd* showed a stern aspect to the enemy and had drifted closer. But, the enemy had not fired a round. Apparently, she too had lost power, but why did she not fire. It was a mystery he would never solve. But, as the current pushed the bow farther to the left, it unmasked the rearmost gun mount, which until now had been silent. The flooding throughout the lower decks balanced out the list; *Halberd* now had a solid firing angle. In desperate anger, the men of "Y" gun mount poured in deadly fire at close range. Hit after hit straddled the cruiser. After a few minutes, the ship, now also dead in the water, began returning fire, but to no avail. Her previous deadly accurate fire had taken out "A" gun, the bridge, and the engineering spaces. Now without fire control due to battle damage, the enemy's rounds flew aimlessly over the destroyer. Braithwaite could only watch the spectacle in wonderment as round after round landed on the enemy, who responded almost like a punch-drunk boxer in the final, desperate rounds.

"Collingwood, take the helm. See if we still have any rudder control," he shouted. The sub-lieutenant gingerly stepped over the dead sailor at the ship's wheel and grasped the shrapnel-pocked wooden wheel. Stiffness indicated that the wheel still had some control. Collingwood shook his head vigorously as a smile spread across his powder-stained face.

At least that's something, mused Braithwaite. "Try to keep her coming to port. Let's give the "X" and "Y" gunners a chance for some more hits." But as he well knew, without steerageway, the rudder was practically useless. *Halberd* was now subject only to the current and a freshening wind. *It's something at least. Something positive.* His feelings of hopelessness and helplessness lightened if only a bit. Slowly, but perceptibly, the two ships drifted farther apart as dusk turned to darkness. The enemy cruiser could still be seen, highlighted by the flames pouring up from her wounds. As "X" and "Y" guns ceased firing, exhausted gunners, drained of all emotion, collapsed onto the deck. They had done their duty. The cruiser would do no more harm.

On the flying bridge, Braithwaite, now fully realizing his awesome responsibility of command, began to think through his options. He hobbled over to the chart table. With one arm, he brushed the debris of battle off the chart and with the other, grasping a pair of dividers, quickly measured the distance to the safest haven. "Bloody Hell!" Still twenty nautical miles from Scarborough, the best bet. Maybe. Placing all his weight on the good left leg and wincing in pain from the gashed thigh, he pivoted to look up at the mast. *No good.* All the high-frequency antennas were gone, dangling limply and flapping in the gathering breeze. Shrapnel from a hit had cut away all the antenna wires from the mast. *Wireless no use. Flares, maybe flares. Perhaps one of the destroyers of the Seventh Destroyer Flotilla, the Humber Patrol, would spot them.* He dragged himself over to the metal box that held the Very pistol and store of flares, but it had been blown away by the blast.

Minutes passed. The German cruiser now had drifted away toward the horizon, barely perceptible except for the silhouette created by the fires. And then, to the dismay and amazement of the men of *Halberd*, black sooty smoke erupted from the enemy's funnels caught in the glow of the firelight. Within minutes, the German cruiser started to move forward. Braithwaite had been scanning her with binoculars ever since Collingwood had pointed out the smoke. Watching the cruiser interrupted his search for any friendly craft approaching perhaps drawn by the sight and sound of combat. Braithwaite's jaw literally dropped at the site. *How the devil…!* Would the enemy finish her work? What was the German captain thinking? Fight or flight. Surely, he must know that more British warships would be on the way, notified of the enemy presence by the fleeing colliers if nothing else. Then slowly, ever so slowly, the cruiser disappeared over the horizon on a course of 120 degrees true, headed for home and safety. Every surviving sailor on *Halberd* who still could stand watched the German ship disappear. Thoughts of rage, disappointment, and utter helplessness crowded out all other thoughts. The Hun would be safe. Despite *Halberd*'s amazing efforts, the wounded cruiser escaped and there was no means to prevent it. On the bridge, Braithwaite slowly lowered the binoculars. He had never felt such a profound sense of disappointment as he had now. Never before.

A sudden lurch broke his focus on the escaping enemy as well as his stance. Braithwaite pitched forward throwing out his hands; he caught his fall on the now shattered signal-searchlight, victim of enemy shrapnel. Recovering his composure, he glanced over at Collingwood who had ceased manning the ship's wheel. The young officer's face was drained and ashen white. With boiler fires extinguished and turbines seized up, *Halberd* had no hope of getting underway. One by one, aft compartments flooded as cold seawater crashed through doors and hatches. Men topside felt the motion as she slipped further under the surface. Many peered up at the bridge, awaiting the inevitable order to abandon ship. The list had corrected, but now she was down by the stern.

As Braithwaite started aft to survey the damage, Chief Petty Officer

MacWilliams raced up the ladder to the bridge, two steps at a time. "She's nay way, Sir. Down by the stern and going fast!"

Taking a deep breath, Braithwaite hoped to calm his racing heart. He had the command. He had the lives of so many men now in his hands. He must be calm. "Right, Chief. Understand. Can the bilge pumps staunch the flooding? Is there any hope there?" he blurted out almost pleading.

The old sailor shook his head in sad acknowledgment of the inevitable. "Nay, Sir, afraid she's hopeless."

Braithwaite hobbled back to the bridge rail. His gaze dropped to the deck, then to the horizon, then back to the deck. The chief and Collingwood stood by only a few feet away, saying nothing but understanding all. *Halberd* and clearly most of her crew were doomed. The guns had long ceased firing at an out-of-range enemy that had finally disappeared over the horizon headed for apparent safety. Braithwaite turned his gaze toward "A" gun forward. No life. Six men lay dead on the deck. A gunner lay draped over the open breach with the barrel, pockmarked by shrapnel damage, pointing helplessly upward. He turned aft and realized the men of the "X" and "Y" gun mounts and torpedo stations had clustered about the funnels, staring up at the bridge, most with hollow, blank stares. With grimy, sweat-covered faces from the black oily smoke streaming up from burning compartments below, the men simply stared at him. Decision time. At only twenty-four, one should not have to make such life-and-death decisions, but in wartime… wartime. Braithwaite turned crisply about, facing the chief. "Prepare to abandon ship." No ship's commander should ever have to utter those horrible words and yet there it was. He had no choice. He had to save as many men as possible. "Mr. Collingwood, make a survey. See what boats are still useful or functional. Chief, pass the word to all hands to make preparations to abandon ship."

"Aye, aye, Sir," shouted Collingwood as he raced down the ladder to the main deck. The chief nodded in acknowledgment, turned, and proceeded down the opposite ladder. The veteran sailor had once before abandoned ship in a storm. He knew the death tally would be high. Perhaps a few could be saved from the frigid November North

Sea. Perhaps not. "God be with us," he whispered as he reached the main deck below.

No time to spare. Braithwaite hobbled toward the chart table. Reaching under the table, he pulled out a heavy canvas bag. Rolling up the chart that had recorded their movements and location, he bundled it into the bag. He snapped shut the deck log. It too went into the bag along with the ship's long glass and binoculars. Moving aft to the signal area, he saw the signals log splayed out on the deck spattered with the dead signal yeoman's dried blood. Braithwaite paused for a moment; he stared down at the log and then at the sailor, whose wide-open eyes caused him to shudder. Bending down over the young man, he placed a hand over his face and gently closed the eyelids. Slamming the signal log shut, he dragged himself back to the open canvas bag despite the pain shooting up from his ravaged leg and tossed in the log. Standing erect among the carnage, he placed both hands on his hips, then winced. He had, up until now, essentially ignored the pain welling up from the gash. At least the bleeding had stopped. *What else? What bloody else?* He looked about the bridge, left then right, then left again. *Ah, yes.* Reaching down behind the chart table, he pulled up the Admiralty codebook. *Mustn't let the Hun ever find this!* As he pulled the line to close the bag, a thought came to him. What of his captain, who sacrificed his life and ship to save the colliers. The valiant man would go down with the ship in the age-old tradition of the sea, but not his memory. No, not his memory. Braithwaite hobbled over to the officer's body still propped up against the bulkhead. He removed the man's wedding band and a gold ring that his father, also a Royal Navy man, had given him on his commissioning years earlier. Searching through his pockets, Braithwaite found a wallet with photos of the man's wife and children, some letters and other memorabilia. All went into the canvas bag. Finally, Braithwaite removed the shoulder boards from the man's heavy greatcoat and dropped them into the bag as well—black with 2½ gold rings of one of His Majesty's finest officers. The children would cherish these despite the spattered blood from the deadly gash.

Aft, the ship's fantail now lay only two feet above the rising water.

The clanging of boat davits as men struggled to get life-saving gear into the water mixed with the shouts of petty officers directing the efforts broke the otherwise stillness of the gathering dark, Braithwaite cursed under his breath. But, he must be strong—strong for the survivors. A wicked gurgling sound welled up from below as more water rushed into the ship below decks. She lurched again and then settled deeper. Amidships, the starboard boat, dangling from a single line, finally broke free and crashed to the deck. "No use," shouted a sailor. "She's holed." Shrapnel from enemy fire rendered the boat useless. A portside boat had floated free and sunk, torn from its davits by the force of a blast. Only a solitary 20-man raft remained operable. It would have to do.

With the life-saving gear stowed and the surviving raft readied, a deathly quiet soon surrounded the ship as one by one the men gathered in clumps about the deck awaiting orders. The preparations complete, a stiff breeze fluttered the battle ensign that incredibly still flew from the ravaged mainmast. Then, with a jerk and a tug, chief MacWilliams hauled down the flag, the last act of a defiant warship. Two sailors folded the flag, which also went into the canvas bag. Looking out at the horizon, Braithwaite prepared to give the saddest order of his life. He grabbed the megaphone that lay on the deck next to the captain's body, raised it to his mouth, and turned to face aft. "All hands. Abandon ship. All hands. Abandon ship." Men scurried and scuttled to the rail, awaiting their turn to go over and into the frigid sea below. Braithwaite took one last look about the shattered bridge and, without a single word, hobbled down the starboard ladder. Without any hint of panic, the crew abandoned the gallant little destroyer. With a sharp shout of command, the coxswain ordered that all serviceable gear be rescued from the now useless boats and placed in the 20-man life raft. Braithwaite stood silently watching the scene and marveled at the professionalism and efficiency of the seasoned petty officers. But other thoughts crept in as he watched the men standing about the deck or going over the side. There were over fifty men. The raft could only hold twenty and maybe a few more in calm seas. But this was a North Sea November. *How many men will be lost to the frigid seas before the patrol found them if at all?*

"Right then, you lot into the raft. Thirty minutes only. The most badly wounded go first. We'll switch out with the lads in the water," barked Chief MacWilliams. The ship's lurch reminded the men that their destroyer died slowly. Already, the stern lay awash as the bow raised upward in the air. Braithwaite chose to leave the bodies of the dead aboard, especially the captain. It was only appropriate that he go down with his valiant ship. For the rest, HMS *Halberd* would be the resting place of the honored dead.

As the last man went over the side, Braithwaite stepped over the rail and jumped into the freezing water below. Despite his kapok life vest, he sank in over his head. Flailing like a desperate man drowning, he clawed back to the surface, sputtering from the cold shock of the icy water. "Tread water! Tread, dammit," he shouted to himself remembering his basic survival training. A few feet away, several seamen aboard the raft extended their hands to pull him aboard. "No, I'll wait my turn. Wounded only for now. Paddle away. Clear the ship or we will be sucked under." He had not lost his command voice. The men in the raft who still could, paddled desperately; sailors in the water, many already handicapped by the cold and weight of their sodden clothing, struggled to clear the wreck. Slowly, agonizing yard by yard, the cluster of survivors moved to a safe distance from *Halberd*. Crunching and breaking sounds came from the ship as bulkheads gave way to the onrushing water torrent. Within minutes, the ship was completely down by the stern with the bow angled up at 30 degrees. Fires still burned above decks, but gradually surrendered to the oncoming water. *Thank God for that; at least the magazines will not go up.* Thirty minutes later, the second group of men pulled themselves onto the raft as the first batch eased into the water. With the death rattle welling up from his throat, a wounded seaman died, his gashed head slumping over his blood-soaked chest. Without a word, the closest man eased his lifeless body over the side and extended hands to help another sailor onto the raft. And so it went.

More groans came from the stricken ship as she sank faster. In only a few minutes, she passed under the surface, but the survivors could still hear the creaking and groaning for several more minutes. Braithwaite, now in the raft, stared at the bubbles and froth welling up in the water. Silently removing the ship's log from the canvas bag, he opened it to the last page and penned the epitaph.

17.23, 18 November 1914. Lieutenant John D. F. Braithwaite, RN, temporary commanding, ordered abandon ship. Fifty-two men in the water, many wounded.

Minutes later, he squinted to see the page, hands shaking from the merciless chill. He extended his right hand and with his left, he steadied his right hand and continued writing.

18.04. 18 November 1914. HMS *Halberd* sank by the stern. Thirty known dead, including Lieutenant-Commander Alastair Urquhart, RN, commanding officer. We pray their soul to keep. End of log of HMS *Halberd*. Lieutenant John D. F. Braithwaite, Royal Navy, temporary commanding.

Slowly, he closed the log and gently placed it back in the bag along with the pen, a gift from his grandfather years ago. He feared he might lose it the next time he went into the water. In the waterproof bag, at least it would be safe. From the opposite side of the raft came a steady, firm voice, "Our Father, which art in heaven, hallowed be thine name. Thy kingdom come, Thine will be done...." One by one, more men chimed in. "On earth as it is in heaven...." Another wounded man slumped to the deck, his eyes wide open, but lifeless. "Amen."

The men silently awaited the long cold night ahead. Braithwaite closed his eyes and drifted off into a state between sleep and consciousness. At least the pain in his right thigh had dulled. For now.

****

Braithwaite shook. Slowly opening his heavy eyelids, he sensed light and movement. Morning had finally arrived. He placed his palm down expecting to feel the rubbery surface of the life raft. Instead, his hand pushed hard against a grainy wood. And, he detected a strange odor—fish. It smelled of a day-old fish. As he cleared away the fogginess, he realized that only a few inches away stood a face with an enormous, bushy, gray-flecked beard with a stubby old pipe belching acrid tobacco smoke. Braithwaite jerked his head up, not yet fully conscious. The old head jerked backward.

"Easy there, young lad. No great exertions required. You're quite safe now."

He looked left, then right, trying to get his bearings. It was a trawler—a typical North Sea fishing boat common along the English coast. The antique steam engine belched ugly black smoke as it chugged along seemingly impervious to the night's chaos. Around the open deck, he saw men slumped and hunched over, some asleep, some staring at nothing in particular, one crying, and one dying. He tried to push himself up, but the pain in the right leg jolted him back down to the hard deck.

"Easy, lad," cooed the old fisherman. "That's a nasty wound ye got there and ye have lost a lot of blood."

"Where ...." His feeble voice trailed off, lacking the strength to finish the question. The fisherman laid a gentle, calming hand on his shoulder and patted in a grandfatherly way. "You and your men are aboard the trawler *Linda Ann* out of Scarborough. We fished ye out of the water early this morning. I'm afraid some of the lads are close to the end and I'm sorry for that, but we didn't spot your raft until just after sunrise. We searched the whole area, so we got all that made it. I wish I had better word for ye, young officer." The last statement had a definitive sadness about it. The old fisherman knew how many men must have been in the water before they arrived.

"How...how...how many?"

The fisherman leaned back, strained his back as a puff of bluish smoke circled his beard and then whisked away in the wind. His eyes seemed to take on a dull gray shade, but perhaps it was just the light or maybe just his changing countenance as he considered the next response. "Sixteen only. Sixteen souls."

Braithwaite started as if struck by a lightning bolt. "Sixteen? Sixteen, you say!" It can't be!" His mouth fell agape and wide open in astonishment. "No, you must be wrong. Not sixteen. Where are the other trawlers? They had to have picked up more men." He struggled to lift himself up over the gunwale, but only his forehead and eyes could make it up. He searched the horizon—the empty horizon, darting back and forth in a desperate search. There were no other boats. The old fisherman stared at him in sad recognition that the young officer would soon realize the truth. Only sixteen men had been pulled out of the frigid North Sea. After several seconds, Braithwaite, exhausted by the sudden rush of adrenalin and exertion, slumped back down onto the hard deck, his chin drooping down to rest on his heaving chest. "Sixteen…." His hands fell to his lap in the resignation of the sad and awful truth. Fully fifty men had gone into the water just hours earlier. "McDuff? Where's McDuff?" He looked about the deck in quick glances searching in desperation for the seaman who had bound up his bleeding, gashed thigh in the night, and likely saved his life. "Has anyone seen McDuff!" he shouted.

About the deck, those that still could looked up at him, most with simply blank expressions and then dropped their eyes back down to the deck in exhaustion. On the trawler's starboard side, MacWilliams screwed up enough energy to respond, but he could only slowly shake his head no. Then, a small tear welled up in his right eye. McDuff was the old Navy man's nephew. Once again, Braithwaite's head drooped; he squeezed his eyes shut in utter resignation. Sixteen men. The oily, black smoke poured from the single funnel and the humming of the engine increased as the trawler *Linda Ann* picked up speed, determined to make port as fast as her old machinery could move her. In the stern, another man leaned over and gurgled before passing out again. The old fisherman stood straight up and turned to his first mate, nodded, and strode over to the wheelhouse to pilot his precious cargo to home port. By God, he would save his refugees.

Braithwaite stared astern back at the open water now with a slight chop. An autumn North Sea storm had brewed up. November had claimed its due. For several minutes, he simply stared aft as his mind drifted off, no doubt due to exhaustion and loss of blood. His thigh throbbed and he was now conscious of the pain from the great gash as fresh blood showed through McDuff's makeshift bandage. He scanned the open water on the horizon in a desperate last look for some sign of his lost men. He saw only the froth of the gathering waves as the north wind freshened. Gradually, his eyelids fell shut as he drifted off into unconsciousness.

As the trawler chugged along, rising and falling in the gathering swells, no one aboard could be aware of the scene unfolding only a few nautical miles to the southeast. Braithwaite and the *Halberd* survivors learned much later that their two torpedoes had doomed the German cruiser as well. She had limped away making for the safety of Wilhelmshaven, only to travel a few miles before she too plunged under the surface taking most of the sailors with her. In the frigid water in a duplication of the *Halberd*'s tragedy, the *Kolberg*-class cruiser's officers struggled to organize the few remaining survivors as the sea grew rougher. None ever made it back to the Fatherland. No friendly trawler appeared to save them. *Halberd* had done her duty as the collier convoy safely reached the Thames estuary with no men or ships lost. The North Sea made no distinctions but had claimed its due as it had for eons. At the trawler's helm making for Scarborough, the old fisherman with the stubby pipe hummed softly under his breath the "Mariner's Hymn:"

> Eternal Father, strong to save,
> Whose arm hath bound the restless wave,
> Who bidd'st the mighty ocean deep,
> Its own appointed limits keep;
> Oh, hear us when we cry to Thee,
> For those in peril on the sea.

CHAPTER 2

Jerusalem

21 February 1915. The Strand, London.

On a chilly, damp, London winter morning, a lone figure in Navy greatcoat with the collar pulled up around his ears strode down the Strand toward the tiny church that sat in the middle of the road across from King's College. As the figure approached St Mary le Strand, he paused. Here and there Londoners in ones and twos bustled about to avoid the misty chill. Lieutenant John Braithwaite gazed up at the massive doors to the venerable church. He had not been there in years. *A funeral perhaps, before the Navy, before the war? No matter, no matter.* In truth, he had not really been in a church in years—a lapsed Anglican perhaps. He attended the Church of England services aboard ship and station but only because it set the example for the sailors. Now, it was different. He felt drawn to this place, a solitary refuge in the middle of a busy Westminster Street, now practically deserted.

As he stepped in, he turned down the collar. The place felt remarkably warm and comforting despite the chill of the mid-winter morning. Stopping just inside the massive entryway to reconnoiter the situation, he noticed only a couple of worshipers in the front pews. In the chantry, a choir bustled about under the supervision of a boisterous music master, no doubt rehearsing for the upcoming Sunday services. One by one, he unbuttoned the brass buttons and noticed that each had a thin verdigris coating from weeks at sea in the salt air of *Halberd*'s open flying bridge in the chilly North Sea. He often wore the heavy greatcoat even on warm sunny autumn days much to the amusement of the bridge watch—all of them now dead. He had been wearing the coat that afternoon the previous November. How it had managed to make it into the water, then into the raft and not pull him under, he would never know. *Must polish up these buttons when I get the chance.* Braithwaite's head drooped as he shuffled his feet. *How stupid of me! Polishing bloody buttons.* He thought again of his dead shipmates and the image of the dead captain.

Silently, he tiptoed forward and took a seat in the last pew, anxious not to disturb the worshipers or the bustling choir. He sat for several minutes just looking about at the magnificent structure. The great window panes allowed ivory-tinted light to flow in, giving the chapel a hazy glow. Intricately carved panels adorned the walls; white painted and natural wood finished, they gave the chapel a magnificent grandeur. The choir snapped his attention back to the chancery as they began the hymn "Jerusalem:"

"Bring me my bow,"

Hazy thoughts filtered through his mind as the choir sang on:

"Bring me my arrows,"

Braithwaite bowed his head in silent prayer, a prayer for his departed comrades.

"Bring me my chariot of fire."

As the last chords reached a resounding crescendo, the chapel fairly vibrated. Through the cloudy haze, a shaft of light shot through the great windows and illuminated the altar as if by divine design. Braithwaite, not a terribly religious man, could not but be struck by the scene. He gazed in wonderment at the glittering light show. The events of the past few weeks, though, had changed his perspective on life, on God, and on himself. Did it not often do so? The living wondered why they had survived and so many had not? Braithwaite had these thoughts as well; they had weighed heavy on his soul in the weeks since the battle as his ravaged thigh healed.

Gazing at the light beam on the altar as a last chord of "Jerusalem" faded away and as he sat in a chapel in the middle of the Strand in safe and secure London, a revelation slowly evolved in his mind. Moment by moment, the young naval officer's resolve built, slowly yet keenly. He must return to the fight. Whether by divine inspiration or by fiat, here he sat in an old chapel where others for centuries had bowed and prayed for divine guidance. Now he did the same. He had entered the chapel beaten down by the sorrow, grief, and the weight of guilt at having survived. Now as the light faded, shadowed by a passing cloud, he stood, a man resolved to resume the fight—he would return to the fray. Damn the pain he still felt in the wounded leg; Braithwaite would return to action with increased resolve. He would honor his fallen shipmates with all he could muster. As he stood in the back pew, a smile broke across his previously sad, careworn face. He now had renewed purpose. As he turned to exit, he thrust his hand into the greatcoat pocket and felt a piece of paper, ignored until now. Pulling it out, he read the official typed, stamped, and oh so military message as he exited out into the Strand.

> Captain Reginald Hall, RN, Director, Royal Naval Intelligence, requests the courtesy of a call at 10.00 hours on the 21st at Room Number 40, Old Admiralty Building, Whitehall. Signed, S. J. B. Millar, Lt Cdr., RNVR

Braithwaite folded the message, replaced it in the greatcoat pocket, turned up the collar against the breeze, and strode down the Strand toward the Old Admiralty on the far side of Trafalgar Square.

****

"Lieutenant Braithwaite, Captain Hall will see you now."

"Thank you." Braithwaite stood, smoothed the lapels of his uniform jacket, and fell in behind the sailor as he knocked at the heavy oak door leading into the inner sanctum of the Director of Naval Intelligence (DNI), Captain Reginald Hall, known as "Blinker" for his constant eye blinks. Hall sat behind a huge mahogany desk, piled high with papers, message traffic, administrative notes, etc. Braithwaite had heard of this former cruiser and battleship sailor who now commanded a most vital, yet secret service. The staff of intelligence officers—some military, mostly civilians now in uniform for the war—intercepted and decoded the most secret and useful of the enemy's naval message traffic. The new wireless technology had made command, control, and communications of the worldwide fleets and remote stations possible, but it also created a great vulnerability. With expert deciphering and decryption, an enemy could now determine the movements of forces, timetables for ships, operational orders, and a myriad of other naval secrets that had previously been hidden. And, Reginald Hall and the denizens of Room 40 had become experts in the clandestine science of naval intelligence. The Kaiser's navy had no such equivalent. Indeed, since early in the war, the Royal Navy had tapped into the underwater telegraph cables leading out of northern Germany and had been intercepting even the most sensitive diplomatic traffic. Braithwaite stood erect, but his eyes scanned the room noting practically everything about it—the marble fireplace, a painting of some distant naval engagement, a pipe rack on the desk, the antique Persian carpet covering a careworn wooden floor, and a photograph of the king looking somber and dour with a touch of defiance. Wartime. Perhaps His Majesty's countenance meant to convey a warning to his cousin: "Kaiser Bill, with love and affection and all the worst wishes for an unpleasant year." Well, not really but the thought flashed through his mind. Hall never looked up, never acknowledged his presence, but kept scribbling on some critically important piece of administrivia.

Braithwaite had always been adept at what the service called "attention to detail." He noted every aspect of the somber room. Grieg's famous melody, *In the Hall of the Mountain King*, came to mind. As he waited for Hall to react to his presence, he hummed it under his breath—then stopped. He gazed over at the battle painting. The Royal Navy clearly had won the day. A demasted French ship-of-the-line listed to starboard with flames shooting from the gun deck as the British warship loosed off yet another broadside. What caught his eye were the men in the water, struggling to stay afloat, arms raised in desperation, mouths wide open, perhaps begging for their mothers or praying to God for deliverance. Before, he might never have noticed. Now, the unfolding tragedy seared into his consciousness, bringing back that awful night of the previous November.

Hall grunted. The old sea dog looked up, and true to form, blinked several times before speaking. "Lieutenant Braithwaite, please, stand at ease. Be seated." He motioned toward a warm, burgundy leather chair. Braithwaite nodded and gingerly sat down, but with spine erect and arms tucked by his side. He wasn't sure whether to relax or tense.

"Relax, Lieutenant. I am not an ogre."

Braithwaite breathed in deeply and let his shoulders fall back into a more natural stance. "Thank you, Sir."

Hall grunted again as he closed the memorandum pad in front of it. The DNI clasped his hands together and leaned back in his leather chair. "I have read the report of the action of the *Halberd* and the testimony of the surviving crew. You did a most remarkable thing that day young man and the Kingdom is grateful."

Braithwaite nodded, swallowed hard, and whispered, "Thank you." A moment of silence followed.

Hall shook his head and after a few moments, spoke again. "The DSC (Distinguished Service Cross) is well deserved."

Braithwaite nodded again.

"I have also read your medical report. The docs have not cleared you for sea duty as of yet. It states that with your leg wound, you are mobile but will likely require several more months of convalescence to be fit for sea duty again. But, they say that you are fit enough for shore duty. Is that true?"

The DNI had stated the facts in such a fatherly fashion that Braithwaite now relaxed a bit more. "Yes, Sir. I'm fit for shore duty but as you will appreciate, I am ready for a new assignment as soon as possible."

"Understandable. You are clearly a man of action, Mr. Braithwaite. I also have read your file with a great deal of interest. It appears that you are fluent in German and familiar with East Africa."

"Yes, Sir, I am." Braithwaite shifted nervously not knowing the meaning behind Hall's question. "My father spent several years at the

Foreign Office and on diplomatic assignment overseas. I spent several years as a child in Berlin when my father served at the Embassy followed by a tour of duty as consul in Dar es Salaam and in Nairobi. My parents believed in total immersion in the local culture. That meant fluency in the German language and culture. I suppose, under the present conditions that is a burden I carry." He smiled weakly, waiting for the verbal hammer to fall. It did, but of an entirely different nature.

Hall smiled and nodded. "Not a burden, Mr. Braithwaite. It is an asset. I want you to go to work for me."

Braithwaite, momentarily stunned at the unexpected turn of events, let his lower lip drop ever so slightly, but enough for the older officer to cock an eyebrow. "More specifically, Lieutenant. I want you to be a spy."

Braithwaite jolted upward, his neck stiffened and his fingers shot out straight as if struck by an electrical current. *Good Lord! A what? A spy?* He could say nothing, but his mind raced in all directions. *A spy!*

Hall instantly noted the young officer's shock and discomfort. "Well, perhaps, really a gatherer of information. Call it an analyst and observer of enemy capabilities."

The classification did not help. Braithwaite's body language indicated his confusion. He shifted uncomfortably in his chair. "A gatherer of information, Sir?"

"Well, quite right. Yes, quite right."

Perhaps the old man means a cushy desk job at Admiralty. Perhaps translating German messages. That must be it. My German skills. That's it then. "Do you mean, Sir, translating intercepted German signals, that sort of this and that until I'm fit for sea duty again?" The upward lilt in the voice indicated Braithwaite's utter confusion at what had been proposed.

The DNI smiled, a wicked, impish sort of smirk. He placed both hands on the desk edge and pushed the chair away. Rising slowly, he turned toward the marble fireplace and placing his hands in his uniform pockets in the traditional nautical fashion, he strode over to the fireplace. In the midst of a chilly London morning, the room had gone cold. Hall reached out, took a poker, and punched up the coal embers until a small flame appeared. Poker still in hand, he turned back toward Braithwaite. A deadly serious look had replaced the smirk.

"You are a man of action, Mr. Braithwaite. Your entire record indicates that. Do you think that a minor desk assignment would suit you?" Again, the left eyebrow cocked as he blinked several times in succession.

"Truth be told, Sir, no, not really. I was rather hoping to be back at sea on a destroyer or perhaps a new light cruiser."

"And so you shall in due time. But for now, your country needs your special talents in another direction. Though you haven't received your new orders yet, you have been seconded to Naval Intelligence Division until you are finally fit."

Aha! There is the mighty rub! Hall's power and influence runs deep. Already seconded, indeed. Braithwaite's shoulders sank in acceptance of his new reality. He was to be, as the old man had put it, a gatherer of information. *Well, so be it.* "Indeed, Sir. And what would be my task?"

Hall, realizing the man was his, strode over to Braithwaite and hovered over him. He spoke more rapidly now, the excitement clearly welling up. "Yes, Lieutenant. We need you to go to German East Africa and gather information." He paused. "Well, dammit all! You are going to be a bloody spy!"

Braithwaite could only nod his head in somber recognition of his new fate.

"You see, Lieutenant, you possess the language skills and knowledge of the place and its peculiarities to be damned effective. We jolly well need you down there just now. What do you say?" Hall leaned back against the front of the massive desk and folded his arms across his chest.

"I suppose, Sir, I must be that man. There is a war to be won and if that is the way that I can contribute then that is to be." *John old sod, what have you just done?*

"Good!" Hall exclaimed as he slammed his fist down on the desk. Inkwell and papers rattled. He picked up the telephone handset with one hand and dialed the numbers with the other. "O'Sullivan, please send in Commander Millar with his special file."

Braithwaite set motionless like a man in the dock awaiting his fate from His Lordship, the judge. Within seconds, came two swift knocks on the heavy oak door. "Come," shouted Hall as he strode over to the chart table in the corner motioning Braithwaite to follow. In came a short, but solid officer carrying a black leather bag and with the zigzag gold rings of a lieutenant-commander in the Royal Navy Volunteer Reserve or the "wavy navy" as it had been deemed. All three men hovered over the chart table as Hall explained, "Lieutenant Braithwaite, this is Lieutenant-Commander Steven Millar, RNVR, a special assistant." Both men acknowledged each other.

"Good to meet you, Braithwaite. We are most impressed with your service."

Braithwaite nodded, "Commander."

"Right then. Millar, please explain what little junket we have in mind for young Mr. Braithwaite here." Hall ambled back over to the coal fire and thrust his hands toward the heat. Millar pulled a chart out of the black valise and rolled it out on the table, placing various navigational tools to hold down the paper corners. Braithwaite instantly recognized the East African coast—Zanzibar, Dar es Salaam, and down to the Rufiji River Delta. He leaned forward with his elbows on the table. Using a pencil as a pointer, Millar indicated Dar es Salaam, capital of German East Africa.

"There is a ship, the SMS *Aachen* to be specific, operating out of Dar es Salaam and the Rufiji River Delta. That is a damned nuisance. She is the only ship remaining of von Spee's original East Asia squadron based in China before the war and only survives since the Battle of the Falklands due to some necessary repairs that had her in port and not with the main squadron. Then the bugger escaped and now operates here. She forays out and, somewhat remarkably, attacks merchant traffic transmitting up the east coast bound for Suez or India. To date, she has sunk or captured at least twenty vessels that we know of." Millar went on to explain the tactical problem of the Rufiji River Delta that complicated efforts to corner *Aachen*. With several channels leading to the Indian Ocean deep and wide enough to allow a light cruiser to transit based on the draft, the enemy could pick and choose his escape into or sortie route out of the Delta at will. Warships operating out of Mombasa or Simonstown, South Africa, were never numerous enough to cover all the possible channels. Then, there was the mysterious way in which the enemy cruiser always knew where the blockading ships operated at any given day. That was the mystery that Hall proposed to send Braithwaite to East Africa to solve.

Braithwaite's eyes narrowed to a slit as he stared at the markings on the chart, each indicating a lost merchantman. "One would think that coaling would stop him."

"One would," retorted Hall from across the room, "except, several months ago, the bastard attacked the French coaling station in the Comoros Islands and got clean away after loading up from two captured colliers. Both ships are gone now, we suppose, but he managed to stash enough coal for several sorties."

Braithwaite, his mind now whirling with the possibilities, fired the next question. "Then Sir, how has she managed to avoid our cruiser patrols?"

Hall strode back over to the table. He had lit a fine old meerschaum pipe and puffed away as he spoke. "That, Mr. Braithwaite, is what you need to find out. Every time we think she is cornered, she simply vanishes over the horizon. Every time we attempt to catch her, in port or at the anchorages in the Delta, she seems to know we are coming. *Aachen* knows where the blockade ships are whenever she slips in or out. The same applies to the occasional port visits for supplies in Dar es Salaam. She always avoids our blockade ships and random patrols. When we think we have cornered her, she seems aware of our presence in advance and merrily sails over the horizon out of gun range. Frankly, it's a deuce of a mystery how she knows where we are and how she is able to escape. And as to fuel, every time she attacks a vessel, she always captures the coal bunker before sinking the victim. She will run short of ammunition at some point, but how much damage will she do in the meanwhile?" Hall slammed down hard on the chart, rattling the dividers, compass, and parallel ruler. "Your mission is to find out what she is about and how she is evading the hunters."

Braithwaite nodded in understanding. *A gathering of information indeed. Well, so be it. It's off to Africa.*

Millar spoke again, "You will take passage in the cruiser HMS *St Andrews* through Suez and on to Zanzibar. She departs from Portsmouth the day after tomorrow. Once in Zanzibar, you will rendezvous with our man in Zanzibar. For security sake, you will only know him by his codename—Minstrel. He will be able to supply what you require in terms of logistics, information, lodging, and so forth."

"Minstrel, right." Braithwaite's excitement built in his voice after weeks of convalescence and inaction. He was finally going back into the fray. Not quite what he had envisioned perhaps, but into the fray nonetheless.

"Yes, Minstrel. By the way, do you know the tune 'The Minstrel Boy?'"

Braithwaite thought for a moment. "'The Minstrel Boy.' Isn't that about the minstrel boy to the war has gone with his wild harp slung behind him?" Braithwaite began to whistle the old melody. Millar and Hall both grinned.

"Indeed it is. Don't forget it. That's how you will recognize Minstrel. He will find you and be whistling the tune. You are to respond with the same tune as a recognition signal."

"Right then!" Hall clapped both hands together. "Lieutenant Braithwaite, please be here tomorrow morning, 10.00 hours sharp for a full briefing and pack your kit. That is all."

"Aye, aye, Sir." Braithwaite snapped to a smart attention, pivoted and strode confidently toward the door, not having any idea how his life was about to change. First things first. He headed back to his lodgings on Talbot Square up near Marble Arch. On the tube ride back, he reviewed all the recent happenings in his life from his cadet days to assignment to the beloved destroyer through the terrible night in November and the tragedy of so many good men lost to the frigid North Sea and the German gunners. As the underground train raced from station to station, he gradually became more and more ashamed of himself. The self-pity and anguish of the past few months deeply disturbed him and, in truth, embarrassed him. The men of *Halberd* had given their lives for King and Country. He had bled a bit. He thought of Lieutenant-Commander Urquhart and the ghastly scene on the flying bridge. He thought of the morning that he visited the captain's family in Aberdeen—a grieving wife and three "wee bairns" as the skipper called them. He presented the man's belongings to the widow—all that physically remained of her husband. All these thoughts now steeled his resolve. Very well. He would not go back into the fleet just yet. That would be in due course. For now, he would head back to East Africa, a place he remembered well. He would discover the secret of the ghost cruiser and so bring about her downfall. He would do so to his utmost. In a sort of fashion, the morning in the chapel in the heart of London and in the inner sanctum of the Navy spymaster, he had a new beginning—a genesis of sorts.

****

22 February 1915, North-Northwest of Madagascar.
"How's it going?" asked the first officer as he slid into the cramped pilothouse. The second mate just nodded. Tired after another long watch, all he wanted to do was to have a quick breakfast and then hit the rack for some well-needed sleep. The watch turnover was simple, routine, and brief. The first officer looked over his daily schedule before putting the binoculars up for a horizon scan. Other than an early morning fog bank, the sky shone bright blue and cloudless—a regular day. But then, something odd on the horizon caught his eye.

The 5,200-ton steamer SS *Wallaby Dawn* out of Perth, Western Australia, carried Chilean nitrate from Valparaiso bound for Cape Town and the South African munitions factories. Nitrate formed a vital ingredient for gunpowder; the shells manufactured in South Africa would eventually be fired in the small-scale war raging in southern Africa between German and British colonial forces. Old, but still serviceable, the ship had been given a new life by the war and the critical need for shipping. And, it needed skilled seamen. The first officer, a medically retired Royal Australian Navy officer, had been badly injured when his ship had been damaged in a typhoon several months earlier. If His Majesty's Navy no longer needed an experienced officer, the Perth shipping company certainly did. He had made the nitrate run in the old tramp steamer several times without incident. Today would be different.

Maintaining course and speed north of Madagascar, *Wallaby Dawn* plodded along at 8 knots—about all the antique reciprocating engines could muster. The object on the horizon appeared to be closing fast. "What the devil?" the first officer muttered to no one in particular. He maintained his observation of the strange closing ship for several minutes and then his naval recognition training kicked in. Clearly silhouetted by the dawn's light, he recognized a warship, a German light cruiser of the *Dresden* class. He leaped to the tarnished bridge to engine room voice tube and snapped open the cap. "Engine room, bridge. We have a ticklish situation here. Can you give me more speed?"

From deep within the hull with the pounding noise of the engines in the background came the reply from the second engineer, a veteran of many such runs. "I'll pour on the coals. I can squeeze maybe a couple more knots out of her. What's the situation?"

"I'll advise. Keep me apprised." The first officer grabbed a message pad from the chart table and quickly scribbled out, "From SS *Wallaby Dawn*. Latitude 10.2 degrees S, longitude 050.35 degrees E. Sighted *Dresden*-class German light cruiser bearing 225. Estimated speed 20 knots. Estimated course 110. Intentions unknown. Will try to evade." Tearing the paper from the pad, he thrust it into the hands of the surprised mess steward, who had just arrived in the pilothouse with morning tea. "Quick, roust out the wireless officer and tell him to transmit to Perth and Admiralty as soon as possible. Now go man, quickly."

The steward placed the wicker tray on the chart table with a clatter of china cups, turned, and raced down the ladder almost bowling over the master coming up from his sea cabin.

"Morning, Mr. Evans, what's the situation?"

The first officer pointed toward the approaching German, now only a few thousand yards distant. "Warship. German. Approaching fast. No idea what she's about, but no good, I'll warrant."

The master grabbed a second pair of binoculars as both men leaned through the open pilothouse windows, peering at the mysterious ship. "I don't like this Mr. Evans." Looking about, the master noted the fog bank now rolling in from the west. "Let's make for that fog bank and hope for the best."

"Concur," replied the first officer, who turned toward the now ashen-faced helmsman. "Right 40 degrees."

"Right 40 degrees, aye," came the reply as the helmsman spun the ship's wheel. The ship vibrated, a clear sign that she had picked up speed. Ten minutes later, the fog completely shrouded the ship. For the next few minutes, the first officer ordered zigzag turns, a technique learned in the navy. Once safely inside the bank with no way for the German cruiser to tell their location, the first officer ordered All Stop. The engine order telegraph clanged to All Stop. Five minutes later, the ship lay dead in the water with fog so thick that the tense men in the pilothouse could barely see the bow. A quietness settled over the old steamer. Meanwhile, the no longer groggy wireless office taped out the frightening message to company headquarters and the British Admiralty, both several thousand miles away.

"That should do it. Let's give it an hour or so and then resume course and speed."

The first officer nodded in agreement and wiped his sweating brow with a well-worn handkerchief.

The first rounds landed only twenty yards off the starboard beam.

"Good God!" shouted the first officer. "All engines ahead full! Quick man!"

The helmsman grasped the engine order telegraph handle and cranked to Ahead Full just as a second volley of 4.1-inch rounds crashed into the pilothouse. The ship lurched wildly with no one at the helm. She started drifting to port as the engines resumed their thrum, thrum, thrum. Moments later, a third volley landed nearby, but one pierced the thin hull and exploded in a cargo hold full of explosive nitrate gases. In a flash, the ship erupted in a cloud of flame and smoke. The shattered hulk sank quickly with no survivors.

CHAPTER 3

Zanzibar

10 March 1915. Zanzibar.

The sea felt good. It filled his lungs with fresh, salty, invigorating air. He loved London even in the darkness of a wartime capital, but the heavy, choking London fog, a mixture of humidity and coal smoke couldn't compare to the clean, crisp sea breezes. The passage from Portsmouth to the Mediterranean and through the Suez Canal had been uneventful. Despite being winter in Northern Europe, the balmy Mediterranean breezes helped. The constant stiffness and occasional pain in his thigh had almost disappeared. Braithwaite felt close to 100% ready for action. The daily routine of shipboard life had a wonderful healing effect. Braithwaite was in his element. As the days grew warmer, he felt better and better. Warm humid nights replaced the damp and chilly North Atlantic evenings. As HMS *St Andrews* emerged from the Red Sea, the days grew sultry and damp and downright hot-winter in the tropics. A quick layover at Mombasa gave him a chance to go ashore; he savored the British ales and lagers available at the Royal Navy officer's mess. Strolling through the colonial outpost brought back memories of his youth—three years as a young teenager—in colonial East Africa before heading back to Britain for school.

As they approached Zanzibar, the captain gave him his final briefs.

Several documents marked MOST SECRET came from the old man's safe, still crisp despite the humid air. HMS *St Andrews* had spent much of late 1914 in the Western Indian Ocean hunting the mysterious and elusive enemy warship. As the captain briefed him, the frustration poured out. How the devil could the German always know where the Royal Navy was? How did the bugger know when to flee despite several ambushes set up to trap the *Aachen*? More than one British and Australian captain came away utterly frustrated. They also came away with a deep, abiding determination to finally settle the score, and a grudging admiration for the German who had eluded so many traps. Many a merchant seamen survivor reported that the German cruiser simply appeared on the horizon with no warning as if she knew exactly where to find the target. Some even thought it to be a ghost ship. Braithwaite knew better. The Germans must have developed some new technology. No other rational explanation fit. And, his task was to find out and report back to "Blinker" Hall. He didn't have a clue as to how he would accomplish the mission but was determined to succeed. Many lives depended on his success.

The captain of HMS *St Andrews* would have the task of shadowing and eventually sinking the German raider. Thus far, it had been a frustrating and humiliating failure chasing down the ghost cruiser. The Admiralty sent him back into the contest once again but, this time, Captain George Peacock had two great advantages. One, he had two other light cruisers and a pair of destroyers and although he had no clue yet as to what a weapon it would turn out to be, he had Lieutenant John D. F. Braithwaite, Royal Navy, DSC.

As they progressed southward, the captain, as time allowed, briefed Braithwaite on the action thus far. He had seen the *Aachen* only once and firmly believed they had landed a round on the enemy's superstructure, but with minimal damage. During a thunderstorm with wild tropical electricity all about them, *St Andrews* had managed to ambush the raider as she came out from under a rain squall. For the briefest of moments, the enemy's magic failed him, and the *Aachen* stumbled into the Royal Navy's gun sights. Surprised, but not panicked, the German went to full ahead and dashed back into the rain squall, never to be seen again. A week later, a desperate SOS from a French freighter alerted the world that the raider had returned.

Braithwaite absorbed every detail from Peacock. *Aachen* operated out of the Rufiji River Delta about 125 miles south of Dar es Salaam. Generally, but not always, she pulled into the port every few weeks to take on food and supplies. Neutral ships still sailed in and out of Dar es Salaam unmolested bringing needed supplies and likely replacement contraband, including 4.1-inch shells. Britain could never catch all of them by the distant blockade, but a Norwegian and a Swedish ship had been caught smuggling ammunition and had been interned in Zanzibar. To Peacock's frustration, he simply did not have enough warships to implement an effective blockade. Most amazingly, the raider always managed to slip in and out of Dar es Salaam at night, even in foggy or rainy weather eluding his few ships. When *St Andrews* returned to Portsmouth for desperately needed maintenance, he had raced to Admiralty to plead for more assets. The Admiralty, frustrated at the enemy cruiser's effectiveness and no doubt influenced by a parade of ship owners and merchants complaining about their shipping losses, detached the flotilla of light cruisers and destroyers from the North Sea Dover blockade, sending them back under Peacock's command. Additionally, two more destroyers and a French light cruiser were on the way as well. With these assets, Peacock would have sufficient forces to implement a more rigorous, tighter blockade. *Aachen* had been bold in Peacock's absence, sailing into Dar es Salaam by day and staying over, giving her crew a few days of much-needed shore leave.

This fact gave Braithwaite his opening. He had to see the ship firsthand. If he was to learn her secret, he had to have a good visual orientation; the resident agent, Minstrel, had the task of making that possible. As African ports went, Dar es Salaam was large and populous. Braithwaite could easily pass for a German resident, and with little to no security on the waterfront, he felt competent and confident that he could get close enough to observe. Hall supplied diagrams of the enemy ship and, on the passage, Braithwaite studied and memorized every detail of the enemy's interior and exterior. With close observation, he might detect any anomalies, modifications, or unusual appearances that indicated the cruiser's secret. The enemy's hubris in sailing boldly into port in daylight would be the critical vulnerability leading to its destruction.

As the flotilla crossed the equator east of Kenya, the uninitiated and detestable pollywogs underwent the time-honored rites of passage and became honored shellbacks in the traditional ceremony of crossing the line (equator). Braithwaite had become a shellback years earlier in a previous command while transiting the east coast of South America before the war. With great amusement, he observed the ceremonies from the bridge wing as King Neptune and his court inducted the rookies, turning them from lowly pollywogs to proud shellbacks—true men of the sea. As the ceremonies concluded, his mood turned from spirited to somber; he realized that many of these newly initiated men would not survive the war. Though months had passed, the horror of that night in November seldom left his conscious thoughts. But the thoughts steeled him to his purpose. The German would send no more men to Davy Jones' locker if he had anything to do about it.

****

Zanzibar. Out of respect, he waited until the entire crew went ashore before heading down the accommodation ladder to the grimy, oil-laden pier. Years of neglect showed in this outpost of the British Empire. Although Zanzibar represented an important staging point for operations against German East Africa, civilian contractors remained wary of sending ships and crews into the area for fear of the German raider. So, Zanzibar would have to await happier times. Otherwise, the ancient city on an island remained much as he remembered. Sights and smells of Africa, the Orient, and the West blended in a curious mix. Hanging above all was the sweet aroma of spices, especially cloves. After all, Zanzibar was known as "Spice Island." Despite the typical urban odors of human waste, poverty, and the ever-present tropical decay, to him, Zanzibar reminded him of a comforting childhood kitchen with warm fire and magnificent pastries and cakes.

One impression had changed. He noted the military presence as he strolled down the main street leading out of the dock area and into Stone Town, the old quarter of Zanzibar. Wartime. After all, the enemy lay only a few miles across the water. Machine gun emplacements and barbed wire surrounded the waterfront manned by an Indian Regiment just rotated out of France and destined eventually for Bombay and home. The Sikhs—magnificent fighters—stood typically over six feet tall and with their turbans appeared even more so. These stout warriors still held the defiant look of stern determination despite their horrendous experience of war on the Western Front. Though in civilian clothes so as to disguise his mission, he mentally saluted a pair of machine gun posts as he passed out of the dock's main gates.

The island's cosmopolitan nature struck him as he strolled through street after street. Asians, mainly Indians, Omanis, and Chinese, operated the many small shops. Africans owned the open-air market as push carts hawked all manner of fruits and vegetables. Here and there, a European appeared, most a bit shabbier than he remembered, clearly a result of wartime shortages and rationing. Although he had been issued a city map, he remembered much of the layout and had memorized the street details before debarking the ship. Though a novice at this spycraft, he knew enough not to be seen reading a map stamped Admiralty while undercover. Prior to departure, Millar had issued his instructions. "Proceed to Great George Street in New Town Zanzibar upon your arrival. In the northeast end of the town, you will find a Mrs. Potter's tea room. Order a tea and two tarts, one apple and one custard. Open this copy of *The Times* dated 16 January this year. When you hear someone whistling "the Minstrel Boy," that will be your contact in Zanzibar. Do nothing overt. Fold the paper, whistle the tune, then roll the paper, and place in your blazer pocket. We will fit you for the blazer later. That will be the signal to Minstrel that you are the agent. He will then make contact. Safeguard your identity. Though you are in Imperial territory, Germany has many agents and spies operating in Zanzibar. Do avoid compromising your presence straightaway—very bad form, old boy."

He strolled casually through the narrow streets and alleys of Stone Town where houses, mosques, bazaars, and small shops all competed for space. Shop owners crowded about him hawking their wares. He politely declined despite their insistence and strode on. The coral stone used to build most of the old city, hence the moniker, "Stone Town," gave the city a warm, reddish glow. *Barazas*, the elevated long stone benches mounted along the outside walls of buildings, allowed for pedestrian traffic even in the monsoon season when flash floods racing through the narrow, confined streets created an annoying, if not sometimes, dangerous hazard in the cobble-stoned streets below. Many buildings had large verandas protected by wooden balustrades. As a young man, while his father served as an assistant to the British Resident, he had always been intrigued by the elaborately carved doors on many of the buildings throughout Stone Town. Depending on the religion of the owner, these carvings tended to be either Hindu such as lotus flowers or Islamic, displaying Quranic text carved in bas-relief.

He passed the Old Fort. The first Portuguese colonists had begun construction of the defensive works centuries ago. When the Sultanate of Oman captured the island in the late 17th century, they completed the structure as the main defensive post for the town and harbor. Most of the stone houses surrounding the Old Fort dated from the 1830s, but he noticed that like most of the old town, wartime shortages prevented the constant maintenance that coral-based stone required. By the Treaty of Heligoland–Zanzibar of 1890, the Sultans of Zanzibar lost control of the island as well as East Africa to the British and German imperial powers. Zanzibar became a British Protectorate. Not quite a colony, it might as well be since the real power in the region was the British Resident, essentially a colonial governor but without the actual title.

Taking his time to soak in the marvels, he strolled past the House of Wonders or Palace of Wonders on the Mizingani Road along the seafront. Built for the Sultan in 1883, it had been damaged in the Anglo-Zanzibar War of 1896. He paused for a few minutes to gaze at the Sultan's Palace, a multistory structure that still showed signs of the British naval bombardment. The shortest war in history occurred there in 1896 as a rebellion by the Omani population against British rule was quashed in forty-five minutes by the guns of the Royal Navy. Such was the power of the modern rifled naval artillery.

In the previous century, slaves and spices dominated the economy and Braithwaite could sense the constant sweet and pungent aromas of spices from all over Asia and Africa as he wandered through the narrow Stone Town alleys and streets. The British had suppressed the East African slave trade in the previous century, but, despite the war, the town still did a robust trade in other commodities with the parts of the world not at each other's throats in Europe and the Mediterranean. The North American market flourished, but these were dangerous waters. The German ghost cruiser attacked freighters of all types and only after boarding would the German sailors realize that the target carried only spices bound for San Francisco, Vancouver, Seattle, or Los Angeles. Still, the trade flourished and he breathed in the wondrous aroma of cloves and other valuable spices.

Braithwaite crossed the causeway that enclosed the protected inner harbor and made his way through the New Town. It had a different look and feel. Here, one could almost imagine being in some European city. Wooden flower boxes graced the windows. Some homes looked almost Tudor in design, no doubt some architect's idea of the idyllic English country village. Most of New Town had been built in the late 19th century and had much wider streets, not the narrow alleyways of Stone Town. Here, the odors were less noticeable, both that of spices and human habitation. He paused to wipe his brow with a handkerchief. It was hot. Although warm and humid year round, this was March—a hot month and the start of the rainy season. After a pause to catch his breath in the super-heated, humid air, he pressed on and turned the corner onto Great George Street.

Mrs. Potter's occupied the corner of Great George Street and Hanover Road in the New Town. The shops and homes along the street reminded him of an urban mews of late Victorian years with comfortable townhouses intermingled among the shops. The pale blue and yellow sign painted with flowers on one side and a pink teapot on the reverse fit right in with the area's tone. Inside, lace tablecloths covered small tables adorned with a vase and a single flower, no doubt purchased every morning from the flower seller three streets down. He chose a table by the window that gave him a view of the entire room. A few patrons sat about enjoying a late morning coffee or tea and chatting quietly. Mostly female or elderly, he did not see anyone likely to be Minstrel. Millar had intentionally not briefed him on the agent's appearance for obvious security reasons. But now, Braithwaite grew anxious. Surely Minstrel had observed the cruiser's arrival that morning. Surely, the man simply waited to be sure that no German agent or local spy had followed Braithwaite. *Yes, that's it. Merely a security precaution. That's all.* Nonetheless, as the minutes passed, his anxiety grew. As he scanned the room again, his right hand started to quiver. *Good God! Am I to give myself away before the mission even begins! Steady on, lad, steady on!*

"Good morning, Sir, what will you be having this fine morning?" The petite, Irish waitress' kindly, sweet voice calmed his tensions for a moment."

"I, yes, well. A tea, black Ceylon. And, perhaps two, yes, two tarts, one apple, and one custard. Would that be available?"

"Certainly, Sir." She smiled, curtsied slightly, turned and headed back to the kitchen in the rear.

He scanned the room trying to identify his contact. Braithwaite felt adrift without a firm deck under his feet. What if Minstrel had been captured or killed? What if he had not received the message or had confused the rendezvous arrangements? As each minute passed, his anxiety grew. Tiny sweat beads formed on his brow. To the casual observer, it would be from humidity and heat. Once more, he scanned the room, his right hand now noticeably trembling with anxiety and anticipation.

An elderly couple sat in a booth quietly chatting. *No, too old.* Two ladies clearly of the local aristocracy sat oh so properly at a table by the window. *No, too proper.* In a corner table sat a young woman quietly sipping a steaming coffee. *No, too ... no, just a very attractive young lady probably in her midmorning break from one of the professional offices.* As he gazed, she looked up and directly into his eyes. He quickly turned his head, clearly caught staring. She only smiled and then looked back down at her newspaper spread out on the table and gingerly took another sip.

The waitress arrived. "Sir, your tea and pastries."

Shaken out of his almost trancelike state, he mumbled some incoherent thank you and looked back down at the table with obvious embarrassment. The waitress just smiled and began setting his order down. With another curtsy, she twirled and, with a tray under her arm, started back toward the kitchen door.

He ate and drank slowly hoping that Minstrel would show up and relieve the ever-growing tension. Over and over, he ran the various scenarios in his mind's eye. *If Minstrel did not make contact, what to do? What had Millar said? Dammit all. Now is not the time to lose focus. Think man! Think!* He raised his cup again to his lips. It was a stall. He had long before finished the tea, but he could not yet abandon the post. No one new had entered the tea shop. The elderly couple paid their bill and departed. In the window booth, the two prim women had also departed. Behind the counter, the Irish waitress counted receipts, oblivious to his presence. *If Minstrel fails to make contact, go immediately to the naval headquarters and ask for Commander Armitage. He will pass to you further instructions.* Those had been Millar's directions. Braithwaite had been in the tea shop for about an hour. He would give Minstrel another ten minutes.

From somewhere behind them, he heard a familiar tune. *A familiar tune! The minstrel boy to the war has gone in the ranks of death ye shall find him.* Braithwaite's hand shot straight back as if fired from a cannon. The voice ceased. He jerked his head around. No one was there except the young lady reading the paper. Had she heard it too? The woman made no hint of having heard a thing. He quickly scanned the room. *No one here. No one.* The waitress had returned to the kitchen. *Minstrel. He must be outside.* Trying to appear as nonchalant and casual as possible, Braithwaite craned his neck and peered at the open door, then over to the bay windows, then back to the door. *Nothing! No one here!* He laid the teacup down and brought his right hand over to his face, rubbing gently across his mouth and nose trying to stifle the panicked look.

"*The minstrel boy to the war has gone, in the ranks of death ye shall find him.*" The voice came from the corner, a distinctly feminine voice this time. Braithwaite jerked around and stared at the young woman who continued reading her paper. *Could this be his contact? Could Minstrel have sent this woman in his place? It had to be. No one else in the room could have sung the verse.* He slowly turned back toward his table, trying not to appear panicked or as bumbling a field agent as he truly was. He took in a deep breath and closed his eyes.

"*His father's sword he hath girded on and his wild harp slung behind him.*"

Braithwaite bit down hard on his lower lip in nervous anticipation. Seconds passed. Then, he heard the rustle of silk and crinoline. A feminine rustle. A dress. The young woman had left her seat. The tapping of leather heels on the polished floor indicated that she came near. Without a further word, she pulled a chair back from the table and ever so delicately sat, hands folded in her lap. She said nothing but simply stared at the nervous naval officer before her. Another sweat bead rolled off Braithwaite's nose and splattered on the table.

"You are a very nervous man, Lieutenant. That's very poor field craft." She now looked down at the table. Only her eyes looked up as she spoke, then went down again. Braithwaite could only blubber. No coherent words came out even though his lips moved. The young lady, head still down, smiled at his discomfort.

As if on cue, the waitress reappeared. She strode over the table and in a jovial voice, asked if she could bring more tea. Braithwaite sat stunned. His new table companion quickly looked up at the maid and ordered two more teas. The waitress nodded and returned to the kitchen. The woman simply stared at him.

After a few more embarrassing seconds, he screwed up his courage and looked the woman directly in the eyes and spoke, "Did Minstrel send you?"

Without breaking stride, she responded, "I am Minstrel."

Braithwaite felt as if the ceiling crashed in on his head. Stunned, he could only shake his head in disbelief. He placed both hands down on the table, palms up as if in total surrender.

"I do beg your pardon," he sputtered.

As matter of fact as before, she simply responded, "I am Minstrel."

Both sat silent for a minute or two. Finally, and thankfully, the waitress brought the tea, chatting aimlessly about nothing in particular. Braithwaite and Minstrel said nothing, simply staring at each other. Finally, after the waitress had disappeared back into the kitchen, Braithwaite spoke haltingly, "I was led to believe that Minstrel was... was...."

"A man?" she chimed in. "Yes, old "Blinker" can have a sense of humor... rarely... but on occasion." She looked about the empty tearoom ensuring that no one heard. They were alone. "You see, Lieutenant Braithwaite, the Germans would also expect a man. This little ruse protects my cover. But we shan't tarry. Too many curious eyes. I have secured a safe house on Royal Charles Street in Stone Town. It's close enough to my flat for easy access, but far enough so as to be discreet." As any proper Edwardian lady would, thought Braithwaite, now recovering some balance.

Both took a few sips of the hot, dark tea so as to make good appearances, then he rose and gingerly pulled his chair back from the table. "Shall we go, Miss... Miss... Minstrel?"

"Droll, Sir, very droll." Both grinned. His panic now subsided, the old Braithwaite humor returned. He dropped several coins onto the table. As they exited into the deserted, dusty street into the glaring, blazing African sun, she cocked her head slightly toward him with yet another smile. "It's Mrs. Alice Hallwood."

The flat on Royal Charles Street was basic and spartan, but adequate, he thought as she showed him the several rooms. With only an occasional grunt, he seemed pleased with her efforts at his lodgings. "It will do nicely, Mrs. Hallwood," he finally responded with an approving nod. She motioned toward a straight-backed chair in what appeared to be a breakfast nook equipped with only a table and two chairs.

"I should hope, Sir. We wouldn't care to waste the DNI's money on overly extravagant digs. This is where we will operate from. I can come and go by a hidden back entrance. Please understand, Lieutenant. I have built a careful cover story as the grieving and unapproachable widow. We must be discreet in our meetings lest enemy agents become suspicious. *Grieving widow? Excellent cover. Wonder if "Blinker" invented that one, unless… no… dare not inquire.* He blushed. The moment of embarrassment passed. She stared at him as if to get the measure of the naval officer clearly on his first field assignment. He would have to do better. Unvarnished emotions will get you killed in the spy business. He had a lot to learn.

"Both are true."

Braithwaite's head bobbed up. Her statement startled him. "I beg your pardon?"

"Both are true. I am a widow and I am grieving."

Braithwaite's jaw dropped awkwardly as his eyes grew wider. He stumbled over the words, "I… I am truly sorry, I didn't know. I… I apologize, Mrs. Hallwood."

"No, you wouldn't have known."

He had noticed previously that she wore the gold band of a married woman. *Damn! Stupid git! I have to learn. The Germans will figure me out.* For the first time since that day in Hall's office, serious doubt crept in. *Had the old man made a mistake? Was he not the man for such a field assignment with little preparation or training?* Alice stood and turned toward the small window where lace curtains fluttered in the late afternoon heat. She stared out the window for several seconds, her head bowed. "My husband was a naval officer as you are. Lieutenant-Commander Adrian Hallwood, gunnery officer on HMS *Aboukir*."

Braithwaite understood immediately. Three older British cruisers— *Aboukir, Cressy,* and *Hogue*—had been sunk in the same engagement the previous September by the same German submarine, a testament to the deadly threat of that new naval weapon. Many British sailors perished that day as some of the war's first maritime casualties. Now he began to understand. Perhaps that is why this elegant young woman had gone to Zanzibar—to seek vengeance for her loss. Braithwaite felt the crush of embarrassment come over him. He started turning the empty glass on the table, not really knowing what else to do and stammered, "Oh. I am truly sorry. I wasn't aware."

Alice turned toward him, her back to the open window. She smiled but the sadness in her eyes belied her true emotions. "Quite all right. You wouldn't have known. It's as the French say, *c'est la guerre.* Many wives lost their husbands that day."

Braithwaite bowed his head, more embarrassed at his clumsiness than anything else. As she stood silhouetted by the late afternoon light with the swaying lace curtains behind her, he finally, genuinely noticed her appearance. He had been so nervous and on edge, before that, he had hardly concentrated on the features. Now, it occurred to him what a strikingly stunning young woman stood there. Of medium height, she had a slender waist accentuated by the high-waist dress popular before the war. Her deep auburn hair pulled into a bun atop her gently rounded face set off her amazing emerald-colored eyes. She had long, delicate fingers and well-developed arms—clearly a woman of some physical strength despite the diminutive size. No European lady would dare display bare arms in public, but not the case in the steamy tropics. Her arms showed the deep rich tan of the tropics. Her loose blouse fluttered in the breeze, displaying an obvious well-toned figure. In short, Mrs. Alice Hallwood was a stunningly attractive woman. He pondered for a few seconds whether she had many local suitors.

"No, I do not."

"What, I, what…?" The question caught him off guard and completely unarmed.

"I have no gentlemen admirers here. That is the question you are considering is it not?" She reached into a wicker basket and brought out a bottle of local wine and a bag of crusty bread. As she poured the ruby red wine into the tea glasses, she continued. "So sorry to be so blunt, Lieutenant Braithwaite. I suppose in polite society, one does not speak openly of such things." She sat facing him across the table. "The truth is, I must ever play the unapproachable war widow. I believe in the trade it is known as a cover." She raised the glass to her lips and sipped. Braithwaite did likewise, his eyes fixed on her glowing face with its delicate but determined features.

"Yes, I suppose so. Entanglements just wouldn't do."

"Quite right and damned inconvenient!"

The remark startled him. *Terribly forward for an elegant European lady. Damned sure wouldn't hear such language at the Savoy Grill or the Derby!"*

"Do I startle you, Sir?" *She is forward. Perhaps old 'Blinker' did get the measure of this remarkable young widow.* Alice began slicing the bread placing it on an old chipped, but still serviceable plate as she continued. "You see, life is different here in the colonies. I spent much of my younger years on a farm near Nairobi. My father was one of those hale and hearty—what do the Americans call them—pioneers. We came to Kenya just after the Boer War. My father fell in love with Africa then and resigned his commission in 1902 just after the war. Lieutenant-Colonel Rupert MacKenzie of the Royal Scots Fusiliers." She glanced at his plate. He had not touched the bread slices. "Oh, please eat. I apologize. Rations are scarce these days and I fear this is all I have for now. No butter and jam, I'm afraid."

"Damned uncivilized, I say!" He grinned. He had now fully recovered his composure and smirked yet again. "A jug of wine, a loaf of bread, a bit of, well, no cheese, but there is thee." So began the dance. So it began. Alice chortled heartedly. "You have a keen sense of humor, Mr. Braithwaite. Don't let the Huns or the tropics diminish that." An implied hint of harsh times to come came with that comment.

For the next several hours, they both drank the so-so wine and downed the excellent crusty bread—wonderful even without the luxuries of an English tea. "The strawberries and Devon clotted cream should be here any moment." Both laughed, loud and lustily. *So, this young field agent has a bit of wit about her. He would learn much from her in the art of spycraft.*

Each told their stories. In 1910, the MacKenzies returned to Scotland to the old estate. He had detected the lilt of the Edinburgh dialect in her speech, though clearly it had been tempered by years out of the country. There, Alice met an up-and-coming naval officer, Lieutenant Hallwood of His Majesty's armored cruiser *Aboukir* at a wardroom soirée when the ship had visited Rosyth. A whirlwind romance and marriage followed, and a two-year shore tour graced their early years. Then, Sarajevo happened, the assassination in the Balkans that plunged the world into chaos. Hallwood went back to sea on *Aboukir*, never to be seen again. Lieutenant-Colonel MacKenzie rejoined his regiment, but a nasty wound at the retreat from Mons sent him back home, ending his military career. When Alice received the word of her husband's death, she reacted as one would expect—a grieving war widow. And then, as one would not expect, in late October 1914, she gathered up her courage, marched into "Blinker" Hall's office at Admiralty, and promptly volunteered to assist the DNI based on her intimate knowledge of East Africa. Hall, clearly impressed by the young woman's grit and determination, asked if she would consider going to Zanzibar to keep an eye on the enemy just across the channel in German East Africa. She leapt at the opportunity. Clearly, this young woman, steeled in the harsh environment of the African plain and disciplined by growing up in a military family, could carry off the assignment. Hall always assessed the mettle of his subordinates quite well, thought Braithwaite. Perhaps the old blighter had seen the same in himself or so he hoped. Nagging doubts gnawed at him. He had much to learn about himself. So, with a carefully crafted cover, she arrived in Zanzibar the previous November to take up her role as a spy for King and Country. And, she became the British agent known in London as Minstrel.

Braithwaite marveled at the young woman's adventurous story. His was remarkably mundane by comparison. The son of a prominent Oxford don, a professor of history, and diplomat, he had grown up in the late Victorian and Edwardian comfort of upper-middle-class privilege and the cocoon of social conformity. Graduation from Eton and Balliol College, Oxford meant a wealth of career options and open doors. He chose the Navy. His parents had wanted young John to pursue the family business of academia or a post with the Foreign Office as had his father and the Braithwaites for several generations back. His father had served in the Oxford and Buckinghamshire Light Infantry during the colonial wars and had been cited for valor in one of the ever constant clashes on the Khyber Pass with a stroppy band of Afghan tribesmen who, somehow, failed to appreciate the benefits of being part of the Empress of India's empire. But, young John, fresh out of the cloisters of Oxford, longed for more adventure. The Royal Navy offered two things—a king's commission and a chance to see the world. Graduation from Dartmouth, the Royal Naval College, had been a breeze. While other younger cadets struggled, Braithwaite conquered navigation, seamanship, gunnery, and ship handling with ease, no doubt due to his passion for sailing and things mechanical. There existed another aspect to Braithwaite. Appointed as a member of the ambassadorial staff in various embassies, his father had traveled to distant places such as Berlin, Dar es Salaam, Nairobi, Mombasa, and Cape Town. Thus, young Braithwaite was exposed to a great deal of the world outside Britain. More importantly for the particular mission, he spoke fluent German with a distinct Berlin accent and he understood East Africa. Commissioned in 1910, he served in a dreadnought battleship, HMS *Vanguard*, for two years before reporting aboard HMS *Halberd*, the noble little destroyer now a war grave for so many of his former comrades.

When he got to the story of the previous November events, he stumbled. A long pause interrupted the free-flowing conversation. Dusk had arrived and, in the still of the early evening, he sat immobile, staring off into some nonexistent space. For fully a minute, he said nothing, simply staring out the window. She understood. Alice had those occasional moments as well. The random tragedy of war strikes hard at the heart and soul. As he stared at nothing in particular, a line from Shakespeare's Macbeth came into his thoughts:

Tomorrow, and tomorrow, and tomorrow,
Creeps in this petty pace from day to day,
To the last syllable of recorded time;
And all our yesterdays have lighted fools
The way to dusty death.
Out, out, brief candle!
Life's but a walking shadow, a poor player,
That struts and frets his hour upon the stage,
And then is heard no more. It is a tale

Told by an idiot, full of sound and fury,
Signifying nothing.

A soft, gentle hand on his brow jerked his mind back to the present. She said nothing, but the emerald eyes indicated she understood. "*Tempus fugit*, Lieutenant Braithwaite. Time flies and we have much to do before you can charge into the fray. I should leave now. It simply would not do for a single lady to be about unescorted after dark. Appearances must be kept up. You'll find bedding and toiletries here about. That should do you for now. I'll return in the morning and start your briefing. Rest well, sailor man. We have much work to do."

With that pep talk, she stood and with a gentle shake and nod of her deep auburn mane, whirled about, strode out the door, and into the street. Braithwaite slowly ambled to the window and, in the gathering dusk of an African eve, watched as the remarkable young lady strode away down the cobbled street. He began to hum the tune again and softly mouth the words, "the minstrel boy to the war has gone, in the ranks of death, ye shall find him. His father's sword he hath girded on, and his wild harp slung behind him." Alice MacKenzie Hallwood—a most remarkable young lady, indeed. He smiled broadly and simply shook his head—amazement and admiration all rolled into one.

CHAPTER 4

Jasmine

11 March 1915. Zanzibar.
The morning light through the open windows jolted him awake. Despite the potential relaxation of the sea trip through Gibraltar to Malta, through the Suez and Mombasa eventually to Zanzibar as just a passenger with no responsibilities, he had slept fitfully. What had originally seemed like an adventure had turned into an intractable and agonizing problem—how to crack the secret of SMS *Aachen*. Hall and Millar had given him precious little insight on how to approach his mission. He had to rely on Minstrel's intelligence and his own wits. The gravity of his mission weighed heavily on his mind as he pondered his dilemma. A quick cold-water face wash helped clear away the clouds of a restless night. Minstrel would soon arrive and perhaps bring some clarity. A sharp knock at the door jolted him to attention. He tensed. Millar had warned him that even in British Zanzibar, enemies abounded. Vigilance and caution. Slowly, he walked over to the door and cautiously cracked it open. An otherwise nonthreatening and middle-aged Indian fellow smiled broadly revealing many missing front teeth.

"Sahib. The magnificent lady sends morning greetings and this." The man thrust a scrap of yellow paper into his hand, bowed gracefully from the waist, pivoted, and strode away.

Braithwaite stood in the open doorway in amazement for several seconds. A quick glance about revealed no watchers—no one who should not be there. Stepping back into the room, he unfolded the note. It revealed a simple message—1050 Commonwealth Road, 10.00. *Very well, he would be there.*

He arrived a few minutes early. Although a novice in the spycraft, he instinctively understood that surveillance meant safety. From a discrete alcove down the street, he observed the building at 1050 Commonwealth Road, a nondescript row house in New Town Zanzibar. After several minutes and satisfied that no one observed him, he quickly strode to the door and knocked.

"Welcome, Sahib." The Indian who had delivered the message earlier greeted him with the same toothless smile. "Come, Sir."

Braithwaite followed the man down a narrow hallway and into a darkened office. His eyes, still adjusting to the bright sun outside took a few moments to adjust, but he was aware of two people sitting at a rickety table quietly conversing. The Indian bowed and disappeared.

"Come in, Lieutenant. Please. Take a seat." The man stood and offered a plain wooden chair across the table. He glanced over to see Minstrel, who nodded indicating all was well.

"Thank you." Braithwaite slid out a chair and sat quickly.

"Commander Bill Armitage. Happy to make your acquaintance," said the man dressed in a typical colonial planter sort of khaki outfit, extending a firm handshake.

"Lieutenant John Braithwaite, Sir."

"Commander Armitage has come down from Mombasa to help us with our little problem. He has the latest intelligence on *Aachen*," Minstrel finally spoke up.

"Quite right. I am the First Lieutenant of HMS *Bristol*, but on temporary duty to CinC Cape Station as a liaison officer in Mombasa while the ship undergoes some repairs in Simonstown. We had a bit of a dustup with the Hun three months ago and several of my chaps bought it. Bad business that. We were especially keen to send the bastard to Hell. She came out of a fog bank and we never detected the rotter until she landed a few rounds on the fantail and then disappeared again into the mist." The rancor in his voice clearly indicated his bitterness at losing the engagement with the elusive German cruiser. "Here's what we know." He rolled out a chart of the Western Indian Ocean with Zanzibar and Dar es Salaam circled. "She hides in the Rufiji River Delta, but never at a constant or consistent anchorage. They're fairly clever at hiding her. Apparently, there are at least three prepared and protected anchorages, perhaps more. We've attempted to intercept her transiting out, but there are several exit channels—here, here, and here."

Braithwaite leaned over the chart. The Rufiji River Delta spread out to the Indian Ocean through several wide channels. Any one of them gave access to the sea for a ship with as deep a draft as a light cruiser. He shook his head in acknowledgment. "What about a blockade?"

"Right. Tried already. We never have enough warships to mount an effective blockade. The damned cruiser has a lot of observation stations and a telegraph system stationed at every possible channel entrance that gives them a significant defense, including Maxims and some 37mm guns posted at all the channel entrances and guarding all the approaches. These are manned by trained troops. In order to make it up the channel, a ship must fairly well stick to the center of the channel and that, Lieutenant, removes any maneuverability from the equation. To complicate this picture, these chaps are quite good at spotting and reporting our movements off the coast, so a close blockade is highly problematic. Any ship attempting to run past those defenses is, quite frankly, a 'sitting duck.' Then again, when they spot a ship moving up the channel, they report its presence and the blighter is just waiting at the anchorage manned and ready, already at action stations, with 'rings on their fingers and bells on their toes,' so to speak." All smirked at the intended humor. "The moment we move off the coast to where we think the bugger is exiting, she moves. It's the damnedest thing I ever saw!"

"Could an attack by land be mounted into the anchorage—a 'damn the torpedoes' sort of thing?" asked Braithwaite, still carefully eyeing the chart.

"Tried that as well with God-awful results in January. The Cape

Squadron sent in a predreadnought battleship, the *Goliath*, along with a pair of cruisers coordinated with a landing on the coast just above one of the channel entrances. Unfortunately, the German forces were simply too well-entrenched and repelled the attack. To add to the insult, the battleship ran aground before she got halfway up to where we thought the *Aachen* had anchored." Commander Armitage leaned back in his chair and placed both hands atop his bare head as if in a deep contemplation. "It's just no good. The channels are too narrow with little sea room to maneuver and anything more than a light cruiser just can't make it. It took us all day to get *Goliath* off the bloody sandbar. No, we will have to catch *Aachen* out to sea or in port at Dar es Salaam."

Just then, the middle-aged Indian entered the room carrying a metal tray with a teapot that had seen better times and a plate of McVitie digestives. He set the tray down and exclaimed, "The last of the McVities. I fear they'll be none until another supply ship arrives from Mombasa. Many apologies."

Braithwaite looked up at the dark-skinned man and in a wash of realization, it occurred to him that this native was not a lowly servant. The man had the air of military and status about him. And, his English was impeccable. Minstrel nodded in acknowledgment on the biscuit shortage, grateful for the ones they had. As she reached out and began to pour hot water into each cup, she explained the odd Indian with a wry grin. "Lieutenant, you have met Amrish—Sergeant Major Amrish Patel, late of His Majesty's 2nd Bengal Lancers."

"Very pleased to make your acquaintance, Sahib," responded the Indian extending a hand to Braithwaite, who responded in kind.

"Sergeant Major."

Minstrel placed the tea strainer over a steaming cup. "No fresh milk, either, sorry."

"War is hell!" chortled Armitage. All laughed.

"We shall make do then," added a cheerful Minstrel as she handed a cup first to Braithwaite, then the Patel, and finally to Armitage, already munching one of the prized McVities.

Braithwaite turned to Patel and spoke, "2nd Bengal Lancers?

Damned fine regiment, I hear."

The Indian's back stiffened with pride. "Indeed, Sir. That it is. I am sadly retired now from active service courtesy of the Germans." Patel broke a biscuit into several pieces, grinned, and explained, "Artillery fire during the retreat from Mons back in August. Shrapnel took out all my front teeth and part of my left leg. It's a damned shame and meant a medical discharge," he exclaimed popping a small piece of biscuit into the toothless mouth. "I have put in a claim with His Imperial Majesty Kaiser Bill, but no response yet." All laughed heartily.

Minstrel explained, "Amrish's family have lived in East Africa going on three generations. They were prominent merchants, but when the war started, the German authorities in Dar es Salaam confiscated all their property in German East Africa. They escaped to Zanzibar and eventually Mombasa."

"You see, Sahib, I have a vested interest in the Kaiser's demise in this part of the world." The Indian popped in another biscuit morsel.

Braithwaite leaned forward taking one of the biscuits. "Why not have the teeth fixed? Surely that would be more practical."

"Ah," he responded, "for a very practical reason, Sir."

Minstrel broke in. "You see, Sergeant Major Patel is a very effective spy. Without his teeth and with a good deal of play acting, he can come and go about Dar es Salaam appearing to be a simple lowly native. He has actually been there several times in that guise and even aboard the enemy ship."

This news stunned Braithwaite causing him to gulp a large mouthful of hot tea, burning the roof of his mouth. He leaned forward in his chair. "Then you must know the secret of their ability to appear and disappear at will and avoid any naval patrols?"

"No, Sahib, I fear not. I have not seen anything unusual or out of order. But then, I am a simple cavalryman. I know horses and saddlery, but not things of the sea."

"Which, by the way, is why you are here," piped in the otherwise silent Armitage.

Braithwaite put his hand to his mouth as one does in contemplation. Then he leaned forward and placed his index finger directly on the port at Dar es Salaam. "You say that you have been aboard? How is that possible?"

Minstrel cocked her head to the right and raised her eyebrows, giving an impish look that Braithwaite would soon learn to love. "On occasion, almost always at night, *Aachen* pulls into Dar es Salaam to take on fuel and supplies when she feels safe. This is generally when the Cape Squadron ships must pull off station to recoal themselves. She is always gone by dawn. But, in order to resupply, she hires locals, mostly Asian workers, to carry the goods aboard. This is how Amrish was able to get aboard."

"You see, Sir, I have many friends, cousins, and old acquaintances in Dar es Salaam and they keep me informed of gossip on the ship. We have just heard through the victualing agent—a fat German who, shall we say, can be bought with women, wine, and song - that he expects *Aachen* in port tomorrow night.

The revelation struck Braithwaite like an arrow. At last—action, opportunity, a task. For too long in the transit from Portsmouth, he had chafed at the inactivity. He craved action and challenge. Here, now came his chance. Leaning forward over the chart, he pointed to the port of Dar es Salaam and explained his fateful decision. "Then, by all means, I must get aboard that ship."

****

Zanzibar sweltered. Despite being early autumn south of the equator, the midday temperatures soared. Braithwaite sat quietly in an antique wicker chair so typical of the tropical colonies, dozing gently off and on. An even more antique-looking fan slowly revolved overhead. The aroma of cloves wafted through the open windows combining with the odors of human activity. He imagined that a foul-smelling London must have been this way prior to the modern 20th-century sewage and sanitation systems. Then again, human and working animal odors had been replaced by the pungent aroma of thousands of coal fires and the new monsters—automobile exhaust.

A knock at the door shook him out of his lethargic trance. He tensed. Was it his fellow spies or some German agent? Silently, he padded over to the open window that gave him a view of the doorway. He breathed out quickly when he saw Minstrel, Patel, and Armitage nervously checking out the street for unwelcome observers. Braithwaite quickly unlatched the heavy wooden door and all rushed in. Once all sat about the plain kitchen table, Minstrel explained the plan. Patel had heard from a cousin across the water in Dar es Salaam that *Aachen* definitely would be expected after dark and that the obese and always nervous victualing agent had put out the word for the usual local native porters. Braithwaite and Patel would be among them. Minstrel laid out the plan as Patel spread out a nautical chart.

"We have a fast boat that departs from here," she pointed to a small cove a few miles south of the city, "at exactly 19.00 hours. It should take us less than three hours to reach Dar es Salaam at best speed if the weather cooperates."

Armitage jumped in. "It looks good for now. Calm winds and a mild sea state. We should have no troubles."

Minstrel nodded in acknowledgment. "Very well, then. We have used this boat on previous jobs and it is more than reliable. Once we reach here," she drew a very long, delicate finger across the chart to the town, "Commander Armitage and I will cast off and loiter offshore as you make your way into town. That should take about an hour. You will have plenty of time since the call for porters doesn't occur until midnight for security reasons." She turned to Braithwaite, whose bright, shiny, English face stood out against the other three tanned by nature or the hot African sun.

"And you, Sir, with your lily-white complexion—we must do something dramatic."

Braithwaite blushed, turning from lily white to a shade of bright pink. Smirking, he only nodded in acknowledgment. "Indeed!" All chuckled. "In my school days, we did many a dramatic production where we needed skin darkening for certain characters. Wet coffee grinds applied liberally to the skin does an amazing job of turning a European complexion to that of the warmer climes. That should do the trick."

Patel placed a hand on Braithwaite's shoulder and smiling a broad, missing several teeth grin, exclaimed, "Congratulations, you will now be one of His Majesty's colonial subjects—if for only a few hours." All laughed aloud.

The process of skin dying took several hours and with the gathering heat and humidity, added to Braithwaite's already distinct discomfort. But, it worked. When they finally washed the coffee grinds off his face, neck, and hands, he had that distinct light brown look of a son of India. Though not quite as dark as Patel, it would pass, especially at night among others of varying skin tones from deep ebony to light tan.

Braithwaite peered in the mirror atop the old battered oak dresser. It will have to do. As he turned his face from side to side to ensure complete coverage, he noticed a darker face behind them. Patel grinned. "Yes, Sahib, that will do nicely." It was as if the Indian read his mind. But with a start, he realized that the retired cavalryman of His Majesty's 2nd Bengal Lancers now had front teeth—shiny white teeth against his light brown face. Patel snickered. "Yes, Sahib. I do have teeth, dentures actually, courtesy of His Majesty's Royal Army Medical Corps, although I did pay extra for the much-improved version. His Majesty is most kind to this humble servant."

Braithwaite turned toward him with an equally broad smile. "Sergeant Major, you continue to amaze me."

The Indian nodded his concurrence. "So now we must finish the job. Your light brown hair will no doubt alert the bastard that all is not as it should be." With that, Patel pulled from a sack a swatch of dirty gray linen and carefully wrapped Braithwaite's head in the traditional Indian turban. Minstrel handed him a tin of bootblack. Splotches of the dark paste covered the hair that stuck from beneath the linen turban. Minstrel and Armitage both nodded in approval after a cursory inspection.

"It will do," said an approving Minstrel.

****

The trip of about forty-five miles across the open water took just under three hours in the fast, sleek motor launch. The fact that the boat had been previously owned by the German governor-general of German East Africa added to the irony. Just after dark, they pulled into a small, but protected cove about three miles north of the city. Minstrel and Patel had used this cove often as did smugglers avoiding the colonial customs agents. Truth be told, they simply appeared to be smugglers. Even had they been discovered, the customs agents would not interfere. After all, they had families to feed and the pitiful government salary didn't go far, especially in the inflated economy of the wartime colony cut off from the imperial homeland by the Royal Navy's command of the sea. A few well-placed marks kept the customs agents silent and absent.

The motor launch glided silently onto the sloping beach. Braithwaite and Patel splashed through the foamy surf and raced for the protection of a palm grove a few yards inland. Meanwhile, Minstrel eased the launch away. She would pull out a few hundred yards and await the signal of three quick flashes of a torch hidden under old palm fronds. Patel had left behind his dentures and again took on the appearance of a toothless and lowly Indian laborer. Not only did he look the part, but his accent blended perfectly since he had grown up in the region. Braithwaite, so as to not reveal his disguise, would act deaf and dumb. Both men wore the traditional garment of the East African coast. It gave the additional advantage of not only comfort in the humid air but allowed both men to carry Webley revolvers hidden underneath and tucked securely in their belts. Patel had made the boarding of *Aachen* previously and knew that the sailors never searched the work crew. Braithwaite questioned this lack of security, but Patel assured him that the Germans needed to depart quickly before dawn and viewed searches of the over a hundred laborers as time-consuming and unnecessary. No laborer would have stolen anything either from the ship or the supplies. German justice was sharp, swift, and deadly. The flowing robes also allowed the two intruders to conceal anything of value smuggled off the ship. Braithwaite particularly wanted navigation charts. He had a very good working knowledge of the ship's layout, especially the bridge and chart house. A quick message to DNI earlier that day resulted in a coded signal with the specifications. Braithwaite had spent most of the afternoon reviewing again the ship's layout.

Both men crouched low in the palm grove. Assured that all was clear, they began the walk into the city, which by the road along the water's edge, took less than an hour. As they passed other travelers, Braithwaite hung his head low so that his northern European features did not give him away. By 23.00, they arrived at Patel's cousin's house in the Indian quarter. The two relatives greeted each other heartedly as if they were long lost friends. On seeing Braithwaite, the cousin let out a huge belly laugh and shook his head in amazement exclaiming, "Amrish, it is good that it will be dark!" Both Indians laughed at Braithwaite, feeling more uncomfortable by the minute. He could only muster a forced grin. Self-doubt as to his ability to carry out the deception had been building all day. But, he had a mission, a vital mission, and he had to quell his fears and doubts. Many men's lives depended upon it.

By 23.30, they reached the staging area and simply milled about with the gathering crowd of hired laborers, making sure to keep well away from the victualing agent. The German glanced over at the crowd, then nervously checked his pocket watch. At precisely midnight, a motor whaleboat departed the ship's port side carrying an officer and three armed sailors along with the coxswain and engineer. Braithwaite drooped his head. Would they pick him out? Would the armed sailors check every hired man and realize who he was and was not? As the boat made the landing and the engineer leapt out to secure the lines, Patel leaned over and whispered, "Steady, Sahib. Steady on."

Aachen rode at anchor about a hundred yards out in the harbor. A milky-looking cloud of funnel smoke drifted above the ship. Clearly, she had steam up and was ready to sortie at a moment's notice should British warships appear on the horizon. Deck lights brightened the ship, giving her a festival appearance. Braithwaite admired the cruiser's physical beauty. He had always marveled at the clean lines and elegant appearance of the Kaiser's warships. Compared to them, Royal

Navy ships appeared doughty and clunky, but functional. Yet he also knew that a ship was only a collection of metal, wires, and wood. The crew made the difference and he knew the British tar was the world's finest. That made all the difference.

As he scanned her bow to stern, he noticed an oddity that had not appeared in any of the elaborate architectural descriptions sent by the DNI. Atop the mainmast, a large flat rectangular device rotated slowly. It looked to be a set of bed springs stood on its side; it seemed to have no discernible function. He stared at the device in wonderment and curiosity. Shouts from a tall man in traditional Indian dress shook him out of his fascination with the strange bed spring. In an instant, panic set in. He looked over at the cousin standing by the warehouse door with arms folded across his broad chest. The man locked eyes with Braithwaite and barely nodded indicating all is well, no cause for alarm. Slowly and one by one, the throng of workers—Indians, Africans, and Omanis—formed into a line and under the guidance of the overseer, moved one by one through the warehouse door. Patel hoisted a burlap sack and then tugged at Braithwaite's sleeve indicating time to move. With his head down, he shuffled along playing the part of the sturdy, but deaf and dumb local. As he went past the warehouse doorway headed toward the waiting motor whaleboat, in his peripheral vision, he saw that the armed sailors had positioned themselves on the landing for security and seemed to have little interest in the men making their way toward the motor whaleboat. The German officer, peering at his watch, appeared more interested in getting aboard and underway than in the gaggle of men now tossing sacks of food and supplies into the boat. Meanwhile, two more ship's boats arrived at the landing. The captain intended to be fully loaded and gone before first light. Although the harbor was wide, the channel leading into the harbor provided a natural chokepoint and the Germans fully realized this vulnerability to blockade from the sea.

In the warehouse, Braithwaite and Patel both hoisted heavy bags of some sort of fresh vegetable, most likely potatoes. In a pensive moment that could be thought of as bizarre considering the present circumstances, he thought of the excellent German potato salad that he had loved while living in Berlin as a child. A sharp bark by the overseer jolted him out of his daydream. The Indian directed him and Patel over to the side. A sense of desperate panic welled up. *Had he been found out! Run or surrender?* Other men followed them off to the side until about twenty had gathered. The overseer pointed toward one of the newly arrived launches and men began shuffling toward it. Patel clenched his fist twice, a signal for all is well. While awaiting nightfall and departure, they had worked out a series of hand gestures to communicate. Braithwaite took in a deep breath and let it out slowly in obvious relief.

The crowd of laborers lay down their sacks in the open launch and began to sit in the bilges and about the gunwale. The cousin had made certain that he and Patel had been designated to go aboard *Aachen* as the receiving crew to offload incoming loads and carry the goods to the proper storage places. As the launch approached the accommodation ladder that led up to the quarterdeck, he observed a bored-looking petty officer with clipboard in hand standing between the clearly nervous officer of the watch and an armed sailor. As each man struggled up the accommodation ladder with his sack, the petty officer pointed in one direction or another. Several sailors appeared and led each gang to separate parts of the ship. The cousin had arranged for Patel and Braithwaite to go with the food group, thus putting them into the galley area. From there, Braithwaite could temporarily disappear and make his way to the chart house, two decks up. If challenged, he would put on the deaf and dumb act and hope for the best. Dropping the vegetable sacks in the dry stores locker, the group went back to the quarterdeck for the next load. After several such runs, Braithwaite felt more confident. As he progressed, he scouted the various passageways and noted possible spots to duck into should he be spotted. Inside the ship, the red nightlights cast a warmish glow about the deck and bulkheads. It was enough to navigate by, but not enough to aid in his disguise.

On the fourth run to the galley area, he intentionally waited for the last man to pass. The sailor leading the men could not see the end of the line and could not tell that the last man had peeled off. No one had bothered to count the bearers, so he would not be missed. None of the laborers observed or even seemed to care about it—they simply wanted to finish the job without a fuss, collect their wages, and go home.

Stealthily, he made his way forward and up the decks toward the bridge with the chart house just aft on the same deck. By this time, there were several dozen laborers going in all directions so his chances of being discovered out of place diminished. As he approached the bridge area, voices came from the pilothouse. Two junior officers discussed the channel markers, making sure they were familiar. His German, being excellent, gave him confidence as he slunk into an unoccupied space letting the two officers pass him without notice. But, they had just emerged from the chart house and this gave Braithwaite his chance. He darted into the red-lit space. Before him, on a table, lay a British Admiralty chart of the Dar es Salaam harbor. *Droll, very droll. The bugger is using our bloody charts!* One by one, he slid open the metal drawers of the chart table searching for whatever seemed of importance. In the third drawer from the bottom, he struck gold. On a chart of the Western Indian Ocean covering the area from Mombasa to Mozambique, there appeared in pencil, the route of the cruiser and more importantly, dates and times. From his previous briefing from Armitage, he knew the significance—it was the date that the raider had sunk a Cape Town-bound Belgian freighter and had almost been cornered by the searching ships of the Cape Squadron. He stared at the chart for a full minute in amazement. At one point the cruiser's course had been a straight south-by-southwest. Then, she had suddenly turned to a north-by-northeast heading. Written at the very point of this radical course change appeared a notation: "machine detected enemy force, bearing 220 degrees, range 50 thousand meters." As if a lightning bolt struck, he read and re-read the notation—50,000 meters was well over twenty-five nautical miles. Even the dirtiest smoke from a fast-moving warship could not be seen at that distance. Based on the height of eye from the ship's foretop, eleven miles to the horizon was the most possible. *This can't be correct* he thought. Looking about, he saw the dividers and rapidly measured the mark from the turning point to the spot indicated for the enemy ships. Indeed, the marks were some 50,000 meters apart. This is not possible he pondered. As quickly as he could, he replaced the chart and continued the search. In the next drawer down, he discovered an even more valuable chart of the Rufiji Delta with all the possible entry and exit channels clearly marked. But, as Armitage had indicated, the deep draft of any warship larger than a light cruiser would soon put a ship aground in the mud. In each channel, the possible depth would barely be enough for a few inches below the keel and each channel was extremely narrow. Only a skilled ship handler with intimate knowledge of the channel would avoid being run aground in the mud. He quickly rolled this chart up and stuffed it into his belt under the flowing robe.

Footsteps! Braithwaite desperately glanced about for some secure hiding place. Anything might do. The footsteps came closer. Heavy footfalls clanked on the metal ladder one deck below. Then another set of shoes clanked on the hard steel steps. Two Germans climbed the ladder. Almost in a panic, he saw his out. Through an open door there appeared to be a darkened space next to the chart house. He strode over and darted into the dark room just as the two officers emerged from the ladder and the deck below. He squeezed as tight as possible against the bulkhead. Despite the torrid, humid heat outside, the steel bulkhead felt cool and dry. As his pupils adjusted to the dark space, he noted the surroundings. It looked to be a fan room with machinery that probably sucked in outside air and sent it below to the fire room several decks below. A low hum came from the slowly turning fan. That's when he realized that his breath came in short, panicky breathes. Thankfully, the hum masked his labored breathing. Slowly, ever so slowly, he took in a deep breath, then let it out again. Three more deep breaths. He felt his heart pound, but now his breathing had come under control and, most importantly, made no telltale sound.

The two sailors had gone into the chart house; he heard a metal drawer sliding and the rustle of chart paper. One officer, clearly senior, probably the cruiser's navigator with some authority, spoke first. The more junior officer, probably still in training, responded with an occasional *Jawohl*. Braithwaite strained to pick out the words, muffled by the steel bulkhead. Between the rustle of the charts and the sound of shoes shuffling across the metal deck, he could only pick out a few sounds. His curiosity rose. These were not words he expected of a warship at sea. He cupped his hands against the bulkhead separating the fan room from the chart house. He distinctly heard some phrases—"*Herr Doktor* Steinweiss" and "the machine" and "Station Wilhelm" came out clearly, repeated several times.

The machine? Station Wilhelm? Steinweiss? He furrowed his brow in confusion. *Here is a mystery.*

Verdammt! The senior officer muttered. Braithwaite put his ear directly to the bulkhead. *Had he been detected? Fight or run.* His instinct told him to run, then no, stick. *Fight it out if necessary.* Then he realized the man cursed at having just spilled some hot coffee on the chart table. Braithwaite heard the rustling of the hand across the paper chart, no doubt brushing away drops of hot coffee. He let out a slow breath in relief. He clearly heard the junior officer chuckle and comment that the captain would not be pleased to see the chart coffee stained. The older man just laughed.

After a few more minutes and more sounds and references to the three strange terms—Steinweiss, Station Wilhelm, and the "machine"—he heard the sliding of the drawer and the sound of a chart being replaced. He squeezed back into the bulkhead as tight as possible as the two Germans exited the chart house. As they passed the open door to the darkened fan room, Braithwaite noted the older man's head, or at least the back of it. No doubt bleached by months in the tropical sun, it appeared silvery blonde, almost white and cut high on the sides. He let out a long slow breath as he heard again the clump of shoes on the ladder leading below.

For several minutes, he stood immobile in the dark fan room contemplating his next move. He knew he had to have a look at the charts, but the fear of discovery froze him to his spot. *Must move. Can't stay here.* Then, from somewhere near, he heard the distant rattle of dishes. He remembered that he had to be somewhere near the wardroom. Then he heard voices, muffled, but distant—it must be mealtime for the officers. That made sense—take a quick meal before getting underway again. The bridge, chart house, and wardroom were officer country. With those not on duty receiving, stowing, or supervising the stores loading, likely all hands not on watch would be below in the crew's mass or in the wardroom. Now came his chance—his best opportunity and safest time to investigate. Quickly and as quietly as he could, he padded softly out into the pilothouse and darted into the chart house. The two officers had switched off the white overhead lights and had switched on the red nightlights. All the better. In the dim red glow, chances of discovery lessened.

On the far side of the space, an open doorway led out to the pilot-house, also bathed in a reddish glow. He thought about removing his leather sandals, but then he would need footwear should he have to make a quick getaway. As he tiptoed softly toward the door leading into the pilothouse, a strange object against the rear bulkhead caught his eye. He had not noticed it previously. On a metal pedestal, welded to the deck and clearly not of the ship's original construction, sat a black painted box. The front was simply an open grate. He tiptoed over to inspect the unusual object. Inside the box sat some sort of electronic device. It had a glass face and a green background behind the darkened face. He wanted to inspect it closer, but the heavy pad-lock prevented him opening the grate. The boys and girls in Room 40 had not prepared him to pick a lock. *Damn the poor tradecraft.* He made a mental note to advise Hall about this discrepancy in training. In addition to the darkened round glass, there appeared several knobs and toggle switches. He had enough experience with naval commu-nications to recognize the device as some sort of wireless gear, but he had never seen anything like this. From the back of the device, several shielded cables ran up the bulkhead and through the overhead, appar-ently leading up to the mainmast above. Perhaps the odd bed springs noted earlier had something to do with the device. Voices nearby scotched any further examination attempt. He crouched down again behind the pedestal until the interlopers had moved on. On the main deck below, a crowd of laborers had gathered. *Best move along, old sod. Your train is departing.* He took a final gaze at the strange device and shook his head in wonderment. Whatever the thing was, it had to be important to be locked away.

Pausing to listen for any approaching footsteps, he gloated silently—*I have you, you bastard!* As he turned to leave the chart house another thought occurred. What about the odd terms used by the two officers—"Steinweiss, Station Wilhelm," then the "machine." His curiosity aroused, Braithwaite gently slid open the top drawer and pulled out a rumpled map of German East Africa with a recent coffee stain. With his left index finger, he traced the route of the Rufiji River inland then overland to where was marked with a red grease pencil, a spot marked "X" and labeled Station Wilhelm. It lay on the eastern shore of Lake Nyasa. *Most curious. Indeed, most curious.* Though he did not know why, his intuition screamed. *This place is important. It has to be. Could it be related to the device in the corner of the chart room? Did this place on a distant lake hold the secret of the Aachen and who was Docktor Steinweiss?* Quickly, he rolled up the map and stuffed it in his belt alongside his other booty. Smoothing out the robe to hide any bulges from the hidden chart and map, he put his ear near the open doorway. *Clear, no one about. Move. Quickly!*

Treading silently while staying close to the bulkhead, he headed for the ladder leading down to the main deck. The commotion caused by several dozen native laborers gathering by the gangway to board the ship's boats for the ride to the shore masked his movements. As he approached the gaggle, he saw Patel looking about an anxious expression on his face. Braithwaite had not seen the man display any nervousness or overt concern; the look on the Indian's face was jarring. *Was something wrong? Had he been missed? Were the Germans looking for him?* Now concerned, he picked up the pace. *Stupid! Stupid! You'll give yourself away!* He slowed down to an amble, put his head down and tried to appear as an exhausted and weary laborer. Patel finally saw him and, with a slight nod, indicated that the coast was clear. Without a word, Braithwaite slid next to Patel just as the crowd moved toward the gangway and down to the waiting boat that bobbed up and down in the gathering swell. Within a few minutes, both men stood on the quay. Braithwaite looked back at the ship and smiled—a smile of self-satisfaction. He had pulled it off. *By God, he had done it!* What to make of this find, he didn't yet know, but one thing was certain. He had found an intelligence treasure. Not wasting a moment of darkness, the ship would soon weigh anchor and gracefully glide down the channel and into the open sea beyond.

"Hurry, Sir. We must be gone before anyone realizes who we really are."

Braithwaite shook his head, maintaining the deaf-mute persona. With no further word, the two men strode off north toward the rendezvous where Minstrel and the launch waited. The two men arrived back at the smugglers' cove just as the sun broke the eastern horizon. They quickly located the torch under a pile of dead palm fronds, secure in the same spot where they had hidden it. Clearly, no one had disturbed the site. They had not been discovered. The signal sent, the boat raced to the beach, and the spies were safely away. They arrived back in Zanzibar by early morning. Pilfered chart and map in hand and happy with the results, Braithwaite stepped out of the motor launch very near to Minstrel who had just completed tying off. As his face passed only inches away from hers, he detected the distinct aroma of jasmine.

CHAPTER 5

Indian Country

13 March 1915. Zanzibar.
Braithwaite leaned into the map of German East Africa laid out on the kitchen table in Minstrel's tiny flat. He furrowed his brow almost in confusion and placed a finger at the spot marked in German—Station Wilhelm. *What is Station Wilhelm? Why is it significant? Why would Imperial German naval officers be concerned with such a secluded spot on Lake Nyasa, hundreds of miles inland?* He shook his head, bewildered, but intensely curious. He stood to his full height and crossed his arms. Silently he contemplated—it must have something to do with the odd device he had seen in the chart house.

"Tea?"

"Please," he responded as Minstrel brushed past him and laid a steaming earthen mug on the table by the open map. As her cheek passed close to his, he again detected the faint aroma of jasmine as he had at the boat landing earlier. Despite the oppressive humidity of tropical Africa and the obvious personal hygiene problems thus created, Alice Hallwood always smelled fresh and clean. She is a remarkable lady, he thought to himself. One day, when all this is done, he must tell her that. "Thank you, smells delightful."

She smiled broadly revealing a perfect set of ivory white teeth under her full, perfectly formed lips. She nodded and raised her own mug to sip. "Station Wilhelm again. 'Tis a mystery. Do you suppose it has to do with the *Aachen* secret?"

"Likely so, Memsahib," spoke up Patel sitting on the plank floor, cleaning a Webley revolver.

Braithwaite turned toward the Indian, arms still crossed across his chest. "I concur, Sergeant Major. It does seem most likely. The question is, what do we do about it if it is?"

Patel uncrossed his legs, gently laid down the disassembled revolver, stood, and moved to the table and the map. "Perhaps, when Mohammed goes to the mountain," he said raising a right eyebrow, "as we most likely will be doing, perhaps we shall find out and then the connection will appear obvious."

Braithwaite smiled. He had been thinking the same thoughts. "The question is, Amrish, old sport, is how does Mohammed travel to that mountain? I suspect camels would be a bit rare here," he chuckled.

"And dangerous," added Minstrel from the other side of the table. Her long, auburn hair fell over the map as she leaned down for a closer look while her mug stayed perfectly poised above. "One would have to cross over several hundred miles of German territory, not to mention simply the hazards of travel in this land."

"Concur, concur. When my father served in Dar es Salaam at the consulate, we took a safari to Lake Nyasa. It is a rugged trek even in the best of times or conditions. No, I don't expect that is a viable option." He again furrowed his brow in frustration.

"Very much so, Sahib," spoke Patel. "What if by water?"

Braithwaite stared at the Indian in amusement at first and then in curiosity at the brash statement. "By water, you say? How, Sergeant Major? How might that be done?"

"Well, Sir. Not easily, I assure you. But, it could be done." The former Bengal Lancer placed a dark tan finger on the mysterious German station and began to trace a possible journey as he outlined the bold proposal. "If one backtracks from the station along Lake Nyasa, you come to the Shire River. That is a tributary of the Zambezi River—here in Portuguese East Africa. It joins the Zambezi here." He pointed to the two rivers' junction. "Then, the Zambezi flows south by southeast into the Indian Ocean, just here. A small riverboat could easily make the journey."

Braithwaite uncrossed his arms and leaned back over the table now very much intrigued. "Very well, but how does one obtain such a river craft. I didn't see one for sale in the bazaar." All smirked at the sarcastic remark.

"Well, Sahib, there is the trick now. It also helps to know the locals. There is a boatman, a black native by the name of … well, I can't quite pronounce it in his native tongue, but he does go by the name of Tom."

"Yes, I've heard of him," Minstrel responded. "I believe he is quite well known among the local smugglers and he does operate a very nice boat indeed. But, why might he provide us the transport, especially for such a hazardous mission? Truly, what would he profit from such a venture?"

"Just so, Memsahib. He might be game because he has an intense hatred for the Germans. It seems that before the war, while he was on a cargo run up the Zambezi, the local German magistrate took a company of askaris from another tribe and raided his village. They claim that the village had not paid their taxes. They apparently ran a marvelous business in ivory and skins. Be that so or not, I suspect it was more a case of vengeance by the tribe not his own for some long ago slight. Perhaps *Herr* Magistrate simply wanted the taxes, but the askaris simply wanted blood. Nonetheless, Memsahib, everyone in the village was murdered, including Tom's entire family except for the son aboard his boat at that time. He has no love for the Germans, I'll warrant."

Braithwaite raised a hand to his stubbly beard and rubbed it slowly, considering the possibilities. "So this chap may well be willing to help, particularly if we can pay him with enough of His Majesty's guineas."

"Just so, Sahib. Just so."

Braithwaite paused for several seconds to stare at the map below. "Then, how do we get this Tom, his riverboat, and ourselves to the mouth of the Zambezi?" The silence continued for several seconds. Braithwaite took a long drink from his now lukewarm tea.

"Perhaps, we could convince the Royal Navy to take us and the boat aboard one of their ships from Mombasa and offload as they passed the river mouth. They are constantly calling here in Zanzibar transiting along the coast to Cape Town," volunteered Minstrel.

Braithwaite raised his eyebrows as the plan formulated in his mind. With her suggestion, Braithwaite began to see the possibilities. Perhaps this would not be a fool's mission after all. Perhaps Mohammed might come to the mountain. "We would need a great deal of logistical support," he proposed.

Minstrel slowly straightened up, her rich auburn hair cascading over her narrow shoulders. She raised a delicate but strong hand up and pulled the flowing mane back behind her head and wrapped a bright blue ribbon around the hair. "It could be arranged. The Navy could supply the goods."

Braithwaite nodded. "We would need rifles, probably machetes, knives, rations, jungle clothes, binoculars, and so forth. And of course, money."

"It can be done," responded Minstrel with a broad smile once again revealing her magnificent teeth. "It could be done. But we would need approval from "Blinker." I'll contact Room 40 tonight and then Commander Armitage in Mombasa."

Braithwaite nodded in agreement. His military mind began to click into high gear, running through a list of all the needed items. Energy surged through him. As a man of action, intense action, he had been frustrated by the lack of a plan ever since they had returned from Dar es Salaam two nights before. Now there was a plan—a risky one, indeed, but a plan nonetheless.

"Tom should be returning from his nightly smuggling run this evening. I'll approach him in the morning," volunteered Patel.

"Concur," whispered Braithwaite. "Concur. We have a plan. Also on the *Aachen*, I overheard a reference to a Doctor Steinweiss at Station Wilhelm. Ask Hall if we have any intelligence on this gentleman. Perhaps he is a clue to the device." All shook heads in acknowledgment.

That evening, two coded messages went out on the wireless transmitter that Minstrel kept hidden in a secret closet of the flat. The first went to London and Room 40. The second to the Royal Navy at Mombasa, attention Commander Armitage, the designated liaison with the Navy.

★★★★★★★★★★★★★★★

01 April 1915. Zanzibar.

Braithwaite stood silently on the quay as the first line went over. He had been up early that morning to greet the new arrival from Mombasa, HMS *St Andrews*. The cruiser glided into the berth and had all lines over in a matter of seconds. He marveled at the efficiency and sharpness of the cruiser men, mostly young chaps who must have come in as recruits since the war's outbreak. The threat of deadly violence at any moment and the need for vigilance, alertness, and efficiency made veteran sailors quickly in wartime.

"Secure all lines," came the shout from a young officer into a megaphone on the bridge wing extending outward from the pilothouse. Braithwaite was momentarily taken aback by the youth's appearance. He could not be but eighteen or nineteen, fresh out of school, and yet he had the bearing of an old salt-competent and self-confident. Sea duty will do this. It makes or breaks one. So did war. As he watched the sailors scurry about securing lines to bollards with others cranking out the gangway, he thought of his last ship and the very same type of young sailor as those. His head bowed down. To anyone watching, it would seem only to block out the glaring sun just coming up over the easterly horizon. He shuffled his feet on the gravelly quay. In his quiet thoughts, he remembered his own crew—the same fresh-faced kids who had made HMS *Halberd* seem like a living being. Almost embarrassed by the revelation, he realized that he had not thought of the ship, the captain, and the crew from that November night at all since he had been in Africa. A touch! Muscles tensed. His right hand shot out toward the Webley secure in the hidden holster at his waist covered by the loose cotton shirt.

"Easy sailor!" Came the calming, feminine voice followed by the firm grip of a soft hand on his elbow. He slowly turned his head and stared into Minstrel's emerald green eyes. His arm relaxed as he moved his hand away from the hidden revolver. Even in British East Africa, one carried arms regularly. It was prudent even in peacetime. Alice smiled—a thoroughly disarming smile.

"Most sorry. Not quite Piccadilly," he whispered as he gingerly moved his hand away from the concealed holster.

Over her shoulder, he saw Patel standing a few yards back with folded arms and a knowing, sprightly smile. With a wink, the Indian turned away and ambled farther down the pier. It wouldn't do to be too public. If the British had agents in Dar es Salaam, it was an even bet that German spies roamed Zanzibar. No doubt, the officials in the German city would hear of the cruiser's arrival within hours. Braithwaite wondered if this intelligence could be the secret to the enemy cruiser's success. No, perhaps not. How could *Aachen* know where British or French warships would be once at sea and how the devil did she always escape their ambush attempts. No, the secret lay elsewhere, and he was damned determined to find it out. The new, fast warship just arrived was to be an instrument in that quest. He turned back toward the ship now with all the lines over and secure with the gangway firmly on the concrete below.

The low to high to low shill blast of a boatswain's pipe announced a flag officer going ashore. A stately officer in spotless, pressed tropical white uniform strode down the brow. Peacock had arrived. Per arrangement, the Royal Navy officer neither greeted nor even acknowledged the watchers on the pier. He strode by followed by two junior officers and an armed ordinary seaman and headed straight for the harbor master's office farther down. But as Peacock passed, Braithwaite noticed a change. On the black shoulder boards, a broad gold stripe appeared. Well, well, Captain Peacock was now Commodore Peacock, RN. Well done, he whispered under his breath. *Well done, Sir.* He would congratulate Peacock in private.

Minstrel slipped her arm inside his. To any observer, they were simply the typical colonial couple out for a stroll before the unbearable heat of the tropical morning arrived and observing the hubbub of the ship arrival. In the shadow of a coconut palm, several yards away, another pair of eyes, silent and intent, observed the very proper British couple. The silent figure reached nervously into his flowing robe and fingered the hilt of the long curved blade—an assassin's blade. It was a nervous habit to be sure, just like the Englishman who had been startled by the touch of his lady. The stranger eased his fingers back off the ugly knife. In time he thought. In time.

****

The man turned a corner into an alleyway. Behind him, the bustle and commotion of the vegetable market quieted to a hum, not like the cacophony of noise as before. He breathed heavily. The moist, humid tropical air still caused him to labor. Used to chilly northern climates, he had not yet grown accustomed to the sultry tropics. He leaned over and put his hands on his knees to gulp some fresh air and to take his bearings. Removing a not-so-fresh handkerchief from his back pocket, he wiped sweaty beads off his brow and the back of his neck. It was dusk, but here just south of the equator, it was still hot and he felt every degree. With the coming sunset, the temperature would drop a few degrees—only a few. The ever-present bluish-gray mist enveloped the island city. Finally, catching his breath, he stood upright and looked left then right. It was a market day in the main street with all types of fresh fruits and vegetables. Produce brought in by the boats from the mainland and other parts of the island gave a flowery, pleasant aroma to the vegetable market, but tinged with a fetid smell of the fish market a few blocks distant. Even fresh catch brought in the morning by the fishing fleet had turned rancid smelling by the afternoon. Never a fan of seafood despite always having lived near the coast, he made sure to avoid the fish market area. The man still had several minutes before his sunset rendezvous, so a pause in the flower and vegetable market seemed just the refreshing interlude. The hustle and bustle of the market also allowed him to blend in. There, he was simply another colonial out to buy fresh vegetables for the supper table or a bouquet for the lady at home. He had learned this lesson from Minstrel. In the tradecraft, it was known as hiding in plain sight.

Ever since leaving his lodgings in an old and ramshackle boardinghouse in Stone Town near the piers, he had felt uncomfortable as if someone watched him—as if someone followed him. Several times, he had turned and looked about to no avail. In the streets crowded with shoppers and merchants hawking their goods, he felt the malevolent presence, but spotted no one out of place or too interested in the colonial.

Dammit all. Must get better at this game. Bloody amateur! He quietly railed at his lack of preparation for the spy trade. Why had he not been instructed more thoroughly in the art of spy versus spy and countersurveillance? He mentally noted to make a point in his after-action report to Hall. Field agents need a lot of tradecraft preparation and training. He hoped he had not already compromised the mission before it began. Then again, with a crooked grin, he had to have some skill in his daring jaunt several nights earlier. He had actually been aboard the enemy cruiser, in disguise, and not detected. What might be the secret to the German's seeming invincibility had been noticed. And truth be told, he had pirated successfully the Rufiji Delta chart and the map of German East Africa with the odd spot called Station Wilhelm. He smiled more broadly. *Yes, perhaps I do have some tradecraft skills after all. Bloody Hell!*

Standing erect, his breathing fully recovered, he looked about. Craning his neck, he scanned back at the market area. Nothing. Women in their long, flowing cotton robes carrying fruit and vegetable-laden baskets on their heads milled about as vendors packed up their street stalls. Still…. Still, the menacing presence wore on him. He felt a cold chill running up his spine. Imagination? Perhaps he was just overly worried. After all, since his arrival in Zanzibar, he had rarely gone out in the streets without either Minstrel or Patel or both. Seeing nothing out of the ordinary, he turned and strode down the dark alleyway. In the street beyond, he turned left and headed toward Minstrel's flat in New Town across the causeway. As he turned the corner, behind him, darting into the alleyway from the market street, a dark figure, face obscured by an Arabic turban, crouched down. The figure crept down the alleyway, a hand gripping the ugly curved knife at his belt.

✳✳✳✳✳✳✳✳✳✳✳✳✳✳✳

"Tea?"

"Sorry, what?" Braithwaite had been staring out the window through the parted Belgian lace curtains at the street. The presence still disturbed him despite no evidence of any follower.

"Tea?"

"Oh yes, of course, thank you."

"And you, Sir? Tea?"

The Royal Navy man stood up from peering at the map rolled out on the kitchen table. "Indeed yes. But, I should point out that I would much prefer a stiff whisky," snickered the officer with an impish smile.

"I'm so sorry, Sir. We just served the last of our single malt to the gorilla who lives next door," responded Minstrel as she poured a second cup of the steaming brown brew.

"Cheeky girl! She will seduce my entire squadron with that bloody tea, she will!" A hearty laughter erupted all about the tiny room. Patel sat in the corner cross-legged by the door smoking his treasured pipe carved in the shape of an Indian elephant. A smoke ring wafted toward the ceiling and disappeared.

"And you, Sergeant Major?" She cocked her head, smiling at the Indian, who always refused to sit when smoking—something about enjoying a smoke of his antique pipe, apparently a family heirloom, while in the cross-legged position.

"I have known you British all my life and I still can't quite fathom your strange sense of humor, I daresay!" Another hearty laugh erupted.

"It helps us cope with the damnable British weather," snorted the Commodore.

"Just so," smiled the Indian, releasing another ring of bluish-gray smoke.

Minstrel lay both cups on the table while trying to disguise a mirthful smirk.

"Well gentlemen and seductress, shall we be about our business?" Braithwaite turned and placed both hands on the table. He leaned in over the map. With a jab of an index finger, he tapped the spot marked as Station Wilhelm. "There's the key, I'll warrant." He turned toward Patel who had raised up and also gathered around the table.

"Your plan, Sergeant Major, is certainly creative. Bloody dangerous though," said Peacock, eyes squinted in a concerned look.

"Perhaps, Sir, but we really have little choice if you intend to inspect this place."

Braithwaite sighed. "Well, to use a phrase from our American cousins, it's Indian Country." The others stared up at Braithwaite.

"Indian what?" exclaimed Peacock.

"Ah, well, Sir. I believe it refers to the red American Indian. No slight, Sergeant Major. Simply their term."

The Indian grinned. "None taken, Sahib. It simply means dangerous territory ahead, I believe."

"Colonials. Never understood them. Outstanding people—just never understood them," responded Commodore Peacock, shaking his head. The others just grinned at each other.

"So, Sergeant Major, what of this foolhardy expedition to Lake Nyasa," said Braithwaite, chastened after his attempt at humor had fallen flat.

"Indeed, Sir. I propose that we proceed up the Zambezi River by the riverboat to here." He pointed at the juncture of the Zambezi and Shire rivers. "The Shire is a tributary that flows out of Lake Nyasa, here." He traced the river's roots to the source at the lake's southern end. "From there, we skirt the eastern shore until we reach this interesting place and investigate."

Peacock leaned in, squinting at the lines indicating waterways. "And what about this riverboat and the crew? Can we trust them?" All eyes shifted to Patel.

"I believe so, Commodore. The boatman is a well-known smuggler with a fine riverboat. I believe he is reliable and friendly. As I understand, he has plied all the rivers from Nyasa down to the Cape for nigh on thirty years. Although he had told the story previously to Minstrel and Braithwaite, he covered the essential details for the Commodore's benefit. Just after the war started, a company of askaris and their German officers raided his home village, raped and killed his wife and daughter, and kidnapped some men to serve in their army, at least those that survived the attack."

"None too fond of the Bosch, I suspect," interjected Peacock.

"No doubt, Sir. Hatred might be the better term. Since then, he has operated out of Zanzibar smuggling in goods from the mainland. The port authorities turn the other way and don't molest his business. Yes, I believe he is reliable and perhaps eager to strike a blow against the Germans."

Braithwaite took a sip of tea and blew the steam off the top. "What of this riverboat?"

Patel folded his arms across his chest and nodded. "Indeed, yes, the riverboat. Very good. I have seen it. Most lovely craft. Built by Mitchell Brothers in Greenock, Scotland as are many of the boats. It is very sturdy and the engine is new."

"Can it make the distance?" shot in Braithwaite.

"Tom says yes. If coal runs short, it runs as easily on wood from the jungle. Fuel is not a problem, Sahib."

"Tom?" replied Peacock, suddenly anxious about the plan.

"Yes, Sahib. Tom. He has an African name—very hard to pronounce. He simply goes by Tom."

"Tom, then. And what about any crew?" Peacock worried more about the reliability and loyalty of any additions to the expedition than the Germans, truth be told.

"Not to worry, Sahib. Only Tom's son will be with us. His only surviving son. He goes by Dick."

"Good God above," snorted Peacock. "And, I suppose Harry will join you along the way?"

Braithwaite and Minstrel chuckled. The joke went right over Patel's head and he could only look quizzically at the three. Odd folk these Britons, he thought to himself.

"So, Patel, myself, Tom, and Dick into the heart of Africa," responded Braithwaite.

Minstrel, who had been quiet until now shot a menacing glance at Braithwaite. He had never seen this from her and he rocked back on his heels, momentarily surprised.

"And I suppose you think this is a boy's night out, do you?" She shot another menacing glance at Braithwaite, whose mouth dropped open at her boldness. "No girls allowed?"

A few seconds of uncomfortable silence followed until finally Braithwaite broke the tension. "I suppose that you propose to go along on this frolic?" He had recovered his composure and went into an older brother demeanor.

"That, Sir, is precisely what I intend!" She placed her hands on her hips in a defiant stance and glared at the three men. Patel glared back, but he knew the tenor of this lady and her reaction was totally in character. Braithwaite pursed his lips. Peacock simply shook his head. "Gentlemen. I have been in Zanzibar as a resident agent for months without any trouble. I grew up in East Africa. I know the region. I am as equally comfortable on the Serengeti and in the jungle as I am in Piccadilly Circus. I have made many safaris with my father and brothers in the past. Can any of you say that?"

All three men stared at the defiant, but firm young lady. She shook her head slowly as if to answer her own question. The silky, flowing auburn hair swirled about her shoulders. This woman has some gumption thought Braithwaite. Most unusual and quite refreshing. "I can shoot with the best man and, believe me, Sirs, you may well need an extra gunner on your little adventure."

Braithwaite smiled. As the days had passed since he arrived in Zanzibar, he had grown ever admiring of this wildcat. She knew her business and truth be told, as an old Africa hand, her knowledge and experience could be of great value. No, she is an asset, not a liability. Old "Blinker" knew his stuff sending this young woman out to a remote but vital station. "I shall now amend my remarks. Patel, myself, Tom, Dick, and the unflappable Mrs. Hallwood will crew this expedition."

"Very well, then," responded a not quite so convinced Peacock, but he definitely was much impressed with Minstrel's gumption. "We can procure all the supplies and gear that you need including Lewis guns and ammunition. Let's hope you shan't need that particular item. We will load the riverboat as soon as possible and be underway. It wouldn't do for prying eyes to observe the loading, so I'll arrange it with the harbor master for pier security. Right then, on to Lake Nyasa for you lot. God Speed!"

By midnight, the planning session ended. While not physically exhausted, Braithwaite felt the strain and tension. Mentally drained, he looked forward to a long sleep. With the plans laid, all would rest. About midnight, an armed guard of Royal Marines arrived from HMS *St Andrews* per Commodore Peacock's previous orders. Although generally safe at night, Zanzibar teamed with refugees from the mainland escaping the fighting; even with the constant constabulary and military patrols, desperate persons hung about. Both Braithwaite and Patel each carried a Webley revolver concealed under the loose-fitting khaki shirts—just in case of trouble.

Once back aboard, Peacock would signal Mombasa with an interesting shopping list of items ranging from rations to freshwater in jerry cans to binoculars to a pair of Lewis guns with several hundred rounds of ammunition. The gear would arrive in a few days. Meanwhile, HMS *St Andrews* would continue a routine patrol while the three British agents laid out of sight. In the interim, Patel would make final arrangements with Tom and Dick for the hire of the riverboat, which the African had named the *Ulysses Belle* after the ancient Greek mariner and warrior. Braithwaite chuckled when he heard this bit of intelligence. Ulysses was about to go into the heart of Africa for another odyssey.

Braithwaite and Patel waited for several minutes before departing. Should anyone be observing the flat, upon seeing Peacock's departure, one might assume a liaison of a senior officer with the extraordinarily attractive widow who lived there. In tradecraft, as Braithwaite came to learn, deception and diversion are among the field agent's most valuable tools. By 01.00, the two men felt safe in leaving. Patel's flat lay several blocks from Braithwaite's in Stone Town. The two men walked briskly, but silently, through darkened streets. In the rain-soaked street, animal droppings gave the foggy air a foul, fetid smell. Both men carefully stepped over and around little piles of animal dung. As the men approached the intersection where each would go his own way, they nodded in acknowledgment, turned, and strode off in their separate directions.

As he approached the final intersection before his street, the feeling of a malignant presence returned. Braithwaite's first thought was to dart into one of the darkened doorways. *No, that will show panic and might cause an attack. What was it Minstrel had said?* Thoughts churned over in his mind; it raced. He felt panic coming on. *Steady, old boy, steady.* Slowly, carefully, he moved his right hand toward the concealed revolver. Maintaining his pace, his eyes darted left and right, desperately searching for an intruder. Up ahead, under a flickering gaslight, he saw his street. He fought the urge to quicken his pace. He had an advantage. The intruder might think he had an unaware victim, but Braithwaite had the upper hand—he was alert to the danger and prepared.

In the dim glow of the gas streetlight, he saw a flash, a glint of light off metal. *A blade! The game is on!* He dodged to his right just as the arm appeared from the recessed doorway. Braithwaite's sudden movement startled the attacker, who slashed in the air where Braithwaite should have been. Braithwaite's hand came crashing down on the attacker's elbow. The man howled in pain but held on to the ugly blade. He slashed again but as before, Braithwaite was too quick. He stepped to the left and the blade just missed his shoulder. The man's face came into view as he sprang fully from the alcove. He lunged at the intended victim, but Braithwaite managed to bring a knee up into the man's groin. The knife fell clattering to the wet cobblestones as the attacker howled in pain and bent over.

"No Marquis of Queensberry's rules here, mate," Braithwaite shouted as he brought his fist down hard on the exposed back of the man's neck. The assassin stumbled and yelped in pain. Remembering his form when he was a college boxing champion, Braithwaite assumed a fighter's stance, tight fist raised even with his head. He could now either strike out or parry any blow to his head or chest. Amazingly, the man recovered his balance and spun about. Rather than swing a fist, he lunged at Braithwaite. With the unexpected attack, Braithwaite staggered backward as the enemy crashed into him full force. Braithwaite tipped backward and lost all balance. As he fell, his legs giving way under them, he lashed out, grabbing the assailant's dirty, ragged jacket at the shoulders. Both men crashed to the street with the opponent now on top. His face only inches away, Braithwaite gagged at the opponent's fetid breath, now coming in heaves. The assailant's eyes, hate-filled and wide open, flashed in the lamplight.

Braithwaite pushed as hard as he could. The man would not budge. He was larger and much heavier, clearly not a local ragamuffin. The man's right arm shot out, fingers stretched, trying desperately to reach the knife. Now! Braithwaite kicked up into the man's kneecap. The brute howled in pain as the toe of Braithwaite's boot struck the exposed kneecap. He pushed as hard as he could against the man's chest, but no good. The man had him pinned. Braithwaite felt hard, cold metal jabbing into his spine. *No good.* The Webley lay pinned between him and the cobblestone.

Out of the corner of his eye, he saw a flash—a metallic flash. But it came from well above, not the attacker. In one swift stroke, a fist came down on the man's head from above, a fist with something metal in it. The man howled in pain and panic. Again, the hard fist struck. The assailant's grip loosened as he tried to push up on Braithwaite. *Now! Push!* With every muscle, Braithwaite pushed as hard as he could against the deadweight pinning him to the street. The man rolled over as a third blow struck him in the face. Blood spurted from a broken nose. As yet another blow threatened, the man rolled away. The blow fell harmlessly away. With a screech, the attacker jumped to his feet, turned, gasped in terror and then ran as fast as he could down the street into the darkness and away from the hard fist holding the butt of a British service revolver.

Braithwaite closed his eyes momentarily. Now armed with violent anger, he jumped to his feet, ignoring the savior standing beside him, reached back, and jerked the Webley from his belt. He swiftly raised it to a firing position. A brown hand shot across and lay on top of the revolver, pushing the barrel down.

"No, Sahib, no. Let it go."

Braithwaite stared in the face of Patel with a look of absolute amazement. "What, I have a shot. He's getting away!"

"No, Sahib. Very unwise. Gunfire in the night attracts unwise attention. And, how do we explain a dead body in the street? No, Sir, better letting go and suffering pain in regret and remembrance." The Indian broke into his customary broad, knowing grin.

Braithwaite felt the tension start to drain. He slowly lowered the Webley. His shoulders drooped in utter exhaustion. "Yes, quite right. I have much to learn about fieldwork."

"Indeed, quite so, but not here in the street. Come, Sahib, quickly. This way."

Just as he was about to step off, Braithwaite noticed something shining in the lamp light—a coin. He reached out and picked up a bright silver coin—a German coin. He held it up to the light for Patel to see. Both men simply looked at the coin, then at each other.

"I think, Patel, old chap, the sooner we get this operation underway, the better."

"Yes, Sahib, you are most correct. As you say, we have now entered Indian Country.

The two men strode down the darkened street as quickly as they could out of the lamplight and safely back to their quarters. The enemy had now revealed a key concern—they knew of Braithwaite's presence. The sooner the journey up the Zambezi and Shire Rivers to Lake Nyasa and the mysterious Station Wilhelm got underway, the better.

CHAPTER 6

Revelations

04 April 1915. Dar es Salaam.

A tall man, neatly dressed in the white linen suit common to the African climate, stepped lively down the grimy street pockmarked by mud holes and turned a corner. Up ahead, he spotted a ramshackle market stall. His formally pristine white suit indicated signs of wear. The frayed trouser cuffs showed the effects of many wearings. In the hot, humid dampness of East Africa, linen and cotton fabric did not last long. One wore what one had from before the war. The enemy blockade meant no goods in from the Fatherland. One did as best as one could. Hopefully, the new offenses would break the allied will and defeat the British, French, and Russians and the balance in the world order of 1890 would be restored. To the casual observer, the man appeared like the other hundreds of German businessmen and colonists trapped in the squalid city by the maelstrom of a world war. Perhaps to convey that image to passersby, he appeared like a local resident, his downtrodden look revealing the desperation so common in the city. But if one looked carefully, his closely cropped light hair, made almost silver by the tropical sun and many days at sea, and stark, hard set crystal blue eyes revealed a different sort—clearly military and more so, an intense and determined soul. Try as he might to shamble and shuffle along so as to not be noticed, his erect, tall frame and determined stride could not be hidden—clearly a man on an important mission.

He wore the linen suit acquired from an Italian tailor when SMS *Aachen* made port in Naples on her journey from Wilhelmshaven many months ago. The quality of his red silk foulard tie and pressed white shirt revealed a man of taste and sophistication. It was, however, a perfect disguise. Yes, this was still German territory and would remain so despite the enemy's efforts. Nevertheless, it did not do to advertise the fact he was actually a German naval officer. The creaking and desperate city had many who might attempt a robbery or worse. Then again, the British likely had spies everywhere among the native population, especially in the Indian business community held virtual hostage by the war. He took no chances. Tucked in under his belt and hidden by his jacket, his service pistol, a Model 1908 (P08) Parabellum (Luger) was hidden just in case.

As he turned the final corner, he headed straight for the stall where a middle-aged native peered carefully from under the frayed Persian carpet that formed a canopy shelter from the grueling equatorial sun. The man appeared to be part European and part Omani, no doubt a common site as the races intermingled since the Fatherland acquired East Africa decades earlier. The officer stopped suddenly and pawed through a pile of carpets and rugs as if interested. After a few minutes, without saying a word, the proprietor motioned toward the doorway leading into the shabby shop. The officer looked first left, then right, still holding a carpet in his hands. *Good, no one about.* He nodded slightly and replacing the carpet, followed the vendor into the shop out of the sun. The shop was cool and comfortable. It reeked of some unknown odor but the man ignored the smell. The carpet vendor did not speak but merely motioned to a careworn chair away from the window. The officer brushed off the thick red clay dust with several sweeps of his hand and sat without a word. He interwove his fingers in front of his face and bowed his head as if in prayer or somber contemplation. The vendor began to sweat profusely in nervous anticipation. Finally, after a disquieting and to the vendor, interminably tense and lengthy silence, the German officer spoke.

"So, *Herr* Abel, what have you for me today?"

The vendor took a seat close by and spoke in a firm, but soft voice, his tension now beginning to drain away. If the British could have spies among the natives, so too could the Kaiser. "It seems, *Herr* von Donop, that there is a new player in our match of wits. I cannot say as to his purpose. But, I have not observed him previously."

The officer leaned forward and asked in a low voice, "And, how do you know that he is not of here or simply one of the Zanzibar colonists?"

The carpet vendor sat up straight, somewhat irritated that the German would question his judgment or competence. "Because, *Herr* von Donop, he is too light-skinned to have been in Zanzibar for very long."

"And why might he not simply be one of the new British colonists come to East Africa?"

"Because, Sir, the other night in the streets, I attacked him."

The German officer bolted upright. This was an incredible violation of protocol. This man Abel was too valuable a spy to have revealed his actual role by such a crude and stupid act of street violence. The officer raised his eyebrows in amazement at the vendor's rash act.

"He travels with an Indian. I have long suspected the Indian of being an agent or worse. Both men are definitely military. I could tell by the way they fought. They are strong and well-drilled in self-defense—not like the typical soft British colonist or their Indian lapdog servants. No, they are both military and I suspect they mean us harm."

The German let out a long, slow breath. If true, this was a bad sign. With Zanzibar a short boat ride across the separating channel, it would be all too easy for an enemy spy to come into Dar es Salaam and report the cruiser's comings and goings. But, port calls were necessary. While, over the months, the *Aachen*'s crew had built a substantial coal supply at the Rufiji anchorage, mostly taken from the many merchant victims, the ship's boilers consumed coal by the ton and that had to be replenished. But for *Aachen*, the current stop had exhausted all the coal stores in Dar es Salaam. There would be no more from that source. And, they had to have fresh food, which meant a port call in Dar es Salaam. They had no other option. A British spy would be especially dangerous. *Do not take this intelligence lightly.* "Very well, then, Abel, maintain a sharp surveillance on these two. If necessary, you must do what you must do. I wish that you had not attacked them in the street. You might have compromised yourself."

Abel snorted, "Sir, I can see to myself. I am not compromised. To those two, I was simply a desperate native hoping to steal money for bread. As to an attack, I had to see if my suspicions were true. And, as it were, they are."

The German nodded. "Quite right, I understand. But, do not be careless. Think before you act, *Herr* Abel. And thank you for the report. There is one more thing, *Herr* Abel. On our previous port visit here, something went missing. It seems that one of the hired porters made off with a chart and a map from the ship's chart house. While we have replacements, of course, we should not want them to fall into enemy hands. Scout about the city and if you find out who the culprit is, then, well, you know how to deal with this sort of thievery. Oh, and if you can recover or destroy the items, do so immediately." With that, the German officer reached into his jacket pocket, pulled out a few silver coins, and spoke loudly in case any nearby ear strained to catch their conversation. "Thank you, Sir, I'll take the red and black Kermanshah. It will look splendid in our bedroom chamber." He stood up and dropped the coins in a brass pot on the table.

"It is wonderful to do business with you, as usual."

The German smiled, white teeth set against his tanned face with the piercing blue eyes. He leaned forward and whispered, "The Kaiser will never forget your service to the Fatherland, Mustafa." The carpet vendor shook his head in acknowledgment and gratitude.

With no further words, the officer strode out of the shop, picked up his new purchase and departed. He took a circuitous route to the fleet landing to await the next boat out to the anchored cruiser. With no sign of British interference, *Aachen* had taken the risk of pulling into Dar es Salaam in daylight hours, a highly unusual move. Nonetheless, it gave von Donop the chance to meet with his agent ashore, the half-German, half-Omani Mustafa Abel. *Aachen* would sail with the evening tide. The carpet would look fine in his cabin. First, though, he must brief the captain on this perhaps troubling new revelation. Ignoring the need to appear as just another local German colonist, von Donop strode confidently back to the waterfront, clearly the Prussian military aristocrat that he was.

****

The captain nervously paced the bridge. His racetrack course from one bridge wing to the other, pausing at the compass for a quick glance at the course heading, then to the quartermaster to check the ordered speed and finally to the opposite side and back around to the front of the bridge had ceased to annoy or worry the watchstanders. They had become so accustomed to the commander's nervous quirk that they had actually nicknamed him "Old Derby." It seems that a particular helmsman had lived for several years in America—Louisville, Kentucky to be exact—and being a horse lover, had attended the Kentucky Derby on many occasions. The correlation between an American horse race around an oval track and the captain's concise course about the bridge bemused the crew. Despite their understandable confusion on the origins of the nickname, the crew loved and admired "Old Derby." He had kept them safe and alive. He had shown magnificent seafaring skill. And, most significantly, he had inflicted incredible economic damage on the hated enemy. Quirks could be tolerated. But this particular steamy tropical morning, *Korvettenkapitän* Helmuth von Augsburg appeared especially agitated.

"Maintain a steady course, Bergmann."

"Aye, *Herr Kapitän*," replied the helmsman as von Augsburg nervously stepped behind the speed indicator, clucked his tongue in agreement with the ordered speed, nodded, and then strode over to the left bridge wing. And so it went, over and over. *Aachen* had departed Dar es Salaam in the late afternoon following an intense day of coaling and replenishment. The captain always worried that a squadron of British and Commonwealth warships lay just over the horizon in ambush. But, as usual, nothing appeared. As *Aachen* plowed through the moderate swells at best speed making for the safety of the Rufiji Delta, the sailor sitting attentively in the chart house located in the rear of the bridge every few minutes called off, "No contacts, *Herr Kapitän*." The man stared at a small, round glass plate lit in green light, but with no display of any sort. A low electric hum emanated from the device.

"Twenty nautical miles to Point Baker." The quartermaster of the watch hunched over the nautical chart running his dividers across the chart. Point Baker represented the turning point into the Delta and safety. "*Ja, danke*," responded the officer of the watch in the voice tube that connected the open flying bridge to the chart house below. The youthful officer turned toward the captain who had come onto the flying bridge and spoke confidently, "At this course and speed, estimate ninety minutes to Point Baker."

"*Danke*, very good." He turned to the officer of the watch. "Maintain course and speed."

"*Jawohl, Herr Kapitän.*"

Relaxing a bit, von Augsburg plopped down in his chair, lifted the binoculars to his eyes and slowly scanned the horizon. *No sign of the British this afternoon. Good!* He had had no sleep for over a day. Coming into Dar es Salaam worried him and he had been personally observing the loading and victualing. He trusted his crew and they were the best he had ever served with or commanded. Nevertheless, he dreaded the possibility of being caught at anchor with no way to maneuver or fight the ship. Fortunately, the British did not have the assets to maintain a constant blockade of Dar es Salaam and *Aachen* had always been able to slip in and out at will. Then again, von Augsburg had come to trust the odd, humming device. It had never failed to warn him of enemy warships. Nor had it failed to indicate targets of opportunity. For this, the British, Commonwealth, and French merchant mariners had paid a great price. In the six months since they had a arrived in German East African waters, twenty enemy merchants had been sunk or severely disabled. Truly, SMS *Aachen* had done its part for Kaiser and Fatherland. But this particular afternoon, the captain worried more than usual. In a routine check of the charts prior to getting underway before their last sortie from the Rufiji two days prior, the navigator found a chart and a map missing—one of the cleared and secret channels into and out of the Delta anchorages and a map indicating the secret Station Wilhelm on the eastern shore of Lake Nyasa. The map was the most sensitive and potentially dangerous should it fall into enemy hands. How had they gone missing? Who would've taken them? Surely no crewmember would and surely the ever-reliable and efficient navigator and his expert quartermaster would not have simply misplaced them. No. Someone had deliberately taken them. *Had some British agent or spy been able to board the ship? No, not likely.* The agent, despite his slothful manner and appearance, had always proven reliable and careful in supplying laborers and would have easily detected an enemy spy. Most likely, one of the natives had simply stolen the charts as a souvenir. *Yes, that had to be it. Simply a souvenir. Pray to God that was the case.*

Two officers and the chief quartermaster quietly entered the now crowded chart house, whispered a few words, and then exited up to the open bridge and approached the captain's chair. He dropped the binoculars to his chest and pivoted around to face the men.

The navigator spoke first. *"Herr Kapitän.* We have searched the entire ship. No charts have been found. I can only suspect that as you proposed, one of the porters took them as mementos. There can be no other explanation."

The captain nodded, hoping with all his heart that the ship's navigator was correct. "Very well, we shall assume that is the case. Can you replace the missing charts?"

"We can easily do so, *Herr Kapitän.* We have several duplicates."

The captain turned again, raised the binoculars, and scanned the empty horizon. The younger officer nervously shuffled his feet and stared down at the metal deck plates. As the assistant navigator, he was responsible for the charts. The leading quartermaster, a crusty old sailor, stood at stiff attention, but finally spoke up. "I concur. A souvenir hunter. Nothing more."

The captain nodded and spoke again, never taking his eyes off the horizon.

"Very well, Hans. From this point on at all times at anchor or moored in Rufiji or at Dar es Salaam, you will post an armed guard at the chart house. Is that clear."

"Very clear, *Herr Kapitän.*"

Just then, the gunnery officer, *Kapitänleutnant* Georg von Donop came on to the flying bridge as von Augsburg pushed himself off the chair. "To the chart house, *Herr* von Donop. You three carry on with your duties." The navigator, assistant navigator, and leading quarter-master snapped to attention, twirled about, and exited the flying bridge in their most crisp, military fashion. Once inside the chart house, von Donop, the third senior officer after the first officer and chief engineer, silently opened the bottom drawer of the steel chart table and pulled out duplicates of the missing map of German East Africa and the surrounding British and Portuguese colonies. Spreading it out on the table and smoothing it with his hands, brown and tan from months in the tropical sun, he leaned over and pointed to the spot labeled Station Wilhelm. He looked up at the captain, awaiting a response.

The captain leaned over the chart. He held the binoculars tightly in his right hand to keep them from hitting the metal table and pointed with his index finger. He looked up at the gunnery officer and raised his eyebrows. "We must ensure that all is well there. You understand, Georg?"

The officer nodded in agreement.

"It is imperative. We must make certain that *Herr Doktor* Steinweiss is secure. When we reach the Rufiji anchorage, take a platoon of *Hauptmann* Steiner's askaris and go to Station Wilhelm. Stay there until you are certain that Steinweiss and his laboratory are secure. I suspect that he is in no danger, but we shan't take a chance. Are you clear?"

"Completely clear, *Herr Kapitän.*"

Despite trying to convince himself that the theft of the chart and map held no sinister significance, von Augsburg was truly worried. Before they sailed, von Donop had returned after visiting his man in Dar es Salaam, who regularly kept watch on the British in Zanzibar. The agent, a carpet vendor named Abel had reported a curious story. He had observed a new arrival in Zanzibar. Britons coming and going into the town represented nothing out of the ordinary, but the agent found this one curious and suspicious and claimed the man was clearly military. He had no real evidence that the man was dangerous—only a nagging suspicion. Nevertheless, he needed watching. *Could the British be up to some scheme? Are the missing items somehow connected to the curious newcomer?* Once back in the anchorage, he would send von Donop and a platoon of askaris—native troops in German pay and uniforms—to make sure all was well. He had already determined that course of action as he turned again to scan the map of East Africa. He let out a slow breath. After a moment of silence in the chart house, he again spoke in a hushed whisper. "The safety of the ship and the crew depend on the security of that station. It must be protected."

"I understand, *Herr Kapitän*. I shall not fail." The navigator snapped to his best military attention.

"Just so, just so," muttered the captain as he spun on his heels and strode back onto the bridge. The navigator remained at his stiff attention for a few seconds longer, then peered down at the map on the table. He whispered, "Station Wilhelm. *Ja.* Station Wilhelm."

Two days later a German officer departed the quarterdeck of SMS *Aachen* now safely in her berth at the hidden base well up the Rufiji River. At the head of the brow, a leading noncommissioned officer saluted. On the landing below, in perfect formation and at a crisp attention, stood a platoon of native askaris, twenty-five in all. Milling about behind them stood a crowd of native porters bearing the necessities of a long jungle trek. A stout white horse pawed the dusty trail held in check by an askari corporal. The German officer mounted swiftly, issued a few sharp orders, and turned in a westerly direction toward the interior, Lake Nyasa, and a rendezvous with *Herr Doktor* Steinweiss at Station Wilhelm.

✳✳✳✳✳✳✳✳✳✳✳✳✳✳✳

Two knocks.

"Come."

The first officer entered the captain's cabin silently. Von Augsburg preferred working in the dark with just a small desk lamp above the metal fold-out desk. Other than a simple cot, a single leather chair, and a clothes cupboard, the metal fold-out desk represented the only furniture in the otherwise spartan sea cabin located just below the *Aachen's* bridge. The captain generally preferred to keep the lights off claiming that it kept his otherwise stuffy sea cabin cooler in the tropical heat of the Rufiji Delta. No matter, thought the first officer. *He is a good commanding officer. None better even if he can be a bit quirky at times.*

"*Ja*, Friedrich. What do you have for me?"

The first officer cleared his throat. It was not good news. "*Herr Kapitän*, I have the fuel report from the chief engineer." The first officer handed the clipboard to von Augsburg with no further word. The fuel report was self-explanatory.

Captain von Augsburg took the clipboard with his left hand, never looking away from the letter that he wrote to a mother in Hamburg explaining how her son had died gallantly in action against the perfidious British. There was no truth there. Her seaman son had died of dysentery brought on by malaria so rampant in the tropics. But, as every commanding officer in wartime knew, the letter to family, wife, or parents had a far greater purpose than simply informing them of their loved one's death. It had to glorify the man's actions so as to make his death have meaning and purpose. He had to die in brave sacrifice to the Emperor and the Fatherland. Sadly, *Korvettenkapitän* Helmuth von Augsburg had become quite adept at such letter writing. As distasteful as it was, he understood the necessity and thus, though grudgingly, he did his best to comfort the man's mother.

The captain glared at the fuel report. *Could this be true? Were they really down to less than two hundred tons of coal? How can I fight a ship if I can't leave this wretched river for fear of going dead in the water for lack of coal?* He knew the numbers were true. The meticulous chief engineer was never mistaken. The *Aachen* had enough coal for one more sortie out into the Indian Ocean, perhaps two. Then again, should they encounter a victim, they could confiscate the enemy's coal stores before sinking it. That evolution was always fraught with danger. While the "machine" gave warning of any approaching vessel or worse, a British squadron, taking on a beaten opponent's coal was always the most dangerous period as they sat dead in the water lashed to the victim. Perhaps they would come upon a collier headed to Mayotte or bound for Cape Town. At any rate, they desperately needed fuel. They had already exhausted the stores at Dar es Salaam. And, just breaking out of the Rufiji meant locating the blockade ships with the "machine" and then avoiding them. That evolution was always risky, so a trip to Dar es Salaam, even though only about 125 miles north, always flouted danger. No matter. Dar es Salaam had no more coal anyway.

The captain leaned back in his chair that squeaked loudly. "I must have the engineers lubricate this chair. It is most annoying, is it not, Friedrich?"

"Jawohl, Herr Kapitän, laughed the first officer. "And if not, the horrendous noise will likely alert the British that we are coming!" Both men laughed. It was gallows humor at its finest.

Von Augsburg glared again at the fuel report, picked up his pen and, with a flourish, signed the depressing document. Without a word, he handed it back. Just as the first officer reached the door and was about to turn the knob, he turned back toward the brooding commanding officer.

"One more thing, Sir."

"Ja?"

Neimeyer has just transmitted yet another request to the Naval Ministry in Berlin requesting a coal supply be sent out if at all possible."

Oberleutnant Neimeyer, the ship's wireless officer, had sent a message to Berlin every few days always with the same request—could a *Hilfsschiff* (supply ship) be sent to their aid with coal and other stores, including ammunition for the 4.1-inch main battery guns. The request had been routine for weeks with no response from the Naval Staff. Nevertheless, the *Aachen* dutifully sent the request. Hope springs eternal.

"*Danke,*" sighed the captain, sure that the most recent transmission would result in the same disappointment. He was wrong.

✶✶✶✶✶✶✶✶✶✶✶✶✶✶

05 April 1915. Room 40, Old Admiralty Building, Whitehall.
The phone on Hall's desk chirped twice. He hated the deuced thing. Why not see him in person. Nonetheless, he answered. It was Commander Millar ringing up from the analysis section of Room 40.

"Sir, I believe that you should see this latest intercept regarding the *Aachen*."

The DNI's eyebrows raised. *Well, well, well, our old friend Captain von Augsburg speaks.* "I shall be right there." Hall hurried out from his office and on to the floor of Room 40. He strode over to the analysis desk where the code breakers translated the intercepted wireless and cable transmissions. The *Aachen* had been transmitting desperate requests for coal and supplies for weeks with no response from Berlin. Today was different.

"Right. What do we have?"

Millar noticed "Blinker" blinking, a sign that he was particularly interested in anything pertaining to *Aachen*. "Sir, it seems the German Admiralty has responded and are sending help to our friends."

The cryptologist, who had translated the series of messages handed the piles of paper to Hall, who leafed through them wordlessly other than an occasional nod of the head and a grunt.

"So, our German colleagues have sent out the SS *Bordeaux* with several thousands of tons of coal—apparently high-quality stuff. *Bordeaux*, isn't that a French ship?"

"Indeed, Sir. She had the bad fortune of being in Kiel when the war erupted last August and was interned. I checked with Operations Division. They suspect that she escaped the blockade flying a false flag—Swedish, I believe, and evaded the chaps keeping watch. She is sailing under the name *Tonberg*. What is even more interesting is that the Naval Staff has ordered *Aachen* to coordinate by wireless with *Tonberg* and arrange for a rendezvous somewhere off the Rufiji Delta. The commander is one *Leutnant zur See der Reserve* Bruno Christiansen, a merchant mariner called back to active duty. We know that he is a well-known and quite a competent seaman and was engaged in the commercial trade with German and Portuguese East Africa before the war."

"Hmmm. So he would likely know of the protected anchorages where the two ships might meet, given that *Aachen* can evade the blockade, however, the rotter does it."

"Indeed, Sir. That is the likely plan. What captains von Augsburg and Christiansen most likely do not realize is that we have broken the code used by Aachen for all wireless transmissions. Since they have not been to homeport in Wilhelmshaven since before the war, they are using an outdated code that we broke last autumn."

The civilian cryptographer, still seated at his work desk just grinned. He had broken the code using his mathematical skills as a Cambridge lecturer in mathematics and physics.

Hall rocked slightly back and forth on his heels, taking in the good news and enjoying the triumph. "Very good. Keep me informed on the progress of our two ships. I shall report this to the First Sea Lord. I suspect he will be most pleased."

Within hours, a message went out to the commander of the North Sea blockading forces-allow *Tonberg* to pass. With luck, Commodore Peacock might bag both ships.

✶✶✶✶✶✶✶✶✶✶✶✶✶✶✶✶✶

18 April 1915. Rufiji Delta, German East Africa.
Korvettenkapitän von Augsburg stood on the bridge quietly observing the sailors bringing aboard crates of fresh fruit. At least we have that, he mused and, in general, given the conditions, his crew had been relatively protected from diseases due to their ability to obtain fresh fruit and vegetables. The wireless officer approached holding a sheaf of messages.

"*Ja*, Neimeyer?"

"Signal from *Tonberg, Herr Kapitän.*" She reports that she will arrive at the rendezvous at Mafia Island by dawn tomorrow. Mafia Island, just off the Rufiji Delta, was large enough and contained sufficient small coves for a rendezvous to go unnoticed unless one knew of the date, time, and location in advance. What neither of the two ship captains knew was that the commander of the blockading squadron knew exactly where and when the *Tonberg* would arrive. Cruisers and destroyers from the Cape Squadron would be there as well to welcome Captain Christiansen back to East Africa.

✳✳✳✳✳✳✳✳✳✳✳✳✳✳✳✳

Aachen slowly made her way down the channel at dusk. Captain von Augsburg intended to exit in the dark of early evening with no running lights. While the "machine" allowed her to detect any British warships guarding the various outlets of the Rufiji, in the dark against the land mass behind, it would be very difficult to spot the cruiser from seaward. As the sun set in the western sky, *Aachen* slowed to bare steerageway. At high tide, just after dusk, she could easily make it over the bar at the mouth of the Simba-Ouranga branch of the Rufiji Delta. At about five meters of water under the keel, the ship would pass safely over the bar.

"Any signs?" the captain quizzed the petty officer manning the "machine" in the chart house just behind the bridge.

"*Nein, Herr Kapitän.* No contacts."

The captain nodded in acknowledgment. No contacts. That was good. What von Augsburg and the *Aachen* crew did not know was that due to the need for escort protection against submarines and torpedo boats for the battleships engaged in the Gallipoli operation farther north in the Aegean Sea, most of the blockading ships had been pulled away for duty in that theatre. Thus, *Aachen* had free rein to come and go as she pleased on this early April evening. What blockading ships remained had been pulled off station to beef up the ambush force waiting on the far side of Mafia Island for the *Tonberg* and *Aachen* to rendezvous.

With a dark and overcast night, detection would be even more difficult. No contacts appeared on the "machine's" green glass faceplate. On the bridge, nerves became tender as the minutes passed. Where were the blockade ships? In past sorties, the "machine" had given the

Aachen several minutes warning of a ship over the horizon and there had always been sufficient time to alter course to avoid the enemy. Simply, no contacts appeared. The officer of the watch entered the chart house and peered over the shoulder of the petty officer.

"Rhein, are you certain this device is working?" he asked nervously.

"*Jawohl*, Sir. Do you see the outline of Mafia Island just there," he said as he pointed to a whitish glow in the northeast quadrant of the scope.

The officer of the watch leaned further in. Very clearly he could make out the form of the western end of the very familiar island, a landmark that indicated that they neared the Delta. Satisfied, he returned to the bridge and reported to the captain.

A few minutes later, Wireless Officer Neimeyer came onto the bridge with a single scrap of paper. The young officer could hardly contain his excitement. "*Herr Kapitän, Herr Kapitän*. Signal from *Tonberg*." He thrust the message paper toward von Augsburg, who snapped it up swiftly. The message was a single word—arrived. The captain's formerly dour and worried expression changed into a broad smile. He turned to the seaman manning the engine order telegraph that sent speed orders down to the main engine room: "*Biede Maschinen äußerste Kraft voraus!*" (both engines full speed ahead). Within seconds, the whine of the turbines could be heard as more steam poured over them. In daylight, such a dramatic speed increase could give away a ship's position as black smoke poured from the *Aachen's* three funnels. But on this dark night, the only visual indication was the increase in the foam and white water kicked up by the bow wave. *Aachen* shot forward at 20 knots.

"Quartermaster, course to rendezvous?" demanded the captain.

"*Herr Kapitän*, steer course 060 to rendezvous." *Aachen* plowed through the dark Indian Ocean night only vaguely aware of the disaster unfolding ahead.

With the information supplied by the crypto boffins in Room 40, the Cape Squadron arrived at the projected rendezvous point just ahead of *Tonberg*. But, *Tonberg* arrived too early. She stumbled upon the British warships waiting to ambush *Aachen*. Not familiar with the silhouettes of warships, the lookouts—civilian merchant mariners—misidentified the lead British light cruiser as *Aachen*. As they approached the rendezvous point, Christensen realized the error. *There are two ... no... three...Gott im Himmel! Four enemy ships!* He ordered a hard left turn, but too late. The first salvo landed astern of *Tonberg*, throwing up a wave of frothy sea water onto the ship's fantail. The second salvo from the opposite direction hit home carrying away the forward funnel and mast.

Slaughter ensued. Most of the ship's crew made it off the ship as she slowly rolled to port capsizing as she took on ton after ton of sea water. The fires caused by salvo after salvo of 6 and 4-inch shells set fires below decks causing ammunition to cook off blowing great gaping holes in the steamer's sides. Captain Christiansen sadly gave the order *"Schiff verlassen"* (abandon ship). For the survivors in the water, two dynamics saved them—the warm water meant no death by hypothermia and the closeness of the shoreline allowed the men to safely swim to the beach. They would be marooned on the island, but at least they were safe. Captain Christiansen and his crew could only stand on the beach and watch in horror as their ship, their home, their livelihood burned furiously mixed with the occasional boom of exploding ordnance as it lit up the East African night sky. However, as they prepared to abandon ship, Christiansen had raced into the wireless room and quickly tapped out a signal to *Aachen*—"ambushed stay out."

On the *Aachen's* bridge, Captain von Augsburg sighed as he read and reread the simple but powerful three-word signal. Without a word, he handed the paper back to *Oberleutnant* Neimeyer, whose bowed head told the entire story of disappointment and frustration. "It is not a concern, Mr. Neimeyer. Please return to your station and monitor any further message traffic." The young wireless officer slowly turned without a word and quietly exited the bridge. With no other option and fully half the remaining coal bunker expended, *Aachen* returned to the Rufiji anchorage just before dawn, having seen or detected not a single enemy warship.

CHAPTER 7

A Bodyguard of Lies

07 April 1915. The Strand, London.
A solitary figure strode down the Strand, intent on reaching his destinations in a hurry. He turned up the collar of his Burberry trench coat. The sudden wind whipped up sending a chill and causing him to shudder and curse silently under his breath. *Bloody cold and damp!* Even for London in mid-spring the air lay heavy, unseasonably cold, and damp. The warm fireplace at his destination and a good whisky would go a long way toward relief. The happy thought comforted him as he picked up his pace down the thoroughfare toward the Savoy Hotel. Here and there, a solitary pedestrian passed without noticing, equally intent on keeping out the drizzly rain and wet chill.

The figure turned sharply to the right, his destination reached—Simpson's-in-the-Strand. Wartime food shortages had not yet cut into the famous restaurant's bill of fare or reputation for good solid British beef, Scottish salmon, and hearty meals. That, no doubt would come soon enough.

"Good evening, Sir!" The porter, a veteran of many seasons at the storied eatery, extended his hand for the man's trench coat and bowler hat. He had no umbrella—unusual for the weather thought the porter. Many things, though, seemed out of sorts in London these days. No matter.

"Thank you, Amesby." The man clearly was a familiar customer.

"Very good, Sir. Please follow me. The rest of your party has already arrived. This way please."

The man fell in behind the ancient, but still nimble porter. Being mid-afternoon, few diners sat about the main dining room, mainly elderly ladies taking in an early tea. In peacetime, even at this hour, Simpson's would have been buzzing with the clank of cutlery and crystal as the white-aproned waiters raced to and fro from kitchen to dining rooms and back. War changed all that. Few of the ladies or the occasional gentleman glanced up as the two men passed, more intent on biscuits and tea than who might be passing. In the rear of the main dining area, they arrived at a solid oak, very medieval looking door, clearly a private room. The porter knocked twice with a bony hand, waited a few seconds, and then opened the heavy door. The man in the uniform of a Royal Navy captain ceased his conversation in mid-sentence, looked up and nodded to the porter.

"Thank you, Amesby."

The porter acknowledged the greeting and backed out gracefully, gently closing the oaken door behind him after the new guest stepped inside. The four men seated about the table all stood to greet the new guest. The Navy man spoke up first. "Gentlemen, I believe you all know Mr. Churchill, First Lord of the Admiralty." How do you dos, good to see you again, Winston, etc., all around. Churchill took each man's hand and shook firmly with a nod and a smile.

"I believe you know all here," said "Blinker" Hall, going around the room with introductions. "You know, of course, Captain Jackson, Director of the Operations Division, Commander Brandon from the Intelligence Division and Major Neville Pankhurst, Royal Marines, who will be briefing us tonight.

"Yes, indeed, Gentlemen, good to see all of you in such fine fettle."

"How is it at the front, Winston?" inquired the Operations Division Director, referring to the planned amphibious assault on the Gallipoli Peninsula following the failure of the Navy to break through the Turkish defenses and capture the Dardanelles in March.

"Bloody awful, I should say." Nods all around. "Neville, you old sod.

I see they railroaded you back on active duty for this little punch up, eh what?" grinned Churchill as he vigorously shook the major's extended hand. Jackson shot a quizzical look toward the two. Churchill smiled and responded, "Oh yes, Neville and I go back. We were school chums at Harrow those many years ago. Neville played a mean scrum half in those days. My knees still ache from chasing him all about the rugby pitch!"

"Dammit, Winston, I played hooker as you well know, but I did tackle you many times in the intramural games." Both men chuckled.

"Major Pankhurst retired from service several years ago to go out to Nairobi representing Sir Thomas Lipton's company. I talked him back into the service when I relieved Captain Oliver as DNI. I felt I needed an old Africa hand in the division—got him a promotion to major as well," chortled Hall.

"I damned well deserved it and you know it, Sir," smiled Pankhurst. The five men all let out a great guffaw, prelude to more serious discussion. A sudden stillness lay upon the room. The coal fire crackled. Hall rose up from his chair, grabbed a poker, and prodded the flames back to life and, still facing the marble and Dutch tiled fireplace, began the more serious discussion. "As each of you knows, Churchill and Pankhurst here spent several months in South Africa during the Boer War, so they have seen war at its worst. Well, then, let's see what we might do to get this present thing over a wee bit quicker, shall we!" Nods, hear, hears, good show all around as chairs scraped and scuffled on the hardwood floors. "Well, gentlemen, to business." He turned to face the table with arms folded across his chest. "Serious business it is." His hard, steely stare for which he was rightly famous, emphasized just how serious. "We have received a coded cable from our man in Zanzibar with the situation report on the SMS *Aachen*." Everyone in the room knew that the "man" was, in fact, a lady, codename Minstrel; but for security sake, Minstrel would only be referred to as "our man" in Zanzibar. "Major, please read the cable."

"Indeed, Sir." Pankhurst read aloud the report telling of Braithwaite's escapade on board the *Aachen*, the discovery of the strange location labeled Station Wilhelm on the stolen map, the proposal to travel inland to Lake Nyasa by riverboat to investigate, and the attack by an unknown assailant. The cable concluded with the request from Minstrel for assistance in the endeavor. The others listened intently and silently. Churchill stared off in the distance, admiring the antique oak paneling that had graced the almost century-old restaurant, wondering how many plots and schemes had been formed within this private room. As the words from Minstrel and Braithwaite echoed off the smoke-darkened paneling, he thought to himself, damned audacious, but a most interesting proposal—take the fight to the Hun. It appealed to his natural aggressiveness.

Pankhurst finished reading and laid the cable on the brightly polished dark oak table.

"When we received this message, I immediately got in touch with Winston here. He's the most cleverly devious chap I have ever known and we forged a plan to aid Lieutenant Braithwaite and Minstrel in this mission."

"Indeed," responded Hall, now seated and leaning forward in his chair, his eyes blinking away as he always did when his blood was up. "This is why the First Lord has joined us this evening."

Churchill grunted, "Quite right. We propose that our friends in Africa need a proper disguise. It just wouldn't do to have a Royal Navy officer tramping about German East Africa without a proper story. This morning, Neville and I consulted a mutual friend at the Home Office. It seems they have—how do I put it—ah, yes, a guest of His Majesty's Government, a famous criminal, the noted thief and forger, one Ronnie Carper."

A hint of recognition came over Brandon's face. "Yes. The Dolefield counterfeit scandal of a few years back. The man is a deuced genius. Crooked as a country lane, but a genius, no less."

"Just so," responded Pankhurst. "We propose that Mr. Carper, who in exchange for working with the government in some unusual forgery endeavors aimed at economic operations against the Germans, has had his sentence commuted. Thus far, he has done quite well."

Jackson took a long draw on his pipe and blew out a smoke ring that rose above the table toward the dark paneled ceiling. "So, how can this excellent craftsman help our people in Africa?"

Pankhurst turned toward Churchill who, after a long draw on his whisky, set the tumbler back down on the table. "What if we create for Lieutenant Braithwaite and Minstrel a fictitious identity that if confronted or worse, will give them a foolproof disguise? We looked into Braithwaite's dossier. He speaks fluent German. Minstrel attended school in Zürich and speaks fluent French and German. What say they go into the fray as Swiss neutrals? Our man Sergeant Major Patel, late of His Majesty's 2nd Bengal Lancers, being a native, can go as a valet or some such manservant. There are some Swiss neutrals still operating businesses in the region. The new identities should protect them should they run afoul of the local authorities."

Jackson interrupted, "And how does our forger fit into the scheme?"

"Mr. Carper can produce the forged documents to support the fiction. They will require passports, travel documents, identity papers, and the like. Carper can produce these quickly and expertly. Then we can send them on to Zanzibar by the fastest ship available," responded Pankhurst.

Jackson turned toward Hall and leaned in. "So, Reggie, why am I here? This seems like your division's bailiwick?"

"Very simple, Tom. It will take a couple of days to produce the documents and we need a fast ship for Zanzibar to deliver them."

The Director of Operations leaned back in his chair, which creaked under the movement. "We don't have anything currently scheduled to depart for East Africa for another few weeks. Are you asking me to detach a fast destroyer to simply transport a packet of forged documents? That's a heavy request, Reggie."

"Just so, Tom." Hall stood up and faced the crackling fire with his hands folded behind his back. The firelight glinted off the four gold rings on each of his uniform sleeves. "Just so. Our concern is that time is of the essence. If we can break the secret of this ghost cruiser and, in the process, save some British lives and ships, time is of the greatest importance." He turned back toward the table with as stern an expression as anyone had yet seen. "Braithwaite and Minstrel believe the key to this mystery lies at Station Wilhelm. Then there is the issue of the attack a few nights ago. They fear that their identities and perhaps their mission may be compromised. Yes, Sir. We must be prompt."

"Understood," responded the Operations Director.

Pankhurst reached into his locked leather briefcase and pulled out a map of East Africa. All stood and leaned over the map as he spread it across the table. He ran an index finger across the map from Zanzibar toward Lake Nyasa. "I propose to deliver the packet to our people in Zanzibar. They will travel by warship down to the Zambezi River Delta. Minstrel reports that they have a quite reliable chap under hire—a local smuggler and trader well-known in the area, who has a genuine hatred for the Germans. She vouches for his reliability. Once there, they will make their way upriver to the Shire and then north into Lake Nyasa posing as Swiss merchants until they arrive at Station Wilhelm. Meanwhile, I will take a party of Royal Marines overland from Zanzibar across northern German East Africa to the lake. There is already a platoon of marines stationed at Zanzibar. They are seasoned, well-trained in jungle and long-range reconnaissance patrolling, and have been used on such special operations inside German East Africa against the enemy forces operating in the interior. They will do nicely. I personally know their commander—a chap by the name of Barrington-Smythe. Excellent officer. Theoretically, we will extract our Swiss merchants about here north of the station and escort them back to friendly territory." After pointing to a spot at the northern end of the lake, he placed his hands on his hips in clear satisfaction.

"Why not simply send overland expeditions to this mysterious Station Wilhelm," quizzed Jackson.

Hall interjected, "Yes, well, the jungle drums are never silent, are they. That might cause them to shut down the station. On the other hand, if the Germans hear of a single British expedition heading across their territory, it might well distract their attention away from a solitary riverboat carrying a Swiss businessman and his lovely bride. If they don't react to Major Pankhurst's force, so much the better and that provides our party cover and an armed escort out of danger. And, the most critical issue, as I point out, is time. Braithwaite and Minstrel can travel much faster by water than an overland expedition. And, I might add, far more clandestinely."

Jackson leaned back in his chair and nodded. He looked at Churchill, then Pankhurst, then Hall. "You're a devious crew Reggie, a damned devious lot. I'll release a destroyer for the delivery. We can carry Major Pankhurst and the documents. HMS *Midas* is a fast, new Admiralty "M"-class destroyer. She is scheduled to depart Portsmouth for duty with the Mombasa force in several weeks, but, in truth, she can be ready to sail almost immediately if necessary."

"Excellent!" Hall clapped down hard on the table. Waterford crystal glasses clinked. "Neville, put the plan in motion. I'll brief the First Sea Lord. Be prepared to sortie in three days."

"Aye, Sir. We will be ready."

A silence descended on the room. Only the cracking of the fire broke the quietness as each man pondered the seriousness of the situation and the gravity of the mission. But, the enemy cruiser had to be stopped. Many lives depended upon it. It all hinged on a deception and a finely crafted plan. Churchill struck a Swan Vesta match across the box and tossed it on the table in front of them. Slowly, but deliberately, he lit the end of a fine, Cuban cigar. A cloud of bluish smoke engulfed his face. Raising his glass, he drained the last of his single malt, excellent whisky, crossed an arm across his chest, and leaned back in his chair. "In wartime, gentlemen, the truth is so precious that it must always be protected by a bodyguard of lies." The three other men raised their glasses in acknowledgment.

****

07 May 1915. Zanzibar.
The hot, humid, muggy oppressive air weighed on him. Sweat came down from his brow and ran into his mouth, salty and mixed with the dust of a Zanzibar backstreet. He had been in the country for some weeks now, yet still had not yet acclimatized. East Africa needed thin blood; the North Sea required the opposite. He would adjust eventually, but until then, he breathed heavily in the still, damp air. Aboard

ship, he exercised regularly. In Zanzibar, the less he was seen, the better. He could tell the effects of physical inactivity. Though well after dusk, the humidity and temperature, still stifling, made his breathing heavy and labored. Minstrel enjoyed great delight in his discomfort. Even when her tanned face and arms glistened with beads of sweat, she always showed incredible energy and stamina. She liked to joke that in Zanzibar, at night, it cools to a comfortable 98°F temperature and 98% humidity. *Incredible!*

He turned the corner down another dark street, gripping his hidden revolver tighter. It had been several weeks since the encounter with the attacker, but he took no chances. *Was this man simply a local who saw an opportunity to rob a European or, God forbid, could the man be a German informer? Did the Germans already know that this interloper, clearly military by his look and demeanor, had arrived in Zanzibar?* For this reason, speed had been emphasized in the cable report back to Room 40. Speed is life. He turned another corner and a light flashed in his face. Blinded for an instant, instinctively, he gripped the revolver, then eased off slightly.

"Sorry, Sir—can't be too careful tonight. Please pass on." The Royal Marine sentry lowered his torch and slung his .303 Lee–Enfield.

"Thank you. Careful watch," responded Braithwaite.

"Aye, Sir. Especially careful. Have a good evening, Sir."

Peacock had thrown an extended cordon of sentries out several streets from the piers. No one could see what went on that night lest it compromise the mission. No one could see the riverboat being loaded onto the fantail of HMS *St Andrews*. As Braithwaite rounded two more corners, he saw ahead the beehive-like activity on the piers. Two ships, a new Admiralty "M"-class destroyer and an "L"-class destroyer, some of the fastest in the fleet, were tied up pierside, starboard side to. Both took on stores as usual with a port visit, but rather than the regular crowd of native contract laborers, all the men passing stores from the idling lorries and up the gangway to the quarterdecks were sailors and marines, mostly bareback and sweating profusely. Little of the usual chatter and banter could be heard. The men had strict orders—all quiet—and as quickly as possible.

He nodded to the petty officer who headed up the roving security patrol. Without a word, the sailor escorted him to the *St Andrews'*
gangway and saluted smartly. Already aboard, he saw Minstrel, Patel,
the ship's commanding officer, and Commodore Peacock waiting on
the quarterdeck. As he reached the quarterdeck, he acknowledged
the sub-lieutenant holding the long glass, symbol of his officer of the
watch duty that evening. Without a word, the officer of the watch
pointed toward a ladder leading down to the deck below. Following
another petty officer, they made their way aft to the wardroom located
near the stern. Only then did they speak. Minstrel whispered, "Glad
you could make the show."

Braithwaite responded, "Damned glad to be here."

Minstrel smiled, her brilliant white, perfect teeth sparkled against
the perfect oval face in the glow of the red light illuminated passageway. As they entered the wardroom, they heard the clink of china on
the metal table and the grinding of an electric motor. On deck, the
chief petty officer in charge of loading the ungainly riverboat cursed
at the slowness of the operator manning the crane charged with lifting
the riverboat out of the water and depositing it on the cruiser's fantail.
He had his orders—get that bloody boat aboard and lashed down as
quickly as possible. Behind him stood two native Africans, one older,
perhaps in his 40s, and one younger. The older man grimaced and
clenched his teeth as his precious riverboat—his livelihood, really—
swung to and fro in the wind. With a clang, the metal hull landed in
the makeshift boat stocks hurriedly crafted by the ship's carpenter. The
riverboat didn't quite fit, but no matter. It would have to do. With the
speed and skill honed by months at sea, the ordinary seamen of the
deck gang quickly lashed down the riverboat after securing the broad
canvas tarp. Once covered, no one could tell precisely what lay under
the tarp other than simply another large ship's boat. The chief beamed.
His crew had done well despite his bellowing. He turned to the older
African. "Best of luck, Tom. God speed."

In the wardroom, all stood to attention as the ship's captain and
the commodore entered. A quick "as you were" followed and all then
took a seat around the green felt cloth-covered table. Spread out over

the table were nautical charts and two *Geographer's Guide* maps of the East African interior indicating the Zambezi, Shire, and Lake Nyasa regions.

"Proceed, Mr. Dunlap," ordered the ship's captain.

"Very good, Sir." The navigator stood and pointed a divider at the mouth of the Zambezi River where it emptied out into the Indian Ocean. "Once we are underway, the transit will take four days at standard speed with the two destroyers in accompaniment. That includes a fueling stop in the Comoros Islands." He pointed the divider at the French Navy fueling station at Mayotte. "Once off the Zambezi Delta, just here near Chinde, you will head into the Chinde River," pointing to a spot a couple of miles off the coast, "where we will debark the riverboat and crew. The Chinde is the northernmost branch of the Zambezi Delta. It intersects the main river farther inland." He turned to Braithwaite and Minstrel sitting directly across the table. "From there, you will proceed up the Zambezi to the junction with the Shire River. That's roughly a hundred nautical miles upriver. Your boatman chap, Tom, has made the run many times and knows the area quite well. Fortunately, the only dicey spot is the Lupata Gorge at about your 200-mile mark, but that's well upriver and you will have made your turn into the Shire River well before reaching the gorge. That area is quite narrow and fronted by high hills on either side."

"Just a perfect place for an ambush, I should say," piped in Pankhurst.

With that remark, Braithwaite shifted uncomfortably in his seat. As a sailor, he was used to wide open spaces with lots of sea space for tactical maneuvering, not a narrow river gorge.

"Quite so, Major."

Patel let out a not-so-subtle snort.

"The Sergeant Major knows precisely the meaning of ambush in a confined space," responded Peacock.

"Just so, Sir. Just so. Too much time spent at the Khyber Pass," the Indian responded.

The navigator continued, "That is a danger, should the mission and their identity be compromised. However, you will have turned north well before the gorge. Otherwise, the Lower Zambezi from the Delta up is primarily wide and flat. Should there be any interference, you will see the approach from a goodly distance. Nonetheless, I recommend the utmost caution in that area."

The navigator had placed several photographs of the river region on the table prior to the briefing. Braithwaite picked up the top one labeled "Lower Zambezi River, July 1894." He lay it aside and began shuffling through the stack of very old photos, noting that the Delta and upriver was very flat and marshy. "Fuel could be a concern."

The navigator continued, "Quite right, and I recommend that you maintain a goodly store wherever you might find it. The Lower Zambezi is essentially fronted by dense brush with the occasional evergreen forest and palm groves, so there is firewood available. There are, however, considerable mangrove swamps and some sandbars might obstruct the route. Again, your river boatman knows the route quite well."

"Palm trees and evergreens—not the best fuel for a boiler, is it?" questioned Braithwaite, his concern clearly showing.

"Well, it still bloody burns, doesn't it?" shot in Pankhurst, ever the contrarian, but smirking nonetheless. Sniggers all around followed.

"Quite so, Major Pankhurst," responded the navigator.

Braithwaite, relaxing a bit with the levity of the moment, shot back, "Well, Sir, I suppose we could take along all your Royal Marine fancy dress uniforms and burn them in the firebox should we run short of wood!"

"Touché, Mr. Braithwaite, touché. Well played," responded the good-natured marine officer. Meanwhile, Minstrel had lowered her head trying to disguise her own smirk.

"Right then, chaps, why don't we get back to business. Once on the Shire headed north, well, I'm afraid it's a bit of a sticky wicket as you close with Lake Nyasa. This area here, just south of Lake Malombe between Matope and Chikwawa is a problem. The elevation drops over 1,300 feet as you come out of the highlands into the coastal plain. There are numerous gorges and rapids that prohibit passage, I'm afraid."

Braithwaite turned and looked at Minstrel quizzically who raised her shoulders in surprise. They had not heard of that singular problem. Braithwaite turned back toward the navigator. "And how do we…." He left his obvious question hanging in the air.

The navigator grinned and finished the question. "Not a problem, Sir. Since the Shire is a major artery in these parts, there is a company run by a Portuguese chap by the name of Almeida. He will place the riverboat on a mule train and portage you around the rapids to… about here, just north of the Thima rapids. There are actually three rather large rapids that make navigation in that area impossible—here is the Thima rapids. Here is the Toni Rapids, and just about here are the Mbinjewanda rapids. Then there are several falls, most notably the Nkula falls just south of Mbinjewanda rapids, here, here, and there. The portage is normally about five days and you are clear of the rapids here." He pointed to a small bend in the river that formed a natural harbor. "There's an excellent anchorage there that riverboats frequent. It is also the last place to secure reliable supplies before you reach enemy territory, so take advantage of the opportunity." He pointed to a spot north of the harbor. "Not to worry. Your riverboat chap, Tom, is well known to Almeida and the locals. And, a few extra guineas from His Majesty's treasury ensure his discretion."

"Understood. Where do we meet this Portuguese chap?" Braithwaite replied.

"He has a business office in Chikwawa, which is where the portage starts. It's about a three-to-five-day effort—roughly 50 miles—so do plan on a bit of a walkabout." Dunlap's Australian outback roots began to show through despite his otherwise British upper crust demeanor. "The total distance up the Shire is roughly 250 miles and added to the Zambezi transit, at 5 knots per hour, assuming a twelve-hour travel day that should place you at the entrance to Lake Nyasa in about ten days or so depending on how long it takes to transport the boat around the gorges and rapids. You will pass through Lake Malombe just south of Nyasa—nothing unusual there, though I understand the hippos are quite common and you should have some interesting sight-seeing opportunities."

A low rumble came from the commodore. "I doubt they will be

very much interested in the local flora, fauna, and damned hippopotami, Lieutenant."

"Right, quite right, Sir. Apologies. Note also, that near the confluence of the Shire and the Zambezi, there is an area of rather stagnant water called the Elephant Marsh. It seems that the explorer Dr. David Livingstone discovered the Marsh in the 1850s and reported seeing over 800 elephants in one sighting. Quite extraordinary, really. That should not be a problem and again, your boatman has passed there many times. Just be careful to enter the river with a good load of fuel since if you run out and go dead in the water, there's little current to push you to shore. There have been instances of floating mats of loose vegetation trapping riverboats for days. As this is the dry season, that is a hazard to watch out for. Do be wary of the local crocodiles, though."

"And will they be observing more native animals this time, Mr. Dunlap?" snorted a now-amused Commodore Peacock. Several guffaws erupted about the wardroom.

The navigator chuckled. "Only if they need a fresh water wash down, Commodore. I understand the largest of those elephant beasts can shoot a spout from their trunks thirty or forty feet out." More guffaws followed.

"Carry on, Mr. Dunlap," responded a smiling commodore.

"Right then. Once you pass into Lake Nyasa, your target is just about here—the spot marked on the map that you so delicately pinched from under the Huns' noses!" Laughs and guffaws went all around the table. "The lake transit looks to be roughly 300 miles and all open water. So, you should be at the destination in two to three weeks, give or take. That's about the long and the short of the water transit." He handed the dividers to Major Pankhurst, who stood and clasped his hands behind his back.

Braithwaite leaned into the table peering intently at the map. He furrowed his eyebrows as a not too pleasant thought came to mind and looked up directly into Pankhurst's face, only a few inches away. "What can we expect in terms of enemy presence on the lake—other than this Station Wilhelm?" The question had been nagging at him throughout the entire briefing.

"Ah, yes, well, that might be a concern," answered Pankhurst. "Just after the war started our gunboat the *Gwendolen* found the only German military vessel on the lake at the time—I believe it was the *Hermann von Wissman*—in a bay near Spinxhaven. That is a small port in German East African waters. It seems that our lads disabled the enemy boat with a single shot from quite a distance."

"Damned fine shooting," added Peacock.

"Indeed, Sir. That is a fact," responded Pankhurst, who was noticeably miffed at the interruption. Nonetheless, he continued. "However, we now believe there is a second similar river gunboat operating on the lake that our fellows from British Central Africa and Nyasaland have not been able to track and neutralize. But, we know that the *Wissman* is out of commission. That leaves the smaller patrol boats. We are certain that they are still operating out of Spinxhaven, but they don't venture too terribly far out into the lake for fear of running into our patrols out of Nyasaland. They tend to stay on their side of the lake, but they are a factor, which is why we are arming you with Lewis guns as well as small arms. Tonight, my team of Royal Marines will transit across to Bagamoyo, north of Dar es Salaam, then overland to rendezvous with you here, just north of Station Wilhelm at a promontory we will call Point OK." With his officer's swagger stick, Pankhurst pointed to the spot labeled Point OK. That's an overland transit of some 500 miles. Barring any significant delays, we should arrive at Point OK at about the same time as you. That, of course, depends on how delayed you are and what you may find at Station Wilhelm. My chaps are all highly trained in jungle operations. Not to worry, we will be there. If you are not there on "Z" day, we will set up the camp and await you."

Minstrel stared at Pankhurst, her green eyes glowing with a steely edge. "And, Major, what if we don't make it through?"

The marine let out a long breath. "Then, Ma'am, we must assume that you are lost and we will take Station Wilhelm and destroy whatever is there."

The implication was clear. What would they find at Station Wilhelm?

Was it an armed camp full of danger? Would their deceptive identities hold up? Who was the mysterious Dr. Steinweiss and how might he react to them? Could they indeed solve the riddle of the phantom cruiser or would their mission come to naught? Questions abounded, but there were no answers. Only time and events would tell.

"Let us hope for the best," Peacock finally interjected.

"Indeed," responded Pankhurst. "Now then, as to your cover story. You, Lieutenant Braithwaite, are now *Herr* Peter Zimmermann, buyer for a Swiss mining consortium, late of Bern. *Frau* Zimmermann, you are his lovely wife Salome from Zürich, recently wed, and you, for better or for worse, are accompanying your new husband on his buying mission into deepest, darkest Africa.

Minstrel chuckled. "Silly girl! And Salome, a strange name, but I suppose I'll get used to it."

"And you will. Since you both speak French, German, and English, you should be able to pull off this Swiss identity with no problem. Mrs. Zimmermann, as you were educated in Switzerland, you are well able to pull off the deception. Sergeant Major Patel, you will appear as their Indian manservant, valet, and bodyguard."

"Very good, Sahib. They are in good hands."

Braithwaite chuckled. "Yes, I have seen you in action."

Patel just grinned broadly, his ivory white teeth shining across his broad, square-jawed, brown face.

"Here are your packets. Please use the transit time to memorize the details and then leave them aboard the ship. Any questions?" queried the hitherto silent ship's captain. There were none. "Well, then, thank you, Major Pankhurst, Lieutenant Dunlap. We should be getting underway in a few minutes. The less time here, the better for security. We don't want the rotters to see what we are about." All agreed. With the scrape of chairs against the metal deck, all stood at attention.

"Lady and Gentlemen, I wish you well on your journey and best of luck. Your King and Country are relying on you to carry through this vital mission …." As Commodore Peacock droned on with the usual best wishes and how important this mission was and so on and so forth, Braithwaite stared at Minstrel. She did not see his rapt attention to her, but Patel did. The former Bengal Lancer just smiled and nodded his head. He had become the young woman's surrogate father and regarded her as a daughter he never had. He had in the months that they had watched over the German activities just across the water in Dar es Salaam become quite fond of Mrs. Alice Hallwood, not in any sexual manner. Rather, he saw himself as her protector and guardian. He would fight to the death to save his charge. As to Braithwaite, he initially had the normal reaction of a senior noncommissioned officer toward a newly reported junior officer—that of a "sea daddy," a mentor if you will, whose role lay in teaching the young officer the ins and outs of the service. But, with this one, the Indian recognized almost immediately a raw talent for this sort of fieldwork. And, he felt very fond of young Lieutenant John Braithwaite. He would protect him as well. That the Royal Navy officer was clearly infatuated with his surrogate daughter pleased him no end. Thus, he watched Braithwaite staring at an unknowing Alice as the commodore droned on.

They raised their glasses and clinked them together in a toast to the King, to the Royal Navy, and to the mission. With that, Commodore Peacock opened a small wooden box that he had previously placed on the sideboard. He pulled out several excellent Cuban cigars. "I have been keeping these cigars for the right occasion. I do believe that this is the right occasion," he exclaimed as he handed one to each of the men in the room. When he came to Minstrel, he blushed.

"Commodore Peacock," she giggled, "I believe that I shall demure, but thank you, Sir, just the same."

His face returned to its normal hue. "Indeed, Ma'am, indeed. Right then, it's late and we have much to do. I suggest that we all get a good night's rest."

As the commodore and ship's captain departed, from up on deck, they heard the last of the chains lashing down the riverboat. Just as he exited the wardroom to go ashore, Pankhurst turned back toward Braithwaite and, with a smirk, commented, "Well, old boy, be mindful of the crocs. The Germans, I am told, don't eat much, but the river crocodiles …well, quite a different matter."

Braithwaite laughed, "Cheeky bastard. Don't be late."

****

In the dim light cast by the full moon, Braithwaite stared down at the churn and wake created as the cruiser cut through the Indian Ocean water below. Leaning against the railing on the ship's fantail, he stared down at the roiling sea rippling out away from the stern. He turned and looked up at the ship's superstructure. As the ship stood out toward the dangerous sea, he felt a sudden rush of exhilaration; his heart raced. *Back at sea, by God.* In the moonlight, he could make out the faint outline of the superstructure and mast. The lack of any noise but the swish, swish, swish of the four propellers beneath him churning out over 20-knot speed drove the ship along at a hurried pace. In the dim distance, he could see one of the two escorting destroyers—a new Admiralty "M"-class with its fuel oil-fired boilers turning three shafts that could make up to 34 knots top speed. But, with only a fuel oil bunkering capacity of 255 tons, the prudent captain needed to preserve oil lest they needed to put on turns for an emergency run or if facing combat. Nonetheless, 20 knots indicated that Commodore Peacock meant to reach the Zambezi Delta in what the Yanks might call a "New York minute." Braithwaite was impressed. Peacock, embarrassed so many times by the mystery cruiser's ability to escape destruction, meant to bag the fox once for all. As to the fuel oil situation, destroyer sailors never liked to run down their bunkers below 50%. Thus, the flotilla headed for the French Navy coaling station at Mayotte in the Comoros Islands off Madagascar to top up the fuel bunkers before making a run for the Delta. *Prudent planning.* Braithwaite concurred.

The night lay quiet over the ship. She traveled at darkened ship— no running or navigational lights. Although His Majesty's Royal Navy ruled the seas, the ever-present chance of meeting up with the Kaiser's ghost cruiser lay heavy on every crewmembers' mind. The sailors had dubbed the *Aachen* as the "Gray Ghost of the African Coast." All knew of the carnage that the mysterious raider had inflicted on imperial shipping all the way from Kenya to the north and the Cape of Good Hope to the south. And, all knew as well that two other Royal Navy warships and a French light cruiser had fallen prey to the inscrutable enemy, ever lurking in the waters, and striking at random with no warning. How did the German find such targets and how had it eluded effort after effort to find and destroy the enemy warship? It befuddled the Admiralty in London and flummoxed the Navy men seeking its destruction.

As he turned again and gazed at the roiling water below, his wonderment increased. *How did they do it?* Certainly, the secret must lay with Station Wilhelm. It simply had to. And, his mission had become clearer now. He must seek out and find the secret and the mysterious Station Wilhelm. His answer lay somewhere up the Zambezi and Shire Rivers on the eastern shore of Lake Nyasa. As he stared out, he thought again of his lost shipmates; a momentary sadness came over him. His head drooped. But, in those moments, their memory only steeled his resolve to solve the mystery and destroy the foe. He would and could do no less.

In the distance, against the moon glow on the dark water, he could make out the dim outline of the two accompanying destroyers, the only indication of their presence being the bow wake of white water and the bright greenish-orange phosphorescence astern. On they raced through the East African night. He thought of the men on the bridge, strong, confident men who knew their jobs and carried with them equal resolve to destroy the confounding enemy. They would do their duty well; he felt this in his heart and soul. They would do their job well when the time came. He must now do his.

"Evening, Sir." The sudden intrusion on his thoughts startled him for a moment. He jerked back and settled again. "Wonderful evening. So peaceful like. Seems like there's no blink'in war on it all, doesn't it, Sir." The after lookout, a young gunner's mate, had approached silently from only a few feet away. The momentary rush of adrenaline subsided as Braithwaite regained his composure. "Sorry to startle you, Sir."

"Not to worry. I was just pondering."

"Yes, Sir, sorry to intrude." The lookout nodded as he turned and walked forward toward the "Y" gun mount to resume his watch. Braithwaite turned back and resumed his own private vigil staring at the roiling water below. A phosphorescent glow came up from the foam-sea life, plankton, billions of microscopic sea life churned up by the rapidly rotating brass propellers, glowed greenish-yellow. Braithwaite stared at the wondrous light show, completely mesmerized. *A whiff of jasmine. Jasmine!* He spun as the faint trace of an elegant perfume filled his nostrils. There stood Minstrel a few inches behind them. Wordlessly, she stepped up to the rail and stared down into the water below. Braithwaite turned again as he regained his composure. An onerous thought crept into his mind-vigilance and awareness. As each day went by on this mission, he realized that to stay alive in this cat and mouse game of intrigue that is intelligence fieldwork, he must be vigilant. He must be alert. To allow one's mind to drift off even in the least threatening environment could mean attack from an unseen enemy. It could mean death or worse; it could mean mission failure. Lives depended on him—seamen's lives, fellow Navy men's lives, comrades and shipmate's lives. He must not fail. He must be vigilant.

After several moments, Minstrel finally spoke. "The sea is a wondrous thing is it not, especially in the moon glow with the stars above. My late husband used to comment on it frequently. He loved the sea. He would, after a long duty day on watch, just stare at the water below. I see it has the same effect on you."

Braithwaite nodded. This woman certainly impressed them. Perhaps it had been her upbringing in the rough-and-tumble of colonial life in this harsh continent. Perhaps it was just her nature so unlike the prim, proper, and oh so demure Edwardian ladies and London socialites. Feminine, yes, extraordinarily attractive, yes, but strong-willed, confident, and capable. Indeed. "Blinker" Hall had chosen well, this young widow as Naval Intelligence Division's "man in Zanzibar." Any doubt about her ability to carry out her role in this dangerous and critical mission had long since dissipated.

"Yes, I do find it relaxing—the sea at night with the moon and the stars and all quiet."

She placed a hand on his shoulder as she spoke. He'd always been amazed at how delicate her hands appeared with long, elegant fingers and always immaculately manicured nails. How she kept herself like that in this climate and with the physical work that she did always amazed him. Indeed, it had been a topic of conversation between himself and Patel when she was out of earshot. After a moment, she withdrew her hand, placed both hands on the railing, and turned to face the sea again.

After another few moments, Braithwaite finally spoke. "Well, Mrs. Hallwood, we are in for quite the adventure, I daresay."

She chuckled, "*Jawohl*, Herr Zimmermann, you are perfectly correct—an interesting journey. I'm not altogether sure who said it, but may we live in interesting times." Both chuckled. "I believe I'll turn in. Good night *Herr* Zimmermann."

Braithwaite nodded. "Good night, *Frau* Zimmermann. Sleep well."

She smiled again, turned, and strode forward to the hatch and down the ladder leading to the wardroom and officer country. They had been assigned adjoining cabins just aft of the wardroom. No doubt the senior officers displaced and forced to bunk with the junior officers and midshipmen had some grumbles, but no matter—just a temporary arrangement. Patel berthed in the chief petty officer's compartment as befit his status as a senior noncommissioned officer in His Majesty's Service.

Left alone to his thoughts again, Braithwaite remembered the fine Cuban cigar that the commodore had presented him at the conclusion of the initial briefing. Peacock had passed around several of the cigars acquired some weeks earlier in London for good luck and to celebrate his promotion to flag rank. He boasted that he would smoke the last one when he saw the *Aachen* turned turtle and going down to Davy Jones' locker. Braithwaite crouched against a ventilator to shield against the wind and lit the cigar using a match from a box labeled the Hotel Beau-Rivage, Geneva. The matchbox had been part of the cover disguise kit sent out from London and brought by Major Pankhurst along with the "official papers," passports, and other deceptive gems to support their identity as a Swiss businessman, his wife, and Indian valet.

An orange glow from the cigar's tip provided the only light from the darkened warship other than the red-lit instruments on the bridge. But, no one could see the lit cigar as he puffed away. Braithwaite coughed a couple of times. *But a strong cigar. But a good cigar. Strength. Will need all the strength I can muster for this adventure, old boy. Bloody great strength.* Could he carry it off? Could he be the Swiss business-man and fool any potential enemy. Once again, doubts crept into his thoughts as he puffed away. *Blast it! Must be strong. Have to carry it off. I must be this man and fool the Germans.*

****

As three warships lay in the harbor of Mayotte, each, in turn, pulled alongside the fueling pier. French sailors hopped to and fro rapidly and efficiently pumped the fuel into each ship. The Navy ran on beans, bullets, and now black oil and the flotilla would sortie with full fuel bunkers by the end of the day. As the fueling operation continued, in *St Andrews'* wardroom, Chief Petty Officer Proudfoot, a gunner's mate by rate, had laid out the weapons for the journey into Lake Nyasa. On the table, he had placed two .303 caliber Lewis guns, invented just before the war by the American Colonel Isaac Newton Lewis and, by 1914, had become the standard light machine gun of His Majesty's forces. Along with the Lewis guns were four .303 Short Lee–Enfield Mk III rifles, four Webley model Mk VI .455 caliber revolvers—stan-dard issue military handguns—a box of Mills bomb No. 5 model hand grenades, several machetes and piles and piles of round Lewis gun ammunition pans, Lee–Enfield preloaded stripper clips with five rounds each, and boxes of extra shells for both the Webleys and the Lee–Enfields. What a deuced arsenal, thought Braithwaite as he eyed the assortment of instruments of death while Proudfoot meticulously explained the operational characteristics of the Lewis gun.

"The pan contains 97 cartridges, but be sure to only fire in short bursts, say three-to-five-second rounds at a time. The firing rate is 500 rounds per minute, which, of course, means five to six changes of drum. I doubt, Sir, you desire to do so," the chief smirked. All nod-ded in obvious agreement. He continued. "The gun is gas operated and air-cooled, which is quite the advantage and makes it far more portable than a heavier, water-cooled gun. Nevertheless, it weighs just shy of two stone, so you will likely not be marching about too much with these. If you need firepower off the boat, I suggest the Enfields." The chief then proceeded to demonstrate the loading and operation of the standard issue, but highly deadly and reliable rifle. Finally, he briefed the Webley and Mills bomb operations. "Questions, gentlemen? Ma'am?"

There were none. All were already quite familiar with the weaponry; nevertheless, all appreciated the chief's briefing. At that moment, a young sub-lieutenant, barely a teen it appeared, stuck his head through the curtain that separated the wardroom from officer's country. "Pardon me, Sir, ready to get underway."

"Very good, Simpkins. Alert the bridge that I'll be up shortly," responded the captain, who had stood in the shadows, arms folded across his chest, observing the briefing. "Well, there it is. Best of luck and good hunting."

"Tally ho the fox," piped in Braithwaite as the captain departed up the ladder to the main deck. No one smiled or laughed. The array of deadly weapons on the wardroom table before them bespoke the seriousness of their mission and the risks they now undertook. All was silent for several seconds. Finally, from the opposite end of the table, Patel whispered under his breath, "I am become death, the destroyer of worlds."

PART II.
ANTIMONY Rising

CHAPTER 8

Chinde

11 May 1915. Off the Zambezi Delta.

HMS *St Andrews* stood off the coast of Portuguese East Africa near the port city of Chinde by about three miles. Although technically neutral, the local port authorities much preferred their allies of over two centuries, the British, as opposed to their overbearing new northerly neighbors, the Germans. If the local naval commander just didn't see the three British warships standing off the mouth of the Zambezi River while launching what appeared to be a standard, run-of-the-mill, African riverboat, well, so sorry Lisbon, it must have been the bad weather, poor visibility, and don't you know, just bad luck, etc., etc., etc. Even the investigating port patrol boat stood off at several hundred yards and never hailed or otherwise interfered with the offloading operation. So it is with undeclared allies. The Royal Navy would get no trouble from the locals this day.

Braithwaite, Minstrel, and Patel stood on the bridge wing with Commodore Peacock observing the offload. The boatswain's mate handled his men and equipment with grace, efficiency, and speed. Despite the relative acquiescence of port authorities, no one wanted to linger long at all such was the fear factor engendered by the mystery cruiser, which had the unfortunate habit of suddenly appearing on the horizon at battle stations. Typically, the German announced his presence with a couple of 4.1-inch rounds flying over the bow. Prudence dictated caution and, even though several hundred miles south of the Rufiji Delta, all three ships had gone to action stations before dawn.

The chief boatswain's mate had rigged special davits to lower the riverboat. The on load in Zanzibar had been relatively quick and easy using a dockyard crane, but manhandling a heavy metal-hulled riverboat over the side into the water presented an engineering challenge. But, as they did with all things, the chief boatswain's mate and his crew had rigged a perfectly suitable workaround using the ship's boat davits. Within minutes, they had the riverboat into the water. As she bobbed alongside riding up and down over the slight ocean swells, she bounced off the cruiser's hull occasionally with no problems, thanks to the rubber bumpers installed earlier. The 3-foot swells raised the boat's bow, which lowered back down into the troughs with ease. Three able seamen clambered over the side and down the Jacobs ladder into the boat, ready to receive the gear and supplies lowered on the after boat davits while the line from the fore davit held the riverboat fast to the side.

Braithwaite glanced at Patel, whose grimace told all. A landsman to be sure, the former Lancer had ridden out the transit from Zanzibar with relatively little queasiness. But, as his new digs on the water lifted up and down, he felt the symptoms of seasickness. Braithwaite grinned.

"We'll turn you into a proper sailor yet, Sergeant Major!"

All on the bridge wing chuckled. Patel shot a foul look back at the Navy man. Mustering all that he could, he retorted, "Bloody swabbies! Fie on your heads. Give me a fast mount instead." The banter lightened the previously somber mood.

As the minutes passed, they watched load after load of food, water, gear, and weapons go down into the riverboat as the sailors quickly and efficiently stowed the gear in the prearranged spots. Although Tom would stop the boat at several stations along the two rivers heading into Lake Nyasa for supplies and fuel, the boat carried enough fresh water and food for the entire journey. They dare not rely on the periodic supply even though they would stop at riverfront trading posts and towns along the route, especially for fresh provisions and fuel for the boiler. The imperative was to maintain the illusion of just another commercial riverboat carrying the usual European merchants upriver. Every stop along the route brought the hazard of discovery. As he watched the loading, Patel noticed several cartons labeled bully beef go into the boat's stores. As a Hindu, he avoided the tinned meat, but he had heard the horror stories from British comrades who often subsisted on the preserved beef product for days on end. He made a mental note—avoid the bully beef and stick with the vegetables. Fortunately, he saw box after box of relatively fresh fruits and vegetables go over the side and into the boat.

Finally, a large gray canvas bag came down and with it came the devil's arsenal of Lewis light machine guns, rifles, pistols, hand grenades, and hundreds of rounds of ammunition. The ship's carpenter had constructed a large wooden box in the ship's bow to stow and hide the armaments from curious observers, yet still be readily accessible in an emergency. The sailors lashed down the canvas tarp over the weapons box making it appear to be simply more cargo or a small deckhouse. With minimal road and rail infrastructure leading in from the coast, riverboats carried most of the goods into the inland towns and settlements. No one would question the oversized canvas-covered cargo loaded in a riverboat's bow. Braithwaite, Minstrel, Patel, and Tom had been issued keys to the ammunition box. It would not do to have a curious customs inspector or casual observer inadvertently open the box, but the interlopers had to have quick access.

Braithwaite had christened the riverboat the *Zambezi Belle*. Her actual name—*Ulysses*—would not be used to further obfuscate the mission and so that no enterprising German agent could trace the boat's true origin. Braithwaite simply referred to it as the *Belle* and the name stuck. Typical of the best African riverboats before the war, she had been built in Britain and launched in 1910. Tom had been sailing the *Belle* up and down East African rivers ever since, and her presence on the Zambezi and Shire Rivers, and Lake Nyasa should not arouse any suspicion—a bodyguard of lies to protect the true mission. At forty feet long with a beam of ten feet, she drew only two feet of draft making her easy to navigate in shoal or shallow water. It also meant that she could hide in protective coves if necessary and avoid unfriendly or overly curious river or lake traffic. There was a large deckhouse that sat amidships providing cover from the elements for the crew and passengers if needed, but its primary purpose was to store cargo and gear that might be spoiled by foul weather. Into the deckhouse went the perishables—fresh fruit and vegetables, extra clothing, navigational gear and charts, and other necessities for a river voyage. A large, brown canvas tarp hoisted up on six sturdy metal poles covered most of the boat providing shade from the blazing African sun.

Although the deck space was crowded with the main deckhouse, the newly constructed weapons box up forward, the boiler and firebox, engine, and tiller, there was still sufficient room for sleeping space. The Navy had loaded tentage and camping equipment, but, given the presence of river crocodiles and other less than hospitable creatures, the better choice was to always sleep aboard the boat at night. Food could be prepared ashore and a small encampment set up as a staging point for gathering fuel and so on, but no one wanted to risk camping on the beach. Then, there was the problem of security. Should they be suddenly discovered and must make a hasty departure at night, since they were all already aboard, that escape could be hastily accomplished. At night, a watch would always be maintained in four-hour shifts. Watch duties included maintaining minimal fire in the boiler. Should they have to depart in haste, there would always be sufficient steam for getting underway. It would not be very high speed, but at least they would have some ability to escape the shore and danger in a hurry. Only the anchor was ever used to hold the *Belle* fast as well as a single line going over from the stern to the beach. In an emergency, the watch was to chop the line with a swift blow of a machete stowed next to the cleat, shout as loud as possible to sound the alarm, race forward, and haul in the anchor. With the relatively slow-moving rivers, there was always the danger of the current causing the boat to drift away from its mooring, but that was a minimal hazard. The more important imperative was a quick getaway.

Her engine had been upgraded in Zanzibar by the Royal Navy engineers and she could run at a top speed of 10 knots, easily outclassing anything else on the water. A single propeller was always a hazard for the riverboats and often the prop and the shaft would be bent or damaged in shallow water by striking an unseen rock. To account for this case, the *Belle* carried a spare propeller, a replacement shaft and the tools necessary for a quick change out. The major disadvantage was the fuel. The hundred-gallon boiler could make steam in a hurry, but it chewed up the fuel. Anything that would burn went into the firebox, but the plan was to bivouac overnight in protected anchorages. The first order of business by Tom and his son Dick, the only crewmen, would be to re-stoke the fuel supply by foraging while Braithwaite, Minstrel, and Patel set up camp and prepared an evening meal. At a normal, economic cruising speed of 5 knots, they could make sixty miles per day. Depending on the nature of the portage at Chikwawa past the rapids and gorges, the journey would take a fortnight barring any delays or worse—trouble—or so the calculations went. But there is always the fog and friction of war. Braithwaite understood this all too well and the watchwords on this jaunty little African excursion were be mindful, be alert, and be prepared. The journey up the Zambezi had begun.

****

Farther north, another expedition made its way across German East Africa commanded by a German naval officer leading a platoon of native askari troops in German service. The expedition included a half-German, half-Omani whose devotion to German colonial East Africa in the Kaiser's new African Empire knew no bounds. He knew that the recently arrived Englishmen and his two partners—a female and an Indian—meant nothing but trouble for his empire. He did not know what, but deeply suspected that it had to do with the party's destination—a tiny experimental research station on the eastern shore of Lake Nyasa. The man had failed to stop the Englishman and his Indian companion in Zanzibar on a dark, deserted street. Failure had not cooled his ire or his lust for their destruction. Among the

African askaris, they simply called him "The Beast" and avoided contact whenever possible. It did not do to tangle with the devil himself.

****

The Zambezi Delta spread out over miles and miles as the great river poured into the Indian Ocean. The Delta area had been well-charted by the Portuguese merchants and sailors. Doctor David Livingstone had traveled up the Zambezi and the Shire rivers in the previous century, the first white European to do so. While the charts were fairly rudimentary, and more or less accurate, traders and travelers relied on the experience of veteran riverboat men such as Tom and Dick to safely navigate the waters. By design, they chose the most heavily traveled route. The appearance of a standard African riverboat, even in the era of reduced traffic caused by the war, would arouse no suspicion at all. It was the best cover for their mission. Although they carried plenty of supplies for the entire journey, they would always make a show of purchasing the normal supplies of fresh fruits, vegetables, bread, and so on—standard for all boats traveling upriver. The key to the deception lay in appearing as simply another riverboat transporting goods and passengers upriver, nothing more, nothing less.

By late afternoon, all the supplies and equipment had been loaded aboard. During the several days prior to the expedition's departure from Zanzibar, the marines commanded by Lieutenant Thomas Barrington-Smythe, RM, secured supplies and equipment in preparation for the expedition and did some last-minute training in jungle skirmish tactics. As soon as Pankhurst arrived at their depot, they departed to a location north of the town of Bagamoyo on the German East African coast just north of Dar es Salaam where they landed unobserved. From there, the expedition headed inland through the jungle backcountry toward a small promontory on the northern end of Lake Nyasa at a place designated Point OK. Going overland, their journey would take many more days than the riverboat's, a reason for striking out as early as possible and as soon as the ships departed. If all went as planned, the marines would arrive at Point OK at about the time the *Belle* arrived assuming that all went well at Station Wilhelm. But, as the great Prussian theorist General Carl von Clausewitz wrote, war is the realm of chaos and uncertainty. Such thoughts rarely left Braithwaite's mind for very long.

As the boat loading concluded, Minstrel, Braithwaite, Patel, and the crew headed aft to where the deck gang had set up the Jacobs ladder down to the boat, still gently bobbing in the gathering swells. Tom and Dick went over the side first and stood in the boat holding and steadying the ladder. Minstrel came down next. Dressed in a khaki safari outfit of loose trousers and blouse jacket with several wide pockets and brown leather high lace-up boots all topped by the standard tropical pith helmet, she looked every bit the part of the European traveler. Patel came next and none too happy with the prospect of climbing down a rickety rope ladder into a boat that rose up and down with the swells. As the Indian placed the second foot on the top step, he gazed up at the sky as if in a silent prayer. Braithwaite noted the pose and commented while trying not to be sarcastic or critical of the land lubber's discomfort.

"Steady on, Sergeant Major, steady on."

Patel shot back a glance that would seemingly melt tempered steel had it been a bolt of energy. Fortunately, Braithwaite took the rebuke in stride.

"Think of it, Patel, like mounting a horse for the first time and press ahead smartly."

With that bit of levity, the former Bengal Lancer grinned as his head disappeared over the rail. A few seconds later, his feet landed on deck successfully, much to his great relief. He looked up at Braithwaite, who now peered over the rail at him.

"You see, Sir, just like mounting a new one. Did I mention that I was the regimental trainer of new lancers in the fine art of horsemanship?"

With that, Braithwaite laughed heartily as he hoisted himself over the rail, the last to board the *Belle*. As the sailors on deck tossed the bow and stern lines over into the boat, the chief petty officer overseeing the loading snapped to attention and rendered a smart salute, which both Braithwaite and Patel returned with equal crispness. Tom turned the valve on the firebox, and as more steam coursed from the boiler through and over the turbine blades that turned the propeller shaft, he angled the tiller and *Belle* shot ahead toward the beach and an unknown destiny.

****

By dusk, they reached the trading post town of Chinde and made fast to a berth alongside other riverboats preparing to journey up the Zambezi to the many riverside hamlets and trading posts that serviced the interior. Many had just returned from upriver loaded with cargos of ivory, hides, sugar from the inland plantations, and other African commodities treasured by the rest of the world. Several bobbed in the current awaiting their turn to offload cargo at the trading concession still operated by British merchants and licensed by the Portuguese government. Before the war, Chinde had been a bustling port city as the major entry point into central East Africa via the Zambezi and Shire rivers. It was the major port of the old British Central African Colony that had become Nyasaland in 1907. Large ocean-going ships of the British Union Castle line and the German East African line called at Chinde to conduct trade and land passengers bound for the interior. Small river steamers then took passengers and cargo upriver. The steamers, largely 40 tonners of the African Lakes Company, Ltd., traversed the Zambezi River to Katanga, the head of navigation for the Shire River. Many then turned north heading toward the trading stations on Lake Nyasa. Other British companies operated smaller 20- to 30-ton steamers as well as various trading stations in addition to the Chinde concession. The 1884 Congress of Berlin in 1884 declared the Zambezi and its tributaries as free navigation to all nationalities and in the decades since, thousands of merchants, missionaries, and fortune seekers traveled the waterways. The Anglo-Portuguese Treaty of 1891 granted the British the Chinde concession for a 99-year lease to operate the port facility and trading station. But with the war, few freighters made port and even fewer of the large river steamers called at the concession. The loss of trade showed in the relative poverty of the town, especially the outer environs where the impoverished population lived. Bereft of the jobs as stevedores and porters, many of the natives had left the town and returned to their traditional tribal lands. Still, the British government maintained official offices and a few of the warehouses and chandleries stayed open to service the remaining riverboats and occasional merchant freighter. Most of the remaining trade focused on the sugar exports from the Portuguese plantations further upriver, a commodity less impacted by the war compared to other luxury goods, such as ivory.

Braithwaite and Minstrel avoided the official government site. German agents spied on what little traffic remained and they wished to avoid any British or Portuguese officials who might be overly curious about the two Swiss travelers. The Portuguese customs officials made no effort to inspect the boat or the cargo. After all, the *Belle* had made many stops in the years before the war and Tom was well known among the officials. To further disguise the mission, Braithwaite and Minstrel went ashore in their role as Swiss travelers to play out their part. The authorities summarily checked their passports and transit documents so carefully forged by Mr. Carper in London. The impeccable papers passed through easily, thanks to the forger's great skill. As the couple was waived on through by the almost totally disinterested customs agent, Braithwaite marveled at how easily the mission had started. The timing was well-planned. By arriving just at dusk, the men in the inspection station wanted nothing further than to close the shop and head home to their supper. Patel remained aboard the *Belle* with Dick. The plan called for one of the three to always remain aboard in case of trouble and to be prepared to get underway immediately should there be any. None came. Tom meanwhile arranged for the purchase of supplies, especially fuel, and also fresh food and other supplies. The plan called for maintaining a full fuel supply, should they run into trouble and must make speed fast. They would top up the fuel at every opportunity and never let the boiler go "cold iron."

Minstrel had made the point earlier that should they be stopped and boarded by any authorities, how long would their false identities as Swiss merchants hold up with nothing but British goods and rations aboard. The well-hidden weaponry could be kept secret—not so basics such as matches, dried food rations, cookware, and so on, all the necessary logistics for a riverboat making a trading run to the interior. Tom easily made the necessary purchases from the traders and suppliers that lined the almost deserted commercial waterfront. Just another upriver run with a couple of Swiss merchants and their Indian manservant—nothing to see here, nothing at all. The hired German spies, who dwelled like river rats along the waterfront, would have nothing unusual to report that day.

As they strolled as calmly as possible around the shamble of nautical gear, crates, and boxes of trade goods piled on the waterfront pier awaiting loading and around the occasional river sailor cursing his lot or straining under a heavy load, Braithwaite felt his blood pressure rise as the tension mounted. Minstrel, as expected, seemed as calm as a gracious lady at a garden party. They spoke little as they strolled through the narrow, muddy streets. The port customs clerk gave them directions to a small café that Minstrel indicated had been referred to her months earlier, one of many along a crowded market street where Europeans stopped in for a last drink and food before heading up the river. Dressed in the traditional European safari attire, they appeared as simply more of the gaggle of European neutrals who still pursued business interests in Portuguese East Africa despite the war. After several minutes, they arrived outside the tavern. A crudely painted sign hanging from a rusted railing announced the place—Ricardo's. Interesting name for a pub owned and operated by a native of Scotland, thought Braithwaite. The customs clerk had said the owner, an expatriate Scotsman, was a bit crude, but definitely served the best food available on the waterfront and seemed to have an unending supply of British beer and spirits, no doubt black-market contraband. It would do for a quick pint before departure. As they entered the dark and shabby-appearing café, they did not speak until reaching a small table in the corner. Braithwaite realized how much he had to learn about the field agents' tradecraft. He initially chose a table near the bar. Minstrel, with a nod and raised eyebrows, steered him to the table in the corner near the doorway. She knew that should things go wrong, they needed a quick exit route. *Damn! Good thing she knows what she is about. I have a lot to learn.* With a back sweep of a hand, he brushed away the red clay dust so prevalent in East Africa from the tabletop and the two chairs.

The place, dark and musty, appeared as one would expect. The publican had decorated the place like an Edinburgh tavern, not so much as a reminder of home, but more as a marketing tool to appeal to the British and Imperial sailors who pulled into port and enjoyed a quick liberty call. Then again, a number of young ladies of trade made Ricardo's their place of business. The owner didn't mind. Everyone needed to make a living and, well, it did bring in the sailors fresh off weeks or months at sea, flush with pay, and eager for entertainment. The traditional Scottish Highland crossed broadswords on the round shield (*targe*) graced the white-plastered walls. Prints of Scottish Highland soldiers, resplendent in tartan kilts and Kilmarnock bonnets adorned with dyed ostrich plumes—fierce warriors from a martial culture—appeared about the walls and over the bar itself. The publican's pride, a print of the trooping of the colors featuring the Scots Guards from Her Majesty Queen Victoria's Diamond Jubilee Celebration back in 1897, in which, as a much younger soldier, he had taken part, graced the space over the doorway that apparently led back into the kitchen area. Such a place would naturally attract German agents sniffing about for intelligence on merchant or warship sailings and any troop movements.

Wordlessly they sat. Braithwaite appeared nervous. Though not in enemy territory, the feeling of fight or flight that he had felt in Zanzibar the night of the attack returned. Minstrel sensed the tension. She placed a hand on his and squeezed gently. He got the cue—don't betray us accidentally before the mission even starts. He took several deep breaths and felt his heartbeat slow. He might have had cause for concern normally. Being so obviously British and attracting many British, Indian, and Australian sailors, the opportunity for German agents to overhear an indiscreet mention of a specific sailing or arrival was ever present in such a place. But, he need not worry this evening. The bar was empty save for the man behind the counter drying freshly washed beer glasses. The barman lay down the pint glass he had been wiping and ambled over to the table. Clearly, he was the owner described by the customs inspector. Burly, with a bushy flame-red beard and broad shoulders, he appeared every bit the archetypal Scottish Highlander.

"Aye, Sir, Ma'am, German?"

In his best German, Braithwaite replied, "Nein, Swiss-neutral."

The publican, visibly relieved, simply nodded. "Speak English?"

Braithwaite glanced quickly over at the imperturbable Minstrel. She sweetly smiled as she responded, "Yes, *Mein Herr*. We speak passable English and French. We are merchants on a buying trip up the Zambezi and Shire to Lake Nyasa. I am *Frau* Zimmermann and this is my husband *Herr* Zimmermann. We are from Zimmerwald near Bern.

"Good day to you both. Welcome to Ricardo's. What's your pleasure, Ma'am, Sir?"

Braithwaite swallowed slowly. *Don't ruin the disguise. Careful, old sod.* He spoke very slowly and deliberately. "Two steins of whatever is available, *Mein Herr*. We are weary travelers and are not too particular. And, whatever is fresh today, please."

Minstrel smiled ever so subtly. She approved. He had not stumbled.

The Scot just smiled. "Two steins of our finest lager, such as it is. And today, we have some fresh black bread and cheese with some bratwurst fresh from Dar es Salaam. Will that do?"

Minstrel smiled again, "Quite good, Sir."

Braithwaite stared at the petite, but powerful lady next to them. *This lady knows her tradecraft. What extraordinary presence she has.* They sat in silence for several minutes while the publican poured the warm lager from a crusty old barrel beside the bar. From under the bar, he pulled out the plates and dished up two servings of the pale gray sausages and generous hunks of cheese and black bread. Meanwhile, an employee, a native, came through the swinging doors that led from the kitchen into the main room. A shout at the native—something about dishes to be washed up in the back—caused the man to scurry back into the kitchen. No other customers graced the place. Still, the publican gazed about the empty room and out the open entrance. No one appeared. Bringing the two plates over followed by the two lagers, he placed them on the table and amazingly winked at Minstrel. What incredible cheekiness, thought a thoroughly surprised Braithwaite. The subtle wink startled him, but only for a moment. The Scot leaned over the table as if to wipe off a spot of spilled beer and whispered, "Compliments of 'Blinker.'"

Braithwaite's mouth shot open in surprise and shock. Good God! Minstrel returned the wink. The publican nodded with another smile, "*Herr* Zimmermann, *Frau* Zimmermann, please do enjoy the supper—the best in the town." He turned and strode back to the bar.

"Bloody 'Blinker' Hall," he whispered to Minstrel who simply sipped her lager, a shy grin on her lovely, sun-tanned face.

"Captain Hall has many friends." She reached for a slice of black bread and said no more. The burly Scot, owner of Ricardo's pub in a ramshackle port town in Portuguese East Africa, formerly of His Majesty's Scots Guards, former Queen's Piper, veteran of the Boer War, and since retirement from the army a decade earlier, a simple pub keeper serving the colonial Southwest African trade, was also in fact, Naval Intelligence Division's man in Chinde. His mission— track any German activity up and down the Zambezi and monitor the Portuguese East African coast for any signs of enemy activity, particularly in support of *Oberstleutnant* (Lieutenant Colonel) von Lettow-Vorbeck, whose force of German colonials and askari troops operated in the interior. Hall's man, indeed. An ally to be sure. Braithwaite now understood why Minstrel had been so insistent on coming into town into this particular pub even though they exposed themselves to possible detection once off the *Belle*. They had checked in and all was well. Only later did he learn from Minstrel that the Scot's signal that all was well had been a towel draped across his right shoulder. The same towel over the left shoulder meant trouble or be careful.

After a solid meal and a second round of the warm but delicious lager, Braithwaite and Minstrel returned to the *Belle* where Tom and Dick were stoking up the boiler to make steam. All the supplies had been brought aboard and stowed. They stayed the night at Chinde tied to the dock. No one traveled the river after dark. The northernmost navigable branch of the Zambezi River Delta would be their route in the morning. In the rainy season, the depth of over eight meters allowed for larger steamers to head upriver. But in late spring, before the summer rainy season, the sandy river bottom lay only four meters below the *Belle*'s keel—plenty of room for the shallow draft riverboat to navigate freely as *St Andrew*'s navigator had briefed them the night of the departure from Zanzibar. All felt comfortable with the geography and terrain. The shallow water was actually a blessing—it meant less river traffic and thus less chance of an accidental observation by any unfriendly locals. That night, a coded message from Chinde reached London and Room 40—mission secure and underway.

****

Dawn. Streaks of purple to blue to red, orange, and finally yellow colored the eastern horizon as Braithwaite stirred awake. He had had a fitful night. Nightmares of the carnage on the North Sea kept him agitated and constantly awakening him from what little sleep he could muster. The nervous tension made him fidgety and anxious. Patel and Minstrel seemed calm enough as if they were out on a lark or some sort of adventure. Braithwaite attributed it to their past several months on the knife's edge dodging enemy spies and agents, known and unknown. It had steeled their nerves. Then again, he had the added apprehension of not knowing if he was up to the task ahead. The field agent game—a new endeavor—had been thrust upon him with little training or preparation. But, old "Blinker" must have seen something in this young naval officer, bloodied and combat-tested at barely twenty-four. Nonetheless, the gravity of the mission bothered him constantly as he sought to overcome the doubts and worries. Then again, sleeping on the *Belle*'s hard teak deck in a thin bedroll did not help. He would never again complain about the sleeping arrangements aboard His Majesty's warships. He rotated his shoulders left and right followed by a stretch and a great yawn.

"Good morning, Ma'am. Slept well, I trust," he whispered to

Minstrel as she stretched to knock out the kinks from having slept on her rudimentary bedroll laid out on the *Belle*'s foredeck. She shot him an "evil eye" look and laughed softly.

"You promised me the Ritz, my dear husband, not a hard wooden deck under the stars." Both chuckled softly so as not to awaken Patel, still snoring away by the deckhouse.

Within a few minutes, Dick had set up the camp stove. Tom had bunkered the coals in the boiler so that they were still hot and smoldering in the morning. Dick shoveled some of the glowing embers into the small, portable cast iron stove, threw in some kindling and sticks and within minutes had tea brewing while Tom stoked the firebox with fresh fuel to get up steam for getting underway.

"Most sorry, Bwana John. We have no milk for tea," apologized Dick.

"Not to worry, Dick. I'm just grateful for a hot cup of tea," replied Braithwaite. In truth, the tea tasted bitter without the softening of some good fresh milk. Then again, this was Africa, not Devonshire and one did the best one could. He slowly sipped the hot liquid. Truth be told, it did help cut the "slag" in his mouth. Dick broke out a jar of Robertson's orange marmalade and some crusty bread purchased the night before in Chinde. Although they had no fresh butter, it still tasted wonderful.

As the eastern sun rose, so too did the temperature and humidity. Braithwaite felt the beads of sweat forming on his brow as they prepared the *Belle* for getting underway. Farther up the river in the Middle and Upper Zambezi, the temperature cooled to a comfortable daytime high of 70 degrees Fahrenheit. That was in the highlands and high savanna where elevation made for a far more comfortable and drier day especially at this time of year, which was technically approaching winter in the southern tropics. On the Delta at sea level near so much water, even in winter, the daily temperature and humidity rose to uncomfortable heights even for those who had spent their entire lives near the Indian Ocean coast. Braithwaite wiped his brow with a bandana and retied it around his neck, an action he would take many times in the coming days.

All finished their bread and tea breakfast and stowed away the loose gear on deck. Bedrolls went into a waterproof canvas case which was then stored in the deckhouse. Dick shoveled the remaining coals and embers from the camp stove back into the boiler's firebox. It would not do to have the *Belle* catch fire due to an unattended stove. Despite the potential hazard, all were grateful to have the stove. It meant hot tea in the morning and warm meals. With no refrigeration, they could not keep any fresh milk, cheese, or meat, so rations had to be fairly basic—salt pork, dry flour, beans and peas, and so on. But, they could fish and Dick was most proud of his prowess as a river fisherman, a skill he would demonstrate over the next few days. And, depending on the environment and potential threat situation, they could hunt for fresh meat to be boiled or fried over the small stove. The river, wide and calm as it coursed across the coastal plain, featured ample wildlife. Antelopes, gazelle, zebras, and other native animals came to water at the river's edge or at the small pools created by the sandbars and marshes. With the dry season between January and May and the river level down, many of these pools provided excellent watering holes. In the wet monsoon season when the river ran high and more swiftly, the wildlife moved inland to find watering spots. But, with the seasonal shallow river and multitude of watering holes close by the water's edge, the opportunity to lurk near a pool gave the possibility of fresh game for the evening meal without straying too far from the boat. While in Portuguese East Africa, they were not too worried about foraging, gathering wood for fuel, or hunting away from the *Belle*. In German territory, however, a different dynamic played out. But for the trip up the Zambezi and the lower Shire, the pools provided an opportunity for humans to stalk the prey. But, the pools also became the hunting grounds for lions, jaguars, and the occasional leopard in search of a kill. Such is life in the wild and death.

It had rained the night before as it did almost every evening as the daytime heat receded. Thankfully, the *Belle*'s deck was covered with the canvas tarp, which kept them dry. The tarp even had a fringed border indicating some level of affluence. Tom explained that a fringed border on one's deck tarp indicated a sort of riverboat aristocracy.

Braithwaite, Minstrel, and Patel saw it somewhat differently—the tarp not only kept the deck in shade, but everything underneath dry. Anything wet in this climate quickly deteriorated, especially clothing and bedding.

Braithwaite glanced over at the canvas-covered box near the bow where the weapons and ammunition were stored. The padlock kept it secure and prevented any accidental discovery should they be visited by strangers with a curiosity about the odd addition to the riverboat. Should they be officially inspected and forced to open the box for inspection by some customs officer or other official bureaucrat then that would be problematic. Braithwaite feared this situation. They might be able to explain Enfield rifles and Webley revolvers. After all, this was Africa and threats human and fauna meant no one went into the interior unarmed. The Lewis guns and Mills bombs though, well, there was a different matter altogether. They might be accused of gun running or worse. He hoped that they would never have to unlock the box, but in his heart, he suspected that would not be the case. The cruiser's carpenter had done a fine job in constructing the box and, for extra protection, had added an oilskin, waterproof cover over the contents. That, along with the deck tarp, would keep the weapons and ammunition dry and functional. Their lives might well depend on that factor.

Finally, with all the gear stowed, the stove secured, and breakfast completed, the *Belle* stood ready for action. In an offhand way, it reminded him of the preparations for getting a warship underway with the stations fully manned, the officer of the watch ready to give orders to line handlers and the helm, the engineers below standing by far ahead or astern bells and ready to spin the wheels that allowed steam to shoot over the turbine blades that drove the propeller shafts. Exhilarating! It suddenly occurred to him that this was his first command at sea—not what he had envisioned in what seemed like those many years ago as a cadet officer in training. He had always envisioned himself as a new commanding officer astride the bridge of a fast, sleek destroyer standing out to sea and danger in his first command with smart sailors in neatly pressed white uniforms all about him. The captain, the commander, was the one upon whom all responsibility, authority, and accountability rested—that would be his first command at sea. Instead, he now commanded a tiny riverboat with a crew of two natives adorned with a fringed tarp, and headed up a remote river in a remote colony in a remote part of the world. So be it. War creates strange and often bizarre realities.

"Are we ready to get underway, Tom?"

"Yes, Bwana, most ready!" Using an oar lashed to the *Belle*'s side for an emergency should they lose steam or suffer a propulsion casualty, he poked at the tarp to spill out the last of the tiny puddles of rainwater that had pooled in the night. Stowing the oar and then to announce their departure, he pulled the steam whistle chain in a long blast in accordance with the local maritime rules to signal underway and departure. The steam whistle had other uses on the rivers and lakes, particularly when a mist or fog rolled in, a common feature created by the high humidity and heat. The long blast caused other riverboat crews moored along the shabby waterfront to glance up, many waving. They too would soon be heading upriver—the fraternity of boatmen.

"Cast off forward," shouted Tom.

Dick, standing on the dock, immediately and swiftly in two turns, undid the line from the bollard on the dock, tossed it into the bow, and, before the Belle could drift away from him, he leaped into the bow.

"Cast off aft!"

Patel, standing at the stern did the same as Dick and landed on the stern with a heavy thud.

"Amrish, my friend, we will make a river boatman of you yet," laughed Minstrel.

"Beg pardon, Memsahib. But I still prefer a sturdy mount." All laughed loudly.

Tom put the wheel over to the starboard and the *Belle* eased out into the river. Once well clear of the dock, he pulled the chain and with two blasts of the whistle, signaled that he was coming left to head up the river. The *Belle* and the mission were now underway and headed up the Zambezi into a dangerous and unknown future.

CHAPTER 9

Declination of Aries

11 May 1915. The Zambezi River.
The *Belle* chugged along at a steady 5 knots. Against the outflowing current as the Zambezi emptied into the Chinde River and flowed inexorably toward the sea, the *Belle*'s sturdy engine proved sufficiently powerful for the task. Braithwaite leaned against the gunwale just staring at the passing scenery. His time living in East Africa as a youth had familiarized him with the savanna wildlife, but not the rivers. He spotted pelicans, herons, and egrets all of whom ignored the intruders or just squawked and flew away as the boat approached. He glanced over at Minstrel. Eyes closed, she slept gently, impervious to the river's attractions. *She's a steely one, all right.* He'd certainly grant that. With each passing day, he grew more confident and comfortable in her abilities and her strengths—what the Yanks might call "grit." She would be fine and, truth be told, she played the role of a Swiss wife ever so well. *I must ask if she has any theater experience.*

He turned back toward the riverbank view just as a river crocodile passed silently and effortlessly down the starboard side. Braithwaite grinned and whispered under his breath, "not today, Sir Crocodile, no British delights for your belly." He chuckled softly. Suddenly a dark cloud passed overhead, blotting out the sun and throwing a great shadow over the boat. At that moment, a sudden stab of nervousness jolted him out of his daydreaming. He jerked up and looked about in all directions. Nothing. There appeared no unusual thing or person or animal. As a dark rain cloud moved away and the glaring sun reemerged, he calmed down again, but still, his nervousness jolted him. Outwardly, he appeared calm. What was it that so bothered him?. He had had this feeling of unease ever since they left Chinde that early morning. It was as if a dark shadow hung over the boat, inexplicable, but definitely present. Perhaps it was just nerves. After all, he was a seagoing officer, a maritime warrior, almost completely out of his element in this game of field intelligence. Was he up to the task? Had old "Blinker" misread him? Had the DNI made a tactical blunder in sending a neophyte on such a mission? These doubts plagued him every now and then ever since he first arrived in Zanzibar weeks earlier. Only time and events would tell. Time and events. But, many lives— his own shipmates and fellow warriors lives—depended on breaking the mystery of the "machine." Could it be just that factor alone that gave the enemy such advantage in the cat and mouse game on the open sea? He resolved to find out; he must succeed. Still, the dark apprehension remained as if they were being watched. He could not shake it. *Alert. Be on guard. Be vigilant. Expect the unexpected and react accordingly.* Minstrel had admonished him in a quiet moment just before they departed the ship. Through it all, she had been a rock of calm and resolve. He had lost friends and shipmates to the enemy. She had lost her husband. Count on her. Still, the shadow remained.

Up in the bow, Dick shouted as he pulled on his fishing line. The cane pole bent with the stress arching down to the water. He reached out and pulled on the line as Patel held the pole. In seconds, they hauled aboard a large river catfish. As it hit the wet deck, its tail flapped hard on the teakwood as it flailed about, gasping for breath. A solid whack of a wooden paddle ended its struggle. It had to be half a stone at least. Braithwaite smiled. He now knew what would be dinner. He did not particularly like seafood but so be it, when in Rome, etc., etc. *Tonight we dine on river catfish!* And so it went as the sturdy boat chugged gracefully through the calm waters from the Chinde River Delta and into the wide Zambezi River and into the heart of the dark continent and the unknown.

At a steady 3 to 5 knots, the *Zambezi Belle* traveled easily up the Zambezi River. In the distance, they saw zebras, giraffes, and occasionally a herd of elephants. The catfish caught by Dick was delicious when grilled over the small cast iron camp stove. Other species of fish thrived in the Zambezi and Shire Rivers, so they were assured of a constant supply of fresh food to supplement the tinned beef and pork and other dry goods and certainly added to the edible but not very appetizing official rations loaded aboard the *Belle* from the cruiser. The landscape around the Zambezi River was essentially open grassland where lions and leopards stalked their prey. Buffaloes could be seen off in the distance. Patel even spotted a hyena. Birds of all sorts flew overhead. Pintales, African graybills, storks, and a great white pelican were spotted. On the second day, they passed by a herd of hippopotami gracefully watering themselves in the shallows of the river and every now and again spewing a geyser of water into the air. The noise was stupendous. Animal cries amid the trumpeting of elephants and hippos resounded all about them. Braithwaite was always amazed at how truly noisy Africa was.

The lower Zambezi was still fairly shallow. But, with its shallow draft, the *Belle* easily traversed from shoreline to shoreline. For security, they stayed in midstream except when pulling in for the night. Should a hostile party appear on the shoreline, the more distance away, the better for an escape. Should gunfire erupt, distance was a plus. The sandy riverbed allowed them to gently bring the *Belle* into the shore at night. The low reeds that fringed the banks didn't provide much cover from observation. Tom made a point, however, that this should not be a problem since being in Portuguese East Africa, any natives that might spot them would simply note yet another riverboat making its way up the Zambezi and Shire Rivers—nothing to see here. The Shire River ran into the Zambezi about a hundred miles up from the Delta so it did not take long to reach the turning point. Fortunately, Lupata Gorge lay several miles northwest of the Zambezi and Shire intersection. The low, wide, and flat Lower Zambezi provided no obstructions or difficulties, which meant pretty easy sailing. At night, they all slept aboard the *Belle*. Tom made sure to keep at least a small flame going in the boiler partly so as to light off more easily in the morning, but also should they be spotted by someone entirely too curious about their presence or perhaps even someone meaning harm to them, they could get underway fairly quickly. A watch was posted—four hours each. To Braithwaite, standing watch was completely natural; he volunteered to take the mid-watch or midnight watch from midnight until four in the morning. Usually, Patel would take the morning watch from 04.00 to 08.00 and Minstrel the evening watch from 20.00 until midnight. By early morning each day, they had had their breakfast of tinned meat and some fish left over from the evening meal along with any fresh fruit and vegetables procured along the route. Given the climate, though, the fresh fruit and vegetables lasted only the first two days. At each stop for supplies at a trading post or settlement along the rivers and the lake, Tom and Dick procured as much fresh food and bread as possible as would be normal for the riverboats plying the waterways. Not only was this action practical, it aided in their deception as simply another riverboat conducting inland commerce despite the chaos of war. But, should they run into trouble, the *Belle* carried enough fresh water and preserved food to sustain them for quite some time.

****

The bullet whizzed past the man's left ear and struck a massive tree sending bark shards in all directions. The man dodged left then right, knowing what would follow. Instinctively, he dove for cover as more bullets zipped by. From several yards away, he heard the shouts of men—angry men—who knew they had missed their target. The man crawled forward through the jungle undergrowth as carefully and quickly as possible. A simple rustle of leaves might give away his position. His breathing came heavy in the humid, heated air. In and out, he slowly controlled his breathing as best as possible despite the terror and fear. The voices came closer.

Now, a different voice could be heard—not an African voice but European. German. The man hiding under the bushes did not speak

German, but he recognized it and he understood the German officer's agitated shouting, clearly angry at his men for missing such an easy target. The man had walked straight into a party of askaris. He hated the askaris and he despised their German masters. Had it not been a squad of such men who raided his village the year before, raped the women, and killed all the old men before marching off with all the food supplies? The terror tactics had been deliberate as the ferocious war between German East African and British forces turned into a blood feud as the various tribal rivalries and hatreds fired up again, prompted by their colonial masters. He did not especially like the British and longed for the day of their departure. But, given the present circumstances, he cast his lot with the British. His family's death at the hands of the askaris while he had been on a hunt made the choice easy. And now, that choice led to his present predicament. He had stumbled into a German patrol—a patrol now beating through the undergrowth in search of the interloper.

Minutes passed. Amazingly, the shouts and curses seemed to move farther away. He held his breath, daring to hope. Perhaps the spirit of his ancestors guarded him this day. After several minutes, the voices moved out of range. Still, he lay silent on the jungle floor, daring not to move. A half hour after the last curse shouted in German had been heard, he crept up out of the undergrowth. It was all quiet except for the normal sounds of the triple canopy jungle—an array of bird and other noises, but no human sounds could be heard.

The man sprinted back the way he had come along the old jungle path—a trading trail centuries old. It wove from the savannas of the Serengeti out of British East Africa and through the jungles toward Lake Nyasa. As the guide and scout for the squad of Royal Marines, he had chosen the trail for its directness to the lake and for his knowledge of its intricacies, especially likely bivouac sites and fresh water. Now he faced a dilemma. Directly in the path stood a force of the enemy—at least platoon strength, he reckoned. He had stumbled on their encampment without realizing it when a sentry spotted him and raised the alarm. Did the enemy know of the approaching British party? Probably not. It must have been just a random thing, a roving patrol that the German commander routinely sent out to spot incursions from British East Africa. He had made this trek two months previously with no enemy presence. Cursing softly to himself for his bad luck, he carefully trod through the trail back toward his starting point to warn Major Pankhurst and the marines. They must've heard the shots as well. Sound traveled far in the moist jungle air. He had left them more than a mile back to scout out the trail and hopefully they had taken cover, but he must get back quietly to warn the party. As he cleared the danger area, he broke into a trot and then into a virtual sprint all the while praying that a trigger-happy, nervous marine would not open fire on a running man. He need not have worried.

Pankhurst had indeed heard the shots and had spread the men out in a rough skirmish line hidden by the lush jungle vegetation. Either the scout was already dead or he had escaped and headed back. Either way, every man in the platoon fully expected a battle to come. Nervous minutes passed. Each man checked and rechecked his magazine. Some nervously clicked the safety on and off. In the center of the skirmish line, Pankhurst heard a thrashing in the undergrowth. The lance corporal next to him heard it as well and raised his rifle to a firing position. The major raised his right hand—a caution, no firing unless you have a clear target was the watchword. The marine slowly lowered the weapon. The noise ceased. A few seconds later, all heard the password with relief.

"Piccadilly," the native scout whispered, then repeated it louder still, "Piccadilly."

Pankhurst let out a long breath. It was his scout, not the enemy. "Trafalgar." Then twenty yards away in front of the major's position, an African head popped out of the bush, smiling broadly. He had made it. "Over here. Here!" Pankhurst responded as he stood up. The lance corporal next to Pankhurst dropped his chin into his chest in relief. "Bloody Hell!" he exclaimed. Pankhurst nodded in agreement. One by one, the Marines stood at their post, but still craned their necks as if on a swivel looking for any sign of an enemy. The man raced over to Pankhurst's position and dropped to one knee. Despite his heavy breathing, more so from the tension and anxiety than physical exertion, he blurted out his report, "Very bad, Bwana. Very bad."

Pankhurst, not speaking a word, motioned for the scout to ease down to a low squat. In a whisper, after several seconds to allow the scout time to recover his breath, he finally spoke, "What did you find, Gabjanda?"

The native scout nodded, gulped, and took a deep breath. "Bwana. Askaris. Many. Maybe a platoon. They have a German officer. They block the trail ahead."

Hearing the report from a few feet away, Lieutenant Barrington-Smythe with his right hand extended, motioned downward, then strode over to Pankhurst's position. All the men saw the action and quickly and quietly ducked down under cover again.

"Platoon strength, you say?"

"Yes, Bwana. At least. Many men."

Pankhurst looked over at Barrington-Smythe, grim-faced. "How far away?"

"A mile for sure. Maybe closer. The askaris spread out. Maybe closer, Sir."

"Right then. Bad show." Barrington-Smythe nodded in agreement. Just then a shot rang out, then another. Instantly, both officers recognized the distinctive sound of a Mauser model 1898, the standard weapon of German African askari forces. "Christ!" came a guttural remark from the lance corporal on Pankhurst's left as the bullet slammed into the tree and just above his head.

"In for it now," whispered Barrington-Smythe as more shots echoed through the foliage overhead mixed with the cries of the askaris in their native dialects. Then came the distinctive sound of the .303 Lee-Enfield as the marines on the far edge of the skirmish line opened fire. A firefight was not part of the plan. Pankhurst could ill afford to become engaged in combat deep in German East Africa. A prudent commander sent constant patrols into the bush and the savannas to intercept any British raiders. Pankhurst and his marines had the bad luck of running into such a force. *Disengage and retreat.* Pankhurst knew the way forward meant going backward. He shouted the code word as loud as possible over the increasing gunfire. "Kitchener!"

Kitchener!" To the marines, it meant disengage, retire, and rally to the rear. At every third mile along the trail, Pankhurst had designated a rally point in case of such an occurrence. One by one, the men retreated back through the jungle. But the action had not been without loss. Twenty minutes later, the firing died down, but, in that time, three marines had been wounded. None were serious or life-threatening, but in the jungle with thousands of evil microbes and germs, the greater threat had to be infection and gangrene. All the casualties made the rally point, some helped along by their mates. As Pankhurst surveyed the scene, he kicked the turf in disgust. "Damned bad luck," hissed Barrington-Smythe. "Damned evil luck."

"Can't be helped," responded Pankhurst, maintaining a stoic stance despite the damned bad luck. What he could not know was that even though the German askaris had wounded three of his men, nearly a dozen of them lay dead or dying in front of the former skirmish line. The marines' marksmanship had been superb. As he helped apply a bandage to one wounded marine's leg, he considered his options. Clearly, the wounded had to be evacuated. Their best hope for survival lay in returning toward Mombasa. At the border near Jassin, there was a field hospital where army doctors could see to the men if they could make it that far. Alternately, they could head back to the coast north of Bagamoyo and hope to flag down one of the frequent Royal Navy patrols sent out from Zanzibar to maintain a careful watch along the coast. Pankhurst considered his odds. His 20-man force had essentially been cut in half. He would have to send at least six men back to escort and aid the wounded and press on with the remainder toward Lake Nyasa and the rendezvous with the party making their way up the rivers. He turned to the scout. "Gabjanda, is there another trail that leads to the lake?"

"Yes, Bwana. Much less traveled, but much longer. It should carry us clear of the askaris. Yes, much longer."

"Very well, it will have to do." He turned to Barrington-Smythe. "Tom, take the wounded and Corporal Stephen's squad and make for Jassin and the border. If that looks rather a bit dicey, then head for the coast above Bagamoyo. Do the best you can to keep these men safe."

"Aye, Sir." Barrington-Smythe turned to the corporal and nodded. Without a further word, the NCO pointed to his men and motioned to the wounded marines propped up under a whitethorn tree. Wordlessly, the escorts took the men in tow some holding them up by their shoulders, some simply taking off the web gear to lighten the man's load. As the last marine headed back along the trail, Barrington-Smythe saluted smartly. "Best of luck, Sir. I'll see you back at the mess in Mombasa." Both officers smiled.

"Right you are, Tom. Good luck." Without a further word, the Royal Marine lieutenant disappeared into the jungle.

Pankhurst looked about the remaining men before him. He did not see fear or desperation. He saw grim determination. These lads were hard men, rough men, and extraordinary men. They will do fine, he mused. "Right lads. We have a mission." He motioned to the scout, who nodded in acknowledgment and pointed off to the west. The new route would take them wide around the askari patrol. But, it would also add additional days of travel.

To the south, the *Zambezi Belle* slowly made its way up the calm waters of the Lower Shire. Braithwaite, Minstrel, Patel, and crew had no inkling that they now headed into the heart of the enemy without reinforcement. The cavalry had been unavoidably delayed.

****

19 May 1915. The Shire River.

Chikwawa was typical of the settlements and towns along the rivers. In the center, sat the better homes of the colonial elite whose fortunes depended on the river trade. Sugar plantations abounded in the coastal lowlands of Portuguese East Africa nourished by the abundant rainfall in the rainy season, the rich alluvial soil laid down by eons of river flooding during the monsoon season, and the warm climate. Like the sugar plantations of the West Indies in the 18th century, colonists by the thousands flooded into East Africa in search of wealth. Many had brought skills as shipwrights, chandlers, and boat builders, especially the Portuguese from the Azores. Tomas Almeida was such a man. He had come to Chikwawa in his early twenties and had built a fine business in servicing the river traffic. Ever the enterprising entrepreneur, he quickly realized that there was a fortune to be made in transporting riverboats over the portion of the river as it descended out of the lower Shire Highlands onto the plain with a myriad of steep gorges, waterfalls, and rapids. With the backing of investors—sugar and commodities plantation owners primarily who needed the river transport to move their products down to the coast at places like Chinde—Almeida had built himself a profitable company. Although the war made business more difficult, he still paid his expenses and his workers and set aside a small salary.

Chikwawa had a dangerous side for the mission. Although in British Nyasaland and fairly near the colonial capital at Blantyre, German agents abounded taking note of the river traffic. The western side of Lake Nyasa fronting Nyasaland was British territory and the merchants there still needed the Nyasa to Shire to Zambezi to the Indian Ocean water route for trade. The agents, mainly locals in German pay, kept a watch for riverboats carrying British goods upriver or products down the river. But there was another, even darker side of the men who sat and watched along the riverbank–piracy. While the river watchers might report activity to the Germans, they also communicated with the buccaneers who operated on the lakes. With the war and the destruction of much of the Imperial German Navy presence on the German East African side of Lake Nyasa, local pirates proliferated. In truth, Lake Nyasa in 1915 was not altogether unlike the Spanish Main of previous centuries where pirate vessels roamed the waves with relative impunity. The Royal Navy controlled the pirates fairly well on the Nyasaland side—not so on the German side. It was not just as a hedge against German attack that the *Belle* carried a substantial armament. However, for the moment, Braithwaite and the crew worried more about German agent observation and the need to be in and out of Chikwawa as rapidly as possible. There would be no tarrying.

They arrived at Almeida's office just above Chikwawa with no delays or troubles. The Portuguese businessman was no nonsense—

here's the route, here's the time to depart, the time to arrive, and the cost. Braithwaite had worried that this second test of their deception would not hold. He need not have. In truth, the Portuguese business-man neither cared nor wanted to know precisely who his company carried around the falls and rapids, only that they paid the proper fare and caused no trouble for him or his crew. With the cash paid up front, the crew quickly and efficiently pulled the *Belle* into the dry dock, mounted her on the carrying cradle, drained the dock, strapped down the riverboat, and off they went. Braithwaite observed the entire operation with admiration at the native workers' efficiency. Tom, as they prepared to travel, told Braithwaite the story. Each man on the crew was fiercely loyal to Almeida. They were highly paid, well-trained, and taken care of. If a man got injured or sick on the job, Almeida cared for the man's family until the breadwinner was back at work. That is the way to do business, he mused. That is the way he had always treated the men under his command. At that moment, his thoughts drifted back to those lost sailors under his command and it steeled his resolve even further. Observing the men at work and hearing their story reminded him that the success of this mission was not only a matter of national interest, for him, it was deeply personal.

Almeida's transport service was quite elaborate and impressive. He had constructed a small dry dock on the river bank that could be flooded by opening a pair of gates and drained by a pump powered by a mule team turning a capstan. Inside the dock was a cradle. Once the riverboat entered the dock and was held in place over the cradle by native line handlers, the mules turned the capstan that powered the pump that created the vacuum that drained the dock. The riverboat gently settled into the cradle; the line handlers descended into the dry dock and tied down the riverboat securely to the cradle. Then, the cradle was attached to a 20-mule team, which pulled the boat and cradle up out of the dock and on its merry way running parallel to the river in a portage around the gorges, rapids, and falls. Upriver about fifty miles sat an identical dry dock where the process was reversed and the riverboats simply floated back out of the dock and into the Shire. And so it went.

Almeida always gave the river boatmen the option of going ahead and, for a price, would provide a fairly decent room and board at either end of the system. Braithwaite opted to travel with the *Belle*. They could take no chances that the weapons and supplies would be pilfered or disturbed. The journey would take only three or four days depending on the weather and Almeida supplied tents and rations— again, for a good price.

They chose to walk with the riverboat the several miles of the portage. Almeida offered complimentary transportation in what looked like an old stage coach that one might have seen in preindustrial England. They declined. They dare not risk someone finding the Lewis guns and questioning why simple Swiss merchants would be so heavily armed even in a war zone. Then, there was the map so deftly pirated by Braithwaite from the cruiser. That too might arouse some suspicion. No thank you, very kind, Mr. Almeida. We'll accompany the boat and portage crew and etc., and etc. The Portuguese entrepreneur responded with an "As you wish, Sir and Ma'am." Braithwaite, Patel, and Minstrel would keep an eye on the well-concealed secrets of the *Zambezi Belle*. For Tom and Dick, they wanted to keep an eye on their precious boat even knowing that should the mission go as hoped, they would lose her to the flames at its end.

The portage went well. They passed several falls and rapids as the river descended out of the Shire Highlands into the flat coastal plains below. The convoy halted every few miles to feed, water, and rest the mule train. By the third day, they reached the Nkula Falls, roughly halfway to their destination. The crew leader decided on a long stop in the midday heat. As Patel, Tom, and Dick took advantage of the pause for some well-appreciated sleep, Minstrel slowly ambled down to the falls. As the water cascaded over the edge, falling and crashing into the pool below, it created a constant, almost humming sound. Overhead, birds gathered adding their cawing and chirping to the cacophony of sound. Every now and then, one swooped down into the water, caught a fish in its beak and coming up again, swooped back into the air amid loud squawking from other birds who had missed their opportunity for a tasty meal. As Minstrel sat on a knoll overlooking the pool, she spotted a leopard that had come to water on the opposite side of the pool. Looking up at her with suspicious eyes, the wildcat seemed to glare at the intruder.

"Well, Sir Leopard. You stay on your side of the water, and I shall stay on mine," she said aloud, not knowing that Braithwaite had followed her down the path to the lovely pool below the roaring falls.

His first impulse was to join her. Then, watching her unlace her high-topped boots and dangle her long, delicate feet in the cool water below, he stopped several yards short and sat in a patch of tall grass. Despite miles of walking in heavy boots, her delicate feet appeared pristine—no callouses, no bruises, no blisters. Quite remarkable, he thought to himself. She removed her pith helmet, loosened her hair bun, and leaned back on outstretched arms. She closed her eyes and threw her head back staring into the cloudless sky, but with closed eyelids.

He sat quietly for several minutes just observing her without intrusion or interruption. For the first time since the trip began at Chinde, he felt completely relaxed and calm. Although the trip had been uneventful thus far, his anxiety remained with him always. Perhaps it was due to his inexperience in the world of intrigue and intelligence gathering. Perhaps it was going into enemy territory. Whatever drove his nervousness, it was a constant. But, sitting on this patch of grass near a beautiful water pool beneath the Nkula Falls and observing the young lady sitting a few yards away, unknowing of his presence and so relaxed and calm, he started the process of building his confidence in himself and in the mission.

After almost an hour, they heard the crew leader shouting down that they were getting underway again. As quietly and stealthfully as possible, he slipped back up the trail to the ridge where the crew was checking the tie down lines and preparing the cradle to head on upriver. Minstrel never noticed him. She dried her feet quickly and thoroughly. Wet feet, humid climate, and leather boots are not a good combination for hiking along an African trail. She pulled on and laced up her boots. Now fully relaxed and refreshed, she strode back up the trail ready for the next part of their journey—into Lake Nyasa, only a few miles ahead.

Within a few minutes, they were on their way again headed north toward uncertain dangers. The remainder of the journey into Lake Nyasa proved uneventful. But, as they approached German territory, all became more apprehensive. Not only were there Germans to worry about, but lake pirates had been reported in the area. For security, they kept the weapons box unlocked and uncovered at all times. Fortunately, at the higher elevation, the days were more tolerable. The forests fronting the Shire and lake provided much easier access to fuel than down lower on the Zambezi and Shire where Tom and Dick had to often slog through hundreds of yards of marshland to reach the trees. Once in the lake, though, they understood the danger and wariness was the watchword at all times.

****

Moonlight shimmered off the lake's surface creating dancing silver starlets that flickered on and off, on and off, like a thousand fireworks. Since they entered Lake Nyasa, they traveled by night with no running lights. By day, they ran the risk of encountering enemy river patrols. While the western side of the lake was controlled by the British authorities in Nyasaland, security concerns dictated that the mission remain secret. Quite frankly, there were a number of German sympathizers among the tribes in the region, who disliked whatever imperial power controlled the region regardless of British, German, or Portuguese. If they lived in German East Africa, they favored the British and vice versa. Had authorities in Nyasaland known of the mission they might have provided assistance. But, it was a fair bet that had London informed the local authorities requesting assistance or protection for the little riverboat making its way up to Lake Nyasa, the word would soon filter back to German authorities. The result might well have been the abandonment of Station Wilhelm and a lost chance to solve the *Aachen* mystery. While few in number since most of the crews of the prewar river patrol boats had joined von Lettow-Vorbeck's vagabond force in the hinterland, what was left of the Imperial German

Navy's inland lake and river patrol still posed a definite danger. It simply would not do for one of their roaming patrol boats to inspect the *Belle* and find not only small arms but the Lewis guns as well. So, they traveled Lake Nyasa's eastern side by night and hid in protective coastal anchorages by day. Once on the lake and clear of the hazards of river navigation, night steaming posed no particular concern.

Braithwaite stood in the bow staring off into the night sky. Without any man-made lights to obscure the view, thousands of stars appeared almost like a well-lit Christmas tree. He had always marveled at the clear night sky so often hidden by the lights and fog of London and other port cities. Something touched his hand. Startled, he jumped and almost lost his balance.

"At ease, sailor. Merely your cohort in crime."

He turned toward her and with an embarrassed grin, acknowledged her presence.

"Daydreaming, were you?"

He nodded. "Afraid so. Dangerous stuff out here, daydreaming." He turned back toward the bow, a bit embarrassed by the whole scene. She gripped his hand and squeezed.

"Completely understandable." She stepped up beside him, her hips touching his. "Would you, Sir, be willing to tell a poor soul the subject of your wanderings?"

Braithwaite smirked and nodded. "Indeed, my dear wife. The declination of Aries."

Minstrel furled her brow and cocked her head, a shock of auburn hair cascading off her shoulder as she gave him the most charming quizzical look. "I see. The declination of Aries. Most interesting."

Braithwaite snorted a laugh. "Yes, well, quite right." He leaned over the rail observing the water foaming and lapping about the riverboat. "You see, Madam Zimmermann, in my former life as a sailor in His Majesty's Royal Navy, I served as the navigator of the late destroyer HMS *Halberd*. The declination of Aries is one of the calculations that navigators use at sea to establish their position. He pointed to a prominent star. "That is Aries, just there."

Minstrel nodded, though she really could not make out anything but hundreds of visible stars. No matter, let him prattle on. It passes the time.

"I was just pondering what my life would have been like had we not taken on that German cruiser. Would I be at sea somewhere calculating the declination of Aries? It is most interesting to ponder where fate takes us."

She smiled, a wispy, conspiratorial sort of smile. "So, my dear sailor. Here you are in the middle of the godforsaken end of the world Africa on a pitiful little boat steaming into who knows what danger or adventure. Isn't it funny … about fate I mean?"

He stared straight into her emerald green eyes, though in the moonlight, they appeared deep and dark, not sparkling and light as in daylight.

"Fate, Ma'am?" He turned his head away and leaned out over the rail, head down, staring at the dark water below. In the distance, they heard the blast of an elephant and a rush of wings as startled birds flew past the bow, frightened by the sudden noise of the elephant. "Fate, indeed." It was the war. Yes, the bloody awful war that had brought him here. "I never quite thought of it that way."

She only nodded and placed a soft hand on him. Her long, thin, elegant fingers felt warm and gentle to the touch. "Fate, it is then." She turned and leaned against the rail beside him.

Both stood leaning on the rail staring at the stars, not speaking a word. Her firm hips pressed against his. "Fate. Fate and Aries," she finally said after a long while. The swish, swish, swish of the propeller droned on as the *Belle* pressed on through the damp, warm, African night.

****

23 May 1915. Rampole, German East Africa.

The *Belle* bumped hard against the wooden dock. Tom nudged the boat into the small, ill-kept peer and with the bowline in one hand, Dick tossed the line across to the cleats on the shabby, worn wooden dock. As graceful as the gazelles that they had spotted on the shore along the way, Dick leapt swiftly over to the dock and within seconds had cleated down the bowline, securing the *Belle* to its mooring. Braithwaite admired the young man's agility and seamanship. Dick then leapt over and grabbed the end of the boat hook extended out by Tom and quickly pulled in the stern. With a swift turn, both lines secured the *Belle* to the rickety and crumbling dock that had seen better days. Tom had dropped the rubber bumpers along the starboard side earlier. The *Belle* gently eased into the dock. Without speaking a word and no other sound than the slowly turning propeller creating the slow rhythmic thump, thump, thump, Tom pulled back on the handle shutting down the flow of steam to the boat's engine. Moored.

Rampole. The dusty and grimy trading post town on the eastern shore of Lake Nyasa survived on the needs of sailors, but otherwise, offered little in the way of attractions. German lake merchants had established the town in the late 1890s to service boat commerce and little else. Yet it represented something of a haven. Boats could stock up on essential supplies—food, fuel, ammunition, etc. And, of course, there were a few taverns and other less savory places of business for the watermen and their passengers. For Braithwaite and Minstrel, the most critical feature was what was not there—military. The Germans had constructed a pier and fueling station several hundred yards from the public dock, but Braithwaite could detect no activity. With the previous attacks from Belgian forces that came out of the Belgian Congo the previous year, the German station had suffered extensive damage and had not been repaired. He had scanned the station with binoculars from a distance before docking. It seemed safe.

"Not in your Michelin guide is it, Sahib," chuckled Patel.

"Indeed not, Sergeant Major, indeed not," laughed Braithwaite.

"It will do, Bwana," responded a grinning Tom. I can get fuel and provisions here. We are low on lubricating oil. Since the Germans pulled out last year, the chandleries have plenty to sell."

Braithwaite nodded. Minstrel opened a leather satchel and fished about for the documents. Out came three official-looking Swiss passports and other identity papers. "Well, it's a chance to see how good the intelligence boffins in Whitehall are with faked identity papers," she laughed.

She's far more confident than me, thought Braithwaite. At least there doesn't seem to be any official inspectors about. She handed him his passport. Opening it to the photograph, he chuckled. "At least it does resemble me…somewhat." Both laughed.

Minstrel glanced at her passport photo and wrinkled her freckled nose and brow. "Well, I for one, am far more attractive than this chippy!"

In truth, all Hall and the fake papers crew had to work with were some old photos taken at her wedding before the war. They had done the best work possible in finding a model that closely resembled the bride, a stenographer at the War Office. She did roughly resemble Minstrel. Good enough had been Hall's reaction. Will have to do, he grumbled. Braithwaite and Minstrel certainly hoped it would be good enough, either that or a not too particular port official. Braithwaite took both sets of papers and dropped them into an inside pocket of his white linen jacket and patted the packet. With a forced smile, he muttered, "It will have to do, I fear." Minstrel smirked. *I wish I shared her optimism.*

"Bwana, why don't you and the lady go into the town while I visit the chandler and arrange for fuel and supplies. It should be no more than a couple of hours, Sir."

Patel nodded. "Yes, Sahib. You go. I'll stay and guard the *Belle.* Enjoy the time."

Braithwaite agreed. He did not particularly like the idea of leaving the boat, but the tension that had mounted as they made their way up the lake and deeper into German territory, needed some release.

"Bwana, there is a decent tavern on the second street in from the waterfront called the Old Edelweiss. The food is good and the owner is, I don't think, a threat. He's a fine old Bavarian gentleman. I believe his name is Lange. Yes, Lange."

Braithwaite hesitated.

"Oh, let's do. Time to try out our new disguise," Minstrel shot in. Her extravagantly white teeth offset by her deeply tanned face beamed with a broad, confident smile. A plucky young lady, thought

Braithwaite. *Well, let's do.* He tugged at his jacket and smoothed down his hair.

"Off we go then. After you, *Frau* Zimmermann," he chortled as Dick extended a hand to Minstrel, who stepped out onto the wooden dock.

Rampole had that ramshackle look and feel of a once prosperous trading post town servicing the lake and river traffic. But, with the war, many of the businesses had closed shop. Some had returned to Dar es Salaam in hopes of making their way back to Germany. Many had joined the forces as volunteers. Most of the native workers, who had provided many of the service jobs, had either returned to their tribal villages or had been conscripted into the askaris or porters and bearers who served the Kaiser's empire. Still, river and lake traffic plied the waterways and several chandlers, small hotels, and the occasional pub had remained open. Tom recommended the Old Edelweiss on *Friedrichstrasse* as the best. A kindly old Bavarian expatriate had run the establishment for several years, and Braithwaite was willing to give it a try.

As he stepped onto the grimy, rickety pier, he tapped his jacket breast pocket again. *Well, "Blinker," it's time to see if your counterfeiter did a jolly good job with the fake Swiss credentials.* Dressed in an off-white linen suit and straw Panama boater hat, Braithwaite looked every bit the typical European businessman trying to stay afloat in the wash of war. Minstrel, her deep auburn hair pulled back into a tight bun and wearing an oh so matronly cotton print smock, looked the part as well. The appearance startled him somewhat. Until now, he had only seen her in khaki gear with a tan-colored pith helmet. Still, he marveled at how feminine yet strong and independent she appeared regardless of her outfit. She daintily stepped over and around the oil-slicked, water puddles from the ever constant rainstorms. Again, she played the role so well. In Zanzibar, he had noticed that she would be just as likely to plow right through the puddles without a care. She had mentioned that at the very exclusive girls' school in Switzerland, she had taken dramatic instruction as well as the required curriculum on how to be an elegant lady of means. As they ambled slowly down the main street into the town, he knew she would carry off the part. *But would he? He had to. Their lives and that of so many shipmates counted on it.*

As they made the turn onto *Friedrichstrasse*, the Old Edelweiss loomed ahead. It appeared just as he envisioned the place—a little bit of Bavaria in the middle of Africa. Brightly colored window boxes of geraniums in long oblong planters adorned each stained-glass window. The roof tiles were held down by crossbeams and stones in the German fashion. Clearly, the proprietor had spent lots of cash to replicate home amid the dirty and dingy surrounding ramshackle buildings. As he stepped into the cool dimness of the place away from the blistering sun outside, the only thing he could think of was Lord Tennyson's famous line about the disastrous charge of the Light Brigade at Balaclava: "Into the jaws of death rode the 600." He took in a long, slow breath. It smelled of stale beer and cooked sausages. Delightful!

Behind a massive wooden and marble bar, a solitary African wiped down glass steins placing them gingerly in an overhead hanging rack. With the British blockade, they weren't likely to get replacements, so care had to be taken. The man eyed the newcomers and grinned, tooth-less but friendly. "*Willkommen, meine Dame, meine Herren,* Welcome to the Old Edelweiss! Come in, come in." His German, while heavily accented, was passable. "Please, please, be seated wherever you like."

Braithwaite nodded and motioned toward a table near the door-way. He had learned the lesson of sitting back against a wall, facing the inside and near the door both to observe all and to flee rapidly in case of emergency. Minstrel smiled and nodded. She had taught him well in their few weeks together. The was table covered with a blue and white checked tablecloth in the traditional Bavarian pattern. Minstrel daintily took her seat, smiled, and responded, "*Danke.*"

It startled him for a moment. He had never really heard her speak much German before other than a word here or a phrase there. Rather, he had assumed she spoke it well. *Llesson for the future—never assume, be sure of the facts. Learn the environment and blend in.* His tradecraft in this game of spy versus spy and counterspy had many more lessons to learn, but he would improve or perish.

From out of the swinging doors leading back into what appeared to be the kitchen came a presence both dominating, yet friendly. "Ah, *Willkommen, meine Dame, meine Herren.* Welcome to the Old Edelweiss! It is so wonderful to have you with us today." The happy publican strode over to the table, with an oversized hand extended in a friendly gesture.

Braithwaite bowed slightly from the waist as he stood in a friendly greeting sort of way. *"Guten Morgan, Herr Lange."*

The publican smiled broadly, excited to have a new customer know his name. He bowed deeply from the waist. *"Grüß Gott,* It is *wunderbar* to have you grace my simple tavern."

Braithwaite nodded and Minstrel smiled sweetly. "And to you." Her German, precise and natural, impressed Braithwaite. *This is a woman of many talents.*

"Where are you from?" asked the smiling tavern owner. "Have you come far?"

A moment of truth once again arrived. Minstrel glanced at Braithwaite as if to say, the stage is yours, Sir.

"I am Peter Zimmermann and this is my wife Salome. We come from a small village just south of Bern called Zimmerwald." He paused, noticing a quizzical look on the tavern owner's broad face. "We are in East Africa as representatives of an engineering company of Zürich. We are seeking various minerals here in East Africa, particularly chromium. Perhaps you have heard of us?"

The tavern owner placed his hand on his hips in a questioning manner. "Switzerland, you say?" He cocked his head to the right. "And yet you sound more as if a Berliner."

Action stations! Action stations! All hands to action stations! Instinctively, Braithwaite moved his right hand closer to his jacket pocket which held the deadly Webley revolver. Minstrel tensed. *Please, God, don't make me use it.*

Like a lioness quick to strike when the cubs are threatened, Minstrel glanced quickly at Braithwaite and then at the tavern keeper, a broad sweet smile gradually forming on her tanned face. "Of course, *Mein Herr.* You see, my husband grew up mostly in Berlin. His father, you see, was for many years a Swiss diplomatic official at the Berlin Embassy. Truly, *Mein Herr*, he creates great laughter when he speaks at our family events at home in Zimmerwald." Her broad smile and bright eyes completely diffused the potentially disastrous situation.

The tavern owner belly-laughed. "And so it should. Oh, but Berlin is very good though I only visited once in my youth. But München. Now there is a fine city. A wondrous city. A Bavarian city! He beamed with pride. Braithwaite's left-hand edged slowly back away from the pocket concealing the revolver. He breathed out slowly as the tension drained away. He looked directly at Minstrel and winked such that only she noticed. She cocked her head in ever so coquettish way, no doubt saying, touché!

"*Ja*, my lovely wife often rescues me from her most inquisitive relations and assures them of my authentic—from what I shall say is—Swissness."

The tavern keeper laughed heartily. "As well she should, *Mein Herr*." His jovial laughter echoed about the otherwise empty room as all the tension of the moments before dissipated. Minstrel reached across the table and squeezed Braithwaite's hand. It startled him for a moment, but then he recovered. Such a moment might undo their ruse. He had to be more careful and learn his new tradecraft well, or they might pay a deadly price.

"I am *Herr* Lange from Nürnberg originally as you might guess. Oh, but with the war, we get so few visitors these days. It is such a pleasure to see such a marvelous young couple and clearly so much in love." He had noticed Minstrel's hand squeeze. "Please, may I sit a while and talk?"

Braithwaite and Minstrel both nodded enthusiastically. The ruse worked. It occurred to him that this ruddy-faced German expatriate might be an incredible source of useful intelligence, particularly on the level of armed patrols operating on the lake and potential enemy forces. Lange raised a hand and waved. The African barman instantly snapped to attention and began filling their steins. "I'm afraid with this war on we have no supply of beer from the Fatherland and so we must do with the local brew. It is," he shrugged and raised both of his outturned hands, "acceptable, I suppose. We do as we can."

Without missing a moment, Minstrel responded, "*Herr* Lange, that will be wonderful. We have been on the rivers and lake for a so long that any beer will be wonderful and perhaps a reminder of home." Her sweet smile completely disarmed the publican—another hearty belly laugh followed.

The barman arrived with three steins all foaming with the tan-gold brew. Lange raised his glass. "A toast to the Fatherland. To the end of this horrible war, and to our new guests, *Herr* Zimmermann and his gracious and lovely bride." Glasses clinked in unison. To Braithwaite, the beer tasted marvelous. A single malt whisky drinker, he had never really enjoyed beer or ale, but now he made a mental note to give it another try once he returned home—to Blighty. *To Blighty. To Blighty. That's what the troops on the Western Front called Britain.* As he slowly sipped the golden brew, he stared over the stein's top at Minstrel. Somehow, he had completely forgotten that factor. Assuming the mission went well, once completed, he would return home, perhaps to the fleet, and Minstrel would stay in Zanzibar. A moment of sadness suddenly struck him. He had not really considered that reality for weeks—not since he had arrived. *Return to Blighty.*

"You must be hungry. We have today a wonderful goulash. I made it myself and I'm most pleased to offer."

Braithwaite nodded. "Indeed, *Herr* Lange, we would be thrilled to sample your fare."

The publican beamed, then frowned. "Unfortunately, with the blockade and all, I must use, shall I say, some less than top ingredients, but we make do and I am rather proud of my goulash."

"I'm certain it will be marvelous, *Herr* Lange. Simply marvelous."

"*Danke, Frau* Zimmermann. You should not be disappointed." He waddled toward the kitchen, waving his chubby arms at the African barman as if saying nothing but the best for our newfound guests, but without a word spoken. The African understood completely and both men raced back into the kitchen.

Braithwaite grinned. "You certainly have captured his heart, *Frau* Zimmermann."

She grinned as she smiled. "Indeed, Sir. What would you do with-out me?"

What would I do without her? The notion struck him square in the face. *What would I do without her?* An odd sensation came over him, an emotion that he had never really felt, gripped him. Truly, he had never considered this proposition; it bothered him and made him momentarily speechless. He simply stared at the stunning, confident woman sitting across from him in a dingy tavern on a lake in the heart of the enemy's country—Indian country. *What would I do without her?*

After a few moments of this odd silence, Lange returned with two steaming plates piled high with noodles and a hearty reddish-brown topping of beef goulash flavored with spicy red Hungarian paprika. As he placed the plates in front of them, the barman laid out the cutlery, well used and worn, but still serviceable, then bowed deeply from the waist and returned to his post.

"Please, may I join you while you dine. It is so *wunderbar* to have guests such as you to speak with?" A moment of panic swept over Braithwaite. What if the conversation undid their carefully crafted and executed cover? What if he had to use the Webley on this harmless, friendly, cheerful man to protect their mission? He shuddered slightly, not enough to notice, but the thought raced through his mind. After a few moments, he spoke after noticing Minstrel staring directly at him as if to say shall we allow it?

"Why yes, indeed. Please do join us." Minstrel nodded ever so slightly in approval.

The conversation followed for over an hour as he shot question after question about their business, their family, the news of the war, and so on and so on. Both held their story well. Braithwaite marveled at how well Minstrel responded to the queries effortlessly and with great panache. He let her carry most of the conversation. Lange seemed thoroughly charmed by the young woman. Braithwaite silently laughed to himself. *There is no danger here. Situation under control.* He relaxed and with that actually began to enjoy the dish. As the barman cleared the plates, Lange sprang up and raising a finger in the air he exclaimed, "We must have music. We must have dancing!" Braithwaite, startled, stared at the man, who beamed. "Fetch my accordion. We must have music!"

The barman opened a cupboard and out came a well-worn, but still serviceable accordion. Strapping on the instrument to his broad chest, Lange began to play a familiar melody. Braithwaite thought it sounded almost like a Strauss waltz, but he wasn't sure. Minstrel sat quietly but watched closely as the surprisingly nimble fingers raced across the keyboard and buttons. "And for you, my lovely guests, a waltz. The "Schneewalzer!" With great fanfare, he launched into the "Snow Waltz." Braithwaite recognized it immediately. He had heard it many times in his youth in Berlin. "A waltz for you. Please, take your lovely lady to the dance floor for the 'Schneewalzer.'" His nimble fingers raced over the keys, playing the lovely melody.

"*Frau* Zimmermann, may I have this dance."

"Most certainly, *Herr* Zimmermann."

As the couple stood, Braithwaite placed his right hand on her slender waist with his left hand embracing her hand. Step 1-2-3. Step 1-2-3. The couple gracefully slid across the floor, boards creaking beneath their feet. *What a wonderful dancer she is.* Clearly, the Swiss boarding school had taught her the social graces ever so well. The couple twirled about the floor as the publican played the marvelous melody over and over.

He stared into her emerald green eyes, their bodies locked close together. She squeezed his hand. Electricity shot through him—a feeling he had never felt before. As they gracefully glided about the floor, all thoughts of the war, of their mission of death and destruction, vanished. He simply concentrated on the vibrant young woman before him—the one creating the electric feeling. He felt as if the dance could go on and on forever. And then it stopped.

Lange finished playing the "Snow Waltz" with a flourish. Raising his hand from her waist and releasing his other hand, Braithwaite bowed slightly and cocked his head in the age-old gentlemanly fashion. She curtsied and smiled. Then, both turned toward Lange and clapped. The publican blushed and nodded in appreciation. The "Snow Waltz."

Minutes later, having said heartfelt goodbyes, they departed the

Old Edelweiss and made their way back through the dingy, dusty town toward the waterfront. As they strode through the unpaved streets, Braithwaite was confident of three things. They had enjoyed a wonderful and unexpectedly fine meal in the heart of the wilderness. They now had a good idea of the level of enemy military activity on the lake. And, he had experienced some feelings that had never before occurred. These feelings, while confusing, also delighted him; a warm glow spread throughout him as he walked alongside the magnificent Mrs. Alice Hallwood.

CHAPTER 10

Station Wilhelm

01 June 1915. Station Wilhelm on Lake Nyasa, German East Africa.
Lights appeared ahead off the starboard bow. They had traveled several miles up the lake since breaking camp and getting underway just past dusk. They had seen no signs of civilization for several days, just the omnipresent lake creatures and the occasional crocodile. Without a word, Patel tapped Braithwaite on the shoulder and pointed toward the camp ahead. The compound was brightly lit.

"This must be it. Let's confirm it." Braithwaite strode back to Tom manning the tiller. Scanning the shoreline, he spotted a small cove and pointed. "There, pull in just there." Tom nodded his head in acknowledgment and put the rudder over. He eased the *Belle* into the cove and throttled down the engine. Running aground just around the bend from the expedition's target would not do. As Tom cut the steam to the engine, the *Belle* gently glided into the cove. The lead line showed plenty of water under the keel. Dick tossed the anchor over and the boat drifted to a halt.

Braithwaite had already pulled out the map stolen from the *Aachen's* chart house. He unrolled and spread it over the deckhouse roof. As Minstrel and Patel held it down against the freshening breeze, Braithwaite pulled out his navigational tools-dividers, compass, and straight edge. He leaned over the deckhouse and peered at the map for a few seconds, then, laying the straight edge beside the compass, drew a straight line bearing north by northwest.

"From my last fix this morning, dead reckoning at a steady 4 knots on course bearing 020 compass, that places us just here." He turned the pencil slowly with the point at where the line intersected the small promontory. Just ahead of the pencil point with a mark labeled with an "X" bold and prominent, it read Station Wilhelm.

"Then we are here," grinned Minstrel.

He responded, "Yes, Ma'am. It would appear so."

"But, Sahib, what is here?"

Braithwaite looked up at the lancer. "Ah, my friend, that we shall soon see." Despite the banter, an excitement and dread charged with nervous anticipation filled the air. No one knew what they would find. But, if this remote place on the shore of Lake Nyasa revealed the *Aachen* secret, then the journey would not have been in vain.

"Tom, break out the rifles and hide them well. We may be needing them." He turned to Patel. "Amrish, you take the Mauser, just in case." While Braithwaite and Minstrel had been dancing the night away at the Old Edelweiss, Patel had acquired a Mauser rifle and three German pistols from a small shop in town. The rifle, a Model 1898, was the standard German military rifle. Patel thought it might be useful as part of the disguise. Should they need to be armed while in enemy territory, it just would not do to be equipped with British weapons—Webley revolvers and Lee–Enfield rifles. With the Mauser, their disguise as Swiss merchants might be maintained, and they would have firepower as well. The three Mauser C-96 pistols, each holding ten rounds in the magazine, gave them a lot of potential firepower should they run into trouble. No one in the compound would think it odd that travelers carried such arms even into what was apparently a friendly compound, especially given the threat of lake pirates.

"Minstrel and I will go ashore as *Herr* and *Frau* Zimmermann and hope for the best." He nodded to Tom, who started up the engine. Black smoke poured from the stack. Dick hauled up the anchor and the *Belle* drifted until the propeller blade blades bit into the murky, brown water. Slowly, the boat came about to port and chugged back out into the lake as Tom steered around the promontory toward the small, but brightly lit dock.

"Keep the fires up. We might need to make a hasty exit. And the rifles near. Then stay ready as best you can."

"Yes, Bwana, as best we can."

Braithwaite drew in a deep breath and let it out slowly. "Into the jaws of death," he muttered to only himself as he checked the pistol one last time before sliding it into the leather holster on his right hip. He looked over at Minstrel, who patted the side of her holster. What an odd sight, he thought. She wore a fashionable outfit rather than her usual bush kit and the sight of a holstered weapon seemed comical at that moment. Despite that, it was deadly serious with no humor about it.

As the boat rounded the bend, Dick broke out the red and white Swiss flag at the sternpost. The *Belle* slowly chugged toward the dock. On the shore, several men in uniform shouted and pointed. Askaris! Braithwaite let out a long whistling breath, "Oh hear us when we cry to thee for those in peril on the sea."

Two men ran down to the dock and stood awaiting the riverboat. Minstrel looked over at Braithwaite while biting her lower lip. Slowly, her right hand eased over ever so slightly down close to the grip of the pistol strapped at her waist.

"Let us hope the natives are friendly," chuckled Patel. The sergeant major's stone-cold calm in dangerous situations always impressed him. But, as the *Belle* approached the dock, rather than threaten, two men reached out to catch the line as Dick tossed over the bowline. Quickly, they tied it down to a cleat and then the stern line to another. Moored. Minstrel eased her hand away from the pistol, now noticeably more relaxed.

"*Willkommen*," shouted one of the men on the dock. Behind them, an askari sergeant, a dour expression of doubt still on his face, turned toward his two soldiers and ordered them to stand down. Waving a hand, he motioned to the visitors to come ashore.

Ever the gentleman, Braithwaite stepped on to the dock and extended a hand to Minstrel. Nodding politely, she stepped out of the boat and laid on the best smile she could muster. Time to play the role. Patel followed, the Mauser rifle slung on his shoulder. They approached the askari sergeant, who snapped to a stiff attention and clicked his heels. The Hun has drilled him well, thought Braithwaite as he rendered a sloppy, very unmilitary salute.

"May I announce you?" The soldier asked in flawless German.

"Indeed, Sir. I am *Herr* Peter Zimmermann and this is *Frau* Zimmermann. We are Swiss merchants looking to conclude trade agreements along the lake on behalf of my employer of Zürich. And you are…?"

"*Feldwebel* Nkrumu of His German Imperial Majesty's loyal askaris. *Willkommen*, I will notify Herr *Doktor* Steinweiss of your arrival. Please, follow me."

"Of course, *Herr Feldwebel*. As you say, come my dear."

Despite the politeness, all three were intently aware of the two armed soldiers trailing behind at a discreet distance. *Station Wilhelm, no doubt. We shall soon meet the mysterious Dr. Steinweiss.* On the other hand, that seeming lack of operational security surprised them all. Did it mean that Station Wilhelm had no real military importance? Why would the askari sergeant reveal Steinweiss' name to strangers? Braithwaite had a sudden unsettling feeling. Had they made the perilous journey for naught? The name, though, confirmed that they had indeed arrived at Station Wilhelm.

Up the slope, about a hundred yards, sat a compound of wooden huts and some tents. In the middle of the encampment sat a large white-washed wooden building, well-lit and spacious. Off to the side was a large wooden shed clearly for storage or perhaps a laboratory.

The sergeant strode up to the house door and rapped twice. From inside, came a response. The sergeant raised his hand to hold the party and entered. A minute later, he re-emerged through the open door while motioning all to enter. "Please, enter."

Standing just inside what appeared to be a parlor stood a short, dark-haired man with a well-clipped mustache and beard and with thick spectacles. Smiling broadly, he extended a welcoming handshake. "*Willkommen, willkommen*. I am *Doktor* Heinrich Steinweiss. We are so pleased to greet you, *Herr* Zimmermann, *Frau* Zimmermann!"

Braithwaite grasped the extended hand and shook forcefully. A firm grip and handshake established power and they might need some today. In his peripheral vision, he noted a smiling askari. Minstrel politely curtsied the old-fashioned way.

"Please do come in out of the wretched heat. Come, please. My home is simple, but functional for my work."

There! The question they had come hundreds of miles to discover—his work. The house was dark and much cooler—a welcome relief from the heat and humidity on the lake. Both Braithwaite and Minstrel, as discreetly as they could muster, eyed everything that might reveal the station's secret. None could be seen. The house, made of simple white-washed timber with even simpler furnishings, gave no clue. Braithwaite did note a portrait of a dour Kaiser Wilhelm II above the stone fireplace, a reminder that no matter how genial their host Dr. Steinweiss appeared to be, they were in the heart of the enemy's camp.

Unbeknownst to anyone in the site, several miles to the east, a platoon of askaris silently made their way through the jungle undergrowth seen only by the forest denizens. At their head, a white uniform-clad German officer silently cursed the wretched heat and foul-smelling jungle. In the rear, warily scanning from side to side, came a figure in the native dress, his scarred face hidden by a linen turban.

"My house is simple, but it is home for now. Please tell me what brings you to this isolated part of the world?"

A thought passed through Braithwaite's mind as he prepared to spell out the carefully concocted story of a Swiss commercial mineral commodities buyer and his lovely wife plying the dark continent's waterways in search of raw materials to be manufactured in neutral Switzerland. As he started to speak, he suddenly remembered back to his undergraduate days at Balliol College, Oxford, and playing Sir Joseph Porter, KCB, Ruler of the Queen's Navy in the Gilbert and Sullivan Society production of "HMS *Pinafore*." Damn, he had been great, or so said his fellow thespians. The college newspaper drama critic thought otherwise, but no matter. Whatever the damned critics had thought, this time he had to be better. Many sailors' lives depended on his performance this early evening in an obscure part of German East Africa.

"*Herr* Steinweiss. My wife and I are commodities buyers for a trading company in our native Switzerland. We both came to East Africa...." And so it went. Two excellent sherries and a couple of weak teas later, he had told the story. As the tale progressed, *Frau* Zimmermann added those little touches that made the tale so believable that he had learned to appreciate over the past several weeks. The German scientist apparently believed every word, nodding excitedly with every point as the entirely fabricated story grew and grew. Minstrel even added a few new details that certainly enhanced the tale and also made it more credible. The fraudulent couple's confidence increased with every nod from the German. Now for the *coup de main,* thought Braithwaite.

The German fit the perfect "mad scientist" look. Short, somewhat stout, bald with cotton white tufts of hair along the side of his head, he had spectacles that sat far down his long, slender, and ruddy nose. The small oval lenses were more likely for appearance than functionality thought Braithwaite as he sized up the man. Nonetheless, his sparkling eyes betrayed that the chap was friendly and genuinely happy to greet fellow Europeans. While Braithwaite assessed the enemy scientist's affability, Minstrel assessed the man's vulnerability. After all, they had finally found the target of their mission.

"And, *Herr Doktor,* what is your work? What is this, shall I say, remote place all about?" He had drawn in a huge breath before asking the question behind the entire mission. An awkward silence ensued. The German scientist stroked his Van Gogh-style beard as if in great contemplation. Perhaps he pondered just what to say and what not to say to this affable and talkative Swiss couple. The moment of truth had arrived. Braithwaite fiddled with a jacket button, awaiting the response. A long silence followed interrupted only by the tick, tick, tick of an antique clock on the mantle, one of the few signs of European civilization.

"Perhaps you will join me for dinner, *ja*?" Clearly, the man avoided the question. Braithwaite and Minstrel would have to work harder to find the secret. They looked at each other in acknowledgment of the task ahead.

"*Ja*, of course. We really should get back to our riverboat first. Our pilot will be worried."

"*Ja*, of course, say nine then?"

"We would be honored," replied Minstrel.

As the couple hurried down toward the waiting *Belle*, Braithwaite muttered to Minstrel, "'tis a mystery what lies beyond yon door." She did not respond.

Dinner was simple as might be expected—a stew of some animal—better to not know really, and a not-too-bad coarse black bread with butter. The German broke out a bottle of Rhine wine he had been saving and that topped off the meal. Still, Braithwaite could not get the man to divulge the secret and thinking better of it, he did not press. *In the morning, I'll ask again.* First, they had to win his trust. Meanwhile, a few key exclamations about how ridiculous it was that Britain, France, and Russia had started this horrid war and how neutral Switzerland ought to declare for the natural allies, Germany and Austria–Hungary, and so on and so forth. Braithwaite hoped the jingoistic talk would loosen up the German and gain his trust. It seemed to be working. But, Minstrel, keeping an ever watchful presence, diverted the conversation when she sensed he was about to go a little overboard. After a couple of hours, they excused themselves and headed back to the *Belle*, promising to return in the morning. Both spent a restless night aboard, worried about what might happen the next day. Unseen, a few miles away, the thick jungle vegetation masked the cooking fires of the askaris making their way toward Station Wilhelm.

****

With dawn came a hot, hazy, foggy mist over the lake. The seafaring Braithwaite worried. He had seen too many vessels come to a bad end in such weather. Should they need to make a hasty retreat, a dense fog did not help and made safe navigation a concern. But, by about eight, the fog lifted revealing another blazing hot East African morning. Braithwaite, Minstrel, and Patel made their way toward the main house about a hundred yards up from the dock. Meanwhile, as discreetly as possible, Tom positioned one of the Lewis guns under a tarp next to the deckhouse. Several ammunition drums lay within easy but well-hidden reach. Should there be any trouble, Tom and Dick could easily bring out the machine gun, mount it atop the deckhouse, and provide covering fire. Little did the party realize as they made their way toward the main house, that trouble approached only a few miles away. As usual for the place, all carried sidearms discreetly holstered at their hips.

"*Willkommen, willkommen, meine Freunde.* Please do come in." The German scientist welcomed them with arms wide open and a huge, friendly grin. Braithwaite relaxed just a bit, but the squad of askaris just outside still worried him. He noticed Patel and Minstrel both with eyes scanning left and right clearly surveying the place and on the alert for any threat. "Please, do sit. Mboko has prepared a small breakfast for us." The African standing in the doorway smiled and bowed from the waist. Amazingly, the native chef had prepared pastries and coffee, which, truth be told, could rival any café in Zanzibar. It was quite the treat after days of dried and tinned food on the river leavened by the occasional fresh fish. After several minutes of chit-chat, Braithwaite felt ready to pose the key question again. *Caution be damned. They had come all this way to find out what Station Wilhelm was all about so launch right in and see what happens!*

"So *Herr Doktor*, what is it exactly that you are working on here? Truly, it must be something very special," quizzed Braithwaite, trying to be both inquisitive and nonthreatening at the same time.

The scientist seemed taken back. He drew back almost as if in a spasm. Minstrel frowned. Maybe Braithwaite had been too forward and not subtle enough. Slowly, Steinweiss relaxed. He must have sensed no danger with the Swiss neutrals. The German slowly sipped his coffee as if gathering his next thoughts. "Well, that you should ask. The war and all. One must be cautious."

"Indeed," spoke up Minstrel, "but *Herr Doktor*, we are Swiss and therefore neutral. We have no interest in this deplorable war between the imperialist powers. My dear husband, clumsy as he is, is merely curious as to why would such an eminent scientist such as yourself be hidden away in the backcountry of Africa rather than at a university or laboratory back in Germany."

Touché, Minstrel. Well done! Braithwaite blushed. *Bloody Hell, this woman knows her* business!

"Many apologies. We do not mean to pry. We are simply curious, that's all. And you do have an impressive facility here." *That's it, appeal to his ego.* Most scientists and academics have an outsized ego. The tactic worked. The German beamed. The round hit the target. His shield collapsed.

"Indeed, *Frau* Zimmermann. I am most proud of my work here. It is, if I might be so bold in saying so, I am on the cusp of a great scientific and technical achievement. I call it wireless detection."

"Wireless detection?" quizzed Minstrel, looking ever so befuddled. She was none of that.

She had struck home, and the target now was completely defenseless.

"Well, yes, my dear. Wireless detection. You see, when the physicist Marconi proved that electric waves could be broadcast over the air, the great German physicist Christian Hülsmeyer in 1904 theorized that such a wireless burst of energy would reflect off an object at a distance and return to the sending device. But, the great trouble was that while his device could detect a metallic object and it's bearing from the device, it could not determine the range. That was a decade ago. Since then, I have experimented with creating such a device that can detect the returning energy and actually place the location of the object in space relative to the sending machine, both bearing and range."

Time for the killing shot. "And you can actually locate an object with such a device," shot in Braithwaite, sensing the moment. The scientist beamed.

"Indeed, yes. And with some accuracy, I might add. Please, do come and I shall show you." Steinweiss could hardly contain his excitement. Here was his chance to show off his creation, his toy, ultimately his child. *Wicket down* thought Braithwaite, struggling to maintain an air of relaxed detachment.

"Mboko, quick! To the range!" The African who had been hovering nearby said nothing. He nodded, then raced out the open door and down a pathway leading into the brush beyond the camp buildings. "Please, do follow me. This way, *Herr* Zimmermann, *Frau* Zimmermann. Please be careful. Mind your step." The man chattered on and on as he led them through the brush for easily a couple of hundred yards.

Reaching a great clearing, Braithwaite scanned left and right for any sign of trouble. The amphitheater-shaped field, cleared of all brush and scrub, stretched for a further hundred yards and formed a triangular shape with the new visitors standing at the westernmost point. A large metal locked box sat at the entrance to the field or range. Above it was an object that resembled a bed spring similar to what Braithwaite had observed on the *Aachen's* mast, only smaller. Steinweiss fairly danced with excitement with no clue that the three guests were his enemy. Downrange, Mboko stood beside a wooden pole. Atop the pole, there appeared to be a large, metal square. Every moment or so as the African moved the strange object left or right, the rising eastern sun flashed causing them to squint and turn their eyes away.

"Mboko, hold it steady please," shouted Steinweiss as he jangled the keys in his pocket. Out came a ring of keys. "Now yes, yes, here it is. One moment please." The lock popped open with ease indicating that the scientist opened it frequently. "Please. If your man here will help." Patel raised his bushy dark eyebrows and looked directly at Braithwaite, who nodded concurrence. Out of the box came a cylindrical device with opposing crank handles on either side, clearly to create an electrical current. Then came an odd metal box with wires leading all about, in and out. Braithwaite's pulse raced. This is the *Aachen* secret. *Careful now, old chap. Be calm. Don't give up the mission. Not now.* He glanced over at Minstrel. She had that look of minimum curiosity, and an almost distain expression. *What an actress! She has to be as excited as I am.*

Working as fast as a hare in heat, the little mad scientist connected wires to what appeared to be a screen similar to what Braithwaite had also observed in the cruiser's chart house. He ran a cable from the box to the generator beside Patel. "Please, Sir. Do sit just there," pointing to the ground a few feet from the box, "and when I say 'now,' please crank as fast as you are able." Patel pretended not to understand the German's words and looked at Braithwaite and Minstrel quizzically. He understood perfectly; he only played the role of dutiful if not overly bright manservant, a part required for the ruse to work. Flustered, the scientist waved his scrawny arms back and forth simulating a cranking motion. Patel nodded as if he understood, sat down beside the generator, and smiled a great toothy grin, highlighted by his naturally dark complexion.

Braithwaite chuckled silently. *I am surrounded by blooming great actors. There is a West End stage career for these two if we make it through this blasted war.* With all the wires and cables connected, Steinweiss positioned himself behind what seemed to be some sort of round, green glass oval with what appeared to be a compass rose etched into the glass face. Braithwaite crossed his arms trying to appear as nonchalant as possible. He was anything but. The scientist pointed to Patel, who nodded in understanding and began cranking as fast as he could. A low but audible electric hum started slowly and then built to a crescendo. Minstrel cringed a bit at the strange, eerie noise. She squeezed Braithwaite's hand as if in fright. Braithwaite knew better. *Play the part. Play the part.*

Steinweiss waved to the African patiently standing across the field. The scientist flipped a toggle switch and a loud hum came from deep within the odd box. He shouted over the noise. "Come, *Mein Herr.* Here! See this, please."

Minstrel and Braithwaite strolled over and stood behind the seated German. Clearly, on the etched glass, an image appeared—a bright white image clearly outlined against the dark green glass.

"Now watch this," he shouted gleefully as he raised his left arm and motioned to Mboko. Incredibly, as the African moved the metal plate and post to the left, the screen image also moved. When he stopped, the image stopped. Steinweiss then motioned to go right. Again, as the man moved the plate to the right, so did the white image. Braithwaite stood completely mesmerized. The gravity of what he had just witnessed shook and shocked him as if a lightning strike had crashed over him. Both stood motionless, incredulous at what they were witnessing. For several minutes, the African moved left and right and always, the image moved with him. As the power of the demonstration waned, Braithwaite took a deep breath. *Now, strike. Strike while the gleeful man plays with his amazing invention.*

"*Herr Doktor.*" Steinweiss looked up, a broad, satisfied grin on his ruddy face. "This is all rather amazing to be sure, Sir. But, really of what use is this wonderful device?"

"Ah, this is the great and magnificent future. Imagine you are a ship at sea and caught in a fog bank just offshore. If say, a lighthouse whose light cannot be seen through the mist has a metal plate attached, my machine can detect that plate giving the relative bearing and distance to the lighthouse. One can then avoid the danger of shoal water or rocks by knowing where one sails relative to the lighthouse and the shore. Another ship is saved." He punctuated the final word by poking a chubby finger in the air.

Braithwaite nodded. *Now!* "And I suppose that your machine can also detect other ships close at hand through the fog?"

"Just so. Another ship saved."

There it is. There it is. The bloody Hun cruiser is using this device to locate merchant shipping and then detect approaching Royal Navy warships. *Damn bloody devious Huns. One must give them credit though. Damned bloody devious Huns!* "I see. This could be very useful for ship navigation. You have a quite useful device here, *Herr Doktor.*" The scientist beamed, proud of his brainchild. Minstrel shot in the next question. "And, how far away must you be to see, is that the right word, to see an approaching ship?" She asked feigning only a detached interest.

"Well, my dear. I am not sure. We have been able to detect ships up to twenty-five kilometers thus far, and…." He stopped. His face turned red. The scientist realized that in his enthusiasm to show off the device, he had let go of the greatest secret. He then blushed. "Well, I think it is quite far indeed," he stammered while trying to back down from his amazing revelation. Meanwhile, Braithwaite did some mental calculations. With the height of eye to the horizon of roughly nine to ten miles for the typical destroyer, the mad scientist's device could detect an approaching warship well before the visual horizon and well before any Royal Navy ships would even be aware of the German cruiser's presence unless the enemy made too much smoke. Even then, at high speed, the pursuer would never actually see the enemy. This was the *Aachen's* great secret weapon.

Just then, one of the askaris appeared. Breathing deeply, he spoke excitedly. "Bwana *Doktor*! It is the officer from the ship. He comes with a platoon of my fellow soldiers."

Braithwaite stiffened. *Good God. Not now.* He looked at Minstrel who had no ostensible reaction. Patel slowly unsling the shoulder strap of his Mauser, then relaxed his arm by his side.

"I, well … then. Tell your sergeant to prepare lunch for our guests and the officer."

"Yes, Bwana. Right away." The askari departed as rapidly as he had arrived.

"So, we have more guests. I am indeed a fortunate man this day." As quickly as he had broken out and set up the device, he dismantled and locked away the gear. He motioned to Mboko, who dropped the wooden pole and raced over. The scientist pointed to the locked metal box, which the native hoisted onto his shoulder and carried to the house. As they trekked back across the bush trail toward the camp, Braithwaite felt a dread he had not experienced in months—not since the outgunned little *Halberd* had made its gallant, suicidal charge against the enemy cruiser. Once they reached the house, Steinweiss, appearing nervous and tense, locked the box containing the device in a back closet and dropped the key in his front jacket pocket. The indiscreet scientist let slip a critical fact that both Minstrel and Braithwaite overheard. As Steinweiss turned the key in the lock, he mumbled, "There, my pet. You are the only one here and we can't be too cautious, now can we."

****

"So, *Herr* Zimmermann, *Frau* Zimmermann, exactly what is it that you do here in German East Africa? Please explain that to me once more. Do you not know that your nation is neutral in this contest of strength and national destiny?" The blue-eyed German naval officer quizzed, peering over the top of his wine glass. Steinweiss had broken out the best he had—a not-too-bad Cabernet. In intricate detail, Braithwaite went over again the story practiced many times of his and his wife's mineral commodities buying adventure, how had they managed to land at this unusual station on Lake Nyasa, how they were just traveling up the lake, and saw the buildings and were curious, and all that and so on and so forth. Occasionally, Minstrel interjected a point, ever the dutiful businessman's spouse. Meanwhile, a wary Patel stood motionless near the doorway. Nervously, he rubbed his forefinger across the rifle's trigger guard. Fortunately, no one noticed. Behind the German officer stood a quiet, but menacing figure in Arab garb, his face hidden behind a dirty gray linen turban. But, Braithwaite noticed the man's cold, black eyes staring at him constantly.

"And you, *Frau* Zimmermann. Is it not a bit unusual for a lady to be tromping about the African wilds?"

"Indeed, *Herr kapitänleutnant.* You are correct. But, I have often accompanied my dear husband on many of his buying trips—here, to Asia, even to Brazil one year... before the war." She gripped his hand hard under the table. She suddenly realized that she had embellished the story too far. Patel stiffened. Braithwaite froze and did not move. Would Steinweiss remember that they had told him they were newlyweds?

"I see. Very good."

"No doubt, she keeps him out of mischief," laughed the now slightly tipsy scientist.

"More wine, *Herr* Zimmermann?" Thankfully, he was too inebriated to notice the slip or he had not listened carefully enough to their story told over dinner and simply missed the newlywed aspect.

Braithwaite knew he needed to keep a clear head, but to maintain the ruse, they had to remain relaxed and sociable. The scientist leaned across the table and topped up the glass. After several more minutes of banter and idle chat between von Donop of his Imperial German Majesty's light cruiser SMS *Aachen* and the British agents gallantly posing as Swiss merchants, the hard-edged man leaned over and whispered into von Donop's ear. The naval officer's face immediately blanched. He dropped the spoon he had been holding over the coffee cup.

"*Herr* Zimmermann, may I trouble you to see your papers? Merely a formality you understand, it being wartime and all that. Braithwaite stared motionless for a moment, not quite sure how to react.

"Of course." Braithwaite reached into an inside pocket of his beige linen suit jacket, then patted his other side pocket. "Well, it seems that we left them back on the riverboat. If you will excuse us, we will just...."

The officer's hand shot up in the air. "No! Sit. Your manservant can retrieve them." He grinned a most malevolent smile.

"Well, sir. In that case, please allow me to instruct my valet on precisely what is needed. He could fetch our papers, eh?"

Von Donop glared at them. "Indeed." Again, the German smiled and not a friendly one at that. Braithwaite bowed slightly from the waist and motioned Patel over. Both men met in the corner of the room well out of earshot of the table. Meanwhile, Minstrel continued a conversation to lighten the moment even though von Donop clearly ignored her, his cold blue eyes fixed on the two men in the corner.

"Sergeant Major, I fear they are on to us," he whispered.

"Yes, Sahib. I concur. The one in the turban. I know him. He's the man who attacked us in the street in Zanzibar. I'm sure of it. He must've recognized you or me or both."

Braithwaite nodded. "Right then. Get back to the *Belle*. Break out the Lewis guns and wait for us. We may have to run for it. Tell Tom to get up steam for a hasty departure."

"Straightaway, Sahib. I will arrange for a diversion."

"A diversion? What sort of diversion?"

"I do not know yet, Sahib. But you will know it when it happens. Then you and Memsahib race to the boat. We will cover your retreat with the Lewis guns. Braithwaite smiled as Patel bowed as if all were normal and returned to the table. Reaching under the table and unseen by the Germans, he squeezed her hand hard three times. It was the previously arranged signal for "run like Bloody Hell!" He knew Minstrel would know when. Another fifteen minutes passed in useless chitchat, but it was clear that their host had become more and more agitated. For him, an affable morning had turned dark and tense. When Patel did not return, Braithwaite tried once again to win back the tactical advantage.

"I can't imagine what is keeping Amrish."

Minstrel shot in, "Perhaps we had best go see to it. He might not be able to locate the proper papers. After all he…."

"No. *Frau* Zimmermann. That is not possible. We will all wait here for your man to return." The muzzle of a Luger pistol pointed directly at Braithwaite's heart. He tensed. The threat had escalated.

"I see, Sir, you have us at a disadvantage." He gently placed both hands face down on the Irish linen tablecloth and leaned back in his chair, staring coldly at the German officer.

"Just so, *Herr* Zimmermann. Just so. Tell me who you really are. I…."

At that moment, Steinweiss could hold himself no longer. He shot out of his seat, staggered a bit, then slammed his fist hard on the table, spilling the glasses and staining the white tablecloth. He slurred his demand, the result of too much wine. "*Herr kapitänleutnant.* I demand that you put away that evil weapon this instant. Do you hear me, Sir? This very instant. All of you are my honored guests. Do you hear? This instant. I cannot…."

Von Donop cut him off harshly. "No *Herr Doktor.* I will not. I suspect these two are British spies. Sit down, Steinweiss."

At that moment, the tipsy scientist lunged at the German officer, his hands reaching out as if to grab the gun. The German officer swung his pistol about in a defensive motion and struck Steinweiss on the temple. Dazed, the scientist staggered backward, knocking over a chair before crashing to the floor. In instinctive reactions, both Braithwaite and Minstrel bolted up thus making them both a better target as von Donop whisked the muzzle back toward them. The other man dressed in Arab garb drew his weapon and fired two wild shots, both going over their heads. Plaster from above the door splintered and sprayed the room.

Just at that moment, an explosion sounded outside that shook the window panes. The pressure pushed in the curtains, startling von Donop, but just for a moment. Patel, on his way back to the *Belle*, had discreetly loosened the cap on a petrol barrel and tipped it over unseen or unnoticed by the soldiers. As the fuel drained out forming a rivulet of liquid racing down the hill toward the waterfront, all Patel had to do was strike a match and set it off. The flames raced back toward the barrel still draining, but with fumes formed inside the barrel. Once the flame reached the explosive mixture inside the barrel, his promised diversion resulted.

"Now! Now!" Braithwaite shouted. He gripped the table with both hands and with a great heave, pushed it over toward von Donop and the other assailant, knocking their feet out from under them. Within moments, Braithwaite and Minstrel were outside the house, racing toward the dock amid shouts and curses of soldiers punctuated by the tat tat tat tat tat of a Lewis gun. The melee had started.

Up ahead, a burly askari blocked the path to the *Belle*. As Braithwaite raced toward the man, Minstrel did a sharp right turn. Her sudden move rattled the soldier for a moment; within a second, he was on the man, slamming into his chest. The charge hit him in the solar plexus; he whooshed out all the air in his lungs and gasped for air as he staggered backward. A bullet whizzed by Braithwaite's head. Momentarily stopped by slamming into the soldier, he realized that the way to the boat was blocked by several askaris running up from the waterfront. As he ducked behind an oil drum, a jolt of pain shot through his left arm. Numb, it instantly went limp as he rolled over beside the drum into the red clay dirt. Instinctively, he reached for his pistol. *Gone. Damn!* It had fallen out of the holster as he struck the soldier and then rolled behind the drum. The Mauser lay a full six feet away in the open. It might as well as have been six miles, with little spurts of dirt kicked up by the bullets hitting the ground around the drum from the soldiers near the house and storage shed; he was trapped and defenseless. Then a rifle shot, followed by two more rang out from nearby. He jerked his head about and realized that Minstrel had grabbed the rifle dropped by the burly askari, who now lay face down and prone a few feet away. She had downed the man with a well-aimed pistol shot to the head and now began firing at the soldiers near the shed. At this point, he realized how serious his wound really was. Patting it gently, he let out a whistling sigh. No broken bone. Only a flesh wound, but it now throbbed like the devil. *Right, get back into action, old sod!* The askaris who had been charging up from the waterfront had taken cover in the corral behind the horses and goats. Braithwaite saw why. Standing atop the deckhouse stood Patel manning a Lewis gun while Tom held two more ammunition drums. In the bow, Dick had mounted the other Lewis and, though firing wildly, had forced the enemy troops near the house to take cover. For the moment, no one charged the pair. With Braithwaite behind the oil drum and Minstrel taking cover behind a woodpile and plinking away at the askaris near the shed, for the moment, they were safe. But for how long?

They were in what the Yanks called a "Mexican standoff." His Mauser pistol lay in the dirt a few feet away, but clearly in the line of fire from both the house and shed. He shouted to Minstrel. "Cover me." She said nothing but fired two more rounds, then click - an empty clip. Ten feet away lay the dead askari. *Must get to his cartridge belt.* He dove for his pistol despite the numb and now useless left arm. He reached the body just as another round kicked up the red dirt not two inches from his head. He was vaguely aware of a white-uniformed fig-ure standing in the house door pointing a pistol his way - *von Donop!* But, rather than fire again, the German officer raced from askari to askari shouting orders and encouraging them to spread out and sur-round the trapped Britons. That couldn't happen. They had about fifty yards of open ground to the dock. They would never make it. The Lewis guns kept the soldiers in the corral with their heads down, but if von Donop managed to surround them, all was lost.

Using the dead man for cover, he rolled him over and tried to unbuckle the cartridge belt *Damn. No luck.* With only one good hand, it was no use. He glanced over at Minstrel; she shook her head. *Out of ammunition.* He had to get the belt with the ammunition to her. Pulling together all the strength he could muster, he shoved into the body enough to lift it just off the ground and release the pressure on the metal belt clasp. It worked. With a twist, the clasp gave way. Shoving the body again and rolling it toward the house, he managed to loosen the cartridge belt and toss it to Minstrel. She quickly pulled a fresh clip from the ammunition pouch, slammed it into the rifle and fired off three rounds toward the house and the porch where von Donop stood shouting orders to the askaris. One struck home. The German officer howled in pain. It was a nick only, but enough to get his attention. He ducked behind a wicker chair and out of sight. His efforts to rally his men for an enfilade movement had failed. They had too much respect for the two Lewis guns now laying down a deadly fire toward the house and corral. Three soldiers already lay dead, sprawled out on the porch and in the yard. Two more rounds from Minstrel struck the outside of the house.

He was relatively safe at the moment. Minstrel's fire hit home as another enemy soldier pitched forward clasping his throat as crimson blood spurted from the severed artery. Braithwaite took advantage and rolled over and over back behind the oil drums. Safe. For the moment at least. He failed to note the black-clad figure just inches away who now lunged at him wielding a deadly, ugly knife. Mustafa Abel, the strange man in the dirty linen turban and dressed in black despite the heat, had worked his way around the side using the house and shed as cover. He had crawled through the askari camp off to Braithwaite's right unseen and unheard. Now, he raised the knife and laughed. That was all that Braithwaite needed. The man's unnecessary drama had only taken a second, but in that time, Braithwaite rolled to his right; the knife struck the dirt rather than his torso. Enraged, the assailant raised the knife again. But Braithwaite was quicker. He managed to swing about the pistol that he had recovered and pointed it right at the man's coal-black, evil eyes. A flash, a boom, and the back of the man's head blew back, spattering the ground around the oil drums. With the deadly knife still raised in mid-air, the limp body pitched backward away from Braithwaite.

Just as the assailant's body hit the ground, a great whooshing sound came from the shed. Flames shot up out of a window, its pane shattered by the force of the blast. A soldier shrieked as glass shards hit him in the head and back. It must've been a barrel of kerosene used for lamps and cooking. "Now! Now!" shouted Braithwaite. Minstrel fired two more rounds, but it was not needed. Another askari, his uniform aflame, raced out of the burning shed shrieking in agony. Two others tried to tackle the frantic man and put out the flames. Another explosion followed. Flaming pieces of the shed blew across the open space separating the house from the shed, striking the front windows. Instantly, the window curtains caught fire and the house was doomed as well.

In a race toward the *Belle*, zigzagging to avoid badly targeted fire, Braithwaite saw that Dick on the bow had been hit. The Lewis gun fire slackened, but Patel, now with a fresh ammo drum, poured round after .303 round toward the flaming buildings. Braithwaite tripped and pitched forward, his numbed left arm throwing him off balance. Minstrel, just ahead, turned and started to come back to him.

"No! Run! Go!"

She paused for a moment, but then turned and darted for the dock just as Braithwaite righted himself and raced behind her. Both tumbled onto the boat, breathing heavily from the race. Braithwaite could hardly move, but Minstrel leapt up, raced to the bow, and pulling Dick up, she realized that the lad was unconscious. Then, she stood up, defying the bullets now spurting into the water around them from the men who had emerged from the corral when the Lewis gun fire slackened, she opened fire. Straightaway, two men fell as the others dove for cover. Blood still spurted from Braithwaite's ravaged left arm. Between the blood loss and exertion, he began to lose consciousness. The last thing he recognized was the auburn-haired woman, neatly clad in a fashionable dress, blazing away with seemingly no regard for her safety. His eyes closed.

Meanwhile, Tom had thrown off the last line and opened the throttle wide. Smoke poured from the *Belle's* boiler funnel as the propeller bit into the muddy water. Slowly at first, then gathering speed, the riverboat pulled away from the dock and out into the lake. As they retreated, Patel and Minstrel kept up the fire until the rounds danced off the dock. Askari bullets rippled all around them, kicking up water spurts, some striking the boat, but none seemingly inflicted any real damage. But, in the pandemonium of the gunfight, they did not notice that two bullets had pierced the boiler. Geysers of steam poured out of the holed boiler.

As they pulled out of range with two wounded, Minstrel slumped over the Lewis gun, exhausted and shaking. On the shore, two buildings now blazed away, black ugly smoke filling the sky above. On the dock, she saw a German naval officer, an enraged man, waving his arms in the air, shouting curses. She could not hear them, but one could only imagine his words. He vowed they would meet again.

As the riverboat chugged steadily away from the scene of death and devastation, the first part of the mission was complete. They had solved the riddle of the ghost cruiser. It had cost them, but they knew the enemy's great secret. Now, they had to get that intelligence back to Zanzibar and home. As Minstrel looked out one last time toward the smoking wreck of Station Wilhelm, she said a silent prayer, "Lord, please let Major Pankhurst and his marines be there waiting. Please, God, make it so. Amen."

CHAPTER 11

I Will Come for You

02 June 1915. Lake Nyasa.

The *Belle* limped away from the dock at bare steerageway—just enough to move her out into the lake and away from the gruesome battle scene ashore. A few bullets whizzed over their heads, but most landed short into the lake, kicking up tiny waterspouts. Slowly, painfully, the riverboat pulled out of range. Once several hundred yards away from Station Wilhelm, Tom turned the tiller to steer north and out of danger. But, the damage had been done. In the bow, Patel applied pressure to Dick's left leg, which had been struck just above the knee. Although bloody and ugly, the injury appeared to be a flesh wound only; no bones or major blood vessels had been hit. Patel wrapped a cloth tightly around Dick's thigh to further seal the wound and staunch the bleeding. Amidships, Minstrel nursed Braithwaite, who had taken a round through the upper arm. He too had suffered just a flesh wound as the bullet passed through and out with no great damage. It would be painful, though. She dusted the gash with sulfa powder, part of the provision supplied by the Royal Navy. She wrapped his arm as tightly as she could manage. Amazingly, they had suffered no heinous casualties especially given the number of dead and wounded askaris now lying about the devastated compound. No doubt, the steady fire of the Lewis guns had disrupted any chance for accurate return fire by the

German officer or his men.

But, as troubling as their wounds were, it was the damage to the *Belle* that soon became far more serious, particularly as Tom desperately tried to pick up speed. All could hear the slow but steady whistle of hot steam as it escaped through the holes in the steam drum. A third errant round had dented the firebox, but no smoke billowed out. That at least was something positive considering the number of rounds fired at the *Belle*. Tom nervously eyed the steam pressure gauge as the needle inexorably fell off toward zero pressure. He popped open the firebox door and shoved more wood in hoping that with extra heat, they might make enough steam to escape. It would be a close-run thing.

"Bad ju ju, Bwana. Losing steam pressure fast. Maybe 3 knots if lucky and no more damage," the riverboat man shook his head in nervous agitation. "How is my son?"

Patel looked up and shook his head. "He is a lucky lad. It's just a wound in the thigh, but young Dick will survive. Do not worry, Tom. Do not worry, my friend." Patel tried to seem positive, but he had seen enough combat casualties to know that even the most minor wound could go gangrenous, especially in the tropics. That was the real killer, but, once he stopped the bleeding, they could apply sulfa powder, stitch up the lad's wound, and hope for the best.

Braithwaite was much more fortunate. The Mauser bullet, while leaving an ugly gash, had done no horrendous damage. It had hit a nerve, which explained the numbness of earlier. But, by the time she had patched the wound, the feeling in his upper arm returned. Painful, yes. Rough-looking, indeed. But deadly or debilitating, no. He thanked her and, keeping his head low to avoid any final shots from the beach, went aft where Tom had just clamped the boiler door shut.

"How bad, Tom?"

"Very bad, Bwana. We have enough steam pressure to get away from these bad men, but, not far. We must pull in somewhere and anchor. I must patch these holes or we are as you Navy men say, "dead in the water," the boatman grimaced.

"Understood. Do what you can." He was amazed at how calm the man seemed. Despite the terror of the past few minutes, the harrowing escape, and most importantly, his wounded son now sprawled out in the bow, the man remained incredibly calm. Braithwaite knew they had chosen the right man for this mission. "Can you patch it up enough to get us through?" quizzed an increasingly apprehensive Braithwaite.

"Yes, Bwana. I am sure. I always carry spare bits of metal with screws and tools for just such a trouble. But, Bwana, it will take time and we must find a safe spot to anchor. The boiler must be cool to repair. I'm truly sorry, truly."

"It's not your fault, my friend. Just keep us headed north and be on the lookout for a spot clear of the bastards." He placed a comforting hand on the man's shoulder and shook it gently in a vote of confidence. "Do the best that you can, Tom."

Tom smiled through clenched teeth. Braithwaite ducked down and went forward. *Damn! This hurts!* He held his left arm in as close to his chest as possible so as to limit the motion and movement that might set off more bleeding. Patel and Minstrel were carefully unwrapping the binding about Dick's thigh. The lad had grown woozy and almost passed out again. So much the better thought Braithwaite as he reached the bow.

After carefully unwrapping the wound, Patel brought out an ugly clamp sort of device from the medical kit the ship's surgeon on *St Andrews* had provided. The kit contained every form of surgical tool—clamps, scalpel, scissors, and so on. While Patel held down the leg, Minstrel took a clamp and gently pulled aside some loose tissue under the skin, probing for the bullet. Though they could not know it, the bullet had actually ricocheted off the roof of the deckhouse before striking Dick such that it had lost most of its velocity. It had not gone very deep, and Minstrel located the bullet quickly. Without a word, she clamped on the bullet and gently and slowly lifted it out of the wound, then dropped it on the deck.

"Souvenir of our adventure for the future," chortled Patel, still able to maintain a sense of humor amid the carnage and destruction.

"Just so Sergeant Major. Just so," responded Minstrel as she raised a bottle of gin and poured it liberally over the wound, which had started bleeding again. Dick flinched. "Steady on, lad. Steady on," she cooed. She nodded to Patel and he gently put pressure on the wound to close it as best as possible while she deftly sutured it up. More gin followed, and finally, she wrapped the entire wound with a sterile bandage. The surgery complete, Minstrel collapsed in a heap, her head resting against the gunwale, eyes closed tightly.

"You did well, Memsahib. Very well," whispered Patel as he too collapsed onto the deck, exhausted from the strain and stress of the past hour.

Meanwhile, Braithwaite, who had observed the operation, shook his head in admiration. With little practical medical or surgical experience, Minstrel had managed to patch up two wounds with apparent ease. He walked back to the stern and grabbed a few sticks of wood, slammed open the firebox door, and fed the logs to the raging fire. As they moved further from the station, they could not have known that von Donop had quickly regained control over the chaos at Station Wilhelm, reorganized his forces, and within minutes began a quick march up the trading trail that tracked along the lake's shoreline, moving in a parallel course to the *Belle*.

✶✶✶✶✶✶✶✶✶✶✶✶✶✶

"There. That looks like a good spot to anchor," said Braithwaite, pointing to a small cove just off the starboard bow. We should be well concealed there."

"Yes, Bwana. A good place to put in for repairs."

They had only made a few miles, but it would have to do. With a holed boiler, the *Belle* had been steadily losing steam pressure. Tom constantly added water to the boiler to keep it from going dry, but that only added to the problem. With every gallon of fresh water, the boiler cooled even more with an attendant loss of pressure. All morning, they had only been able to make one or 2 knots headway, a critical problem when the imperative lay in escaping the compound as fast and as far as possible. To compound their difficulty a 3-knot current flowed southerly, pushing the boat back directly toward Station Wilhelm and danger. At the current pace, the askaris, now no doubt angrier than a disturbed hornets' nest, could easily outpace them along the shoreline. At some point, they had to make landfall to replenish the fuel supply giving von Donop and his men the perfect opportunity to attack.

Although his arm hurt constantly, Braithwaite pitched in. Dick soon recovered his senses; all were amazed at how quickly he recovered. Despite the painful wound, he bound about the boat with ease. Patel, two decades older and now beginning to feel the woes of physical aging, could only shake his head at the youth's resiliency. As Tom fought to keep the *Belle* far enough into the lake to be out of rifle range from the beach, his wounded son fed the boiler's firebox. Meanwhile, Braithwaite, Minstrel, and Patel took turns manning the Lewis gun mounted atop the deckhouse. If the askaris appeared, a few .303 rounds into the trees would keep their heads down.

Tom put the tiller over hard as Braithwaite scanned the cove with binoculars. Good. No sign of trouble. Maybe they had outrun the enemy or he had given up. Then, the image of von Donop standing on the porch at Station Wilhelm screaming and waving his arms in frustration, rage, and hatred came into his mind. No, the German officer would not give up. He was out there somewhere in the jungle probably just waiting his time to strike.

"This is no good, Sahib," whispered Patel. He spoke low as so as to not alarm the rest, a useless gesture really. All completely understood their plight. The whistling steam rushing out of the two bullet holes in the boiler reminded everyone of their shaky situation.

"Very true, Sergeant Major. Sadly, you are right." Braithwaite turned to Tom, who struggled with the tiller to keep the swift current from pushing them farther south away from the cove.

"How long to repair the boiler, Tom?"

The African screwed up his face in a contortion that told all. "Bwana John. It is bad, very bad. I must allow the boiler to cool. Then I can apply a patch to the holes. Then I must fire up again for steam. After dark for sure, Bwana."

Braithwaite nodded in acknowledgment and turned back toward the shoreline, raised the binoculars and resumed scanning. Meanwhile, Minstrel, who had been on the Lewis gun, dismounted from the deckhouse and stepped up next to Patel—a council of war.

"Well, colleagues. We should set a defensive perimeter," said Braithwaite. "It should be at least twenty to thirty yards out from the beach. Minstrel, you take the left flank, Sergeant Major, the right. I'll cover the center. We'll form a semicircle around the cove. If you hear or see anything coming your way, shout as loud as you can, then run for it back to the boat. We will collapse the perimeter to just around the *Belle*. Dick can man the machine gun while Tom repairs the boiler. Agreed?" All indicated concurrence. Braithwaite let out a long slow breath and shook his head. "A bad show all around. I fear we must make the most of it and pray for time."

The *Belle* glided slowly into the tiny cove, surrounded on three sides by foliage and jungle growth. Quickly, they constructed a barricade of fallen trees, driftwood, and scrub, a fallback defensive position should it be needed. The timber and driftwood could then be brought aboard as fuel. Tom gently beached the *Belle* on the pebbly sand and tossed the anchor over to stabilize her while he worked. He set to work straight away. He doused the fire in the firebox with a bucket of cold water. Steam poured from the funnel as the water hit the hot coals. It would take perhaps an hour for the boiler to cool down enough to begin the patch. As a steam cloud rose high in the air, Braithwaite worried that the cloud and the whistling from the dying fire might be heard or seen by any trackers. He was right to worry. A couple of miles away, an askari pointed up at the sky over the lake as the cloud rose and then dissipated. The German officer spotted it as well; von Donop smiled for the first time since the morning battle. He had found his quarry.

Silently, Braithwaite, Minstrel, and Patel loaded up extra stripper clips of ammunition for the rifles. Slinging the Enfields, each marched off in a different direction to take up their picket post and to await what all expected—an all-out assault. Patel whispered to Braithwaite as they departed, "Worse than the Khyber Pass, my friend. Worse."

Braithwaite could only shake his head in quiet concurrence.

By late afternoon, the boiler had cooled enough to begin work. Tom always sailed with a patch kit. He had several square pieces of metal that could be shaped to fit the round boiler sides. He had screws and some tools—wrenches, spanners, pliers, a hammer, and so on. It would be enough for a quick repair, but with sufficient screws, it should hold. Likely, they would lose some steam pressure, but at least a temporary patch should see them through to Point OK and the hoped-for rendezvous with Pankhurst's marines. At least that was the hope. As he took his post some thirty yards out from the beach, Braithwaite had never felt so alone. True, his shipmates and comrades were only yards away, but well-concealed in the jungle overgrowth. He dropped to one knee. His aching arm made for a tough go of it. He had taken some morphine from the medical kit as they sailed north away from Station Wilhelm, but had refused more of the painkiller since that morning. He had to remain alert. Their lives depended on it.

Dusk came. The banging from the riverboat had ceased as Tom finished making the holes for the screws and shaping and bending the metal patches. He quickly fitted the patches to the boiler sides. Every now and then, a banging came from the beach. It could not be helped. He had to hammer out the patches to fit over the two bullet holes precisely, otherwise, a patch was useless. With each bang of the hammer, Braithwaite cringed. How far into the jungle the noise could be heard he could not tell. But, in reality, it provided an excellent target solution for the enemy troops hiding in the jungle several hundred yards away, awaiting the dark and the signal from their commander to strike. More minutes passed. The banging stopped. Tom now attempted to screw on the shaped patches, but the process proceeded agonizingly slowly. Dick, smarting from the wound and exhausted from the loss of blood and the tension of the moment, helped as best he could. As Tom screwed on the patches, he gathered loose driftwood. They said nothing. Only the gentle lapping of the waves against the sandy beach could be heard along with the occasional metallic screech as the screws turned against the boiler sides. With the last screw turned in place, Tom and Dick quickly stoked the firebox with coals removed earlier and kept alive in the camp stove. Within minutes, they had a blaze going in the firebox and fresh water in the boiler. Steam pressure started to rise, but it would take some time to get the pressure back up enough to turn the shaft. Slowly, the pressure gauge needle moved - slowly, but perceptively. Tom tossed in more fuel to the white-hot flame. He paused and grinned. The patches seemed to hold—no steam leak from around the edges.

A scream! It was more of a screech. Braithwaite instantly crouched down. Shouts came from several yards away in Minstrel's direction. "Alice!" He shouted. Then a shot. He jerked up so quickly that the blood rushed from his head. He staggered, dizzy from the sudden movement and loss of blood. "Alice!" he shouted. More shots. Another scream. Shots came from Patel's position followed by the anguished cry of a wounded askari. Patel had downed one of the attackers. Without another thought, Braithwaite charged through the undergrowth toward where Minstrel should have been.

On the *Belle*, Dick leapt to the Lewis gun, pulled back the bolt and swung the gun from side to side. No targets. The jungle growth masked the action. Tom slammed the firebox door shut and leapt to the beach. He pulled in the anchor, deeply dug into the sand, until it gave way, almost knocking him down. He tossed the anchor into the bow, grabbed the rifle staged on the bow, and took a firing position.

Within seconds, Braithwaite arrived at Minstrel's position. *Gone! Where!* He shouted again and then again. Meanwhile, Patel had also reached the position, having fired off all five rounds in the magazine. Desperately, they both looked about.

"Sahib! Where is she?" he shouted as both desperately scanned the dark undergrowth. Nothing. Then another scream came from off to the right. Through a slight clearing, they both could see for just a second, Minstrel slung over the shoulder of a huge, muscular askari. She pounded on his back, but to no avail. Next to the hulking soldier, another askari took up a firing position and loosed a round in their direction. The bullet rippled through the leaves overhead.

"They have her. They have her!" shouted Patel.

Braithwaite leveled his rifle at the soldier, but could not pull the trigger for fear of hitting Minstrel. "Dammit to hell," he shouted. The two askaris, native to this area, knew how to travel stealthily and quickly through the undergrowth. They had sneaked up on Minstrel unawares and grabbed her. She managed to get off a warning shot and scream. Grabbing her by the waist, the askari had hoisted her over his shoulders while the other soldier kicked away her rifle.

After firing the errant round, both soldiers stood up and started off away from Braithwaite and Patel. Minstrel still struggled to escape. Just as Braithwaite started to run toward them, a blow came from seemingly nowhere. It caught him on the temple. He staggered, somewhere between consciousness and darkness. With one blow from the butt of his rifle, Patel bashed in the man's skull. Braithwaite dropped to his knees, the jungle whirling about. His arms flailed helplessly as he gasped for air. "Must... get... must get to... her... must...," he rambled incoherently. Then in a fraction of the second, his lucid thoughts returned. He reached out both arms in the direction of the retreating soldiers and shouted as loud as he could muster, "I will come for you. I will come for you!" Blackness.

Patel reached out and grabbed Braithwaite by the shoulders as he collapsed. "Come, Sahib. No good. They have her. We must get back to the boat. Come!" The Bengal Lancer dragged the Royal Navy man back toward the beach and the waiting *Belle*. Hoisting him as one would a potato sack, he shouted to Tom, "Underway. Get underway. Quick." Tom leapt over to the tiller and opened the steam valve as a cloud of gray smoke erupted from the funnel. Slowly at first, then picking up momentum, the *Belle* edged off the sand and finally into the water. Braithwaite's limp body hit the deck with a thud. Patel hoped to be gentler with the still unconscious Braithwaite, but there was a greater imperative - speed and get away from the beach. Patel grabbed one of the rifles and quickly emptied the clip toward the jungle. He did not aim at anything in particular, rather, he simply pointed at the beach and let loose the volley so as to force the askaris to keep their heads down. They needed time—time to get out of range. The unconscious Braithwaite would have to wait.

On the beach, more askaris gathered, firing wildly at the retreating riverboat. On the deckhouse, Dick opened up with the Lewis gun. As he raked the beach, several askaris dropped. Others scattered, taking cover behind the remains of the improvised defensive works. Other soldiers scampered into the jungle. Only a few random shots came across the water. None hit the *Belle* as she slowly chugged away from the beach, picking up speed. As they moved out further into the lake and safely out of effective range, no one spoke. The enormity of the past few tragic moments started to strike home. Standing in the boat's bow staring at the beach now littered with askari dead and wounded, Patel softly spoke to no one in particular, "He will come for you, Memsahib. He will come."

****

By the time the *Belle* reached well into the lake at least two miles from the shore and the angry askaris, Braithwaite finally awakened as Patel stood over him like a mother hen.

"Alice… Alice… where…."

Patel placed a gentle hand on his shoulder. "Sahib, the askaris have her. You could do nothing. We could not save her." He choked as he spoke those dreadful words—we could not save her.

Slowly, Braithwaite drew his knees up toward his chin and bowing his head, he placed both hands atop his head—a sign of desperate resignation. *We could not save her. We could not save her.* The bitter words rattled about his still groggy mind. Patel said nothing. He simply knelt down beside Braithwaite and stared at the beach receding in the distance. Silence. No one spoke for several minutes. Only the chug, chug, chug of the engine and the swoosh of water over the bow as the *Belle* quickly made her way up the lake and away from the scene. Dick still manned the Lewis gun in case the askaris somehow managed to give chase. Tom sat quietly at the stern, his right hand on the tiller and his left hand held against his bare forehead, a sign of the desperation and grief that he now felt.

After several minutes, Braithwaite finally lifted his head up and looked back at the beach. His head had cleared. After a minute he turned toward Patel. "Amrish, we must save her."

"Yes, Sahib. We must. And we will."

Tom guided the *Belle* into a small cove covered on three sides by thick jungle growth. But like so many such coves and inlets, the enemy could attack without warning, hidden from view and stealthily. These men were locals and since their livelihood in peacetime relied on their hunting skills, they had become experts at concealment and stalking prey. So, while Patel and Braithwaite made their plan, Dick manned the machine gun, prepared for any action. They did not want to go ashore. That lesson had been learned. But, the firebox needed fuel. While Tom and Patel gathered as much driftwood as could be found on the beach, Braithwaite covered them with an Enfield. Tom remained aboard slowly fanning the Lewis gun from side to side ready to open fire at any instant. Nothing happened. They gathered as much firewood as possible and returned to the *Belle* as fast as they could. Tom got her underway and hauled off toward the lake's center, well out of rifle range.

"We have to go back."

"Yes, Sahib. We have to go back," responded a grim-faced Patel.

"Tom, how far do you think they went?" questioned Braithwaite.

"Bwana John. Not far. Askaris respect the jungle at night. They do not travel in such places after dark. The leopard and jaguar like to hunt by dark. Most likely, the bastards set up camp with a blazing fire to scare off the hunters."

With that, Braithwaite's nimble mind raced.

"Then, we shall be the hunters. Tom, how close can we get to the shore without making a noise?"

Tom raised his eyebrows. He knew that the Englishman had a plan in mind. He leaned over the side and placed a hand in the water. The *Belle* had been sitting dead in the water for several minutes. Only the current moved the boat. After several seconds, he looked up and grinned.

"Very good, Bwana. Current very strong here and moving us to the south. We can stop the engine perhaps a mile up and drift to the beach."

Braithwaite nodded and smiled. He had a plan. "If they have set up camp for the night, it will likely be near the beach for firewood and fresh water. We might be able to spot their fire."

"What are you proposing, Sahib?"

"An attack, my Indian friend. A three-sided assault. What do you think?"

Patel stood, looked over at the beach and back toward Braithwaite grinning, his white teeth shining by the light of the full moon. "A convergent assault, my friend. Indeed. For a Navy man, you're thinking like a Lancer. Most good, Sahib."

With no further word, Tom slowly brought the riverboat about and the *Belle* sailed south aided by a strong current. Back into the fray.

****

"So, *Frau* Zimmermann or whoever you are. Tell me about your plan."

She said nothing. The German officer only smiled a malevolent grin. "Let us try again. Where were you headed, you and your companions?"

Minstrel did not speak. She glared at von Donop. As discreetly as she could, she jiggled her hands about trying to loosen the leather ties binding her wrists behind her back.

"I suspect that you are headed for safe haven in Nyasaland, were you not? Please, it does no one any good to stay silent. We will know the truth soon enough. You should know that I have sent a fast runner back to the station. They will alert the lake patrol at Spinxhaven. There will be maximum river patrols out before dawn and, quite frankly, my dear, your comrades will be captured or killed before they can get across the lake to Nyasaland. Be assured."

Minstrel still said nothing.

"Tell me, *Frau* Zimmermann, what did you and your spy husband if indeed he is that, learn from the departed Herr *Doktor* Steinweiss?"

She simply glared at him as von Donop took in a deep breath, and let it out slowly. "You try my patience, my dear. We will learn your plan. Be assured that they will not escape."

Nyasaland. Nyasaland. He expects us to flee to Nyasaland. Well, well. Then they have no knowledge of the rendezvous at Point OK. She had to escape. If she could get free and head south, the Germans would follow in that direction, while the *Belle* headed north toward Point OK and the rendezvous with the marines. She had to get free. She finally spoke. "They will get to Nyasaland and safety. You have lost, Sir. You have lost."

The German glared at her for several long seconds.

"And where in Nyasaland do they intend to head? It will be ever so much better for you if you talk to me. Please do that much for yourself. I cannot vouch for what my askaris will do, you understand. They are most angry that your spies killed and wounded so many of their friends and comrades. The sooner that you confess your plan to me, the quicker I can get you to safety. Otherwise…." His sentence trailed off, but the implication was clear—rape, torture, and a horrible death awaited her.

Please, dear Lord, they must head for Point OK as fast as they can. The secret to the machine has to be delivered.

The German sat quietly, just tapping his riding crop against his boots. She had to stall. She had to stall long enough for Braithwaite and Patel to escape north.

"*Herr* von Donop. If I told you where they are headed, can you guarantee my safety? Are you a gentleman or a barbarian, Sir?" *That's it! He is an aristocrat. Pray God that he still has some of those chivalric ideals left despite the war. Pray God.*

Von Donop stared at her for over a minute, those cold blue eyes never blinking. Finally, he looked away and tilted his head as if in deep thought. He turned back toward her and leaned in. "Very well, *Frau* Zimmermann. If I get you to safety, you will tell me where your companions are headed?"

"Yes, *Herr* von Donop. That is the agreement. But not before I'm safe from your men."

He leaned back in his camp chair, hands clasped. His fingers interlocked as if in deep contemplation and then he looked away. "You should know, Madam that this is, of course, all academic. The river patrols will find your miserable little boat and sink it and your nest of British spies well before they reach Nyasaland. But, I am a gentleman. I will keep you safe… for now." He leaned forward, a frightful leer on his face, the face with the piercing eyes. "But remember this, my dear, if you attempt to escape or do not hold up your part of this bargain, I cannot vouch for your safety. Do you understand me?"

"Perfectly, *Herr* von Donop. Perfectly."

The tent flap parted as the askari stuck his head in. "Sir, the runner has returned from Station Wilhelm. The message to Spinxhaven has been sent and they have responded. All the riverboats are out on the lake hunting for the British spies."

"Very good, *Herr Feldwebel.*"

With that, the askari ducked back out as von Donop stood. "Very well, *Frau* Zimmermann. I leave you now. Please do remember what we have said here. It would be ever so sad to see you harmed," he hissed in such a malevolent voice that Minstrel cringed. He had made his point and with that, the officer exited the tent.

Minstrel again struggled with the leather straps. *No good. Too tight.* But, she had bought some precious time and had deceived him. As the *Belle* chugged north, the Germans would hunt them to the west.

****

Tom throttled down the engine as the *Belle* drifted slower. Through the binoculars, Braithwaite and Patel could see the flames of the askari campfire. True to form, they had encamped only a couple of miles south of the scene of the carnage. Braithwaite dropped to one knee as did Patel and Dick. All had armed themselves with rifles, revolvers, and extra ammunition. They would each strike from a different direction. Braithwaite reviewed the plan one last time.

"Right. Patel on their left flank and Dick, you hit them on the right." Braithwaite lifted the Very pistol, cracked it open and double-checked that a green flare was properly loaded. It closed with a solid click and he put it back safely in his belt." When I fire the green flare, open up with as many rounds as you can. Don't aim as such. The idea is to create chaos and force them into a crossfire. That should confuse the devil out of the poor sods. Once they start running about, that's when I will strike, find, and pull her out of there. Is everything clear?" All nodded affirmatively.

An hour later, Dick returned. He had waded ashore and reconnoitered the camp. "Bwana John. There are four tents set up in a circle. I guess the larger one is the officer's. No sign of Lady Alice, but I think she is in the big tent."

Braithwaite and Patel shook their heads in agreement. "Right then. We are off."

The three men waded ashore several yards north of the camp. Patel stayed put in the undergrowth while Braithwaite took a post in the center. Dick went wide around the camp until he found a good spot on the right. From there, he had a clear shot to the camp as did Patel from his position on the left. Meanwhile, Tom eased the boat over into the current and allowed it to drift into position just across from the camp, but far enough out to stay undetected. When the green flare went up, he would crank the steam valve to full speed and head for the beach to remain at waiting distance just off the sand. If the plan went wrong and he was attacked, he was to fire a red flare and get underway as rapidly as possible to a spot about a mile up the coast. It had been noted and marked as the emergency rescue point. As the *Belle* drifted toward the beach, he patted the Very pistol and muttered to no one in particular, "Stay put, little Very pistol. Stay put."

Within ten minutes, all were in place. There were three soldiers on sentry duty, but otherwise, the camp seemed quiet except for the blazing fire in the center. Braithwaite waited another five minutes to make sure all was in place. From his position, he could clearly see the entire camp in one direction and could make out the faint outlines of the *Belle*, waiting quietly just off the beach. Another two minutes passed. All quiet.

"Right, old sod. For King and Country!" he whispered. With that, he pulled the Very pistol from his belt, raised it high in the air and pulled the trigger. A whoosh sounded as the cartridge shot high into the air, then exploded lighting up the entire area with a phosphorescent green light. Within a second, two shots rang out, one each from the north and south. Simultaneously, two guards went down. *Good shooting, lads!* He sprang to his feet and raced toward the camp as two more shots rang out. The lone standing sentry bellowed, enraged and stunned. He desperately tried to unsling his Mauser, but just as it came off his shoulder, Braithwaite barreled into him, knocking the man to the ground. With the Very pistol still in his hand, Braithwaite struck the askari twice on the forehead. The man's eyes rolled in his head as he lost consciousness. More shots mixed with the shouts from the tents. Up ahead, a white-uniformed figure appeared at the entrance to the large tent waving a Luger about. He tried to shout just as another round slammed into the tentpole sending slivers of wood flying. As several splinters struck his face, he ducked down and raced toward the fire, shouting to the men exiting the smaller tents.

Now! Move! She is there! Braithwaite shot across the open ground toward the big tent, keeping his head low to avoid Patel and Dick's fire. He reached the tent flap. Von Donop did not see him as he was too absorbed in rousing and rallying his men. Braithwaite charged into the tent, pulling out a knife as he did so.

Minstrel sat in a wicker chair, her hands and ankles bound and with a dirty linen cloth for a gag. Her eyes were wide open. He reached behind the chair and, within a second, cut the leather ties. Bolting around to the front, he knelt down and with one swipe, cut the leather ties as Minstrel, her hands now free, yanked out the gag.

"Bloody fool! You should have left me," she screamed above the chaotic din coming from outside the tent.

"I said I would come for you. No time for idle chitchat, my love. I suggest, we hurry!"

She laughed. It seemed a strange thing to do in such a predicament, but he had apparently not lost his sense of humor. Neither would she.

Braithwaite looked out the tent flap at the chaos. More shots rang out from different directions confusing the askaris. While von Donop raced about attempting to organize a defense, another askari fell, clutching his chest. Others took cover behind anything they could find. Braithwaite paused. *Should they rush into the chaos?* After a few more seconds, he noticed that Patel and Dick's rounds were hitting higher in the trees, clipping branches and leaves. By God, they were aiming high so as to give him and Minstrel a clean, safe exit. He grabbed Minstrel's wrist and grinned, "Everyone into the pool!" With that, they both shot out of the tent and weaved and bobbed behind the row of tents before heading toward the beach and the *Belle*. Then a red flare exploded above their heads, mixing red with the glow of the green flare creating an eerie, hellish site. "Damn!" he shouted.

What they had not seen was that two askaris had run toward the beach rather than take cover among the trees and camp accouterments. They spotted the *Belle* and opened fire. Shooting wildly and still half-panicked, they missed, but Tom immediately turned the steam valve, pulled up the Very pistol and let fly the warning red flare. Crouching behind a huge tree just outside the camp, Braithwaite turned to Minstrel. "Change of plan. We head north." With that, both sprang up and dashed to the right toward the emergency rendezvous point a mile away. They passed Patel who had stayed in position to give covering fire. A minute later, Dick came running up from their right, out of breath, but otherwise in good shape. He and Patel let loose one more volley toward the camp. They rose up and began the race for life. From behind them, they heard the bellowing German officer.

"After them! They're headed north!"

The race was on. In the dark, the three stumbled over roots and undergrowth. Braithwaite fell twice, re-opening his wound. His thighs throbbed. But, halting every hundred yards or so, Dick and Patel turned about to fire a few shots at the pursuers so as to force them to take cover. They raced through the dark jungle lit only by the full moonlight holding tight to Minstrel's hand. She too stumbled but together, they helped each other back up. *Press on, Press on. Can't stop.* In the dark, they started to become disoriented. "Which way ... which deuced way?" shouted Braithwaite. Minstrel shouted back, out of breath, "We could use your bloody Aries star just now, my dear husband!" She still had the wit about her.

The chase went on for a full half hour before they reached the rendezvous point. It had been a trial, tripping over roots and heavy undergrowth and ducking as the occasional rifle bullet shot past them. But, they made it unhurt all three within a few seconds of each other. As soon as he saw Patel emerge from the undergrowth onto the beach, Tom turned the tiller over and drove the *Belle* up to the beach. They tumbled onto the deck, exhausted, but safe. With that, Dick pushed off the sand and the *Belle* was underway again at full speed. As they pulled out of range, on the shore in the full moonlight stood a crowd of askaris and an officer in bright white but blood, dirt, and smoke-stained naval uniform, all raging in frustration at the escapees.

"We head to Point OK, and...."

Minstrel shot in, "Wait, look at the funnel."

The damp wood produced a volcano of cinders that poured from the stack. "Von Donop has alerted the lake patrols. They may be out by now and they will spot those glowing cinders."

"Quite right, Sahib. Best to get safely away and shut down the engine for now," added Patel.

"He thinks we are headed to Nyasaland," she added.

Braithwaite pondered this intelligence for a moment, then turned to Tom. "Tom, turn west toward Nyasaland. Keep those cinders blowing. Once we are well out of their sight, head north for a few miles. Then, we'll shut down for the night and wait for dawn when those blasted sparks are not as visible."

"Yes, Bwana. West it is, "he responded as he turned the tiller to the right swinging the bow round to port.

Braithwaite knew they were right. It had to be done. They traveled a few miles west, then north to be well clear of the askaris. Tom then shut down the engine, leaving only a few glowing coals for the morning.

****

Minstrel slowly opened her eyes. The rising sun's glare caused her to turn her head sideways and squint. For just a moment, she felt disoriented and almost as if she drifted above the earth like a cloud. Slowly, her senses returned. The only sound was the water lapping against the riverboat's side. A wisp of smoke drifted from the funnel, but no cinders. She looked about. Far in the distance, she saw the shore of German East Africa, a thin green line along the horizon. Good. They were far enough out to not be spotted by the enemy ashore. *But where were they?* All through the night, they had drifted with the current. No matter, Braithwaite will be able to do a navigational fix. Patel sat on the bow, rifle in hand, and binoculars to his eyes. He had mounted the Lewis gun on the bow in anticipation of a dawn patrol by the enemy lake boats. Nothing yet appeared.

"Good morning, Memsahib."

"And to you, Amrish," she yawned.

Braithwaite stirred. He had taken the midwatch from midnight to 04.00 and despite the three hours of sleep, was groggy as he stretched. "A fine down pillow and soft mattress at the Ritz would do nicely after this adventure is concluded."

No one laughed or even smiled. After the last few hours, apparently, no one cared any longer for such humor. And, overhanging all, was the worry that at any moment, danger might pop up once again. After a quick breakfast of stale, crusty bread, Braithwaite took a navigational fix while Dick and Tom fired up the boiler. It hurt to even raise the sextant to his eyes, but he had to ignore the painful wound. Meanwhile, Patel and Minstrel kept watch for any enemy patrol boats.

He looked up from the chart of Lake Nyasa spread out over the deckhouse roof. "Not good news, my friends. Not good at all. Apparently, the current is fairly strong here. It has pushed us back several miles south. It makes us roughly ten miles northwest of Station Wilhelm.

"So, we have lost ground?" questioned Minstrel.

"Apparently so."

Minstrel's chin dropped to her chest in disappointment. "I suppose there's nothing for it but to head back on track as best we can," she muttered.

"Sahib, Memsahib! Quickly. On the horizon. A boat!" shouted Patel, who leapt to the Lewis gun mounted on the bow.

Grabbing the binoculars that lay atop the deckhouse, Braithwaite scanned the horizon as Tom slammed the firebox door shut and leapt back to the tiller. Dick cranked the steam lever to full as they prepared to flee.

"Wait," said Braithwaite scanning the distant horizon for any signs of other craft. "Wait. She is dead in the water and I can't see any crew."

Meanwhile, Minstrel had taken up another set of binoculars and also scanned. "This is odd. No crew. And, it appears to be another riverboat just like ours. In fact, it looks to be identical."

"By Jove, you are right. It's the same design as the *Belle*," shot in an astonished Braithwaite.

"Yes, Bwana. There are several of the same boats on the waters. It is a very stout design and very popular," added Tom. "We can be underway in a moment or so." Heavy gray smoke poured from the funnel from the still damp driftwood collected the day before.

"Point OK, Sahib?" questioned Patel, still aiming the machine gun at the strange riverboat.

"Yes…," Braithwaite paused. A thought started forming in his mind. "No, let's investigate. Perhaps they've encountered the Germans and can provide some useful intelligence of any lake patrol. Patel shook his head in concurrence. Within minutes, they reached the riverboat, but still, no one appeared on deck. As they closed to a few yards, Braithwaite shouted, "Ahoy there. Ahoy. May we come alongside?"

As they approached, Patel and Minstrel dismounted the machine gun and covered it with a tarp—ready for action but hidden from view. They lay the rifles down on the deck and out of sight. Still no response. They edged closer.

"Ahoy, I say. Is anyone there?"

As they got within a few feet, Dick put out rubber bumpers and Tom gently guided the *Belle* alongside. The boat gently bumped up against the strange craft. Carefully, with revolvers drawn, Patel and Braithwaite stepped over the gunwales and onto the riverboat. Meanwhile, Minstrel covered them with her Webley. "We are coming aboard. Ahoy."

Despite all they had seen and endured in the past few hours, the site stunned them. Lying about the deck, awash in dried blood, lay four bodies, two Africans and two Europeans. Their throats had been slashed. One man's head hung to the side, almost totally decapitated. They could say nothing as they moved from body to body looking for any sign of life.

"Could the Germans have done this?" questioned Minstrel, shaking her head in disgust and revulsion. She had come aboard when it was clear the pistol would not be needed.

Tom peered over into the carnage. "No, Ma'am. Germans do not do this. Not even their askari do this. Lake pirates do this."

They searched the boat but found no cargo or valuables. All weapons were similarly missing. The pirates had been thorough and ruthless. Everything of value had been stripped, even the men's boots.

"Well, the buggers are thorough. When did this happen?" Braithwaite asked.

"Sahib, from the odor and the state of the bodies, I would guess sometime late yesterday. Not too long. There is the start of decay, but not far along. Yes, I say late yesterday," responded Patel.

With that assessment, Minstrel's fertile mind whirled with the germ of an idea. "This could be us. Yes, it could be us."

Instantly, Braithwaite saw where she headed with the thought. He looked south toward Station Wilhelm. In a microsecond, a plan formed—a bold plan. "What if it were us?" Patel and Minstrel both stared at Braithwaite. Minstrel's eyebrows raised as the thought began to formulate.

"We could make the Germans think we were assaulted and killed by lake pirates."

"And end their hunt for us?" shot in Patel.

"Just so. Just so. We can make this sad craft appear to be the *Belle*. If we put enough gear and supplies aboard to give the impression it was us, perhaps the blighter's will assume just that. The current is taking us toward Station Wilhelm where the Germans could find us."

Minstrel knelt down beside one of the bodies and took a long look. "Yes, this one could easily be you, John. The two crewmen could be Tom and Dick. And, since I'm apparently missing, they might gather that the pirates took me as part of their booty."

Patel grinned a knowing smile. "Indeed, Sahib. We can give these poor chaps a fitting going away. A Viking funeral-flaming boat as you Europeans are so fond of."

Minstrel stood, hands on her hips. "Perhaps these unfortunate souls can serve humanity as their last act."

The plan came together. For the next few hours, they transferred cargo, supplies, and extra clothing aboard. Tom and Dick did everything possible to reconfigure the riverboat just like the *Belle*. Once they completed those tasks, they began the grizzly job of dressing the bodies. Minstrel discreetly looked away as the four men stripped and changed into spare clothing. They then re-dressed the dead men in the clothes that they had worn at Station Wilhelm and since. The bloody garments taken from the unfortunate victims went into the firebox. Fortunately, all four victims were generally their same sizes, give or take. It might not matter if the fit was not exact. A flaming boat should destroy enough to make the deception believable. Pray God it works.

They even transferred one of the Lewis guns over, but without any ammunition. Patel took a hammer from the toolkit and smashed the gun's receiver. The pirates would not have bothered with the damaged weapon but would have stripped the boat of all other weapons and ammunition. Finally, Tom took the Swiss flag from the deckhouse and ran it up the sternpost. Fortunately, neither boat had a name painted on the sides or stern, which would have been a problem. By noon, all was set.

"Now, we wait for nightfall."

✳✳✳✳✳✳✳✳✳✳✳✳✳✳✳

Darkness came. Although they could not yet see Station Wilhelm, Braithwaite had done another navigational fix at dusk. They were only a few miles away, but still too far for casual observation from the shore. They had drifted with the strong current for several miles, but Tom had kept steam up for their getaway sprint. As a last preparation, Patel spread kerosene from the night lamps about the deck and bodies, still in the same place they died. Patel and Braithwaite stripped down.

"Well, Sergeant Major, my old friend. Are you ready for a night swim?"

Patel glared at the naval officer, then laughed. "Indeed, Sahib. Let us hope the crocs have had their supper already." All sniggered at the dark humor. With that, both men eased over the side and took up positions on either side of the unfortunate riverboat after they all said a prayer for the men's souls. It was not quite a conventional funeral, but given the present circumstances, it would have to do. Patel and Braithwaite gingerly pushed the riverboat several feet away from the *Belle* as the current began to catch. Minstrel stood atop the deckhouse with a flaming torch. She gave the torch a great heave; it landed on the riverboat's deck. Within a second, a flame erupted, shooting high up in the air as Patel and Braithwaite heaved the boat in the direction of the beach.

As the stricken boat gathered speed in the swiftly moving current, Braithwaite and Patel swam as fast as they could back toward the *Belle*. Meanwhile, Tom opened the steam valve just as both men clambered aboard. As the flames shot into the night sky from the riverboat drifting away rapidly, all stood to attention and saluted the dying boat. With that, Tom cranked the throttle to full, turned the tiller and the *Zambezi Belle* chugged away north toward Point OK and safety.

****

The askaris found the burned out riverboat and the charred bodies the next morning beached a couple of miles south of Station Wilhelm. Von Donop and his soldiers had returned to Station Wilhelm the previous evening, assuming that the British spies were away toward Nyasaland. He hoped that the increased lake patrols would soon intercept the interlopers and that whatever they had learned at Station Wilhelm would die with them.

That afternoon, by the still functioning HF wireless set at the station, a coded message went out to *Aachen*, now back in her Rufiji anchorage. The detailed message gave all the pertinent details of the recent events—the battle at the station, Steinweiss' death, the destruction of the second "machine," and, perhaps most importantly, the demise of the British spies thanks to the barbarity of Lake Nyasa pirates. In his reply, von Augsburg ordered von Donop to return to *Aachen* by the fastest route possible and to leave several askaris to sort out and clean up the shambles that had been Station Wilhelm. As the cruiser captain read the sentence announcing Steinweiss' accidental death in the fire-fight and the inadvertent destruction of the second "machine" in the fire that followed, the German captain felt a sudden wash of anxiety. He did not know what this matter would ultimately mean, but he had a sudden premonition—a premonition of coming disaster.

CHAPTER 12

Gunfight at the OK Corral

04 June 1915. Lake Nyasa.

"Smoke, Bwana," whispered Tom. "On the horizon. There." He pointed to the north to a wispy trail of dark smoke. Braithwaite flipped open the wooden box lid where they kept the navigation instruments—compass, sextant, charts, and so on. He grabbed a pair of powerful, Swiss-made binoculars and scanned the horizon to the north. *Nothing yet.* Still, Tom was right. Something definitely approached and in this part of Africa, it could be only a bad thing.

"Slow to bare steerageway," he ordered. On the helm, Tom twisted the valve down to slow the steam flow to the engine. Within moments, the *Belle* drifted with the slowly moving current and toward the shore several hundred yards off their starboard bow.

"Chart," requested Braithwaite. Tom, already anticipating the request had pulled up the now frayed paper chart of Lake Nyasa and surrounding territory. Both men hovered over the deckhouse roof, chart spread out on top. Meanwhile, Minstrel grabbed the binoculars and kept a watchful eye on the distant mysterious smoke. As Tom held down the chart against the breeze, Braithwaite extracted the dividers and a set of parallel rulers. With a quick mental calculation and even swifter walk across the chart with the dividers from their last navigational fix at noon, he marked an "X" on the chart and drew a straight line from the last navigational fix spot to the "X."

"I make us just about here," he tapped the "X" with an index finger.

Patel, with raised eyebrows, scowled. "Then, Sahib, we may have trouble." Both men leaned over the chart. Meanwhile, Minstrel joined the two men hovering over the chart, now fluttering in the breeze.

Point OK—a simple place on a map, but a critical place for the mission. That was where they were to rendezvous with the rescue party sent overland from Zanzibar—Pankhurst's Royal Marines. From there, they were to trek overland back to the coast at Cape del Gado on the northern Portuguese and German East African border along the Ruvana River, then by warship back to Zanzibar. Meanwhile, Tom and Dick would continue north to the top of the lake. If queried about the unusual Swiss couple, their cover story would be that they both came down with some strange tropical malady, and, being new to the area, had all perished of the fever, etc. They were buried in the lake as ceremoniously as possible and so on and so forth. Likely with that tale, any suspicious official would very quickly pass them on and move away as fast as possible considering contamination or infection. If they made it to the north, they were to burn the *Belle* and all trace of their expedition and then enjoy the magnificent pension so generously provided by His Britannic Majesty's government.

The *Belle* came to a full stop as Tom shut off the air vents to tamp down the boiler fire and cut out any telltale stack smoke. Drifting dead in the water with no way on, hopefully, whatever craft over the horizon would not notice them.

"Damn!" hissed Braithwaite, barely able to conceal his disappointment as he ran out the dividers from the estimated position and that of Point OK. Barely five miles to the rendezvous point. What if they made a run for it? What if the marines sat at Point OK awaiting their arrival? What if they hadn't arrived and they were alone with no reinforcement? What if the distant vessel was merely another riverboat such as the *Belle*? All these thoughts ran through his mind as he nervously tapped the dividers on the chart. In a flash of decisiveness, he decided. "Right then, we go on as we are and hope for the best," he exclaimed as he rolled up the chart. "Patel and Minstrel, break out the

Enfields and Webleys, but conceal them just in case. If that is the Huns or pirates and they stop us, we need to be prepared for a fight."

"Right away, Sahib," shouted Patel from the bow, already pulling out rifles and cartridge boxes. Minstrel simply shook her head.

"Tom, make steam. Let's proceed as innocently as possible, but make for Point OK. If the marines are indeed there, we want to have as much reinforcement as possible."

Grabbing the leather glove used to protect his hands against the heat of the boiler firebox handle, Tom yanked open the door while Dick, grabbing several large logs, shoved them into the flames. Smoke erupted from the funnel within seconds as the wood began to burn. Slowly at first, but gradually picking up speed, the *Belle* chugged forward. A small wake developed spreading away from her stern indicating the increased speed. Braithwaite doubted they could outrun any German patrol boat, but he was determined to take no chances. They had made a calculated risk in approaching the riverboat days earlier, but now, so close to Point OK, they dare not take another such gamble. Raising the binoculars again to his eyes, he scanned the horizon. The interloper seemed to be maintaining a parallel course and speed to the riverboat. Had they been spotted? Surely the other craft detected the smoke pouring from the *Belle's* funnel. Without any other word, Minstrel opened the weapons box and withdrew three of the Webleys, handing one to Patel and keeping one for herself tucked neatly into the waistband of her khaki safari trousers. She handed another revolver to Braithwaite, who tucked it into his waistband under the belt after checking the chamber to ensure it was fully loaded. Meanwhile, with the firebox completely full, Tom returned to his tiller and steered toward a small promontory a good five miles in the distance.

The cat and mouse game continued with the interloper standing off several hundred yards away, but now clearly on an intercept course. The real question remained—could they make the five miles to Point OK before the interception? If so, they might drop the anchor and quickly scatter into the surrounding jungle. An enemy patrol boat might then confiscate or destroy the *Belle*, but, at least for the moment, they would be safe at Point OK and hope for Pankhurst's arrival if not already there. The problem, as Braithwaite anxiously tracked the approaching vessel through the powerful binoculars, is simply one of geometry. Then, suddenly, a thick cloud of white smoke erupted from the unknown vessel's single funnel. Slowly at first, but more dramatically as she picked up speed, the course changed to a much sharper angle. Braithwaite did a quick mental calculation based on the relative motion of each craft. The geometry did not work. At the interloper's new course and speed, she would likely intercept the *Belle* just a few yards short of Point OK and safety.

"I make her a small boat. Patrol boat of some kind, Sahib. I count four, maybe five sailors. But she is armed. Looks to be a couple of mounted Maxim guns as well as a larger deck gun on the bow, perhaps a 3-pounder," Patel warned.

Braithwaite looked over at the shoreline. He could now make out the distinctive features of the outcropping extending into the lake that had been briefed weeks earlier in the cruiser's wardroom. Scanning with the binoculars, he recognized the ruins of an old stone tower, a relic of an earlier age when Arab traders had ventured in from the coast and constructed defensive works as a precaution against angry local warriors unhappy with the intrusion into their traditional tribal territory. It had made for a convenient and easily recognized rendezvous point based on a German survey map with ever so handy photographs published in the 1890s. God bless that Teutonic efficiency! He scanned the promontory, desperately hoping to sight any signs of the marines. Nothing. He turned the binoculars back toward the approaching enemy patrol boat. As she came into a closer view, his mind scrolled through page after page of ship recognition images studied in the rare downtime while still part of the destroyer patrol out of Harwich at what now seemed centuries ago. She looked awkward as did so many of the river craft built for utility, not beauty—not the crisp, clean lines of a destroyer, the "greyhound of the sea." No, this one was more utilitarian with a wide beam and an open, canvas-covered bridge shielding the ship's wheel from the sun. She definitely was not a sea-going vessel, but she did have the appearance of a civilian riverboat with armaments thrown aboard by the emergency of war. Then it struck him—he recognized the craft. It was a gunboat very similar to the lake steamer *Hermann von Wissman* that had been crippled and put out of action in the first naval battle of the war the summer before. He recalled seeing photographs of that German vessel one morning in late October in the *Halberd*'s wardroom. Everyone thought it most humorous that despite all the great battleship and battlecruiser building that went on before the war between the Royal Navy and the German Imperial Navy, the first actual engagement would be on a lake far away from Europe in the backwaters of the Empire between a couple of converted civilian lake steamers.

The approaching patrol boat appeared old, likely from the 1890s, but still functional on the African lakes. His head drooped. *Could this be the end of the mission?* They could now make out at least two deck guns, one likely a 3-pounder on the bow and what looked to be at least a 50mm rapid fire on the fantail. Quickly, he searched his memory from his cadet days of memorizing the German, French, and Russian Orders of Battle. The result was not comfortable. He recalled that the German weapon that he now saw near the stern of the approaching patrol boat was an SK L/40 model, which fired a 50mm shell—about 2 inches in diameter. The SK L/40 might not do much damage to a large warship, but one round could crush the *Belle*. The enemy vessel could quite literally blow the *Belle* out of the water with a single, well-aimed shot. Mounted on either side of the wheel on the bridge deck was a Maxim machine gun, but only the portside gun was manned. Nonetheless, between the forward deck gun, the Maxim machine guns, and the larger weapon aft, they stood no hope in a shootout. He dropped the binoculars to his chest and heaved a heavy sigh, noticed by Patel.

"Bad trouble, Sahib?"

"Indeed, Sergeant Major. Likely very bad. See those guns forward and aft? Perhaps even worse, she has a crew of ten or more men. We might avoid the guns, but they could simply overpower us," he responded dejectedly. Patel turned back toward the approaching enemy gunboat, saying nothing. *Blasted! To come this far and lose the battle. Maybe, just maybe, the story would hold. Then again, what about the gunfire damage still evident despite their gallant efforts to patch up the Belle. Surely some German would notice.*

As the *Belle* chugged toward the promontory, the German patrol boat raced closer. Braithwaite could now see the officer on the bridge above the main deck, scanning them with his own binoculars. Something seemed odd. Only one other sailor appeared on the bridge, most likely the helmsman—nothing unusual there. But on deck, where a three-man crew would normally man the main battery weapon, a solitary sailor stood behind the gun's breech. Another sailor stood by a Maxim gun mounted on the bridge. More significantly, Braithwaite noticed that the aft gun had no crew. There had to be at least one engineer below tending the engines, but where were the rest of the ship's company? And, where were the boarders who should already be on deck, armed, and kitted out. With this realization, Braithwaite and Patel looked at each other, expressions of surprise on both faces. What the two men did not know was that with the German manpower shortage, the entire crew save the officer in command, a quartermaster, two gunners, and an engineer had been pulled ashore to supplement the land force under *Oberstleutnant* von Lettow-Vorbeck.

Several minutes passed as the enemy craft pulled closer. But, the German did the unexpected and slowed to bare steerageway. Rather than approach closer, the helmsman turned hard to port. The boat's bow swung sharply to the left as the patrol boat glided alongside the *Belle*, but still several yards away. The officer shouted through a loud hailer.

"Identify yourself and no tricks." The intense man on the Maxim gun made it quite clear that the Germans were dead serious. He pointed his machine gun directly at Braithwaite, who instinctively raised his arms in the universal sign of surrender. "I say again, identify yourself."

"We are the *Zambezi Belle*, riverboat out of Chinde in Portuguese East Africa. My wife and I are merchants. Swiss. We are neutrals. We mean no harm."

The officer, a young fair-haired man no older than Braithwaite, looked confused. He whispered to the helmsman standing at the wheel next to him. Both men laughed, no doubt chuckling at the crazy Swiss couple foolishly plodding through the middle of a hot war zone. Braithwaite forced a smile even as a bead of sweat dripped off his brow and down his nose. Not caused by just the heat and humidity, the droplet rolled down the bridge of his nose and splattered on the wooden deck below.

Returning to his serious face, the officer again turned toward the *Belle*. "What business would you have on Lake Nyasa?" *The hook is baited.*

Braithwaite smiled again as friendly and nonconfrontational as possible. Meanwhile, the helmsman relayed orders to the sailor on the bow manning the 3-pounder, who began slinging his rifle. *This is not a good sign.* In his peripheral vision, he saw Patel's right-hand slide off the gunwale in behind his back and clasp around the handle of a knife safely tucked in his belt, a gift from a friend in a Gurkha regiment. Minstrel ever so slightly shifted her left foot under the sling of the Enfield hidden on deck beneath her and out of the German's sight. With a sharp snap of her foot, she could hoist the rifle up in a flash and be ready for action. *Well, Braithwaite, old sod, another moment of truth.*

The patrol boat slowed to bare steerageway as it approached the *Belle's* port side. Tom and Dick waved and smiled. Perhaps a friendly attitude might help. Braithwaite's right hand nervously slid down toward the holstered revolver, his thumb gently rubbing across the top of the wood grain handle. He glanced over again at Minstrel, who rocked back and forth as if a fighter taking the proper stance. Patel stood motionless, immutable, and unflappable. As always thought Braithwaite, who had come to admire the sergeant major's stoic steadiness. With a loud hailer, the German officer announced his authority.

"Prepare to be boarded and inspected. Do you understand?"

"Well, darling wife. What say we do as the gentleman requests," whispered Braithwaite only loud enough for those on the riverboat to hear.

"Dearest husband of mine, let us do."

Somehow, the gallows humor seem to fit their circumstance.

Braithwaite noticed Patel edging closer to the weapons box where the Lewis gun lay hidden. "Steady on, Sergeant Major. Steady on." The Indian grinned in acknowledgment, but still took two steps closer to the bow, his right hand still poised just above the handle of the deadly *kukri* knife. He had taken a position whereby he could throw open the box lid and retrieve weapons in a matter of seconds. Braithwaite nodded in acknowledgment.

As the boarder on the bow prepared to toss a line over to the *Belle*, Braithwaite tried again to head off what looked more and more like an unavoidable and deadly confrontation. He noticed the machine gunner looking more and more agitated. Fearing the next wrong step, he resolved to try again to reason with the officer.

"We are *Herr* Peter and Salome Zimmermann from Switzerland. We are merchants headed to Langenburg on the north end of the lake. We represent a mining consortium, perhaps you have heard of it? *Ja?* We are from Bern. With the war and all, it has been difficult, and we are looking for new sources of chromium. We understand that it might be available hereabouts."

Braithwaite edged closer to the boat's gunwales and shouted again toward the German officer. "We are neutral business people. We have no quarrel with you or the British. We are simply seeking to obtain mineral concessions for our employers."

He was quite capable of being heard from where he had stood. The move was tactical. Should the German sailor attempt to pull the two boats together to board and search, they would be better repelled as the man attempted to cross over rather than once he had a firm footing on the *Belle's* deck. Seeing and understanding the move, both Minstrel and Patel also moved closer to the gunwales. Although the tension mounted, he did his best to stay calm, resolute, and unflappable. "Might I ask who you are, Sir?"

"You may, *Herr* Zimmermann. I am *Oberleutnant* Kluge of his Imperial German Majesty's Navy. You are traveling in a war zone, *Herr* Zimmermann."

On the patrol boat, the helmsman turned and whispered to the young officer, "Swiss idiots, *Herr Oberleutnant*. I do not trust them."

The officer nodded, never taking his eyes off Braithwaite. He then turned to the helmsman and whispered an order. Immediately, steam poured from the funnel as the engine sputtered, then kicked back to life. Slowly, the patrol boat moved forward again.

"Maybe they believed it?" whispered Minstrel, with a hopeful expression on her previously stern face. It was not to be. Turning back to face Braithwaite, the officer shouted, "We are coming aboard. We will examine your papers and search your boat. Everyone move to the center of your boat and please raise your hands in the air. We will tolerate no monkey business, do you hear now. The sailor on the bow leaned over and took up what appeared to be a grappling hook. *Moment of truth.* Braithwaite's hand inched closer to the Webley again. The German officer turned to the helmsman and spoke quietly before turning back to the *Belle*. "Prepare to be boarded." With that, the gunboat's commanding officer turned toward the ladder leading down from the bridge to the main deck.

That's it, then. There are no other sailors aboard. If so, the officer would never have left the bridge. There would be other sailors in any boarding party, probably led by a petty officer, but certainly not the boat's commanding officer. Right then, we may have a chance if this little tea party goes awry. As the German officer made his way around the bridge ladder coming forward, Braithwaite shot a glance toward Patel, who reacted with a slight raise of his eyebrows. As discreetly as possible, Braithwaite looked up at the nervous machine gunner. That was the imperative—take him out first. If he reacted quickly, he could mow down everyone on the *Belle* in literally one short, sweeping burst. He had to be taken out first. Patel dropped his chin to his chest indicating he understood that the Maxim gunner was his target. Minstrel and he could gun down the two boarders, leaving only the helmsman to deal with. Likely, when the shooting started, if Patel downed the machine gunner first off, the helmsman would attempt to leap to one of the unmanned Maxims and open fire. Patel would lay down covering fire against that likelihood. That left only what engineers were below, but it would take time for them to react. If all this worked, then he planned to leap aboard the gunboat and pick off the engineers or anyone else coming up on deck as they emerged from the open hatch clearly in view just astern of the superstructure. *It is a good plan. Well, it's a plan at any rate. Praise God and pass the ammunition. At least they had a fighting chance at survival.*

Braithwaite responded as the officer reached the bow. "I am afraid, Sir, that our riverboat may not take the extra weight of you and your man. We are due for an overhaul in our next port of call and we are concerned that the very fragile hull will not support more weight. Already we have had to jettison many of our personal possessions." That part was true—they had used several sets of clothes and personal possessions in the ruse to make the unfortunate sailors on the pirated riverboat appear to be them and the boat look like the *Belle*. Apparently, it had worked as they had not seen or heard from von Donop and his troops since that night. "Could you please stay aboard your boat? We are most pleased to answer any questions." While the *Belle* had taken a few hits from the fire at Station Wilhelm and in the engagement the following night where they almost lost Minstrel to the askaris, she was a stout vessel and in no danger of capsizing. Nevertheless, keeping the German at a distance was critical.

"Please understand, *Herr* Zimmermann, we are obligated to inspect your craft. Please heave to and prepare to be boarded," he shouted.

Braithwaite could see the nervous sailor on the Maxim gun pulling back the slide and cocking the weapon, prepared for action. No need to antagonize a situation, he thought almost aloud. Turning to Tom at the helm, he nodded. The riverboatman just nodded in agreement and gingerly eased back on the throttle, but the expression of dread and fright on his face was palpable. With a slow whining sound, the riverboat's engine ratcheted down. As the boat slowed, they heard only the shoo-shoo-shoo sound of the steam engine and the swish of water around the bow. The German gunboat also slowed as it edged closer, now only a few feet away and close enough for the grappling line. The *Belle* drifted closer and closer to shore, now only a couple of hundred yards off the starboard bow. Bird calls and other jungle noises could be heard above the gentle wash of the lake around the now slow-moving riverboat.

Braithwaite heard the click of the hammer as Minstrel cocked the Webley hidden behind her back. He took in a deep breath and glanced over toward the Point OK promontory. In the few minutes since they had first spotted the Germans' smoke, they had moved ever closer and now lay only a few hundred yards away. At this point, it might have been miles. Clearly, they could not reach the promontory. The enemy was now upon them. Then, a thought struck him.

"*Herr Oberleutnant.* Might I suggest that we move over to the shelter of that promontory just there," he pointed toward Point OK and the old stone tower, "where we might find some convenient spot. And, your men might then do the search?" They cannot outrun the enemy patrol boat but perhaps they could catch them by surprise. All had their revolvers hidden, but ready and Braithwaite knew that Minstrel still had her foot under the Enfield, ready to pop it up and into action, so in a shootout, they would have the advantage of surprise. He noted that the designated boarder was armed with a Mauser rifle slung over his shoulder. That gave them the advantage. A man leaping from one deck to another lay at a distinct disadvantage—a deadly disadvantage. An opponent drawing and firing a weapon at close range had the upper hand over one desperately trying to unsling a rifle. He glanced at Minstrel. She nodded her head. *Good. She understands what I'm about.* He looked over at Patel, who leaned over the gunwale. The Indian looked directly at Braithwaite, then swiftly glanced at the sailor manning the deck mounted Maxim gun. Braithwaite understood completely. Everyone was set and just awaited his signal, which would be the quick withdrawal of his own Webley from behind his back.

The grappling hook came over and snagged the *Belle* amidships. The riverboat jolted, but no one lost their balance. The German seaman slowly drew in the line until the two ships touched hulls. "Very well, *Herr* Zimmermann. We will pull you to the promontory. Do not attempt to break free as that will go very badly for you."

Meanwhile, the sailor made the line fast to a cleat on the gunboat's deck. The two boats, now inextricably tied together in this little pirouette in a dance of deadly deception, edged closer and closer to the shore.

Crack! A shot! From behind them! A scarlet red bright spot appeared in the middle of the machine gunner's forehead. With a stunned look on his face, eyes wide open, he slumped forward over his gun; it spun around aimlessly, firing off rounds into the air.

"*Gott im Himmel!*" shouted the sailor at the helm.

Wide-eyed with mouth open in shock, the officer spun around and froze for a moment, staring at the gunner sprawled across the top of the Maxim. He turned around again and just as new orders welled up in his throat, another shot struck him in the mouth. Pieces of his skull and brains splattered the sailor standing just behind him. On the *Belle*, everyone dove to the deck and cover. Braithwaite shouted, "Rifles, now!" With one hand, he grabbed the Enfield that had been hidden on the deck below. As fast as he could, he worked the bolt chambering a round. Before he could come back up to a firing crouch, more shots rang out, clearly from behind them in the jungle under-growth. Meanwhile, Minstrel, with an amazing agility as she too dove for cover, flipped the Enfield with her left foot and caught the stock in mid-air. Patel ducked behind the weapons box, took a deep breath, raised up, and emptied his revolver at the crewman on the gunboat's bow. On the bridge, the helmsman grabbed his abdomen and pitched forward. The remaining man forward shouted and cursed as he desperately tried to unsling his Mauser and return fire. A fusillade came from the beach and the loud pop-pop-pop of a Lewis gun erupted as pieces of the boat flew about, shredding the deckhouse and bridge. Minstrel and Braithwaite now had their rifles raised and added to the chorus of gunfire as round after round tore into the German gunboat. Struck in the shoulder, then again in the throat, the helmsman let go of the ship's wheel and it veered right. On the bow, the sailor managed to raise his Mauser and get off a single shot before he too collapsed in a growing rivulet of blood. The bullet whizzed past Braithwaite's head and lodged in the *Belle's* funnel. The sailor who had been manning the engine emerged from the hatch leading below, his face ashen and ter-rified. The engineer desperately raced to the safety of the deckhouse only to pitch forward, a .303 round lodged in his heart. He sprawled across the deck in death throes.

An eerie quiet followed. No more shots. Several seconds passed. A groan came from one of the dying sailors. Then nothing. A round had struck the grappling line holding the two boats together and parted it. The line dropped into the water, releasing the *Belle*. Rudderless, the enemy gunboat drifted into the *Belle*, then veered off after scraping along the riverboat's port side. Smoke pouring from the gunboat's funnel indicated that it had taken many hits. As the smoke escaped into the hot, humid murky, African air, the patrol boat and its five now-dead crew came to a halt a few yards away and now adrift. The action had taken only a few seconds.

"My God!" whispered Minstrel through her clenched teeth as a wisp of smoke rose out of the muzzle of her now empty rifle. Silently each lay down their weapons. Only the click-click-click-click could be heard as Patel, grimacing, chambered another round in his rifle. From somewhere behind them in the thick jungle undergrowth that reached almost to the water, they heard a shout—a full-throated West Country shout. "God Save the King!"

****

Braithwaite leaped over the side and waded ashore through the cool lake water. On the sandy beach, he just sat down and propped his knees up to his chest. The adrenaline of the past several minutes had now begun to wane. He noticed his hands slightly quivering. Whether from the nervous tension now abating or the adrenaline rush that now dissipated, he could not tell. Nor did he care. He had arrived at Point OK. His crew and comrades were all safe if a bit battered from the journey. He was now in the gentle fold of some of the toughest, best fighting men on the planet. He had accomplished the mission thus far and he felt secure. It felt good. He had come to love the riverboat and the two men who sailed her. He would miss the *Belle*.

Braithwaite extended a hand. "Pankhurst. It's awfully good to see you again!"

The Royal Marine officer grinned and, clasping Braithwaite's outstretched hand, shook heartily. "Lieutenant, it appears that we arrived just in time." Braithwaite grinned. "Rather a sticky wicket." The marine scrunched his face against the Western setting sun as he gazed out at the German gunboat drifting aimlessly toward the shore. "We had better see to it." He strode off toward the sergeant major standing at the water's edge. Within minutes, the Royal Marines had rigged an explosive to the gunboat's boiler with a timed fuse. A marine tossed a line to Tom on the *Belle's* stern, who swiftly secured it to a cleat. Two marines clambered aboard the *Belle* as the engine chugged and strained to pull the new weight.

"Can the old girl handle it?" one of the marines questioned.

"Surely, Bwana. She is stout. Indeed, she is very stout," the grinning boatman laughed, happy to have survived not only the gunfight, but the perilous journey.

Pankhurst stepped up beside Braithwaite and with his hands locked behind his back in that very British military fashion and slightly rocking back and forth on the balls of his feet, he explained the plan. "You see, Braithwaite. Once the lads and your boatman drag this Hun boat farther out into the lake, they will light the fuse. It burns slowly, you see. They will then standoff while the bloody bastard blows. It will look as if the boiler overheated and exploded killing all aboard."

Braithwaite's expression remained cold and lifeless. He thought of the youthful German officer, a man his own age, simply doing his duty to Kaiser and Fatherland in a harsh war in an unforgiving outpost of the Empire. Perhaps it was just the adrenaline going away. Perhaps not. Either way, he could see in his mind's eye the fair-haired young man's look of terror as his head exploded in a cloud of bloody mist. *What was it the American General William T. Sherman said? War is hell.* "Excellent plan, Major. Then how do we explain the many bullet holes in the bodies courtesy of His Majesty's Royal Marines?"

"Ah, yes. Quite right. Haven't quite figured that one out, old boy." Pankhurst turned his sunburned, rugged face toward Braithwaite and laughed. "It's rather like the gunfight at the OK Corral, isn't it?"

"The what?" piped in Minstrel who had just joined the two men on the beach at water's edge.

"Mrs. Hallwood. Yes, well. The old American West. Wyatt Earp and his brothers and the Clanton gang. Nasty gunfight that. The OK Corral in Tombstone, Arizona—an appropriate name for the town. Well, we had best be off soon before the blighters detect our little gunfight and come calling." With that, he bowed slightly from the waist and strode over to his men assembled under a palm tree.

They gathered all their gear and piled it at the edge of the jungle. What they could not carry on their backs remained on the *Belle*. The plan was simple. They would return to Zanzibar escorted by Pankhurst's marines. Meanwhile, Tom and Dick would sail the *Belle* to the top of the lake near Karonga. There, they would set her afire and scuttle her. Perhaps it was an unnecessary precaution, but too many Germans had seen her on their passage up the lake and it had to be done to protect Tom and Dick. Going to Karonga in British Nyasaland, they would be paid for their time, effort, and double the value of the riverboat.

Several minutes later, they saw a flash followed by a sharp boom. The gunboat, consumed by the orange-red flames, drifted slowly away, carried by the current, an appropriate final funeral pyre for the five German sailors who had done their duty, but had the bad fortune to come upon the Zimmermanns—Swiss merchants dealing in chromium—and death.

Braithwaite and the others boarded the *Zanzibar Belle* one last time. Braithwaite took Tom's hand and shook, a firm and sincere handshake.

"Tom, we thank you. The British nation thanks you. You have done us a great service, Sir."

The African beamed. "It was my pleasure and honor, Bwana John. And I wish you the best of luck always. May God always smile upon you." A small droplet fell from his right eye. He wiped it away with the back of his hand, but Braithwaite nodded as he stepped over and shook Dick's hand. Minstrel reached around Tom and hugged the boatman. As she did so, she whispered something in his ear and he laughed. She never revealed what was passed between them.

****

Though darkness approached, the party had to move fast. Other

Germans or perhaps curious onlookers might have heard the explosion or the gunfire. By midnight, they had marched fifteen miles inland, backtracking the way the marines had traveled to Point OK from Bagamoyo before turning south. For several days, they tramped across German East Africa toward Portuguese East Africa and safety. Herds of elephants and zebra occasionally passed them, oblivious to their presence. To avoid detection, they bypassed all villages and any native population. As they neared Portuguese East Africa, Braithwaite's thoughts couldn't leave Station Wilhelm, the odd scientist, and the marvelous machine. How to counter it? How to destroy it? Steinweiss had carelessly let on that there were only two devices, the one destroyed at the station and the second operational set on board *Aachen*. Had he lied? Was there another set hidden at Station Wilhelm? If so, had it truly been destroyed in the subsequent blaze? How many more mariners had to perish before the Royal Navy finally cornered the ghost cruiser? How many more good men? There could be only a single answer. The cruiser had to perish. If he could somehow engineer that feat, then it mattered not how many sets had been constructed. The *Aachen* must die.

They eventually came to the Ruvuma River and followed it east to the coast at Cape del Gado. The trek of roughly five hundred miles took almost a month. When they arrived at the Cape, all appeared scraggly and rough. Braithwaite had grown a shaggy beard over the course of the trek. It would have made proud any old salt from the previous century. In those days, any sailor worthy of the title sported a stately beard. But, it was soon to have a practical purpose, a fact that no one yet realized as they sighted the Indian Ocean ahead and safety. They had not lost a single person nor had anyone become any sort of casualty. As they came within the sight of the ocean, a thought struck him. Minstrel stood just ahead of him sipping from a canteen. "I have a plan." She turned toward him and tapped the cork back into the canteen.

"A plan?"

"Yes. It's a bloody awful plan, but it's a plan nonetheless. I must get back aboard the *Aachen*."

Meanwhile, Patel had joined the couple and overheard Braithwaite. "Sahib. You may be cheating death once too often. You were able once to go aboard, but again? Much too risky to one's good health, Sahib."

Braithwaite chuckled. As always, Patel was right on the money. "Quite right, Sergeant Major. Quite right. But necessary, I fear. We must get to Zanzibar as soon as possible. And, I need to cable Captain Hall straightaway."

"Right, lads, off we go. The last leg!" shouted the Royal Marine sergeant major. "On to Cape del Gado and home, such as it is." Waiting offshore stood HMS *Spitfire*, the destroyer that had taken the marines across the dangerous water to German East Africa. Once aboard, she transited back to Zanzibar. That night, a lengthy message went out over the high-frequency airwaves. It made its way from HMS *Spitfire* to the communications station at Mombasa. From there, it was broadcast to Cairo, then to Gibraltar, then to Portsmouth, and finally on to the desk of Captain Reginald Hall, Director, Royal Naval Intelligence Division, in Room 40, Old Admiralty Building, London, the lair of the lion of British naval intelligence.

CHAPTER 13

In War, All is Deception

"All warfare is based on deception."
—Sun Tzu, *The Art of War*[1]

05 July 1915, Room 40, Old Admiralty Building, London.
"Signal from Zanzibar, Sir."

The silver-haired man in the deep red leather swivel chair did not turn around to acknowledge the Royal Navy officer standing at a loose attention on the opposite side of the broad mahogany desk. He had been staring for several minutes at the paneled wall behind his desk and more specifically at a painting of the Battle of the Nile, the 1798 event that launched Vice-Admiral Horatio, Viscount Nelson to national attention and had squashed Napoleon Bonaparte's attempt to establish a French empire in Egypt.

"You know, Millar, Lord Nelson used quite a deception at the Nile. The French thought he would sail his battle line down the seaward side, so they moved guns to that side of their ships. But the blighter sailed down the shoreward side despite the shoal and shallows risk as

---

[1] Sun Tzu, *The Art of War*, trans. Samuel B. Griffith (London: Oxford University Press, 1963), 66.

well as the seaward side and totally decimated Vice-Admiral Bruyes' squadron." "Blinker" Hall slowly turned around to face Millar. Leaning forward in his chair and folding his hands on the blotter, his usual stern countenance even more marked than usual. Millar stiffened to a more formal attention. "Signal from Minstrel and Braithwaite?"

"Indeed, Sir," responded Millar as Hall motioned for him to sit. The commander sat gingerly on one of the straight-backed antique chairs, but remained stiff and formal. The old man was in a dither with a possibility of a major fleet engagement, and informality would be inappropriate. Wireless and cable intercepts indicated the possibility of a sortie by the German High Seas Fleet into the North Sea. Although the message traffic heralded the possibility of intercepting Admiral Hugo von Pohl's battleships and battlecruisers, the valuable intelligence came to naught. The Germans never engaged Admiral Sir John Jellicoe's Grand Fleet and turned back due to inclement weather the following day. Nonetheless, Room 40 buzzed with activity and high anxiety as these enemy sorties throughout the winter and spring always did.

Hall read from the signal received by coded cable that morning. Much of the message was fairly routine until the end. It reported the highlights of the trip up the Zambezi and Shire Rivers into Lake Nyasa, the events at Station Wilhelm, the rendezvous with Pankhurst's marines, and the most intriguing description of the mysterious "machine." The message promised a fuller report on the device once Braithwaite and party reached Zanzibar. Hall chuckled softly. "Well, well, well. So the Germans have invented some magical new device. Clever folk those Huns. We must see to it that the light cruiser SMS *Aachen* can no longer take advantage of this marvelous invention. How, becomes the question, eh, Millar?"

"Quite right, Sir. I recommend that we pass this intelligence to Rear-Admiral Tudor's lads. Perhaps the Third Sea Lord's engineers can develop some counter to this device. Or perhaps, even develop our own version. At any rate, we will first need to see what Braithwaite and Minstrel can give us on the technical characteristics based on their unfortunately very brief observation of the bugger in operation."

Hall nodded in agreement. "It would be nice to actually have a copy, but if this initial report is correct, they believe the original was destroyed at the station and the only other model is aboard the cruiser. A conundrum, Millar. A deuced conundrum." The DNI leaned back in his chair as if in deep thought as to how to solve the problem. He raised his hands with his elbows propped up on the desk blotter, fingers touching as he tapped the tips together in a contemplative fashion.

"Just so, Sir. I fear we have few options other than to actually sink the ship outright."

Hall's fertile mind whirled. *There must be another way to get hold of the German's magic machine.* He picked up the message again and read the final line. As he did so, his bushy eyebrows raised higher and higher as the germ of an idea formed. He read the final sentence aloud. "Lieutenant Braithwaite indicates that he must get back aboard the ship. The machine must be captured or neutralized. Braithwaite proposes to board *Aachen* as a stranded German mariner to disable, capture, or destroy the machine. Assistance required. Please advise." Hall slowly lowered the paper and looked up at Millar. He did not even blink, a rare event. After a silence that seemed like minutes, Hall finally spoke. "Either the man is the bravest of the brave or the most foolhardy, eh what!"

"He seems rather adamant, Sir."

"Agreed. So, how do we assist young Braithwaite in his suicide?" Millar raised his eyebrows, indicating that he had not a clue. Hall nodded and leaned back in his chair. He turned again toward the Battle of the Nile painting, deep in thought, and began tapping his right foot. The tap tap tap on the hardwood floor went on for several seconds. Then it stopped. Hall slowly turned back toward Millar, a wry grin on his face. *The old boy has a plan.*

"O'Sullivan!" He called loudly to the petty officer outside the office, who leapt from his desk and raced into the director's office.

"Sir?" he asked as he snapped to a crisp attention.

"Petty Officer O'Sullivan, if you would be so good as to please set up an appointment with Sir Max Aitken. He is a director of Lloyd's of London. At his convenience, if you will, but as soon as possible."

"Aye, aye, right away, Sir." The petty officer spun on his heels and raced back out the door, barely stopping long enough to pull it shut.

"You have a plan then, Sir."

"Indeed I do, Commander Millar, Indeed I do."

Both men smiled the catbird grin. When old "Blinker" has an idea, not even icebergs or hurricanes could stand in the way, mused Millar.

****

08 July 1915. The Admiralty, London.

"Blinker" Hall sat quietly at the end of the long, highly polished table. As the briefing officer droned on and on with the daily report of sinkings and tonnage losses to the merchant fleet, Britain's lifeline to the Empire and North America, the spymaster's acute mind whirled. Yes, it was true that as DNI, his essential job was collecting intelligence through cryptoanalysis and signals breaking in support of fleet operations. It was also true that he was regarded as a most cunning and creative spymaster. He had created a network of agents around the world with the mission of intelligence gathering; they did their job extraordinarily well. But, it was also the case that His Majesty's DNI conducted numerous extracurricular activities that in more modern parlance would be called "black ops" or more specifically, special operations. The men and women of the DNI were, in essence, the forerunners of the Special Operations Executive (SOE) and MI6 of later conflicts. But in 1915, those field men and women not only gathered intelligence, but operated as covert agents under the direction of Room 40. Given this aspect of Hall's extracurricular activities, no wonder the man's mind turned over and over contemplating the dispatch from Minstrel in Zanzibar received in the previous day's traffic reiterating the proposal - *Braithwaite proposes to board Aachen as a stranded German mariner to observe, capture, or destroy the machine. Assistance required. Please advise.* The young man has gumption and courage all right thought Hall in reaction to Braithwaite's proposal. The DNI knew of the foray aboard the enemy cruiser weeks earlier disguised as a native laborer, a trick that had revealed the odd "machine" and its likely geographic origin. Now, he proposed to re-enter the tiger's mouth. A brave soul indeed.

The First Sea Lord grumbled. Heads jerked up from their day-dreaming that such monotonous briefings induced. The First Sea Lord finally spoke. "Well, gentlemen, what about this business with the *Aachen*?" No response. Finally, after a few uncomfortable seconds of silence, the briefing officer cleared his throat, picked up a paper from the corner of the table and with a perceptible sigh, began.

"Sir. It is my sad duty to report that *Aachen* has once again sortied out into the shipping lanes and done quite a bit of damage. This incident occurred in late April just after the *Tonberg* affair." He looked down at the beige paper with the list. "SS *Meridian*, Australian, refrigerator ship carrying beef for the Egyptian force, bound for Suez, lost with all hands; SS *Punjab*, Bombay registry, troop steamer carrying uniform and small arms for the Indian Army units also bound for Suez, sunk but most hands rescued; and SS *Barnaby*, British registry, tramp steamer, carrying dry goods from Perth to Cape Town, escaped, apparently when smoke on the horizon indicated the arrival of a Royal Navy destroyer. But," he paused, "apparently, the *Aachen* simply vanished. The *Barnaby*'s master reports that there is no way the enemy could have seen the smoke. HMS *Archer* approached from the steamer's starboard side and *Barnaby* barely detected the funnel smoke as she approached. *Aachen* lay at least 10,000 yards off the port side and could not have visually sighted *Archer*'s smoke, yet she simply vanished—sailed away untouched." Hall, the consummate poker player, held his tongue. No need to reveal that he now had a plan to neutralize *Aachen*'s secret. All would be revealed in his own good time and moment.

How had this happened? With the bulk of the Cape Squadron engaged in the ambush operation against *Tonberg* at Mafia Island, only *Archer* covered the southern approaches between Madagascar and the mainland. When *Aachen* discovered the fate of *Tonberg* and using the device to detect the enemy presence nearby, Captain von Augsburg laid in a southerly course to return to the Rufiji Delta. But, with a hunter's instinct for the game, rather than head for the Rufiji, he changed course to search as far south as Cape del Gado. It represented a huge gamble. With dwindling fuel stores and bunkers depleted, why burn ever more of the precious coal chasing an unknown victim? As if the gods of fate and war were with him that day, the three ships of the lightly escorted convoy approached Cape del Gado, vulnerable and unaware. They thought themselves safe since the Cape Squadron commodore knew where *Aachen* would head—Mafia Island and the promise of fresh fuel and supplies. Oh, the disaster of hubris. As it turned out, many sailors lost their lives that day. If there was a bright spot, it was only in that all three merchantmen were well down on their fuel and had been headed to the Mayotte coaling station. There would be no relief for *Aachen* this day as she had burned ever more precious fuel in the endeavor. As she raced back to the Rufiji Delta and sanctuary, von Augsburg understood his dilemma. Sitting at the table in the First Sea Lord's morning brief, so too did Captain Reginald Hall.

The First Sea Lord shifted uncomfortably in his chair. From across the table, the Second Sea Lord expressed the frustration of all, "The bugger is a bloody phantom." Nods all around.

There are moments when a genius has sudden revelations—when all becomes as clear as a beautiful cloudless summer afternoon and when an entire operation suddenly becomes crystal clear in all its parts. The great Prussian theorist of war, General Carl von Clausewitz, called it *"coup d'oeil"* or simply the flash of an eye where the military genius sees the entire picture and intellectually and instinctively knows the precise plan in all its ramifications. Such was the nature of Captain Reginald "Blinker" Hall, Britain's premier spymaster and intelligence manipulator. He said nothing yet, waiting for the right moment to spring the plan that had emerged in his fertile mind in a flash of the eye earlier in Room 40. In the moments of silence and quiet contemplation about the briefing table, with heads down in frustration about the way ahead, Hall's mind whirled with activity. He had a plan, a plan for the destruction of the phantom cruiser. He shuffled his pile of message traffic and found the object that had intrigued him. *Aachen* had transmitted several days back that she was desperately short of coal and could likely only conduct one more brief sortie. The ghost cruiser had been kept steaming by periodic attacks on colliers carrying anthracite, the high-efficiency, cleaner burning coal from Welsh mines that still powered much of His Majesty's fleet. *Aachen* had intercepted and captured several colliers rounding Africa headed for India or the Persian Gulf and the Indian Ocean coaling stations. But, she had not hunted one down lately as the Admiralty had re-routed the colliers into a wide berth well south and east of Madagascar. *Aachen* had not been able to extract any fuel from the three ships recently attacked, thanks to the timely arrival on the scene of HMS *Archer*. But the essential coaling station at Mayotte needed re-supply. This seemingly small fact opened the door wide open for Hall's scheming mind. In a microsecond, he had reckoned that if the Royal Navy laid an ambush and if Braithwaite could somehow get aboard the ship posing as a stranded German merchant sailor and then neutralize the "machine," might *Aachen* fall into that trap? What if Hall sent a message in a code known to have been broken by German Naval Intelligence to the effect that a collier convoy had been dispatched to re-supply the coaling station and was set to arrive on a specific date by a determined route? A key had to be that the convoy would have no escort protection from the time it departed Cape Town to a predesignated rendezvous point somewhere near the Rufiji Delta or Dar es Salaam, close enough for *Aachen* to reach given its limited remaining fuel. Of course, the Admiralty would never send such valuable ships through those dangerous waters unescorted. But perhaps, just perhaps, the *Aachen* so desperately needed coal, that von Augsburg would take the calculated risk that the colliers were not part of a well-planned ruse leading to an ambush. Additionally, it will let slip that two light cruisers – *St Andrews* and *Fearless* - are both unavailable with engineering casualties and are in dry dock. Sort of a sorry, old chaps, but we simply can't provide escort and you will be on your own until you reach the rendezvous with the destroyers coming down from Mombasa. That should attract von Augsburg's notice. The message would also request that the Mombasa station send destroyer escorts to rendezvous with the colliers at a point north of Madagascar. But, in an apparent momentary loss of operational security, the message also had to provide the intended track, base course, and speed of the colliers. What if the desperate captain of *Aachen* sortied to intercept the colliers well to the south of the rendezvous position only to blunder into an ambush? As the silence continued around the table, he thought further and smiled. Indeed, if the compromised message indicated the point at which the colliers would meet up with warships coming down from Mombasa as well as the point at which they would join up well to the south of that point for the transit up the west side of Madagascar, what captain of an enemy commerce raider could or would resist such an opportunity to bag several enemy merchantmen all at once? He could offload their stores and coal well before any opposing warships could interfere. It was a delicious plan. And, if Braithwaite could somehow get aboard *Aachen* and disable or destroy the machine, then the mystery cruiser might well be finally cornered. The entire plan had come together in his fertile mind within seconds and now was the time to strike. The DNI broke the despondent silence of the room that had only been interrupted for several seconds by the nervous shuffling of briefing papers.

"First Sea Lord. I have a proposal."

The briefer glanced over at Hall, seated at the far end of the huge gleaming, polished table across from to the First Sea Lord. Hall nodded his head as if to say, you're doing well, Commander. Proceed. The briefer from the Operations Division cleared his throat, stiffened his back, and carried on smartly. "Sir, there is a plan that Captain Hall has proposed to Captain Jackson and the Operations Division. We have tentatively designated it OPERATION MOUSETRAP. In essence, Sir, we will ambush *Aachen* as she heads for what she presumes is a collier convoy headed for the French station in the Comoros Islands. Once we receive word from our Zanzibar station that *Aachen* has sortied, then the ambush force will proceed to the point where the German expects to intercept the colliers."

With that, Hall sprang up and moved to an easel brought in before the brief. It had been covered with a white canvas flap. The DNI raised the cover revealing a nautical chart of the East African coast and the Western Indian Ocean. He picked up a wooden pointer and began his pitch. Everyone in the room detected his rapid eye blinks. Those who knew him well understood the implication—old "Blinker" was primed and ready for action. The room came alive with anticipation.

On the chart, he moved the pointer to a spot labeled "X." The spymaster began. "Just here is the spot that we shall say is a rendezvous point for an escort force coming down from Mombasa. In sending a message in a code that we know has been broken by the enemy intelligence chaps, *Aachen* will know two things—where the convoy will be and when, and where and when the escorts will join up. More importantly, the false message will indicate this point—call it "Y"—where the convoy will form up assuming that all the vessels are transiting from different directions. Any prudent captain would likely choose just north of that point to attack. We will ensure that it is close enough to the Rufiji anchorage that he feels safe to sortie. Also, the fact that the chap is desperately short of coal means that the closer to the Delta that we place point "Y," the more likely it is that he will take the bait. By placing point "X" much farther north, we are telling the bugger that he can expect no interference from the escorts coming down from Mombasa. He can, Sir, do his business and flee in plenty of good time."

"You are a devious lot over there in Room 40, eh what!" snorted the Second Sea Lord. Clearly, the enthusiasm in the room built as the plan unfolded.

"Indeed, Sir, that we are," beamed "Blinker." "What the bugger will not realize is that coming up from Cape Town will be a force of cruisers and destroyers, which will form a blocking position between *Aachen* and the Rufiji Delta or Dar es Salaam, whichever he chooses to flee to. Then, the attack force will assume a position just here," he again indicated a spot on the chart with the pointer, "right where *Aachen* should expect to intercept the colliers now formed into an unprotected, unescorted convoy just ripe for the picking. Meanwhile, I have coordinated with Sir Max Aitken over at Lloyd's. He has agreed to insert a false entry in the shipping report establishing a lost Argentine ship, probably due to foul weather off Madagascar. If the Germans swallow the report, it gives Lieutenant Braithwaite the cover to go back aboard *Aachen* posing as the sole survivor and as a German national and experienced seaman. With just a little bit of luck, he can disable the device at some point prior to her arrival at point "Y." Based on Minstrel's report of what they found at this Station Wilhelm, and the observed actions of the enemy, we can safely assume that this device somehow gives them advance warning of vessels in the area."

The First Sea Lord broke in, "And what if our chap Braithwaite cannot disable or destroy the device? What then, Captain?"

Hall smiled and responded. "Then, Third Sea Lord, we will hope that the *Aachen* sees either the blocking or the attack force on the device and presumes them to be the colliers. Both forces will be sailing in a loose formation as merchantmen would so as to create that illusion."

All in the room had been previously fully briefed on Braithwaite's exploits aboard *Aachen* earlier as well as the details of Station Wilhelm and the amazing "machine." The First Sea Lord smiled—the first time since the brief started. "And what of this Braithwaite chap?"

"Indeed, Sir. That is the wildcard. If he can successfully get aboard, then hopefully he can disable the device. He saw it in operation at this Station Wilhelm and then previously when aboard disguised as a native laborer. He is a resourceful young chap and we have every hope that our little magic show will give him enough of a clever story to get back aboard disguised as this stranded German merchant sailor who only wants to serve the Kaiser and the Fatherland by joining up. I suspect that the *Aachen*'s captain will welcome the additional crewman, particularly since we will plant the fake record that the chap is an experienced quartermaster and coxswain. That should appeal to the rotters."

"A bit of skullduggery and trickery. Ha! Hall, you should have gone into the theater with that bit of illusion," responded the Second Sea Lord. Hear, hear, well done, good shows came from all around the table. The deception coup had been brilliantly conceived. What might the Kaiser think had he known that a British agent was about to go on board his phantom cruiser again posing this time as a German sailor?

Hall spoke up again, "Lieutenant Braithwaite was clever and resourceful enough to make his way to Lake Nyasa and discover this mysterious device. Now, we can only hope he is clever enough to disable it before the Huns figure him out. Likely, Sirs, for this officer, this is a suicide mission." Silence about the room. After several seconds of the tomb-like silence, the Second Sea Lord spoke up. "Brave lad. Assuming that the Germans don't catch him, he is likely to go down with the ship once our chaps sink the bugger. Bad business this—so many brave lads." Mumblings of agreement came from around the room. A sudden quiet chill seemed to dampen the enthusiasm of a few moments earlier as each man contemplated the sacrifice and toll. Such is war.

Hall finally broke the gloomy silence. "There is another imperative for young Braithwaite to go aboard the *Aachen* despite the risk. While this scientist chap Steinweiss indicated that only two copies of the "machine" existed – the one destroyed in the fire and the one aboard *Aachen* - what if that is false? What if the design has already been sent to Berlin? Imagine the horror of many more enemy warships so equipped? Imagine if their submarines have such capability. Sirs, that is a horrific scenario. In short, we must have the device or the Germans must not. If Lieutenant Braithwaite can somehow purloin either the key components or the operating manual, perhaps our own scientists can replicate or at least devise a counter. As risky as it may be, we must have Braithwaite carry through his operation. At worst case, he can disable the device and make her vulnerable to our ambush. At best case, he accomplishes that task as well as escape from the ship with vital information or components that we can work with. And, there is another imperative. Apparently the device is also used to provide more accurate fire control. If Braithwaite cannot destroy or disable the device, we may well launch into the ambush with inferior gunnery compared to the enemy and suffer the consequences. No, Sirs, for this operation to succeed as we hope, Lieutenant Braithwaite must get aboard, pull off the ruse, and neutralize the device while hopefully escaping with some useful intelligence such that we can replicate the damned thing."

"Why have we not tried such an ambush before, Captain Hall?" queried the Third Sea Lord.

"Very simply, Sir, we have not had the available assets. Between the need for cruisers and destroyers in the Med for the Dardanelles operation and the requirement to hunt down the enemy submarines or at least blockade them in the North Sea, we simply could not allocate those ships to such an operation. But, Commodore Peacock now has what he requires – an overwhelming force, albeit, it must be temporary. And, if Braithwaite accomplishes his mission, we can blind the bugger just as he is sailing into harm's way and our ambush."

"Well, gentlemen. We can only hope and pray for young Braithwaite's safety and bad luck to the *Aachen*. Captain Hall, Commander, thank you for your excellent briefs. Please keep me up-to-date on the operation's proposals."

"Indeed, Sir. As current as we are able," replied Hall.

The First Sea Lord pushed his chair back and rose. The assembled staff stood in unison and with murmurs and whispers, all exited the room. Only Hall and Jackson remained standing about the table. Shaking his head and pursing his lips, Jackson grumbled, "I hope this Braithwaite knows his business. He goes in with his head already halfway in the noose."

Within an hour, the word came down from the First Sea Lord's office—"Initiate OPERATION MOUSETRAP immediately."

****

10 July 1915, Berlin.

The short, blond-haired civil servant turned toward the corner on the *Bendlerstrasse*. He walked with a natural limp, ostensibly a war wound from the Eastern Front fighting in the early months of the war. This day, he was a bureaucrat, a minor clerk in the Ministry of Marine at the German Imperial Naval office. To what few friends he had, he was simply Heinrich. Day after day, he took the same route from his cheap flat to the more elegant section of Berlin to labor away as a clerk in the records office where he maintained navy and merchant marine personnel records. Noted for being ever so precise and accurate in his recording of seamens' lives, their employment, and occasionally their deaths at sea, he often joked with his comrades that he was a victim of that "bloody-minded Prussian efficiency." It was good for a laugh at the beer garden near his flat. Thus, he toiled away in seeming obscurity, grateful for the imperial government's largess and kindness in finding him a living after his war service and wound. He rounded another corner. Up ahead lay the target.

The *Bendlerblock* was a massive office complex built just before the war to house Imperial German Navy headquarters. In the fashionable *Tiergarten* district astride the *Landwehr* canal on the *Bendlerstrasse*, this massive complex had been his work place for several months. Without a word, he went to his desk in the records office and toiled away all that fine early summer, July day. At times, he wished he had a window office rather than the plain institutional bland workspace of the minor functionaries. As lunchtime approached, his friend from the next office popped in for a chat and invitation.

"Heinrich, are you game for lunch with the lads at Heidi's?" The small beer and sandwich shop, popular among the lower staff, was tempting, but not today.

"Sorry, Dieter, not today. I am well behind on some filing and need to catch back up before you know who loses his temper again. *Danke,* all the same." The friend nodded, headed back out into the passageway, and into the raucous crowd departing the office. He sat motionless for a full ten minutes, listening for signs of anyone still plodding away at their tasks. Nothing. Slowly, he rose, limped to the doorway, and scanned the row of offices. Nothing. All quiet. He smiled broadly. As quickly as he could move, he strode over to the main records filing room where merchant mariner records were stored. The navy kept a record of all merchant seamen serving in German flag vessels as well as in foreign-owned ships. The high command wanted the ability to recall any German national with merchant service in time of crisis or war. But, since most of the German vessels in neutral ports had already been interned and their crews interned or returned to Germany, not that many sailors remained serving on foreign-flagged or German ships. Many had already been absorbed into the fleet or the supporting auxiliaries.

He went straight to the "S" drawer and gingerly pulled it open. He

thumbed through the index cards until he found the right place—
SCH. "Bloody-minded Prussian efficiency!" he muttered to himself.
Little did his work comrades, now enjoying a hearty lunch at Heidi's
place, know that their simple friend and colleague, Heinrich, was
actually one Josef Kwiatkowski, a Polish nationalist. He had been
wounded in the early months of the war, but not on the Eastern Front
and not in the Kaiser's army. Sub-Lieutenant Joseph Kwiatkowski, he
of the Polish father and Scottish mother, had been commissioned an
officer in His Majesty's Royal Navy just before the war. He did indeed
walk with the decided limp, except, it came not from the Eastern
Front action, but in the Battle of the Falklands in December 1914 in
the South Atlantic. A shell fired by one of Admiral von Spee's doomed
cruisers had shattered his gun mount on HMS *Inflexible*, wounding or
killing his entire gunnery crew. If Kwiatkowski hated the Germans for
the subjugation of the Polish people, he despised them even more as
he lay in sickbay, his left leg badly wounded by shrapnel. Once back in
London, he volunteered for duty in whatever capacity possible. Since
he spoke fluent German with a decided East Prussian accent, he had
come to the attention of Captain Hall. To his mates at the *Bendlerblock*,
he was simply Heinrich, a minor but dedicated civil servant, gratefully
and efficiently secured from the Kaiser's army. But to "Blinker," he was
simply known as Lorelei, one of the spymaster's most able, dedicated,
active, and efficient field agents.

Thumbing through the index cards, he came to his target. Several
SCHs served in the navy and in various merchant ships. *Ah, there it is.*
Schmidt, a common enough name to be sure. Reaching into his deep
jacket pocket, he pulled out an index card identical in form and style
to all the other thousands in the file cabinets. Into the appropriate
place, he gently inserted his clandestine and fake record that read:

Schmidt, Heinz Peter. Merchant seamen. Qualified coxswain.
Qualified quartermaster. German national. Home of record,
Berlin. Current employment aboard SS *Mount Pleasant*, stores
ship, Argentine registry, homeport Buenos Aires. Reported overdue, presumed lost in Eastern Indian Ocean, last reported 20 May
1915. Status unknown. Age: 25, height: 1.9 m. Distinguishing

features, scare on right thigh. Brown hair, brown eyes.

His work done, he slid the drawer shut. Smiling broadly, he limped back to his desk, leaned back in his chair, locked his arms behind his head, and chuckled softly. A good day's work. Perhaps he would join his comrades at Heidi's after all.

That evening, a coded message went out via a dead drop to another of Hall's clandestine agents in Berlin and was sent swiftly on its way to Room 40.

****

12 July 1915, Rufiji Delta.
The chief yeoman knocked on captain von Augsburg's sea cabin door and waited for the order to enter.

"Come," responded the captain, hunched over the small metal desk, pouring over the depressing morning fuel, oil, and water reports. Damn the chief engineer, thought the captain. Then again, the man was doing the best he could to preserve what little coal remained. The ship had gone to "water rationing" to reduce the need for the evaporators to produce feed water. Instead, for personal needs, the crew boiled water drawn from the river, thus reducing the need for the ship's steam for the fresh and feed water condensers. That would not do for the boilers. They required almost pure condensate water turned to contamination-free steam. Otherwise, the sludge of minerals and other contaminants would quickly foul the boiler tubes and destroy them. With no way to take down the boiler tubes for cleaning and repair, such a mundane aspect of maritime engineering would render the magnificent and deadly raider null and void. River water, if sanitized by boiling or treated, was fine for consumption, cooking, washing, and so on, and little else. No one dared to consume the river water untreated or unsterilized. Who could tell what form of bacteria and parasites dwelled in the murky, muddy waters of the Rufiji Delta.

The hazards of keeping the boilers operating at a very low level lay in the danger of the British sending warships up the river. Without enough steam already up and the engines more or less ready to answer all bells, the cruiser would be helplessly moored to the shore and unable to get underway to flee or maneuver. Coal, must have coal and soon, thought the captain as he contemplated the depressing engineering report. To conserve the fuel meant everything at this point.

"Daily intercepts, *Herr Kapitän*. Also, this week's Lloyd's of London weekly index of ship losses." Despite the remote location, *Aachen* could still receive the message traffic put out by the major maritime insurance consortium, Lloyd's of London. The weekly index told the world the status of all their ships covered by Lloyd's. Every lost ship went into the books regardless of the cause of the loss whether by accident or act of war. In 1915, the weekly index was always heavy. The captain indicated a small table by the desk. Without a word, the yeoman quickly placed the message board on the table and, clicking his heels smartly, turned and exited. The captain ignored the message board. He would read it later, he concluded. Had he bothered to read the report from the British insurers, he would have seen an entry among the ship losses that read:

S.S. *Mount Pleasant*. Overdue, presumed lost. Cause unknown. Singapore to Cape Town by way of Mombasa. Argentine registry, lost contact, 0012GMT, 20 May 1915.

There followed a list of the crew presumed lost at sea. Had the captain looked even further, one entry might well have interested him. But, the first officer had read the report and noted the entry. Why he did so, he could not say. *Aachen*'s crew had more pressing matters than to pay attention to the Lloyd's index. This random fact played large in the drama just unfolding across two continents.

Schmidt, Heinz Peter, quartermaster and coxswain, German national, aged about 25 years, no listed relations.

The great Chinese theorist of war, Sun Tzu, said, "In war, all is deception."

****

16 July 1915. Room 40, Old Admiralty Building, London.

Two knocks.

"Come." Hall laid down his pen. He had been mulling over the report to the First Sea Lord on progress in breaking a new German naval code. Laying it down, he looked up at the RNVR officer standing before the mammoth desk, a beige folder neatly tucked under his left arm. "Good morning, Commander. Any good news for me today?"

Millar smiled broadly. "I do believe so, Sir. Yes, I do believe so." He lay the beige folder marked MOST SECRET directly on the blotter in front of Hall.

"Indeed," responded the DNI. "We shall see." He opened the folder revealing a single ivory-colored form containing only a few powerful words:

MOST SECRET
Signal made 07.15.15 at 10.15 PM
Cipher J219 wave-length 400
From SMS Aachen
Naval Staff Berlin
Time-group 2352
For Operations
Sortieing Rufiji at 14.00 for Dar es Salaam. Then to intercept enemy collier convoy headed coaling station Mayotte. Anticipate intercept roughly late p.m. 07.18.15 west of Madagascar.
BT

Hall smiled broadly. "Thank the Lord that the Hun still refuses to practice wireless discipline and stay bloody quiet about his intentions." Raising his pen as he closed the folder, he scribbled his initials in the appropriate box marked DNI and handed the folder back to the patiently waiting officer. "Get this intercept over to Operations Division straightaway. Commodore Peacock will be most interested."

"I daresay, Sir, and most pleased." Millar spun on his heels and exited swiftly.

Hall walked slowly over to the window and quietly stared out at the lovely summer day. A minute later, two knocks broke the silence.

"Come." "Blinker" Hall did not move. He continued staring out the window at the field beyond. His hands clasped behind his back.

"Signal from Minstrel in Zanzibar, Sir." Hall whirled about and strode toward the yeoman who was startled by the sudden move and rocked back on his heels. The DNI could be sudden like that. The sailor stiffened to attention while simultaneously handing the clipboard bearing the message to Hall.

"Excellent." His eyes darted back and forth across the page, blinking as he went as was his norm. "O'Sullivan, ask Commander Millar to step in, please."

"Aye, aye, Sir." The yeoman did a perfect right about turn and marched out of the office. Hall returned to his chair re-reading the message as he went. He plopped the clipboard down on the desk and returned to his chair smiling. The trap is set.

Millar entered without fanfare. "Sir."

"Steven, the game is afoot."

The commander chuckled. "Sherlock Holmes, I believe."

"Quite right. 'The Hound of the Baskervilles,' I recall. Well, our hound is on the moor now so to speak. Signal from Minstrel. Braithwaite is on board *Aachen* and the German got underway from Dar es Salaam this morning. They bought the story. Now pray God they take the bait and he is able to disable that infernal machine."

"Indeed, Sir. God go with him."

Hall nodded in acknowledgment. "I'll see the First Sea Lord straight away. We'll initiate the second phase of OPERATION MOUSETRAP."

The man, who the American Ambassador to the Court of St. James described to President Woodrow Wilson that "all other Secret Service men are amateurs by comparison," leaned back in his chair. Turning toward the large window that fronted Horse Guards Parade, he stretched his hands out in front of him and chortled contently, his eyelids blinking furiously as they did in such triumphal moments. He murmured to himself, "The mouse now enters the trap."

****

16 July 1915. HMS *St Andrews*, West-Northwest of Madagascar.
"Signal from Admiralty. Initiate OPERATION MOUSETRAP. Repeat initiate OPERATION MOUSETRAP." The wireless officer handed the message board to Peacock, who without a word, signed and returned the message. He turned to the chief of staff. "Signal Captain Thatcher on *Fearless*. Well, it's time. Detach his blocking force to the predesignated position."

"Very good, Sir."

"Oh, and, add this if you will. Good hunting, Nigel." The chief of staff grinned, spun on his heels, and exited the bridge headed toward the wireless room below.

Within minutes, the HF antenna hummed with electricity as the signal went out advising the blocking group that operated off the southwestern coast of Madagascar. The two light cruisers and three destroyers of Captain Thatcher's force drawn from the Cape Squadron had been loitering in that vicinity for several days, awaiting word of *Aachen*'s departure. Northwest of Madagascar in the main attack and ambush force, Peacock had two light cruisers and four destroyers. Signal flags fluttered up the halyards. Flashing lights blinked their dots and dashes as a message went around the force. One by one, the ambush force ships hauled up their signal flags to the top of the mast to acknowledge the order and then hauled them down, executing the command to form line ahead and follow in the wake of the guide. At some point, they would disperse into a gaggle to simulate a loose merchant convoy. But for now, each ship moved smartly into station. *St Andrews* set a new course for a point west of Madagascar but near the Rufiji Delta where they hoped to meet and destroy the ghost cruiser in combat to the death. Within minutes, the ambush force had formed line ahead at 15 knots. If the ambush force didn't get her, by God, the blocking force would. On board HMS *Fearless*, Captain Thatcher ordered all ahead full. They would be in position within a few hours. The mousetrap was set. Now, the mouse must enter that trap, hopefully, blind to the danger. All rested on Braithwaite's shoulders.

CHAPTER 14

Mad Dogs and Englishmen

16 July 1915. Zanzibar.

Braithwaite turned the packet over again, opened it, and re-read it for at least the fourth time that day. He had to be certain of the details. He had to be Heinz Peter Schmidt, stranded German merchant mariner. Hall had transmitted not only the details of his false identity but also a primer on the German merchant marine. If Braithwaite was to pull off the deception, he had to be expert in procedures and terminology. Granted, he had supposedly sailed on a foreign flag vessel, but a real German sailor would have been practiced in the German maritime style. He had studied the primer over and over ever since the message arrived earlier. But he was tired, tired from not only the exhausting forced march across Portuguese East Africa but mostly from the tension and the apprehension of his uncertain future. Could he pull off the deception? Was he convincing or would the Germans see right through his act? He could not know. Enough for today. His eyes hurt. His head ached. He reached for the kerosene lamp on the table and turned it to the lowest setting—just enough to barely light the room, casting shadows about. He needed a good sleep. His eyelids slowly closed.

"Mad dogs and Englishmen."

Braithwaite started. His head jerked up. "What, what…."

"I said, Sahib, mad dogs and Englishmen. Only mad dogs and Englishmen go out in the mid-day sun."

Braithwaite wheeled about and faced the Indian, who sat in the corner hidden in the shadows and the faint glow of the lantern. The sergeant major had been cleaning a rifle.

"Becoming poetic, are we Patel?"

Patel laughed. "Indeed, Sahib. You must be truly mad to go back aboard that ship. And, you are quite the Englishman. We fooled them once. May we be so fortunate as to fool them again?"

Braithwaite leaned back, propping his back against the table. It was a good question. The briefing information was faultless. The cover story convincing. He had studied his role until his head hurt. *Could he pull off the most dangerous of deceptions? Courage man, courage. It had to be done.* The "machine" must be destroyed. The plan was dangerous. The timing critical. Somewhere between the sortie and reaching the intercept point where *Aachen* expected to find a collier convoy loaded with the precious fuel, but where in reality, a Royal Navy battle force waited in ambush, he had to disable the device. It could not be obvious lest the Germans discern the sabotage and flee back to safety. No, the timing had to be near-perfect. He had thought about simply disabling or destroying the "machine," but what if the enemy carried spare parts or God forbid, a spare device on board. If so, his sacrifice would be for naught. No, he had to disable it just when *Aachen* sailed unknowingly into the trap. She had to be sunk and all trace of the device with her. Steinweiss had let slip that only two such devices existed—the one aboard *Aachen* and the one he demonstrated at Station Wilhelm. The old boy had foolishly shown them how the machine operated and all the key components. Like a proud parent bragging about his child's accomplishments, the scientist had revealed all. And Braithwaite had absorbed all. Still, a doubt remained. Had Steinweiss lied? Did he have an extra "machine" somewhere? Surely the one at Station Wilhelm had been destroyed in the fire. No, the *Aachen* had to be sunk. If there was another "machine" on board the German cruiser, it had to go down with her as well. But, if he could get off the ship with both the device and the operating manual, that would be the crowning achievement as Hall had put it in his last message. He would certainly give it a go.

"How do you plan to survive this little excursion?" came a voice, wrought with tension and apprehension. Braithwaite had not noticed Minstrel entering the room from the kitchen carrying a tray of tea. Braithwaite grunted, "There, my dear Mrs. Hallwood, is the rub. I should not like to be a victim of my own fellows' excellent gunnery." He chuckled, but it was a nervous laugh at best. "At some point before we reach the target area, I plan to hide a life vest or ring. Once the trap is sprung, I can flee my post wherever that is. I doubt I'll be missed by the crew at that point. Then, it will be a one-man abandon ship. Hopefully, if we can sink the blighter, there will be survivors in the water and I will be rescued along with the German sailors." He smiled half-heartily. *What a bloody awful plan!*

A knock at the door. Instinctively, as they always did, Braithwaite and Patel drew their Webleys, prepared for any contingency. Minstrel, playing the role that she had so successfully for many months, answered the door. Braithwaite overheard part of the conversation, including the ever so innocent and sweet, hello, who's there as she cracked open the door. But, he heard none of the whispers that followed. Clearly, the African at the door had brought clandestine news. Minstrel gently shut the door and latched it. Slowly, she pulled the curtain edge at the window back just far enough to watch the man head back down the cobbled street and disappear around the corner. Satisfied that no one had followed him, she strode over to the table, sat, and folded her arms. She looked Braithwaite squarely in the eyes.

"*Aachen* arrives in Dar es Salaam tonight. She is in only to take on stores and sortie again before dawn. We move tonight. They have actually done us a great favor. I suspect it will be far easier for you to board her in Dar es Salaam rather than in the Delta."

They had been prepared to travel to the Rufiji by a fast boat, but that transit, fraught with danger, plus the time to get to the ship, would take days. *Aachen* had foolishly transmitted a supply request to the victualing agent in Dar es Salaam giving the date of her port visit. And, the lads and lassies of Room 40 dutifully read the cruiser's message even before the agent. Based on this intelligence, Hall transmitted the false message providing the route, course, speed, and so forth of the false convoy, easily intercepted by German Naval Intelligence and passed on to *Aachen*. Meanwhile, the two ambush forces loitered north and south of Madagascar. However, all hinged on Braithwaite getting aboard. Once Hall learned that fact, he put the operation in final motion.

Braithwaite pursed his lips and nodded in acknowledgment. "It's on then, God, help us." With that, Patel piped in, "May God be more with you, my friend."

★★★★★★★★★★★★★★★

The rain came and went later that afternoon, sometimes hard and thunderous, then a pause. Despite the wetness and stifling humidity, Braithwaite felt dry and warm. After the weeks-long trek back from the rendezvous point, the warmth and shelter of Minstrel's modest flat felt magnificent. He was finally dried out. He scratched his beard. The itching never seemed to stop. *How can anyone tolerate this?* He longed for a decent shave, but the beard had its purpose. Ever since he conceived of the plan of getting back aboard *Aachen* disguised as a marooned German merchant seaman, he realized that he needed to look the part. A scruffy beard and unkempt clothes were an essential piece of the disguise. And, anyone of the ship's crew who had seen them, either in Zanzibar or at Station Wilhelm, had noticed only a clean-shaven, well-dressed man. A shabby refugee it had to be. He scratched again at the still-growing, shaggy dark growth.

"You look magnificent!"

Startled, he jerked about. Minstrel stood in the doorway leading into the kitchen. A soft glow seemed to emanate from her, but he knew it was only the fire in the open hearth behind her. To Braithwaite though, she glowed, angelic and regal. Ever since he conceived the plan, the same thought returned constantly—he might never see her again. At this moment, that thought weighed on him almost as heavily as that of his dangerous mission.

She entered the room and sat at the table, her hands with the long, slender fingers and immaculately shaped nails reached out touching his arm. A tingle shot up his spine with her touch. "*Aachen* will dock tonight about midnight. We have to be quick about it. She never stays in port past sunrise. We'll depart just after sunset. The boat will be at the usual landing at 20.00 hours." She had spent the early afternoon arranging the usual clandestine transportation.

Braithwaite nodded. Into the jaws of death came to mind as he thought about the danger ahead. Was he up to the task? Going about before as a native had been relatively risk-free compared to this jaunty little endeavor. Was he mad? Did he have the fever when he thought up this escapade? Was he bloody suicidal? As thoughts of doubt raced about his head, one kept coming back—the sight of HMS *Halberd*, afire, and down by the bow taking many of the crew with her and then that morning counting the few survivors. A foolhardy mission? Yes. Necessary? Of course. Was he able to pull it off? Unknown. The crackling of a coal fire in the kitchen shook him back to consciousness.

****

Outfitted in the usual manner as local workmen in case anyone intercepted the boat on the transit to Dar es Salaam, Patel, Minstrel, and Braithwaite stood on the ramshackle pier as the boatman revved up the motor. It sounded solid and powerful, belying the shabby appearance of the runabout. Disguised as just an ordinary boat so as to avoid suspicion, the powerful engine could outrun any snooping patrol boat once it entered German waters. Still, disguise and anonymity were best. Patel clambered into the boat and started taking in the bowline. Braithwaite and Minstrel stood close together on the dock. She took his hand and ran her smooth, long elegant fingers across his wrist. A tingling ran up and down his chest almost as if an electric shock had hit him. He had the same feeling as that night in Rampole at the Old Edelweiss so many weeks back. With her face, gorgeous in the moonlight and auburn hair wafting in the breeze, she seemed nothing like the cold, efficient, deadly field agent that she could be when needed. Tonight, she looked the part of the angel, thought Braithwaite, as she stroked his hand softly.

"You will take care, John."

"Yes, as best I can."

"You must come back to us... to me."

They both stared into each other's eyes for a full minute, saying nothing. The boatman, with an anxious expression on his normally calm and resolute face, interjected and broke their spell. "Ma'am, Mrs. Hallwood. Please. We must go now."

Braithwaite reached for a rucksack, pulled out a revolver, checked the chamber, and slid it under his belt. He would get rid of the gun before approaching the ship, but in case they ran into trouble beforehand, it helped to be armed. He turned to Minstrel. "Well, my dear. I'm off to work."

She laughed loudly. "Will you be home in time for high tea, dearest?"

He chuckled. "Likely not. Kiss the children tonight and be a good dear."

Patel stared at them both. Only mad dogs and Englishmen go out in the midday sun. Mr. Kipling surely had it correct. These Britons are certainly an odd lot. In truth, the light banter relieved some of the tension that had only grown since they left Minstrel's flat in New Town.

Silence. Only the gently lapping waves against the boat's sides broke the silence. Without a word, he wrapped his arms firmly around her waist and pulled her toward him. She resisted for only a brief second, then moved her head toward his. They kissed, a long, gentle kiss. She placed her hand on his shoulder, her auburn hair fell down across his arm as he embraced her more tightly. Neither moved. It was only seconds, but to Braithwaite, it seemed eternal. After a few moments, he silently chuckled to himself—the moon, the gently lapping waves, swaying palm trees on a beach of sugary sand, a silvery moon, and the enemy nearby just waiting to shoot all of us as spies—what could be more romantic? And then a feeling of loss came over him. Not for his lost shipmates—that loss would be eternal. Rather, it struck him once more that this would likely be the last time he would ever be with this extraordinary woman, she of the emerald eyes. Alice Hallwood could look so feminine at times yet man a Lewis gun with ease and tromp through the jungle as if on a stroll in Hyde Park. She, who succeeded in a man's world, maintained the grace and polish expected of a lady, unflappable, imperturbable, courageous, dangerous, yet gentle. Surely, he had met no other such woman. And now, he marched off to war perhaps for the last time. He held her even closer, tighter still in the glow of the moon.

Patel coughed. "Pardon me, Sahib, Memsahib. But we had best be on our way." He gently raised his hand and pointed toward the German East African coast and Dar es Salaam. He had broken their trance. Minstrel slowly pulled back but kept her arms wrapped around his waist.

"As always, Sergeant Major Patel is correct. Time to go, I fear."

Braithwaite nodded and smiled. "The next time you're in London, do look me up. With the war and all, fine dining is a bit dicey, but I am assured that the Savoy Grill still offers the finest filet still available in town."

She smirked and flirtingly cocked her head. "Why, Lieutenant Braithwaite, I do believe that you have offered a date. Savoy Grill it is. Next time in London," she paused, "the Savoy Grill. Wear your best mess dress uniform, kind Sir."

He took a deep breath as they unlocked the embrace. "Consider it a date, Mrs. Hallwood, once this bloody war is over if not sooner."

"You had best be off then. Good luck, sailor, God Speed, John Braithwaite."

Without another word, Braithwaite stepped into the boat. He turned and waved to Minstrel as the boatman fired up the powerful engine. As the runabout headed out toward the open sea and Dar es Salaam, Braithwaite gazed back at the solitary figure standing on the dock, her hair still wafting gently in the breeze with the moonlight illuminating her face. He raised his right hand and waved back and forth slowly. She answered with a wave. Both held their hands up until she simply disappeared in the darkness of an African night.

****

Patel and Braithwaite reached Dar es Salaam before 23.00 and made their way through the darkened streets as stealthily as possible. Meanwhile, the boatman stood offshore ready to retrieve Patel, who would escort Braithwaite to the docks and observe from the shadows before heading back to the beach and safety.

Aachen sat at anchor just off the waterfront awaiting the stores' arrival. As they stood in the shadows of the warehouse next to the boat landing where laborers scuttled to and fro with crates and boxes, Braithwaite turned to Sergeant Major Amrish Patel, late of His Majesty's 2nd Bengal Lancers. He extended a hand, and the two men shook firmly. "It has been a pleasure and an honor to know and work with you, Sergeant Major."

"Indeed, Sahib. It has been this lowly noncommissioned officer that has had the pleasure and the honor. May all the gods of the universe look after and protect you from harm. Good luck."

Braithwaite could see the beginnings of a tear welling up in Patel's eyes. The older man had begun to think of Braithwaite as a son just as he had come to think of Alice Hallwood as a daughter but, like all sons, they must leave the protection of home and hearth and stand on their own. In an unusual way, this eternal scene that had been played out between fathers and sons since the beginning played out in the shadows of the shabby warehouse in the darkened streets of Dar es Salaam. Braithwaite reached into his belt, removed the Webley, and handed it to Patel. "I shan't be needing this anymore, Sergeant Major. Best of luck and do take care." Patel nodded but said nothing. With that, Braithwaite turned and strode toward the sentry post down on the dock.

"Halt," cried the nervous sentry posted near the ship's boat loading, pointing his rifle right at the scruffy man's chest. "Halt you," the petty officer standing several feet away who had been checking a manifest of goods about to be loaded, looked up. Putting his clipboard down, he strode over to the nervous young sailor, sweating not only from the torrid heat and humidity but just simple nerves.

"Wer da?" The petty officer glared at the sentry, who pointed at the strange man with the muzzle still aimed directly at his chest.

Braithwaite raised his hands high. Gently, he approached the two sailors as nonthreateningly as possible.

"*Meine Herren,* I am a German sailor." A thought struck him at that moment. *Was his German good enough? Did he really sound like a native speaker? Was he rusty after so many years?* All these thoughts raced through his mind as he approached nearer and nearer to the upraised muzzle. A gush of relief came over him as he stopped a few feet away without being shot yet.

"What is your business?" queried the petty officer.

First wicket down!

"Identify yourself."

"Sir. I am Heinz Peter Schmidt, quartermaster from the S.S. *Mount Pleasant.* We were capsized in a storm and I am the only survivor. I am German—a Berliner. I wish to join your crew. I am a skilled seaman, a coxswain and a quartermaster. I wish to serve the Fatherland."

The petty officer stared at Braithwaite for several seconds, then reached out, touched the Mauser's barrel, and slowly lowered it toward the pavement. "Well, *Herr* Schmidt. Let us see what to do about you." He turned to another young sailor and shouted orders. "You there, find the duty watch officer and ask him to come down if he will. We have a strange situation." The sailor jumped to a stiff attention. "*Jawohl,* at once." He raced down the metal ladder to the ship's boat.

****

"Heinz Peter Schmidt, quartermaster of the late S.S. *Mount Pleasant.* You say you were the only survivor?"

"*Jawohl,* Sir." Braithwaite tried to conceal his tension, yet convey just enough expected of a German refugee wanting to return to the fold. The first officer had come ashore to interview the strange newcomer once informed of the request to join the ship. With an armed guard, the first officer took Braithwaite into the harbor master's office for interrogation. They could take no chances.

"What registry?" quizzed the first officer in an inquisitorial tone.

"Argentina, Sir. Homeported in Buenos Aires. "We were carrying a cargo of tinned beef from Argentina to Persia by way of Cape of Good Hope. We ran afoul of the storm off the East African coast. I was the only one who made it ashore."

"I see, *Herr* Schmidt." Braithwaite noticed that the yeoman had taken down every detail. Good. Hopefully, the Germans in their ever constant efficiency would check for details with the Naval Staff in Berlin—details given to him by Hall and hopefully planted in German records. After several more minutes of questioning, the first officer seemed satisfied with the story, but even so, ordered the master-at-arms to take Braithwaite aboard the ship and down to the mess decks and to keep an armed sentry watching him.

As SMS *Aachen* prepared to weigh anchor just as the sun broke over the eastern horizon, a signal arrived from the Naval Staff in Berlin confirming that quartermaster Heinz Peter Schmidt, a German national, had indeed been presumed lost with the entire crew of the Argentinian freighter S.S. *Mount Pleasant* off Portuguese East Africa according to Lloyd's of London. Details that accompanied the report provided a complete description of quartermaster Schmidt taken from the file records of German seamen safely housed in the records office of the Imperial German Naval Staff at the magnificent new headquarters building on the *Bendlerstrasse* in the *Tiergarten* District of Berlin.

****

Captain von Augsburg looked up from the flimsy message paper and stared directly at Braithwaite, who stood stiff at attention. He scanned Braithwaite again and without moving his head—just his eyes up and down—and waved the paper back and forth. He leaned back in his chair and dropped the message to the desk. "Well, *Herr* Schmidt. It seems that you are genuine, though I am at a loss as to how you survived the sinking of your ship so far from land. You must be an incredibly resourceful and stout fellow. How would you like to serve your Kaiser and the Fatherland in the Imperial Navy?"

Braithwaite beamed. "It would be a pleasure and a great honor,

Herr Kapitän."

"Very well, then. We are short a quartermaster what with Kline dead from some barbarous tropical disease."

"*Herr Kapitän,* we are also down a bridge lookout with the loss," added the first officer.

"Well, *Herr* Schmidt, it seems that you have come at a fortuitous moment. We are getting underway in a few minutes, and it promises to be an auspicious cruise. We can certainly use your assistance and experience."

"I thank you, *Herr Kapitän. I* will do my best at all times."

The captain affirmed with a nod, a sign that Braithwaite—a.k.a. quartermaster Schmidt—was acceptable. He turned to the chief petty officer, who had been standing silently in the corner, ready to react should there be trouble from the newcomer. "Chief, take quartermaster Schmidt to the stores and get him situated. He is an experienced seaman. I want him on the port lookout position as soon as we get underway."

"At once, *Herr Kapitän,*" replied the ship's senior quartermaster. With the click of heels, Braithwaite and the chief quartermaster exited the captain's quarters leaving only the first officer.

"So, number one, what do you think of this?"

The first officer looked down at the deck for a moment then up at von Augsburg. "*Herr Kapitän,* I am satisfied that Schmidt is who he claims and that we can well use his skills. But as to our current sortie, I am leery. Why would the allies allow such a valuable convoy so close to us? And, why would they allow that without a proper escort. That is quite odd indeed. On the other hand, we have Steinweiss' device and should it be a trap we will know well ahead of time to retire. And, considering that our coal bunkers are so low, we will soon be inoperable. This, I believe, is worth the risk."

"I concur. Make all preparations for getting underway," responded the captain. The first officer exited quickly. The captain, exhausted from the tension and stress of dodging the Royal Navy for month after month, leaned back in his chair and closed his eyes. That stress, he noted, had made him appear far older than his actual forty years. He lifted the message paper again and read it aloud to no one but himself.

From: Imperial Naval Staff, Berlin

To: Commanding Officer, SMS Aachen

Schmidt, Heinz Peter. German national, qualified quartermaster, qualified coxswain. Berlin native. Aged about 25. Height 1.7 m. Brown hair, brown eyes, scar on upper left thigh from accident at sea. Last known employment: crew of Argentine flag freighter S.S. Mount Pleasant, homeport Buenos Aires. Lost in a storm off Portuguese East Africa. All crew presumed lost.

He sighed and let the message fall to the desk. A slight breeze through the porthole broke the stifling humid air but only for a moment. The message floated to the deck. "No matter," he muttered, "perhaps we will steal enough British coal to make it home." The ship badly needed repairs and dry docking after months and months in the wet, hot climate. There was no recent battle damage thanks to the device, but the ship was simply worn out from service. *Yes, perhaps, they could finally make it home and rejoin the High Seas Fleet where she really belonged.* He heard a rumbling as the two-shaft reciprocating (VTE) engines came to life below. But, he heard nothing else. Exhausted and careworn, *Fregattenkapitän* Helmuth von Augsburg nodded off in his chair, lost in the knowledge that the first officer and the experienced crew had all well in hand.

✸✸✸✸✸✸✸✸✸✸✸✸✸✸✸✸✸✸✸

Salt spray washed across the deck as Braithwaite slowly made his way up to the bridge. The overland trek had undercut his sea legs, but he would get them back soon. The worst problem was a queasiness he always felt just as a ship got underway. But, being up on deck, with the horizon in view cured that. He never really got seasick, even in the roughest weather.

"Quartermaster Schmidt reporting for lookout duty."

The officer of the watch pointed to the boatswain's mate who grunted, shoved a pair of heavy binoculars into his hands, and pointed to the port bridge wing. Braithwaite acknowledged without a word. He took his station just aft of the doorway leading into the pilothouse, more so that he could look into the chart house at the rear of the pilothouse. Through the salt-encrusted porthole, he spied the device, an exact replica of the one he had seen at Station Wilhelm. As slowly and covertly as possible, he visually traced the wires and cables leading out from the device. One was clearly the power cable that went down to the deck. Another led out of the chart house and up the mainmast to the odd bedspring. From Steinweiss' demonstration, he knew that to be the transmitting and receiving antenna. It rotated slowly, just as had the model that Steinweiss had so gleefully demonstrated. Another cable led to what appeared to be a glass panel, green, but with pale yellowish-white images that danced about. He put the binoculars to his eyes as if scanning the horizon for contacts, but in reality, he observed the shoreline falling away in the distance. There were several small vessels, coastal dhows, and fishing boats, all making for port with their trade goods or morning catch. He covertly glanced back at the glass panel. Very clearly he saw blips on the screen that corresponded to the relative position of the small craft. And, he could make out the outline of the coastline. A sailor sat in front of the glass screen, watching intently all of the blips' movement.

Well, then, no go there. He would have to overpower the sailor manning the screen and likely the navigator. Then there was another quartermaster hovering over the chart table tracing the ship's course, speed, and track as well as recording all rudder and engine orders in the ship's log. *No, no go there. So what is the critical vulnerability? Aim high! That's it—the cable to the antenna.* That clearly was the critical transmission and receive part of the "machine." If he could covertly disable or cut that, then perhaps the crew would assume a gear casualty. But timing had to be just right. He had to disable the device just before they reached the ambush point or at least once there was smoke sighted on the horizon. The device would likely detect the assault force, but expecting a collier convoy, they would assume the blips to be those ships, not a waiting Royal Navy force. A message from Hall received just before they departed for the boat to Dar es Salaam gave the expected or most likely intercept point given the position of points "X" and "Y," but he knew it could never be exact. While *Aachen* might realize that the contacts were warships in time to go to full speed and flee south, with the device disabled, they would not detect the waiting ambush force until too late to escape the trap. The enemy cruiser would be caught in a vice between two potent battle forces. Timing was everything. He drew in a deep breath of salty air.

****

The first watch went without incident. He had spent his time wisely. While seemingly scanning the horizon for contacts as an alert lookout would, he used his peripheral vision to scout out every aspect of the enemy cruiser. From his earlier foray aboard as a native laborer, he knew the rough layout already, but if he was to make any kind of escape in the chaos of the expected battle—assuming he didn't get blasted to pieces first—he would need better situational awareness. By the end of the first four-hour watch, he had a reasonably good idea of the ship's exterior. That left three tasks for the four-hour off time. He would scout out the interior, stow some key survival items that could be retrieved easily, and, most importantly, chat up the sailor manning the "machine" in the chart house. Once relieved, as nonchalantly and unobtrusively as possible, he wandered through the pilothouse and into the chart house. He smiled and silently chuckled. After all, this was the scene of the great heist, an event that set in motion the current escapade and now seemed so distant in the past. He edged over to where the next watchstander stood being briefed by the off going watch on the tactical picture as provided by the device. Nothing appeared on the green glass plate—they were alone on the open sea.

"You there!" The shout startled him. *Fright or flight.* He almost raced back out of the chart house onto the bridge. But, he caught himself and recovered quickly. "*Ja?* Me?"

"*Ja*, you, you, dunderhead! You have been relieved of the watch. Now get out of here and go below. You are a lookout only. You have no business in here, do you understand?"

As sheepishly as he could muster, he lowered his head and responded, "*Jawohl, Herr Bootsman* (boatswain's mate)." He had seen enough. The device was bolted down to the chart table but not as securely as it should have been. He surmised that the Germans ran low on basic repair and maintenance items such as heavy metal bolts. A swift blow from a hammer or other heavy tool would easily break the fragile bolts. A swift chop of a fire axe would sever the cables joining the device to the power source or the antenna. He had two tasks. First, he must disable the cable leading to the antenna, which would blind the ship to the approaching danger. That had to be timed just as the Royal Navy pursuers closed in. Second, if he could, he had to break the device free and make off with it. If not, he might at least locate an operations manual and pirate that document. The science lads at home could make of it what they would. If he couldn't steal it, at least the gear would go down with the ship. As he swiftly exited the chart house under the glaring stare of the irate boatswain's mate, he knew that he had seen enough. *The game is afoot.*

****

He scouted out the ship's interior as best he could. Most sailors slept, played cards, or otherwise amused themselves when off watch, but he made certain to avoid contact. The last thing he needed was to make a verbal slip and give away the deception. Yes, his Berlin accent was damned good, thanks to his being in Germany in his early years, but he had to be cautious. The sailor who manned the device, on the other hand, was a target of opportunity. As he approached the messing area—really just an open space with a few wooden tables and chairs where the sailors could take their rations—he spotted the sailor, who he had overheard being called Mühlhauser. *Tally Ho, the Fox!* "Mühlhauser."

The sailor turned toward the shout of his name somewhat startled, then recovered quickly. "Ah, the new man. Schmidt is it?"

"*Ja.* And I am totally lost. My freighter was laid out much differently from this fine weapon of war." They both chuckled. *Hook in the water.* "Where can I get some rations? Very hungry now," he smiled as he rubbed his stomach so as to make the point. In truth, he was especially hungry having not eaten since the night before at Minstrel's flat.

"This way, my new friend, this way."

Mühlhauser led Braithwaite down the starboard passageway to the galley. Smells of bread, freshly baked filled the air. What most of the sailors queued up outside the galley did not know was that these were the last loaves to be baked. *Aachen* had literally run out of stores and there was little to be had in Dar es Salaam. Fresh fruits and vegetables were in abundance in the city, but not wheat, flour, or meats that normally came from Germany. The captain had ordered the last of the bread baked and the final sausage tins opened and served. There would be no more supplies from Germany. A hearty meal for the hunter the captain had said as they sortied out to find the colliers.

He followed Mühlhauser back to the messing area and sat down to enjoy the feast as well as suck out as much information as possible from the friendly sailor. If he survived and if he could not heist the device, at least between what he had seen and learned at Station Wilhelm, from the overly talkative Mühlhauser, and from observation, he might describe the thing to those that could either replicate or counter it. Black bread with jam, a knockwurst with hot mustard, and strong coffee eased his growling gut. The mess ended, Mühlhauser excused himself. Their next watch came in another three hours and the German was intent on some much-needed sleep. No rest for Braithwaite. He had things, serious things, to do first.

****

17 July 1915. West of Madagascar.
19.00. Braithwaite raised his binoculars to his eyes and slowly scanned the horizon. *Fine German optics. We should be so fortunate.* He had no intention of spotting anything that might be a target or a hunter. How he might assume blindness if others saw distant contacts he had not figured out yet. A small drop of moisture welled up on his forehead. It rolled down the bridge of his nose and dropped to the metal deck

below. In this climate, all sweated profusely. The threat of impending combat made everyone all the more tense, especially for the Royal Navy man deep in enemy territory. He tried not to worry about the coming action. But constant thoughts raced about his mind. Would he be killed by his own side? Could he pull off this deception? He thought of Minstrel and a gentle feeling welled up inside his sweat-soaked chest. He could not explain the peculiar feeling. He had never before in his young life had such feelings. So it went. Overhead, he heard the continuous creak of the antenna on the mast, rotating in a rhythmical arc every few seconds almost as gentle and soothing as the waves gently rolling on the beach at night. If he made it back to Blighty, he would go back to his favorite spot on the beach at Dover where the famous white chalk cliffs met the English Channel, where he often went to be alone, contemplative, and thoughtful.

"Schmidt, keep a sharp watch there. It does us no good if the bastard British catch us with our jumpers down. Understand?"

He wheeled about on his heels. "*Jawohl, Herr Bootsmann.* I understand." He turned in a most unmilitary manner. He had to maintain the deception that while he was a trained, experienced mariner, he was not a navy man and therefore, the imperative lay in not revealing that he could, in fact, not only render a smart salute, but could do a right about wheel exceptionally well. In war, all is deception.

"See that you do," the surly boatswain's mate shouted from the pilothouse.

"I understand completely," he muttered to himself. The gentle grind of the antenna above reminded him again—the mission, the mission, the mission.

20.00—watch relief. He ambled below decks where other weary, sleepy watchstanders rolled into their hammocks, grateful for a few hours rest before the combat to come in the morning and hopeful for another day's harvest of sunken enemy ships. In the captain's sea cabin just below the bridge, the captain, first officer, and chief engineer fretted over the bunker report—only a few more tons of coal remained. They must capture at least one enemy collier. Their existence depended upon it. Finally, the captain stood and raised his glass of schnapps from one of the few bottles left in the stores brought aboard a long time ago. "Gentlemen. To a successful day's hunt!" Glasses clinked. "Now get some rest. First light will bring great fortune to us and the Fatherland."

Braithwaite knew that he needed sleep, but couldn't. Too tense to rest, he re-checked his escape route and his gear safely hidden in a little-used fan room on the second deck below. All there. All secure. Hopefully, once the action commenced, he could break away from his battle station as if in a panic and leap overboard before the ship sank and swallowed him under the water. Finally, alone in a quiet corner out of sight, he finally nodded off into a fitful sleep to await the dawn.

18 July 1915. Southwest of Madagascar.
05.00. Alert now and ready, he crept past the mess decks and retrieved the fire axe he had pilfered earlier from a damage control locker and had hidden in the fan room. As gently and quickly as he could, he crept on cats' paws toward the bridge. In the east, a faint glow signaled the coming dawn. Time to strike. He slid past the pilothouse unseen and pushed himself into a small niche between the mast and the chart house bulkhead where the cable exited and ran up to the antenna. He wore rubber gloves. An electric shock would not do at this stage as he severed the cable. From inside the chart house, he heard through an open portal what he wanted to hear. The captain had entered the chart house along with the first officer and navigator.

"*Jawohl, Herr Kapitän,* We are here. If our intelligence is correct, the colliers should be passing us at less than 20,000 meters very soon."

"Indeed. Let's hope the British sailors are as prompt as we are." Laughter erupted. Braithwaite smiled. Bloody Huns, he thought silently. Let's do hope that.

05.30. Time to strike. Hopefully, the Royal Navy warships were just out of range of that device. *Now, old sport. For King and country!* He raised the axe high above his head and like the headsmen executioners of old, brought down the heavy, sharp axe onto the neck of the evil device's cable. One whack did it as sparks flew about the deck. He stood, frozen in place staring in wonderment, but only for a moment.

Turning quickly, he bolted down the nearest ladder to the main deck below and strode aft away from the scene of the crime. Pausing only to pitch the axe and the gloves over the side, he ducked into the nearest doorway and continued aft toward the mess decks.

"*Herr Kapitän, Herr Kapitän!* The device. It has lost power."

"What!" shouted von Augsburg as he raced back into the chart house. "What!"

"I do not know what has happened, Sir. The display suddenly went dark." Both men huddled over the now darkened glass display as one would over a sick child. Outside, the antenna slowly wound down with a wrenching of gears squealing in the half-light of dawn. The quartermaster raced out and around the mast. His eyes grew wide and he tried to shout, but no words came up from his throat. He reached out and grabbed the cable, loose and dangling about the deck. A clean-cut had severed the cable. *No accident here.* "*Herr Kapitän.* Sabotage! We have been sabotaged." Heavy shoes clanked on the deck as sailors and officers crowded about the dead cable. Captain von Augsburg, with a clenched jaw, glared at the destroyed cable, then whirled about facing the navigator. Calmly and stately, he lowered his head in an almost pensive motion. "Hans, where are we relative to the target?" Calmly to the panicking navigator, he repeated, "I say again, Hans. Where are we relative to the targets' likely track?"

The navigator gulped hard and wiped his brow with a shaky hand. "*Herr Kapitän*, we are dead in the track and should see the colliers within the next few minutes assuming they have maintained their intended course and speed."

The captain placed a firm hand on the young officer's shoulder. "Then, Hans, let us bring the ship to battle stations. Please inform the officer of the watch."

"*Jawohl, Herr Kapitän.*"

Fregattenkapitän von Augsburg clasped both hands behind his back. The first officer stood beside him, having said nothing yet. "Well, Friedrich, it looks to be a glorious day. *Ja,* a glorious day for a fight."

"Indeed, Sir." The sun just cresting over the horizon threw a warm glow across their faces. "A glorious day for a fight."

Metal doors and hatches clanked as the crew raced to their battle stations. In the seeming chaos of the ship readying for action, Braithwaite easily hid from observation. Seeing a clump of sailors headed forward no doubt to man the forward 4.1-inch guns, he melted in as just one inconspicuous sailor among the gaggle. As they peeled off toward their various stations, he ducked under a ladder. Once all had passed, he bounded up the ladder two steps at a time toward the bridge and chart house level. Since he had no official battle station as of now, manning the bridge area seemed like a likely location. With the flurry of activity on the bridge, no one noticed him as he ducked into the chart house. With the navigator and chief quartermaster on the bridge, only the "machine's" operator sat immobile in the chart house staring at the now-darkened glass screen.

"Schmidt. Oh, you. What you doing here?" he queried, spinning around in his swivel chair.

"*Ja*, I don't have a battle station, I...."

"So you came to help me, eh?"

Braithwaite nodded yes.

"Well, then, stow away those charts there. In action, they tend to fly all over—a damned mess, I say." With that, he swiveled about and stared again into the dark, dead glass device.

"Smoke! On the horizon! Many ships!" came a cry from the starboard lookout. Simultaneously, a tinny voice erupted from the brass speaking tube from the lookout in the foretop above. "*Herr Kapitän.* Many smokes on the horizon. I count at least six. It must be the enemy colliers. Bearing 020. Range unknown."

In the chart house, Braithwaite smiled discreetly. Under his breath, he muttered, "The time has come the walrus said, to talk of many things, of shoes and ships and sealing wax, of cabbages and kings."

****

Peacock lowered his binoculars. "Marlton, do you concur?" The officer at his side, now commanding officer of Peacock's old ship, HMS *St Andrews,* lowered his glasses as well.

"Yes, Sir. I do. I spot a single smoke bearing 200 degrees. Range closing. He doesn't appear to be evading as he usually does, Sir."

Peacock grinned. "Then we have the bugger this time. Well done, Mr. Braithwaite. Well done."

From the lookout in the foretop came the word, "Many contacts bearing 210 degrees but further south." The fox was trapped. Hounds to the north. Hounds to the south. There would be no escape for SMS *Aachen* this day.

"Very good. Signals!"

"Signals, aye," came a shout from the signal bridge.

"Signal to all ships. Set action stations. Assume special attack formation."

"Signals, aye." There followed a fluttering of signal flags up and down the halyards. Signal lights blinked on and off around the squadron as ships picked up speed, charging into the attack formation.

★★★★★★★★★★★★★★★★

"*Herr Kapitän.* They are warships! And more to the south! Enemy ships—north and south of us!" A trap, *Herr Kapitän.* It's an ambush."

The first rounds landed short. Another barrage flew over *Aachen* and hit the water on the far side. A third salvo crept even closer. Another salvo landed forward of the pilothouse as yet another one straddled the forecastle. Wounded badly, the helmsman collapsed over the ship's wheel, which spun out of control. *Aachen* lurched to port. The first officer shoved the now dead helmsman aside, grabbed the spinning wheel and yanked it back to starboard. Another round crashed into the deck below, shooting hot metal splinters up and out, taking out a starboard 4.1-inch gun crew. An explosion aft rocked the ship as she lurched again to port. Casualties mounted about the German ship. Cries of wounded men and shouts of petty officers mixed with the acrid smell of cordite filled the air as smoke drifted into the bridge and chart house.

Now! Strike! Most sorry, shipmate. He raised the brass dogging wrench high above his head and struck the sailor just as the man, now slack-jawed with fright, spun back around in his swivel chair. The blow struck him in the temple—not enough to kill, but certainly to stun. He slumped to the deck. As rapidly as he could, Braithwaite loosened the bolts holding down the machine. *No time to ponder. Just get the damn thing and get out.* One bolt didn't budge. Panic started to well up, but only for a few seconds. Another boom and crackle as the mast, hit by a 6-inch round, crashed down on top of the flying bridge above. The ship heeled to port, now totally out of control. Braithwaite grabbed the dogging wrench and furiously beat on the last bolt holding down the machine. Finally, with a loud thunk sound, it gave way. With a spanner, he spun it until it came completely free. *Done!* Pulling chart table drawers open, he searched for the operations manual. *Nothing here! Blast it! Can't be helped. Must be off, old sod.*

Looking around, he spotted a canvas bag under the chart table. Grabbing it, he stuffed the machine into the bag and, like Father Christmas, slung it over his shoulder.

"*Herr Kapitän.* We have lost all power. Main engine room is flooding rapidly. We can't keep up steam," shouted the chief engineer through the voice tube amid all the chaos and clamor.

"We have lost all steerageway," shouted the first officer still desperately manning the ship's helm. As calm as any man could be, von Augsburg responded to the chief engineer, "Very well, you have done your duty. Evacuate the engineering rooms." Just as the last word came out, there came a screech like that of a diving hawk followed by a crash and boom—a direct hit on the pilothouse. The blast decapitated the first officer. He took the full blast of shrapnel and collapsed into a bloody heap. Just at that moment, von Donop charged into the pilothouse. Shielded by the now dead first officer, he staggered backward striking the helm and falling to the deck, wounded. In the chart house, shielded by a steel bulkhead, Braithwaite was shoved back into the chart table, but unhurt. Recovering his senses after being momentarily stunned, he yelled, "Time to go, old sod!" He grabbed the canvas bag and as best he could, staggered back onto the bridge and stopped, staring in stunned amazement. The ship's captain stood staring directly ahead seemingly oblivious to the carnage about him. Brown and black splotches marred his otherwise pristine white tropical dress uniform. Braithwaite looked down at the deck and saw a trickle of blood emerging from the captain's trouser cuff and dribbling across the deck plates. Captain von Augsburg lifted the binoculars to his eyes and calmly scanned the horizon as if nothing was there. Speaking to the now dead first officer, he calmly asked, "First officer, how is the crew? I don't think we have any casualties yet but please make sure that any men who are hurt are well taken care of. I shouldn't want to have anyone hurt."

With those words, *Fregattenkapitän* Helmuth von Augsburg collapsed to the deck. A bright red patch formed on the chest of his white dress uniform, but his eyes remained open. He struggled as if he meant to give orders to the helm. Braithwaite leapt over the body of the dead helmsman and knelt down beside the captain. He placed a hand on the man's forehead as blood poured out of the captain's mouth. A tear welled up in Braithwaite's left eye. He had seen this before. Yes, this man was an enemy, but he was a noble adversary. Even as he fought for his own country, this excellent officer had waged war against all odds for his country. He did his duty as all military men must do theirs. Funny what thoughts one has in the midst of tragedy and death.

A gurgle welled up from von Augsburg's throat. He looked into Braithwaite's eyes struggling to speak. A cough. Finally, he was able to mouth a few simple words, "Are the men all right? Are the men all right?" With that, the captain's eyes went glassy.

Braithwaite could only stare down at the dying officer for several seconds cradling his head under his forearm. "*Jawohl, Herr Kapitän.* Everyone is all right." Another boom from astern reminded Braithwaite of the danger. He gently lowered the captain's head to the deck and with two fingers of his right hand gently closed the man's eyelids. He stood. Braithwaite turned to race out of the pilothouse almost tripping over another officer sprawled over the deck on his hands and knees, but struggling to rise. He looked up. The man's ice-blue, cold eyes bored into Braithwaite like a pair of ice picks. For a moment, there was no recognition. Then like a waterfall cascade, the memories all came back into stark view—Station Wilhelm. "You! You!" shouted the now enraged officer. A bloody hand reached out, just short of grasping Braithwaite's ankles. "You!"

Momentarily stunned, Braithwaite could not move, but then, he regained composure. Glancing at the doorway leading out to the bridge wing, he glared down at the prostrate von Donop. "Sorry, old chap. Afraid, I can't stay for tea." With that, he raced out of the pilot house. Clutching the canvas bag, he leapt over the side into the churning water below. SMS *Aachen*—a deep rumbling noise welling up from the bilges below—began her death roll to port as sailors leapt overboard. Braithwaite kicked and scratched to gain the surface. *No good.* The heavy bag with the "machine" weighed him down like a diver's weights. For a few seconds, he thought of letting go of his precious booty. Then, from above on the surface appeared a large piece of floating flotsam just within reach. Desperately, he kicked as hard as possible—just enough to reach out and grab the floating object. He pulled hard and his head broke the surface. Kicking again, he managed to hoist the bag onto the object, which turned out to be a large piece of a wooden ship's boat. Bereft of the heavy bag, he shot to the surface and clambered aboard the shattered boat. Holding tight, he kicked as hard as ever to get as far away such that the sinking cruiser would not pull him down. Several yards away and drifting in a safe direction, *Aachen* turned completely sideways, her props and rudder completely out of the water. Braithwaite slumped his head against the floating remains of a ship's boat, never before as exhausted as now. *Now, wait for my lads to rescue me.*

Something grabbed his ankle. Stunned, he kicked hard, but to no good. Then a blonde head and glaring, blue eyes popped out of the water. *Von Donop! How the bloody...!* Too late, the German now had him by the waist, breaking his grip on the boat and pulling them both under. Thrashing about to recover leverage, he lashed out with both fists, catching the enemy officer square in the face. But with seawater in the way, his blows barely grazed the man. For the next several seconds, both men spun about, each vainly attempting to pull the other down. Crashing back into the shattered boat, it tipped and the bag tumbled over into the water. Both men desperately clutched for the bag. No good. Down it went.

Then, as suddenly as it began, von Donop's attack faltered. His limp body fell away and started to sink. As all men of the sea know, you never let a man go into the deep, enemy or not. Braithwaite reached out, desperately clutching for von Donop, who drifted slowly away. But the man was just beyond his reach and sinking. Braithwaite's last view was of the eyes, still wide open, staring in rage at him in a death spiral.

Slowly, with as much strength as he could muster, Lieutenant John D. F. Braithwaite, RN, hoisted himself up onto the shattered ship's boat. His last conscious thought before he passed out from exhaustion was the deadly enemy cruiser, SMS *Aachen*, stern high in the air as she plummeted down beneath the waves. Then darkness.

In the distance, HMS *St Andrews* charged towards him with rescue nets draped over the side, bearing down fast toward the German sailors struggling to stay afloat. They were the lucky ones. Their war had ended. On the flying bridge, Commodore Peacock said nothing. Rather, he reached into the pocket of his greatcoat and pulled out a fine Cuban cigar and a beaten silver lighter presented to him years ago by the men he first commanded as a sub-lieutenant. Clicking the lid open, he rolled his thumb across the wheel. Despite a stiff wind, a flame shot out, lighting the cigar's tip. He whispered, "A very good day for a hunt."

CHAPTER 15

Dover Beach

And we are here as on a darkling plain, Swept with confused alarms
of struggle and flight, Where ignorant armies clash by night.
—MATTHEW ARNOLD, *Dover Beach,* 1867.

24 August 1915. Room 40. Old Admiralty Building. London.
"Lieutenant Braithwaite, Captain Hall will see you now. Please follow
me." The polite petty officer gingerly opened the door to the inner
sanctum of the old man and heart of Naval Intelligence Division.
Snapping to attention, he announced, "Sir, Lieutenant Braithwaite."
He then stood aside as Braithwaite stepped through the doorway and
came to an equally stiff attention.

Reginald Hall never looked up, rather, he simply waved his hand
in a come on in fashion. Braithwaite took a seat across from the broad
desk.

"Thank you, O'Sullivan."

The petty officer quietly exited, closing the heavy door behind
him. Hall continued reading without looking up or acknowledging
Braithwaite, who noticed the trademark eye blinking of Reginald
"Blinker" Hall. The silence, however, was not uncomfortable or threatening. Only the turning of pages broke the room's stillness. Finally,

after several minutes, Hall closed the folder, looked up at Braithwaite and grinned.

"An outstanding piece of fieldwork, Lieutenant. Truly exceptional."

Braithwaite nodded slightly in acknowledgment. "Thank you, Sir." He mustered all the energy he could through the exhaustion of the past several weeks, which even the voyage back to Britain failed to alleviate. He had been pulled out of the water by the destroyer *Archer*, unconscious, but alive and unhurt. The destroyer detached that evening carrying German survivors back to Mombasa where they became prisoners of war. After a port call and the off-loading of German sailors and marines, *Archer* sailed back to Portsmouth for a much-needed overhaul and had arrived only the day earlier. Braithwaite received the message from Lieutenant-Commander Millar to report to Hall immediately upon his arrival. The officers of *Archer* had gathered as much uniform clothing as would fit him. Nevertheless, as he took a fast train from Portsmouth up to London, he looked the part of the bedraggled and worn out old man of the sea.

Hall gazed at the man before him who looked pale, drawn, and clearly in need of a long rest. He would ensure that Braithwaite got an extended leave. The DNI leaned back in his chair and placed both hands on the arms in almost regal throne-like fashion. Neither spoke for several seconds. "I have read Commander Millar's report as well as that of Mrs. Hallwood in Zanzibar. Most impressive work I might say." Braithwaite dipped his head in acknowledgment, too weary for more. Hall raised his eyebrows and nodded in an affirmative. "Braithwaite, you have an impressive talent. I might also add that you have been recommended for promotion and a decoration. I realize that some little trinket doesn't equal what you endured out there. That is the cruelty of war, you understand. But, all things as they are, it's the best His Majesty's Navy can offer and well-deserved, I might add."

"Yes, Sir. I do appreciate that." The mention of a medal reminded him of the DSC he had been awarded for his actions in taking command of *Halberd* and saving as many of the crew as he did. Indeed, the First Sea Lord had been amazed that any of the crew survived that cruel night the previous November. In truth, Braithwaite had little memory of that night or his actions from the time they abandoned ship to waking up the next morning aboard the trawler *Linda Ann*. At first, he declined the award. A visit from a previous commanding officer changed his mind. The former commander and mentor reminded him that he must accept the medal not for himself, but on behalf of every member of the crew, alive and dead, who charged into the battle to save the colliers against enormous odds and the almost certainty of death. Lieutenant-Commander Urquhart received the Victoria Cross posthumously, a fitting tribute to that courageous officer. Even so, as Hall announced the promotion and decoration, Braithwaite could only lower his head as he acknowledged the recognition. The mention of *Halberd* shot through his mind. In the flash of an eye, he saw the image of the dying ship and that of his captain lying prostrate at his feet on the open flying bridge. These thoughts, he knew, would never leave his consciousness. "Thank you, Sir." He finally mustered the strength to respond.

Hall leaned forward in his chair with elbows flat on the desk blotter and his hands clasped together almost as in prayer. "Lieutenant, I have a proposition. I would like for you to come to NID to work directly for me on special projects. Mind you, this is not a desk assignment. I have rather extraordinary men and women already on those tasks. No, I would like you for, shall I say, special field duties. You may be aware already that the mission of this division is strictly signals intercept, analysis, decryption, and the like."

"Yes, Sir, I am aware of that role," he chuckled to himself. Everyone knew that NID and Hall's activities far exceeded their advertised mission and role.

"Indeed." Hall smiled faintly, barely imperceptibly, but ever so slightly. The old fox. Just who is he fooling, Braithwaite thought to himself. Hall leaned back again in his chair and grinned broadly. "You may also be aware that I tend to somewhat exceed that assigned duty if, in my estimation, the need exists." Hall's extracurricular activities were well-known throughout the Admiralty or as a later historian would describe him as: "enmeshed in counterintelligence" and, "a devious runner of agents and spies." After all, had not Braithwaite's mission to Africa been something of that nature?

"I realize that it is a lot to ask of a seagoing officer, but do consider a posting with Naval Intelligence Division for our very special little activities. A talent for fieldwork like yours should not be wasted. Do consider the offer very seriously." The old fox's eyelids blinked rapidly in rhythm. Braithwaite looked down at the elegant, antique carpet, then up at the grinning spymaster, then back at the carpet.

"Yes, Sir. I shall give it my utmost consideration."

"Excellent then!" shouted the head of NID. "Excellent. Please take your careful time about it. I have arranged for thirty days of leave for you to recuperate from your African adventure. O'Sullivan has your papers. I'll expect to see you back in a month full of vim and vigor and ready to get underway—whichever way that might be." Hall stood and extended his right hand toward Braithwaite, the four gold rings on his uniform sleeve glinting in the late afternoon sunlight.

Braithwaite stood smartly to attention and grasped Hall's extended handshake crisply. "Thank you, Captain. I shall set my mind to a decision straightaway."

After three solid shakes, Hall responded. "Indeed you shall. Indeed you shall. Take care Lieutenant Braithwaite."

"Thank you, Sir, I shall." With that, he turned slowly and shuffled toward the door, his physical and mental exhaustion clearly evident. Just as he extended a hand toward the doorknob, the director of NID spoke again, almost fatherly in tone.

"Do you know what Antimony is?"

Braithwaite spun around, somewhat befuddled. *Antimony?* He paused for a moment, not quite sure how to respond. Tentatively, he began to speak, not really certain what Hall meant. "I believe it is an element mixed with iron to make it stronger and more resilient, if my school days chemistry still serves me. Why do you ask, Sir, if I might inquire?"

"Antimony. Yes, Antimony. It's a damned fine codename for a field agent making the Empire stronger against an implacable enemy. A damned fine codename. Good day, Lieutenant. Do enjoy your leave and we look forward to seeing you again."

"Aye, aye, Sir." With that, John Braithwaite turned and departed the inner sanctum, the lair of the Director of Naval Intelligence.

****

23 September 1915. Dover Beach, England.

Dusk fell. In the western sky, shaded bright crimson, orange, pink, and yellow by the light filtering through layers of hazy clouds, the sun had about reached the horizon. To the east in a clear, clean sky, stars glinted and glimmered. The moon appeared just over the rim of the white chalk cliffs of Dover, made glowing and multi-shaded by the setting sun.

On the beach, a solitary figure shuffled along the sandy beach occasionally kicking loose pebbles with his feet, seemingly adrift, going nowhere in particular. The lone figure stopped for a moment as he spied some interesting shells. He bent down, picked one up and as if bowling in a test match, tossed the shell into the frothy wave. He could not hear the splash; the early autumn storm still roiled the waves as they crashed and broke onto Dover Beach. He turned and looked up at the cliffs above, then back at the channel toward France. A solitary seagull swooped by, oblivious to the human on the beach. The bird dove down toward the sand, having spotted his dinner, a crab scurrying back toward the water and safety. The human intruder stood tranfixed as the gull bore down on the crab, scooped a claw up in its open beak, and sailed away. He winced. He had seen enough of death in any form. The man turned again and continued walking parallel to the water's edge as foam from the crashing waves washed over his bare feet.

"Ignorant armies clash by night," he whispered over and over again, then repeated aloud the lines of a poem remembered from his school days. Matthew Arnold's "Dover Beach" had always been one of his favorites, but until now, the last line's meaning had eluded him. "Where ignorant armies clash by night." He turned again facing toward the continent. Hundreds of men died daily, suffered wounds or went missing on the Western Front in that interminable war while he stood safely on Dover Beach tossing seashells into the surf.

Another thought crept into his consciousness. The Scottish-American naval hero, John Paul Jones, once wrote: "In human affairs, it is a law immutable and inexorable, that he who will not risk, cannot win." *He who will not risk. He who will not risk, cannot win.* The naval officer clenched his jaw, teeth grinding, eyes almost shut with furrowed brow. *He who will not risk. Interminable war. The dead of HMS Halberd.* But, he had risked, risked all and succeeded. The Kaiser's cruiser had been sunk by his shipmates and removed from the struggle. Had he not done this? Had he not already done his bit for King and Country? Had he not risked all and won? Had he not saved potentially hundreds or even thousands of lives? Could God or man require more? And then, he thought of his shipmates of the *Halberd* and of that horrendous night months earlier.

He folded his arms behind his back as he kicked another pebble into the encroaching surf. A startled gull squawked and flapped away in fright. He looked down as the froth again surrounded his bare feet and then receded back into the dark water. Captain Hall's words sounded loud and clear in his mind's eye: *"It is a lot to ask of a seagoing officer but do consider a posting with Naval Intelligence Division for our very special little activities. A talent for fieldwork like yours should not be wasted. Do consider the offer very seriously."*

In the distance, a destroyer passed close to shore at darkened ship, but still silhouetted against the rising moon on its way to join the Dover Patrol, no doubt. *Where ignorant armies clash by night.* He took in a deep breath of the clean, crisp sea air, turned up the collar of his reefer against the chilly, freshening breeze. A broad smile spread across his face—a decision made. Braithwaite turned back toward the path leading up from the beach to the heights above. As he strode with a purpose, he pulled out the note sent to him earlier by Lieutenant-Commander Millar and read it aloud: "Lieutenant-Commander Braithwaite, we have just been informed that Mrs. Alice Hallwood will arrive from Zanzibar by Royal Navy destroyer this day." *Must not tarry.* After all, he had a date at the Savoy Grill in the Strand with a pair of emerald-green eyes, a mane of lustrous auburn hair, and a whiff of jasmine. As he reached the top of the cliffs, he whispered, "Very well, then, Captain Hall, very well."

On Dover Beach, on a crisp, early autumn evening among the seagulls and the gathering darkness, newly promoted and decorated Lieutenant-Commander John David Fairchild Braithwaite, VC, DSC, Royal Navy, became ANTIMONY. ANTIMONY was born.

The End.

AUTHOR'S NOTES:

We are all the sum of our experiences. Readers may find it odd or perhaps humorous that the origin of *Genesis of ANTIMONY* had its particular genesis at Disneyland. Several years ago, while visiting Disneyland in California with my wife Linda and two granddaughters, we rode the Jungle Cruise ride. While standing in the queue to board, I was intrigued by the posters advertising adventures in Africa via riverboat and airplane. I was especially drawn to the Zambezi River references; that started the mind whirring. I had recently published the World War II action-adventure, espionage, historical fiction novel, *Resurrection of ANTIMONY,* which introduced the character Commodore John Braithwaite as a retired British naval intelligence and seagoing officer brought back on active duty in World War II by William Stephenson, aka INTREPID, the famous spymaster. As I rode the Jungle Cruise, the plot line for the prequel emerged. What if I introduced the character as a destroyer sailor wounded in action and then recruited by Royal Naval Intelligence Division to go to German East Africa to discover the secret of an enemy cruiser that was devastating British, French and Commonwealth merchant traffic in the Indian Ocean and operated covertly out of the Rufiji River Delta? By the end of the day at Disneyland, the plot outline was complete and a central organizing feature of that plot was a riverboat trip up the Zambezi River.

In many ways, the story is not new, either factually or in fiction. The saga of the German light cruiser SMS *Königsberg* that operated for many months out of the Rufiji Delta in the opening months of the First World War has provided fodder for other historical fiction tales, most notably, *Shout at the Devil,* a Wilbur Smith novel set in Zanzibar and German East Africa in 1913-15. The German cruiser (SMS *Blücher* in the novel) plays a major role in Smith's story. The novel was made into a film in 1976 starring Roger Moore, Lee Marvin, and Barbara Parkins. Then there is *The African Queen,* a novel by C.S.

Forester that was made into one of the best action-adventure films of all time in 1951 starring Humphrey Bogart and Katherine Hepburn. In the story, the couple travel by riverboat into a fictional lake where they sink a German patrol ship. Then, reaching back to one of my favorite novels read in Mrs. Phyllis Peacock's senior English class, I recalled Joseph Conrad's *The Heart of Darkness,* another story set on a river in central Africa. With all of these inspirations whirring about in my mind, the story of how John David Fairchild Braithwaite, RN, became the extraordinary British naval intelligence field agent code-named ANTIMONY, came to life. The first words didn't materialize until 2013 and it took until the summer of 2018 for completion. As a Department Head for Strategy and Policy in the College of Distance Education at the United States Naval War College in Newport, Rhode Island, one of my chief responsibilities is to visit the many non-resident Strategy and War seminars around the country, either to conduct a seminar assessment or present a case study lecture. Since these are evening seminars, during the days, I would write at such varied places as Corral Canyon Park in Malibu, California, Fort Stockton in Old Town San Diego, California, overlooking Crystal Lake on Pike's Peak, Colorado, at Surrender Field in the Yorktown National Battlefield Park at Yorktown, Virginia, Roanoke Island Festival Park in Manteo, North Carolina, and on the beach at Naval Station, Mayport, Florida. Over the years, *Genesis of ANTIMONY* gradually took shape.

Since this is an historical fiction novel, several of the characters were real, notably Captain (later promoted to rear-admiral) Reginald Hall, the Director of Naval Intelligence, and the father of modern cryptology and code breaking. The SMS *Aachen* is based loosely on the German light cruiser *Königsberg.* Therefore, some background on the ship and Hall is both interesting and informative.

SMS *Königsberg* was a light cruiser laid down in December 1905 at Kiel and completed in 1907. She displaced 3,400 tons. Her coal-fired boilers drove the 2-shaft reciprocating (pistons) engines generating 13,200 horsepower, which gave her a maximum speed of 24 knots. She carried ten 4.1-inch guns as the main battery as well as two 18-inch torpedoes in underwater tubes. With a crew of 332 officers, petty officers, and other rates, she operated in the Indian Ocean prior to the war based out of Dar es Salaam, capital of colonial German East Africa. Two days after the war broke out, she attacked and captured the *City of Winchester* in the Gulf of Aden, the first British merchant ship casualty of the war. Rear-Admiral King-Hall commanded several older cruisers and set out to sink the *Königsberg*. HMS *Astrea* attacked Dar es Salaam, putting the wireless station out of action and damaging the port facilities. The harbor master responded by sinking a dry dock across the entrance channel thus limiting access. In the novel, however, the plot calls for Braithwaite and Patel to go aboard *Aachen* in Dar es Salaam, therefore, I exercised artistic license to allow *Aachen* to come and go from the port. In retaliation for the British attack, *Königsberg* bombarded Zanzibar in mid-September 1914, sinking HMS *Pegasus*, an obsolete cruiser. Her original intent was to flee back to Germany, but an engine casualty caused her to head back to the Rufiji Delta sanctuary. To guard the ship, the Germans established a number of defended posts and a telegraph warning system along the several channels in and out of the river. In response, Admiralty dispatched the newer cruisers *Chatham, Dartmouth,* and *Weymouth* to deal with the German ship under the command of Captain Drury-Lowe of HMS *Chatham*. In the novel, the HMS *St Andrews* is a *Weymouth*-class cruiser and Captain, later Commodore, Peacock is the fictional version of Drury-Lowe.

The more capable Royal Navy forces then attempted to blockade the Rufiji Delta. They sank a ship in one of the main channels thus limiting the possible escape routes. Aircraft played a vital role in *Königsberg's* eventual demise. Initially, a civilian Curtis flying boat was acquired, but was shot down. She did, however, locate *Königsberg*, forcing her to shift anchorages farther upriver. Admiralty then sent two Sopwith 920 and three Short Folder seaplanes, which served to locate and observe *Königsberg's* movements and provide gunfire spotting. But, the new aircraft could not carry bombs, so they served as observers only. In early March, Rear-Admiral King-Hall took over as the overall commander aboard HMS *Goliath*, a pre-dreadnought battleship. Her 12-inch main battery guns could pound the German cruiser had she been able to negotiate the shallow channels. The admiral called for shallow draft gunboats with the firepower to destroy the cruiser. Accordingly, the monitors *Severn* and *Mersey* were towed from Malta. Monitors mounted heavy guns and with their shallow draft, could easily reach firing range upriver.

On 6 July 1915, the two monitors entered the northernmost channel while *Weymouth* created a diversion farther south. Although the monitors, aided by spotting from the aircraft, hit *Königsberg* at least a dozen times, they did little serious damage and retired having fired over 600 rounds. The cruiser managed a few hits, but inflicted no great damage on the heavily armored monitors. On July 11, a second attack occurred with improved aerial spotting procedures. *Severn* scored many hits, knocking out all of the cruiser's guns and causing secondary explosions. *Mersey* then moved in closer and also landed several rounds on the crippled cruiser. With no other choice, the commander ordered abandon ship and set scuttling charges. However, that was not the end of *Königsberg's* war effort. Over the next several weeks, German salvage crews pulled up most of the main battery guns, which were mounted on carriages and then used in the land war led by *Oberstleutnant* Paul von Lettow-Vorbeck, The surviving crew became essentially foot soldiers and participated in the various German units that fought a long struggle against British and colonial forces for the remainder of the war. The *Königsberg* wreck remained sunken at her mooring until finally salvaged and broken up for scrap in 1962. There are several good historical works on the *Königsberg* and the First World War in East Africa, including *The Germans Who Never Lost: The Story of the Königsberg* by Edwin Palmer Hoyt (1968), *African Kaiser: General Paul von Lettow-Vorbeck and the Great War in Africa, 1914-1918* by Robert Gaudi (2017), and, *The Forgotten Front: The East African Campaign, 1914-1918* by Ross Anderson (2004).

In this novel, the cruiser is portrayed as a Dresden-class light cruiser. As such, *Aachen* would have been powered by a 4-shaft turbine engine generating 15,000 horsepower for a maximum speed of 25 knots. The fuel was coal, which required constant replenishment, a factor that drives much of the plot and the decisions of Captain von Augsburg and his British opponents. At 3,650 tons displacement, *Aachen* would have mounted ten 4.1-inch guns as her main battery with two submerged 18-inch torpedo tubes. Her complement would have been 361 men. She would have been fairly new, having been commissioned about 1910. The commander, Helmuth von Augsburg, is a reflection of *Fregattenkapitän* (roughly equivalent to a senior commander in the US Navy and Royal Navy) Max Looff, of the *Königsberg*, who proved to be a highly capable, efficient, and beloved commanding officer, a characterization given to the fictional von Augsburg. Of note, in the Wilbur Smith novel, an aircraft plays a seminal role as airpower did in the real *Königsberg* saga; however, I chose to not use that aspect of the actual events. Rather, I used the riverboat *Zambezi Belle* as a critical aspect of the plot progression.

Admiral Sir William Reginald Hall, K.C.M.G., C.B. (28 June 1870 - 22 October 1943), Director of Naval Intelligence Division during most of the war, is a fascinating and intriguing character and the perfect vehicle for starting Braithwaite on his career as an intelligence field agent. Hall had commanded the new battlecruiser *Queen Mary* at the Battle of the Heligoland Bight in August 1914, but due to ill health, was relieved of sea duty and in October 1914 assumed command at Room 40 located in the Old Admiralty Building in Whitehall near Trafalgar Square as the Director of Naval Intelligence. Known as "Blinker" for his habit of rapid eye blinking, especially when excited, he guided NID from an encryption and code breaking office to essentially a covert operations and intelligence gathering entity. Hall built a network of intelligence operatives and field agents that actively gathered information on German naval operations, personnel, building programs, etc. But, he did more. His field agents actually carried out periodic covert operations. The activities of Hall's NID presaged the World War II activities of the Special Operations Executive (SOE) and MI6. (The Secret Service). Promoted to rear-admiral in 1917, Hall retired from active service in 1919, and was promoted to vice-admiral and later full admiral on the retired list. He dabbled in Conservative Party politics and represented West Derby in Parliament. There are several good histories of Hall and Room 40, including Patrick Beesly,

Room 40: British Naval Intelligence, 1914-1918 (London: Oxford University Press, 1982), and, David Ramsey, *'Blinker' Hall: Spymaster: The Man who Brought America into World War I* (Stroud, U.K.: The History Press, 2008) (referring to Hall and the famous Zimmermann Telegram affair).

On a technical note, the theory of radio detection actually did emerge a decade before the war. The German scientist Christian Hülsmeyer invented an early, primitive radar called the Telemobiloscope. However, while it could determine bearing, it could not determine a target's range and was never operationalized by the Germans. In the 1930s, British scientists did develop an operational radar (for Radio Detection and Ranging, known as radar from 1940 on), which played an incredibly important role in World War II.

In the Indian Army cavalry such as the 2nd Bengal Lancers, Patel's regiment, the highest enlisted rank was *kot daffadar*. It equated to sergeant major in the British Army. For easy recognition so as to not confuse readers, I have simply used the rank sergeant major for Patel.

There are several wonderful friends and relatives that helped with the technical details of *Genesis of ANTIMONY*. Professor Angus Ross (aka, Commander Angus Ross, RN, Retired), my colleague at the US Naval War College and an expert on the pre-war and First World War Royal and Imperial German navies, provided invaluable assistance with period terminology and procedures. Professor Donal O'Sullivan at California State University, Northridge and a Fleet Professor of Strategy and Policy for the College of Distance Education at the Naval War College assisted with German phrases and language. Note that when German characters speak, it is often mixed German and English. The concept is to create the impression of being German speakers while remaining understandable to the reader. My lovely wife Linda, armed with a red pen as she did for many years as a teacher in the Newport School System, graciously read and reviewed my scribblings and made corrections and valuable suggestion on the plot and sequence of events. My brother, Larry Carpenter, is owed a thanks for the initial idea many decades back of a British agent codenamed ANTIMONY brought back on active duty in World War II to watch over an American nuclear physicist embarking for Africa on a derelict Egyptian liner. That idea resulted in *Resurrection of ANTIMONY* first published in 2009 with a second edition in 2016. Finally, many thanks go to Chancellor-Emeritus Keith Bird, who helped me locate a source for German Navy terminology *(Marinewörterbuch Fünfsprachig)*.

This prequel introduces John David Fairchild Braithwaite as ANTIMONY, ace intelligence field agent. There are a number of possibilities for future novels. At this time, I forecast at least three more ANTIMONY novels set in the world wars and the Cold War. Preliminary titles include *Dry Tortuga: ANTIMONY's Gambit, The Flying Squadron: ANTIMONY's Danger,* and *ANTIMONY's Ninth.* So, for those who enjoy the series, keep your powder dry and all the best!

S.D.M. Carpenter
Portsmouth, RI
August 2018

CPSIA information can be obtained
at www.ICGtesting.com
Printed in the USA
BVHW06s1414280918
528616BV00005B/15/P